Shattered Mind

Stephanie Tyo

Stephanie Tyo

Copyright © 2023 by Stephanie Tyo

All rights reserved.

No part of this publication may be reproduced, distributed, or transmitted in any form or by any means, including photocopying, recording, or other electronic or mechanical methods, without the prior written permission of the publisher, except as permitted by U.S. copyright law. For permission requests, contact contact@stephanietyo.com.

The story, all names, characters, and incidents portrayed in this production are fictitious. No identification with actual persons (living or deceased), places, buildings, and products is intended or should be inferred.

Book Cover by http://www.selfpubbookcovers.com/NorthernLight

First edition 2023

CHAPTER 1

The year was 2077, and the cityscape buzzed with holographic billboards projecting shimmering advertisements into the air. Autonomous vehicles glided silently along the streets, their solar-paneled exteriors gleaming in the sun. People on hoverboards donned form-fitting, tech-infused attire that combined sleek aerodynamics with smart fabrics, showcasing shifting colors and patterns. Safety was paramount, with augmented reality helmets, energy-efficient solar-powered clothing, and levitating footwear, all while expressing individuality through holographic displays and intelligent accessories, seamlessly merging technology, style, and sustainability in their daily lives.

The citizens cruised past with the wind ruffling their hair, conversing effortlessly with friends through the neural implants that connected them to the hivemind of humanity. Robotic vendors sold snacks and drinks from glowing carts while hovering drones delivered goods and services to citizens in need. A holographic projection of the news scrolled across the sky, and everywhere one looked, the streets were alive with tech-savvy citizens living out life in a vibrant metropolis.

Amidst this futuristic world, Dr. Elizabeth Harmon stood at the window of her fourth-story, high-rise office, gazing out across Seattle, the city that never slept. As a successful psychologist, she gained recognition for her expertise in a field that had evolved significantly over the past decades. Her ground-breaking work in understanding the complex interplay between human minds and the advanced technology that shaped their lives had earned her numerous accolades and the respect of her peers.

"Dr. Harmon?" A soft voice interrupted her thoughts.

Elizabeth turned to face one of her patients, a young woman whose eyes were rimmed with dark circles from countless sleepless nights. She could sense the anxiety radiating off the woman like an electric charge. "Yes, what can I do for you?"

"Sorry to bother you," the woman said hesitantly. "But I've been having these dreams again ... the ones we talked about last time."

"Have a seat," Elizabeth replied, gesturing to the comfortable chair that hovered just above the floor that was positioned opposite of her own. As the woman sat down, she took a deep breath, preparing herself to delve into the labyrinth of another troubled mind. She felt a familiar tingling sensation at the base of her skull as her neural implant synced with the patient's permission, allowing her to access the woman's thoughts and emotions.

"Let's talk about your dream," Elizabeth began, her voice calm and steady. "Tell me everything you remember."

As the woman recounted her nightmare, Elizabeth sifted through her memories, piecing together fragments of images and feelings. The patient's heart raced, and Elizabeth could almost feel the cold sweat that had drenched her sheets as she awoke from her terrifying ordeal. She knew that this woman was not alone in her suffering; others had come to her with similar stories—visceral dreams that haunted their waking hours.

"Thank you for sharing that with me," Elizabeth said gently when the woman finished her tale. "I know how difficult it can be to confront our deepest fears."

"Dr. Harmon, why is this happening to me?" the woman asked, her voice trembling. "What do these dreams mean?"

"Sometimes our minds create nightmares as a way of processing unresolved emotions," Elizabeth explained. "But I have a feeling there may be more to your dreams than meets the eye. I will do everything in my power to help you find answers."

"Dr. Harmon, what do you mean that you have a feeling there's more to my dreams?" the woman asked.

"I have other patients that came to me with the exact dreams." Elizabeth said.

"Oh, I see... I hope you can help us all." The woman said.

"I will do everything I can to help you and the others, I can promise you this." Elizabeth said.

"Thank you Dr. Harmon I hope you can and I appreciate your help." The woman said.

As the woman left her office, Elizabeth couldn't shake the nagging suspicion that these shared nightmares were more than coincidence. In the back of her mind, a single question echoed: What hidden truths lay buried within the labyrinth of her patients' dreams? With each passing day, Elizabeth felt an increasing urgency to unravel the mystery and uncover the truth before it was too late.

"Let the journey begin," she whispered to herself, steeling her resolve. Elizabeth did not know at the time, but the path she was about to embark on would lead her not only into the darkest corners of the human psyche but also into the shadows of her past.

As Elizabeth sat at her sleek, glass-topped desk in her office, the holographic display of her recent research paper floated in front of her. It was a groundbreaking study on the effects of virtual reality therapy on patients suffering from post-traumatic stress disorder. Her work had gained recognition worldwide, and her list of clients included high-profile individuals seeking relief from their deepest psychological wounds.

"Your latest publication has garnered quite the attention, Dr. Harmon," her assistant's voice chimed through the speaker on her desk. "The Institute of Psychological Sciences has requested you to present your findings at their upcoming conference."

"Thank you, I'll consider it," Elizabeth replied, her mind drifting elsewhere. Her thoughts wandered to Claire, her late sister, who had died under mysterious circumstances. Elizabeth knew her sister Claire had also suffered from post-traumatic disorder but did not know why. The memory of that fateful day still haunted her, gnawing at the edges of her consciousness like an insatiable beast. She clenched her fists, a knot forming in her stomach as she recalled the unanswered questions surrounding Claire's death.

"Doctor, are you alright?" her assistant asked, sensing her discomfort.

"Of course," she lied, forcing a smile. "Just lost in thought."

"Understandable," the assistant replied sympathetically. "Please let me know if you need anything."

"Thank you," Elizabeth murmured, her voice barely audible as she dismissed the holographic display with a wave of her hand. She couldn't help but wonder if her relentless pursuit of understanding the human mind had been fueled by the unrelenting grief and confusion that engulfed her after Claire's passing. She found solace in the intricate patterns and connections that made up her patients' psyches, believing that unraveling their mysteries would somehow lead her closer to the truth about her sister.

"Elizabeth, my dear," a familiar voice broke into her thoughts. It was Dr. Singh, her mentor and confidante, his lean frame stood in the doorway of her office. His eyes were full of wisdom and kindness, while his white beard showed years of experience. She glanced up, startled by his sudden appearance.

"Dr. Singh," she greeted him, her voice betraying a hint of relief. "What brings you here?"

"Your research, of course," he replied, his eyes twinkling with admiration. "Your work is truly groundbreaking. But more importantly, I've come to check on you."

"Me?" Elizabeth asked, feigning confusion. "I'm fine, really."

"Ah, but are you?" he pressed gently, stepping into her office. "We haven't spoken much since Claire's passing a year ago, and I know how much she meant to you."

"Sometimes ... it feels like an unsolvable puzzle," Elizabeth confessed, her voice cracking as she fought back tears. "I want to understand why she's gone. I need answers, Dr. Singh."

"Elizabeth, sometimes the answers we seek lie hidden within ourselves," Dr. Singh said softly, placing a comforting hand on her shoulder. "You have spent your life unraveling the mysteries of others' minds, but perhaps it is time to confront the shadows that lurk within your own."

As Elizabeth looked into her mentor's wise eyes, a shiver of determination ran down her spine.

Elizabeth's heart raced as she paced back and forth in her impeccably tidy office, the sterile smell of disinfectant hanging heavy in the air. Elizabeth's hands trembled slightly, betraying the turmoil churning within her. Elizabeth couldn't shake the gnawing guilt that clawed at her insides, the feeling that she should have done more to save Claire.

"Damn it," she muttered under her breath, stopping in front of the floor-to-ceiling window overlooking the cityscape. "Why didn't I see it coming?"

As a psychologist, she had devoted her life to understanding the intricacies of the human mind, to uncovering the hidden truths buried deep within the psyche. Yet when it came to her sister, she had been blind, unable to recognize the signs of distress that must have been there all along.

Elizebeth mind drifted to a memory of Claire as she visited her.

It was the year 2076. Claire and Elizabeth, sisters bound by a lifetime of shared secrets and experiences, found a rare moment of joy and laughter. They sat on a sleek, levitating bench in a bustling city park, sipping holographic beverages that sparkled with vibrant colors. The holographic gardens around them, displayed iridescent flowers, that seemed to dance to the melodious hum of the floating cars passing overhead.

As they giggled, Claire's laughter briefly faltered. Her eyes, normally bright and full of life, clouded with a hint of unease. In a moment of vulnerability, she leaned closer to Elizabeth.

"Remember when we were kids, and I used to tell you about those odd dreams?" Claire said, her voice lowered.

Elizabeth nodded, her brow furrowing. "Yeah, you used to say something about experiments being done to you. Why do you bring that up now?"

Claire's gaze shifted towards the holographic trees that concealed them from prying eyes. "Liz, those dreams, they've been haunting me again, but they're different this time. It's like ... like I'm reliving them in a way. The experiments, they feel so real."

Elizabeth's concern deepened. Elizabeth reached out and gently placed a hand on Claire's arm. "Claire, you know you can talk to me about anything."

Claire's lips quivered, and for a moment, she looked as if she wanted to say more. But the distant laughter of children playing and the world around them reminded her to be cautious with her words.

With a forced smile, Claire shook her head. "Nah, probably just stress. Let's not ruin our day with my imagination. I'll be fine."

Elizabeth nodded, but a sense of unease lingered as they returned to their laughter, cherishing the precious moments they could share in their beautifully bewildering world of 2076.

"Perhaps if I'd paid more attention ..." Elizabeth whispered, her voice barely audible over the hum of the high-speed transportation system zipping past her building. "Maybe I could have saved her."

The weight of her grief settled upon her like a heavy blanket, suffocating and oppressive. Elizabeth thoughts spiraled into a dark vortex, images of Claire's final moments haunting her, like ghostly specters. Memories of Claire's last words to her, before tragedy struck, swirled in her mind, the sound of her gentle laughter echoing in her ears. The pain of her loss overwhelmed her, pressing down on her chest and stealing her breath away.

Elizabeth was reminded of other days, brighter days, of the two of them walking through fields of wildflowers, the sun beating down on them. Elizabeth remembered the way Claire's face would light up when she saw something beautiful, the way her smile could make the skies blue. Elizabeth thought of Claire's boundless energy and enthusiasm for life, how she could find joy even in the darkest of times. The weight of her remorse pressed down on her chest.

"Get a grip, Elizabeth," she admonished herself, clenching her fists until her knuckles turned white. "You can't change the past. But you can find the truth."

Determined, she took a deep, shuddering breath and began to construct a plan of action. Elizabeth would delve into the depths of her memories, examine every moment shared with Claire, and leave no stone unturned in her quest for answers. And though the path before her was fraught with uncertainty and danger, she knew she must forge ahead, driven by an unwavering conviction that she owed it to her sister—and to herself—to confront the demons lurking in the shadows.

"Whatever it takes," she vowed, her voice steely and resolute. "I will unravel this mystery and find justice for you, Claire. I promise."

As Elizabeth gazed out at the sprawling metropolis below, she couldn't help but feel a strange sense of foreboding, as if unseen forces were already conspiring against her. And though she couldn't put her finger on it, she knew deep down that the road ahead would be treacherous and unforgiving, testing her resolve and pushing her to her limits.

But she had no choice. The truth was out there, hidden like a needle in a haystack, and she would not—could not—rest until she found it.

"Rest in peace, dear sister," she murmured, her eyes filling with tears as she stared into the fading light of the setting sun. "I won't let your death be in vain."

The room felt colder than usual, the air heavy with unspoken emotions as she sat in her office, reviewing the case files of her latest patient. Elizabeth heart pounded in her chest and her hands trembled ever so slightly, as she tried to focus on the words in front of her. But her thoughts, like tendrils of smoke, kept drifting back to Claire.

"Dr. Harmon?" a soft voice intruded, pulling her back to the present. Elizabeth looked up to see her assistant, Lucy, standing hesitantly in the doorway.

"Sorry, I was lost in thought," Elizabeth said, attempting a smile. "What is it?"

"Your four o'clock appointment is here," Lucy informed her. "Shall I send her in?"

"Of course," Elizabeth replied, motioning for her to do so. As Lucy left, Elizabeth took a deep breath to steady herself, mumbling under her breath, "You can't let Claire's death consume you, Liz. You have patients who need you."

As she greeted her patient—a young woman named Anna struggling with depression. Elizabeth drew parallels between her case and her sister's. Anna's parents had been distant and unsupportive during her childhood, much like Elizabeth and Claire's parents. However, while this led Elizabeth to excel professionally, Claire had spiraled into darkness, leaving behind a trail of unanswered questions.

"Sometimes ... sometimes I feel guilty," Anna confessed to Elizabeth, her voice barely a whisper. "I wonder if I could have done more for my sister before she died. If I'd been there for her, maybe she would still be alive."

"Anna," Elizabeth said, concern etching her features. "You can't blame yourself for someone else's actions. You're only human."

"Thank you, Dr. Harmon," Anna replied, blinking back tears. "But I can't help feeling responsible. Maybe if I'd tried harder to understand her, things would have been different." Anna said gently, "You've helped me so much in the short time we've been working together."

"I'm glad I have." Elizabeth sighed, rubbing her temples as a familiar headache began to blossom behind her eyes. "Anna, instead of focusing on what you could have done differently, try to use that energy to help yourself. Honor her memory by being the best person you can be for yourself."

Anna nodded, wiping away a stray tear. "You're right, Dr. Harmon. That's what my sister would have wanted."

As their session progressed, Elizabeth found herself increasingly immersed in Anna's struggles, allowing her guilt and grief to provide a deeper level of empathy and understanding. The parallels between their stories reminded her of the complex tapestry of human emotion, and how every thread—no matter how tangled or frayed—served a purpose.

"Thank you, Dr. Harmon," Anna said at the end of their session, her voice filled with genuine gratitude. "You've given me a lot to think about today."

"Likewise, Anna," Elizabeth smiled, standing up and guiding Anna out.

"Take care," Anna said as she headed for the door of the room.

"Goodbye, Anna," Elizabeth replied, watching her patient exit the room. As she sat there, alone once more, she closed her eyes and allowed herself a brief moment of reflection. Elizabeth had let her guilt overshadow her ability to help others, and she couldn't allow that to continue.

"Forgive me, Claire," she whispered, her voice thick with emotion. "I promise I'll make this right."

One afternoon, Anna entered the office, her eyes carrying a weariness that betrayed the sleepless nights she had endured.

"Dr. Harmon," Anna began in a hushed tone, glancing around the room as if expecting the nightmares to materialize in the shadows. "I need to talk about these nightmares. They're getting worse."

Elizabeth leaned forward; her concern etched across her face. "I'm here for you, Anna. Take your time. Tell me about these nightmares."

Anna took a deep breath, her hands nervously clasped in her lap. "It's like I'm in this dark, twisted place. I see things—horrifying things. It feels so real, Dr. Harmon. And when I wake up, it's like the darkness is still there, following me into the day."

Elizabeth nodded, her brow furrowing with empathy. "That sounds incredibly distressing, Anna. Can you describe one of these nightmares to me?"

Anna hesitated, choosing her words carefully. "There's this shadowy figure, always just out of reach. It whispers things, things I can't quite make out. But it fills me with this paralyzing fear. I feel like I'm suffocating."

Elizabeth's gaze softened. "It must be terrifying to experience that. Have you noticed any patterns or triggers that coincide with these nightmares?"

Anna shook her head. "No, it just happens. Randomly, it seems. And it's affecting my daily life. I can't concentrate, and the fear lingers long after I wake up."

Elizabeth leaned back, her mind already formulating a plan. "Anna, we need to explore these nightmares together. They might be connected to deeper emotions or experiences. It's crucial for us to understand them so we can work towards alleviating their impact on you."

Throughout the session, the dialogue unfolded as a collaborative exploration of Anna's subconscious. Elizabeth asked probing questions, gently guiding Anna through the details of her nightmares and encouraging her to express the emotions they stirred.

"I just don't understand why these nightmares won't stop," Anna admitted, her vulnerability laid bare. "I thought things were getting better, but it's like I'm trapped in this never-ending cycle."

Elizabeth reached across the table, offering a comforting touch to Anna's trembling hand. "Healing is a complex journey, Anna. Sometimes, our minds bring forth these challenges when we're ready to confront them. It doesn't mean you're regressing. We're navigating uncharted territory together, and we will find a way through it."

As the weeks passed, Elizabeth and Anna delved deeper into the labyrinth of Anna's fears. Elizabeth introduced techniques to help Anna confront and reinterpret the elements of her nightmares, empowering her to regain a sense of control.

"It's like I'm fighting a war in my own mind," Anna confessed during one session, her eyes reflecting both fear and determination.

Elizabeth nodded, acknowledging the intensity of Anna's struggle. "You're incredibly resilient, Anna. We'll work through this war together, and you won't be alone in the battle."

As the session ended, she guided Anna to the door.

Elizabeth's office was a sanctuary of sorts, filled with the comforting scent of old books from a hundred years ago and the soft hum of the futuristic air purifier that floated in the air. With a swipe of her hand, a transparent, shimmering desk appeared before her. Her fingers danced across the see-through surface, and the holographic image of an avatar appeared with a cup of coffee on float above the desk. She picked up the warm mug with both hands and brought it to her nose to inhale the aroma., the rich aroma of roasted beans mingling with the subtle, earthy fragrance of the potted plants that adorned the room. She took a deep breath and savored the sensory experience, allowing it to ground her in the present moment.

The sunlight streamed through the blinds, casting intricate patterns on the polished wooden floor. As Elizabeth gazed at the dancing shadows, she couldn't shake the nagging feeling that she was being watched. It was an uneasiness she'd experienced before—fleeting glimpses of a mysterious figure lurking just outside her line of sight. She shook her head, dismissing the thought as paranoia brought on by unresolved grief.

Elizabeth's journey had been a winding path of self-discovery and professional breakthroughs. With each patient she guided through the darkness, Elizabeth found herself inching closer to understanding the truth that haunted her waking hours.

Elizabeth took a moment to soak in the serenity of her surroundings, feeling the weight of the world lift ever so slightly from her shoulders. She felt the familiar tingling sensation at the base of her skull, the electric charge of anticipation coursing through her as she prepared for another day of delving into the human psyche. Her mind churned with thoughts of her patients, their fears, and traumas like pieces of a puzzle she was determined to solve. Would today be the day she unlocked the secret to the labyrinth that haunted their dreams?

She glanced at her reflection in the glass of a framed diploma, noting the determined expression on her face—eyes sharp with intelligence and empathy, dark hair swept back into a no-nonsense bun. It was the face of a woman who refused to give up, who would stop at nothing to unravel the mysteries that plagued those she sought to heal. As Elizabeth took a deep breath, she allowed herself a moment of vulnerability—a fleeting acknowledgement of the personal demons that drove her forward. Yet, instead of letting them overwhelm her, she harnessed their power, transforming her insecurities into fuel for the fire burning within her.

"Dr. Harmon?" The soft knock on her door was followed by her receptionist's voice, pulling Elizabeth from her reverie. "Your next patient is here."

"Thank you," she replied, straightening her posture as she shifted her focus to the task at hand. As she opened the door to greet her patient, Elizabeth steeled herself for another day of journeying through the labyrinth of the mind, one step closer to understanding the truth that had eluded her for so long.

Elizabeth's journey had been fraught with challenges, both personal and professional. She had faced the darkness within her soul, as well as delving into the shadowy recesses of her patients' minds. And now, in this sanctuary of healing that she had created for herself and others, she prepared to embark on another day of exploration.

A middle-aged man entered Elizabeth's office, clutching his hat in trembling hands. Mr. Thompson, a nervous and slightly disheveled figure, had come to seek help with his debilitating fear of heights. As he took a seat across from Elizabeth, the faint scent of sweat mixed with cologne filled the air.

"Good morning, Mr. Thompson," Elizabeth began, her eyes searching his face with empathy. "I want you to know that you are safe here. There is no judgment, only support and understanding."

"Th-thank you, Dr. Harmon," he stuttered, his gaze darting around the room as if seeking some reassurance.

"Please, tell me about your experiences with heights," Elizabeth gently prompted him, leaning forward in her chair. "When did you first notice your fear?"

Mr. Thompson hesitated, twisting the brim of his hat between his fingers. "It started when I was a child," he said finally. "My father, he ... he used to make me climb trees with him. He thought it'd toughen me up, but every time I got up there, I'd just freeze. I couldn't move, couldn't breathe."

Elizabeth nodded, her brow furrowing in concern. "That must have been terrifying for you," she said softly, allowing him space to continue.

"Y-yes," he admitted, his voice trembling with the effort of reliving those memories. "Even now, I can't stand on a balcony or look out a window without feeling like I'm going to fall."

As Mr. Thompson opened up about his experiences, Elizabeth absorbed his words like a sponge, sifting through the layers of emotion and memory that formed the tapestry of his fear. She recognized the complex web of associations and triggers that had become ingrained in his psyche, and she knew that untangling them would require patience and perseverance—qualities she possessed in abundance.

"Mr. Thompson," she said earnestly, her eyes locked onto his, "I believe that together, we can help you face this fear head-on. We will work on strategies to gradually expose you to heights, allowing you to build up your confidence and regain control over your life."

Mr. Thompson looked at her with a mixture of hope and trepidation, the vulnerability in his eyes a testament to the trust he was placing in her. As they began their journey into the labyrinth of his mind, Elizabeth felt the familiar surge of determination that fueled her every day—the unwavering belief that she could help him overcome his nightmares and find freedom.

"Alright, Mr. Thompson," Elizabeth began, her voice steady and reassuring. "Let's start with some cognitive-behavioral techniques to help you challenge the thoughts that trigger your fear of heights."

As they delved into the tangled mess of fears and anxieties that haunted him from within, she guided him through various techniques, such as examining the evidence for and against his catastrophic beliefs and considering alternative interpretations.

"Remember, our thoughts can greatly influence how we feel," she explained, her eyes gleaming with conviction. "By changing the way, you think about heights, you can gradually change the way you react to them."

Mr. Thompson nodded, his expression a mix of determination and trepidation. Mr. Thompson knew this would not be an easy journey, but he trusted Elizabeth implicitly, finding solace in the empathy and understanding that radiated from her every word.

"Next, we'll try a visualization exercise that involves exposure therapy," Elizabeth continued, her fingers deftly adjusting the virtual reality headset she held in her hands. "This simulation will place you at the top of a tall building. Remember, it's just a simulation—but engaging with it can help train your mind to better cope with your fear."

The headset found its home on Mr. Thompson's head, and as the world around him transformed, he couldn't suppress a gasp. The cityscape sprawled before him, buildings reaching up like jagged teeth biting at the sky, and he felt himself standing on the edge of a precipice, the ground far below him. Mr. Thompson's heart pounded, adrenaline surging through his veins as the familiar terror gripped him.

"Take a deep breath, Mr. Thompson," Elizabeth's voice echoed in his ears, soothing and supportive. "Focus on your breathing and remind yourself that you're safe. This is an opportunity to face your fear in a controlled environment, where you have the power to overcome it."

Mr. Thompson clung to her words like a lifeline, forcing air into his lungs as he tried to calm the tempest within. Gradually, the icy tendrils of fear began to loosen their grip, and he found himself able to take a step forward, closer to the edge.

"Good," Elizabeth encouraged him. "Now, I want you to visualize yourself facing this fear and conquering it. Imagine that you have the power to control your emotions and see yourself standing at the edge without any fear."

As Mr. Thompson's eyes scanned the world that surrounded him, the once-terrifying cityscape took on a new light—a realm of possibility where he could face his fears and emerge victorious. Mr. Thompson felt a glimmer of strength rise within him, fueled by the unwavering support and guidance of Elizabeth, who stood by his side through every step of this arduous journey.

As they continued to explore the complex tapestry of his mind, woven from memories and emotions, fears and nightmares, Elizabeth remained steadfast in her belief that together, they would find a way to conquer the darkness and set him free.

Mr. Thompson's heart raced as he struggled to find his footing on the virtual skyscraper, his hands trembling against the railing. He glanced at Elizabeth with wide, pleading eyes, silently begging for an escape from this nightmarish scenario.

"Remember to breathe," Elizabeth reminded him gently, her voice a beacon of reassurance amidst the chaos of his thoughts. "You're in control here, Mr. Thompson. This exercise is designed to help you face your fears, not be consumed by them."

In response, Mr. Thompson took several deep breaths, attempting to steady himself and focus on Elizabeth's words. With each inhale, he tried to envision confidence filling his lungs, while every exhale expelled the terror that had gripped him so tightly.

"Very good," Elizabeth said, nodding slowly. "Now, can you tell me what you see around you?"

"Buildings....so many tall buildings," he murmured, his gaze shifting uneasily across the virtual cityscape. "And below ... it's just so far down."

"Focus on the horizon," she suggested softly. "Let the vastness of the sky remind you that even when we feel small and powerless, there's always room for growth and change."

As Mr. Thompson reluctantly shifted his attention toward the sunset hues painting the distant skyline, he felt the tension in his chest begin to ease. Inch by inch, he allowed the warmth of the fading sun to seep into his very being, dissipating the cold dread that had weighed him down.

"See?" Elizabeth said, her voice tinged with a hint of pride. "You're doing it. You're taking control."

"I am," he whispered, a small but genuine smile tugging at the corners of his lips. "I am."

With time and patience, they continued to work through the exercise, and Mr. Thompson gradually learned to trust in his ability to face and conquer his fears.

The soft buzz of hovercraft and tall, sleek buildings pierced the sky, reflecting the neon glow of holographic billboards that advertised the latest advancements in technology. In this futuristic world, Dr. Harmon-Brown, a renowned scientist, moved gracefully through the bustling streets, her presence commanding respect and admiration.

As the co-creator of the revolutionary Hive Mind, Dr. Harmon-Brown had dedicated her life to pushing the boundaries of human consciousness. The Hive Mind, a groundbreaking experiment that interconnected human minds, promised to usher in an era of unprecedented collaboration and understanding. Working alongside her husband, Mr. Harmon, they had been at the forefront of scientific innovation, their love for each other and their work intertwining in ways that seemed inseparable.

However, as with any monumental endeavor, the Hive Mind project had its pitfalls. The pursuit of knowledge came at a cost, and the experiment that brought the Harmon-Brown family together also threatened to tear them apart. The lines between professional and personal life blurred, and the weight of their creation became a burden they all bore.

Elizabeth, the daughter of Dr. Harmon-Brown, was a witness to the highs and lows of her parents' work. She watched as their passion fueled late-night discussions and laughter, but she also saw the strain it put on their relationship. Despite her mother's brilliance, Dr. Harmon-Brown had an innate ability to shield Elizabeth and her sister, Claire, from the darker aspects of their research.

One evening, the glow of holographic lights bathed the Harmon-Brown residence as Dr. Harmon-Brown returned home from the lab. The sleek, automated door slid open, revealing a spacious and meticulously designed living space. The air inside carried a subtle hum of technology, a reminder of the scientific endeavors that consumed the family.

One afternoon, the harmonious facade shattered. Dr. Harmon-Brown, lost in thought and burdened by the weight of responsibility, stepped onto her hoverboard. The device, a symbol of progress and futuristic elegance, glided effortlessly above the ground. As she navigated the crowded streets, her mind raced with calculations and hypotheses.

In a moment that seemed to freeze time, tragedy struck. A sudden malfunction caused Dr. Harmon-Brown's hoverboard to falter, sending her plummeting to the unforgiving pavement below. The bustling city, oblivious to the loss of one of its brilliant minds, continued its ceaseless rhythm.

News of Dr. Harmon-Brown's untimely demise reached her family, shattering their world.

In the aftermath of Dr. Harmon-Brown's tragic accident, Mr. Harmon found himself standing at the precipice of a decision that would shape not only the future of the Hive Mind project but also the legacy of his late wife. The once-promising endeavor now bore the weight of sorrow and uncertainty, and Mr. Harmon, a man of both intellect and determination, faced the daunting challenge of carrying on his wife's groundbreaking work.

Surrounded by the shimmering lights of the city, Mr. Harmon immersed himself in the equations and research left behind by Dr. Harmon-Brown. The holographic displays flickered to life, each line of code and intricate diagram a testament to her brilliance. The city, with its ever-present hum of progress, seemed to pulse in sync with the heartbeat of the scientific legacy now entrusted to Mr. Harmon.

With a heavy heart, he made the decision to continue the Hive Mind project, recognizing that it held the potential to redefine the very fabric of human connection. The separation caused by the experiment would not be the end; instead, it became the catalyst for a renewed commitment. Driven by a desire to honor his wife's memory and complete the vision they had shared, Mr. Harmon threw himself into the work.

Days turned into nights as he delved deeper into the complexities of the Hive Mind. The once-shared dream now became a solitary pursuit, a journey marked by both the brilliance of scientific innovation and the melancholy of personal loss. The project became a living tribute to Dr. Harmon-Brown, a way for Mr. Harmon to keep her spirit alive in the pursuit of knowledge.

The hive-like network of interconnected minds, once a source of both wonders and discord, began to evolve under Mr. Harmon's meticulous guidance. He faced challenges and setbacks, but the echoes of his wife's dedication and love fueled his determination. The laboratory, once filled with the harmonious collaboration of the Harmon-Brown couple, now echoed with the solitary footsteps of a man driven by a profound sense of purpose.

As the cityscape continued to glitter with neon lights, the legacy of Dr. Harmon-Brown endured. The sacrifices made in the pursuit of knowledge were not in vain, and the bittersweet reminder of her daring spirit lingered in the air.

Mr. Harmon, now a steward of his wife's vision, navigated the delicate balance between progress and introspection, determined to see the Hive Mind project through to its fruition.

In the heart of the city, where the boundaries of science and emotion converged, Mr. Harmon forged ahead. The legacy of Dr. Harmon-Brown, a beacon of intellect and love, continued to shape the trajectory of the Harmon-Brown family and the destiny of a world hungry for the promise of progress.

The moment Mrs. Ramirez stepped into Elizabeth's office, the air seemed to grow colder, as if the shadows of her nightmares had followed her through the door. Her eyes were rimmed with red, the telltale signs of sleepless nights spent in the clutches of her own tortured psyche.

"Please, have a seat," Elizabeth said softly, gesturing toward the plush armchair across from her desk. As Mrs. Ramirez settled into the chair, Elizabeth studied her carefully; beneath the exhaustion and pain that marked her features, she saw a determination—a will confront the demons that haunted her dreams.

"Tell me about your nightmares," Elizabeth began, her voice gentle yet unwavering. "What is it that plagues you each night?"

Mrs. Ramirez hesitated, her fingers twisting into the fabric of her skirt. "It's...it's hard to explain. It feels like I'm trapped, reliving the same terrifying moments over and over again."

"And these moments," Elizabeth pressed, "are they connected to a traumatic event from your past?"

A tear slid down Mrs. Ramirez's cheek as she nodded, her voice barely audible. "Yes."

"Then together, we'll find a way to confront this trauma, so that you may finally break free from the cycle of fear and pain."

As they delved deeper into the labyrinth of memories and emotions that fueled her recurring nightmares, Elizabeth couldn't help but draw parallels between Mrs. Ramirez's struggle and her journey to overcome the ghosts of her past. And though the road ahead would be fraught with challenges, she knew that with empathy, understanding, and unwavering determination, healing was within reach for them both.

The air in Elizabeth's office seemed to thicken as Mrs. Ramirez's nightmares were laid bare, the shadows cast by the soft afternoon light lending an eerie quality to the room. Elizabeth's heart pounded in rhythm with the ticking of the clock on her wall—each second marking another moment this woman had endured the torment of her past.

"Is there a recurring theme or image within these nightmares?" Elizabeth asked, her gaze fixed on the young woman before her.

Mrs. Ramirez swallowed hard, her lower lip trembling. "There is ... a man. He always appears in different forms, but I know it's him. He's responsible for my suffering."

"Can you recall any specific details about this man? Even small pieces can help us understand the bigger picture," Elizabeth said, her voice steady and compassionate.

"His eyes." She shuddered, wrapping her arms around herself. "They're cold and empty like he's looking through me. And his smile...it's so twisted and cruel. I can never escape him."

"Let's try something," Elizabeth suggested, leaning forward in her chair. "I want you to take a deep breath, close your eyes, and imagine yourself back in one of those nightmares. But this time, instead of being a helpless victim, I want you to envision yourself empowered and in control. What would you say to this man if you had the power to confront him?"

A flicker of uncertainty crossed Mrs. Ramirez's face, but she nodded, taking a few shaky breaths before closing her eyes. The silence that followed was deafening, punctuated only by the faint sound of their breathing.

"I ..." Her voice faltered, but she pressed on. "I would tell him that he no longer controls me, that I am stronger than him. That I won't let him hurt me anymore."

"Good," Elizabeth encouraged, feeling the weight of Mrs. Ramirez's words in her chest. "Now, let's explore that power further. I want you to rewrite the narrative of your nightmares. Instead of running from this man, imagine yourself standing your ground and facing him. How does that make you feel?"

"Scared ... but also ... stronger," Mrs. Ramirez whispered, tears streaming down her cheeks as she clung to this newfound sense of control.

"Remember this feeling, Mrs. Ramirez," Elizabeth said softly. "This is the first step towards reclaiming your power and overcoming the darkness that haunts your dreams."

As they continued their work, delving into the murky depths of Mrs. Ramirez's psyche, Elizabeth marveled at the resilience of the human spirit—its ability to endure unimaginable pain and still emerge stronger. And within her own heart, she felt the flicker of hope grow brighter, fueled by the knowledge that healing was not just a distant dream, but a reality within their grasp.

"Close your eyes, Mrs. Ramirez," Elizabeth instructed gently, her voice a soft beacon in the dimly lit room. "Breathe slowly and deeply. With each breath, imagine yourself sinking deeper into a state of relaxation."

As Mrs. Ramirez's breathing steadied, Elizabeth continued. "Now, picture yourself standing at the edge of the nightmare that has haunted you for so long. See the darkness around you but remember that you hold the power to bring light to this place."

Mrs. Ramirez's eyelids fluttered, her body tense as she allowed herself to be led into the depths of her subconscious. Elizabeth's words wrapped around her like a protective embrace, shielding her from the suffocating shadows.

"Within this dream, you are no longer a victim," Elizabeth said, her voice taking on an authoritative tone. "Instead, you are a warrior, armed with the strength and determination you've cultivated through our sessions together. As the man who has tormented you approaches, feel the power surging through you. You are ready to face him and take back control."

A shiver ran down Mrs. Ramirez's spine as she visualized the scene unfolding before her. She saw herself, standing firm and unyielding, even as the man drew closer. The fear that had once paralyzed her now transformed into a fierce resolve, igniting a fire within her soul.

"Speak to him, Mrs. Ramirez," Elizabeth urged. "Tell him what he needs to hear and reclaim your power."

"I am not afraid of you anymore!" Mrs. Ramirez cried out, her voice trembling yet resolute. "You do not own me, and you cannot hurt me any longer!"

The air in the room crackled with energy as Mrs. Ramirez confronted the source of her nightmares, her eyes still closed but her spirit alight with newfound strength. Elizabeth watched her patient's transformation, feeling a swell of pride and admiration for the courage she displayed.

"Open your eyes, Mrs. Ramirez," Elizabeth said softly, a smile playing on her lips.

As the darkness of the nightmare receded, replaced by the comforting surroundings of Elizabeth's office, Mrs. Ramirez gazed at her therapist with tear-filled eyes. The weight that had burdened her heart for so long seemed to have lifted, leaving behind an unshakable sense of hope and strength.

"Thank you," she whispered, gripping Elizabeth's hand tightly. "I never thought I could be free of this ... but you've helped me see that I am stronger than my fears."

"Remember, Mrs. Ramirez," Elizabeth said, her voice thick with emotion, "the power to overcome your nightmares has always been within you. You just needed to unlock it."

As they sat together, basking in the light of Mrs. Ramirez's emotional breakthrough, Elizabeth knew that this was only the beginning of their journey toward healing. There were still many obstacles to face, but as she looked into the eyes of the woman before her—now blazing with determination—she felt a renewed sense of purpose and conviction in their shared quest for triumph over the darkness.

"Goodbye, Mrs. Ramirez," Elizabeth said, carefully folding her hands in her lap as she watched the woman leave the room, her steps lighter than they had been when she entered. With a deep breath, Elizabeth turned her attention to her appointment book and skimmed her finger down the list until it rested on the name: Alex. A teenager who suffered from severe social anxiety and a fear of public speaking.

The door creaked open hesitantly, revealing a lanky young man with unkempt hair that hung over his eyes like a protective curtain. His gaze darted around the office, taking in its calming ambiance, before finally settling on Elizabeth with an expression of trepidation. She offered him a warm, inviting smile and gestured for him to take a seat across from her.

"Hello, Alex. It's nice to meet you. I'm Dr. Harmon."

"Hi," he muttered, sliding into the floating chair and immediately hunching over as if trying to make himself smaller. His fingers twitched nervously in his lap, betraying his inner turmoil.

"Thank you for coming today," Elizabeth began, her voice gentle and reassuring. "I understand that just being here might be difficult for you, so I want you to know how much I appreciate your courage."

Alex's cheeks flushed, and he ducked his head further, hair obscuring his eyes entirely. Elizabeth could sense the waves of anxiety rolling off him, and she knew that creating a safe space for him was crucial.

"Let's start by talking about your fears and insecurities," she suggested softly. "You don't have to share anything you're not comfortable with, but I'm here to listen and help you work through whatever is causing you distress."

Alex shifted uneasily in his seat, avoiding her gaze. "Well, uh ... I guess I'm just really scared of people, you know? Like, I can't talk to anyone without feeling like they're judging me or ... laughing at me."

"Those feelings are completely valid, Alex," Elizabeth reassured him, her own emotions a mix of sympathy and determination to help him overcome his fears. "But I want you to know that you're not alone. Many people struggle with social anxiety, and together, we can work on strategies to help you feel more comfortable around others."

He glanced up at her, eyes wide and vulnerable, searching for the sincerity in her words. She met his gaze steadily, radiating empathy and support.

"Can you tell me about a specific situation, where your fear of public speaking has affected you?" Elizabeth asked, guiding him gently towards self-reflection.

"Um, yeah," he stammered, shoulders tightening as he recalled the memory. "Last week, my teacher made me give a presentation in front of the whole class. I couldn't even get through the first sentence before my voice cracked, and everyone started laughing. It was...it was awful."

"Thank you for sharing that with me, Alex," Elizabeth said softly, her heart aching for the young man before her. "I know that must have been difficult to relive. But we need to examine these experiences so that we can begin to understand and challenge the fears that hold us back."

"Alright, Alex," Elizabeth began, her voice steady and encouraging. "One technique we can use to address your fear is cognitive restructuring. This involves identifying the negative thoughts that contribute to your anxiety and replacing them with more balanced, rational ones."

"Like, instead of thinking 'everyone will laugh at me,' I could think, 'I'm prepared and capable of giving a good presentation'?" Alex offered hesitantly, his hands fidgeting in his lap.

"Exactly," Elizabeth affirmed, nodding approvingly. "Now, let's combine this with gradual exposure. We'll start by practicing public speaking in a low-pressure situation and then slowly increase the challenge."

Alex swallowed hard, his Adam's apple bobbing nervously. Elizabeth could see the trepidation in his eyes, but she also sensed a flicker of determination—a spark of hope that he might find relief from his crippling anxiety.

"Let's begin with a role-playing exercise," she suggested gently. "Imagine you're standing in front of your class, about to deliver a short speech. First, try focusing on those more positive thoughts we discussed earlier."

As Alex closed his eyes and took a deep breath, Elizabeth watched the tension in his body gradually dissipate. Alex shoulders relaxed, and his face softened into an expression of quiet resolve.

"Okay," he murmured, opening his eyes and looking directly at Elizabeth. "I think I'm ready."

"Great," she smiled reassuringly. "Whenever you're ready, go ahead and start your speech."

With a shaky but determined voice, Alex began reciting a speech they had prepared together earlier. Elizabeth listened attentively, offering both verbal encouragement and silent support through her empathetic gaze. As he continued, his confidence grew, and his voice steadied.

"Very well done, Alex," Elizabeth praised him once he'd finished. "How did that feel?"

"Better," he admitted, a small, proud smile tugging at the corner of his lips. "Still nerve-wracking, but better."

"Good," Elizabeth replied, her satisfaction mirrored in her warm expression. "Now let's increase the difficulty by adding some imaginary audience members—perhaps some of your classmates."

As they progressed through various scenarios, each more challenging than the last, Alex confronted his fear head-on. The visceral manifestations of his anxiety—his trembling hands, erratic heartbeat, and shallow breaths—gradually gave way to a newfound sense of control.

"Take a moment to reflect on how far you've come today, Alex," Elizabeth encouraged, her voice filled with pride. "Remember this feeling of accomplishment and use it as a reminder that you have the power to face your fears."

As she watched the transformation taking place within the young man before her, Elizabeth couldn't help but feel a swell of gratification. Through the combined forces of psychological insight and human connection, they had made tangible progress toward conquering Alex's crippling anxiety. And though the road ahead remained uncertain, one thing was clear: together, they would continue to push the boundaries of fear and self-doubt, forging a path toward healing and growth.

The ringing of the timer signaled the end of their practice session, and Elizabeth looked up to see a new light in Alex's eyes as he finished his final presentation. Now standing taller than before, his voice carried with confidence across the room, each word articulated clearly and deliberately.

"Excellent job, Alex," Elizabeth praised him, her tone genuine. "You've made incredible progress today."

"Thank you," Alex replied, a hint of surprise lacing his words. "I can't believe I did it."

"Believe it," Elizabeth assured him. "You've worked hard to overcome your fears, and it shows."

As they wrapped up their session, Elizabeth couldn't help but marvel at the transformation she had witnessed in all three of her patients that day. From Mr. Thompson's newfound courage in facing his fear of heights to Mrs. Ramirez's emotional breakthrough in confronting her traumatic past, each individual had taken significant strides towards healing and self-discovery.

In the quiet of her office, surrounded by the soft hues of calming holographic artwork, Elizabeth allowed herself a rare moment of reflection. The delicate balance of science and empathy, of guiding and being guided, had led to transformative experiences for her patients. Although the dark shadow of her sister's death continued to haunt her, the knowledge that she was helping others navigate the treacherous waters of their fears and nightmares provided her with a sense of fulfillment and purpose.

"Dr. Harmon?" Alex's voice pulled her from her thoughts, a shy smile gracing his features. "I just wanted to say ... You've helped me. I don't think I could have done this without you."

"Thank you, Alex," she replied warmly, her heart swelling with pride. "But remember, it was your strength and determination that brought about this change. I'm just here to guide you along the way."

As Alex left her office, Elizabeth took a deep breath, allowing the day's successes to settle within her. The weight of her sister's memory still pressed heavily against her soul, but the knowledge that she was making a difference in the lives of others, provided a beacon of hope amidst the darkness.

For now, at least, she could find solace in the notion that through her work, the unyielding grip of fear and despair could be loosened—one patient, one breakthrough, at a time. And as she stared at the fading sunlight filtering through her window, Elizabeth knew that the battles fought within these walls were far from over.

The setting sun cast elongated shadows across the walls of Elizabeth's office, the fading light painting a somber scene that echoed her thoughts. She stood by the window, feeling the cold glass against her palm as she observed the city below teeming with life, yet so isolated in each individual's struggles.

"Dr. Harmon?" The voice pulled her from the introspection, and she turned to see Alex standing timidly in the doorway.

"Come in, Alex," she beckoned, stepping away from the window. "How are you feeling after the presentation?"

"Good," he hesitated, his fingers fidgeting with the hem of his shirt. "But ... I'm worried."

"About what?" Elizabeth inquired gently, guiding him towards the plush armchair.

"About... about the future. What if I can't keep this up? What if I... regress?" Alex's eyes were filled with fear, the specter of anxiety lurking just beneath his newfound confidence.

"Change is a process, Alex," Elizabeth reassured him, her tone soothing yet firm. "We may stumble, we may falter, but it is our resilience and perseverance that will ultimately see us through."

"Thank you, Dr. Harmon," Alex whispered, the gratitude in his gaze momentarily dispelling the uncertainty.

"Remember, I am here to guide you," Elizabeth reminded him. "You don't have to face these challenges alone."

As Alex left her office, Elizabeth could not help but ponder her own words. She had weathered many storms, both personal and professional, yet the undercurrents of her past still threatened to pull her under. And as the night enshrouded the city, she knew that the journey ahead would be fraught with perils—not only for her patients but for herself as well.

Each soul that entered her sanctuary brought with them a unique set of trials, their tangled webs of fear and trauma woven into the very fabric of their existence. As Elizabeth bore witness to their pain, she would also confront her demons—the unresolved guilt, the unanswered questions, the insatiable drive to understand the darkness that haunted both her sister's memory and her psyche.

"Dr. Harmon?" The soft voice intruded upon her thoughts, a gentle reminder of the task at hand.

"Coming," she murmured, steeling herself for the next session. For in this crucible of healing, the battle against fear was an ongoing struggle—one that would test the limits of her strength and resilience, even as it illuminated the path toward redemption.

At the end of the day with a heavy sigh, Elizabeth sank into her chair, her gaze once again drawn to the rain-streaked window. Elizabeth couldn't shake the nagging feeling that the mysterious figure she'd seen lurking in the shadows was somehow connected to Claire's death. But why now? What had changed?

"Focus, Elizabeth," she reminded herself, trying to regain control. She reached for her phone, intending to check her schedule, but instead found herself scrolling through old messages from Claire.

Claire: Hey Elizabeth, I've been having these disturbing nightmares again.

Elizabeth: Oh no, Claire! Tell me about the nightmares you are having.

Claire: They're like vivid visions, Elizabeth. I see myself in some underground place, and people are doing somethings to me.

Elizabeth: That sounds intense, Claire. Do you think there's a reason behind these nightmares?

Claire: Well, hmm, I can't say much right now but what I can say is that I stumbled upon some information. It's like I know things I shouldn't.

Elizabeth: That's concerning, Claire. What information is this?

Claire: It's complicated, I can't tell you, but let's just say I had access to some sensitive documents, andnow I can't shake the feeling that someone's after me.

Elizabeth: Claire, this sounds serious. Have you considered talking to someone about this, like a therapist or a counselor besides me?

Claire: I'm afraid, Elizabeth.

Elizabeth: I understand your fear, Claire, but you shouldn't have to go through this alone

Claire: Thanks, Elizabeth. I appreciate your support. Maybe I should start by speaking with a therapist to help me cope with these nightmares and anxiety.

Elizabeth: That's a good idea, Claire. A therapist can provide guidance and help you navigate these difficult feelings. Just remember, I'm here for you, and we'll figure this out together.

Claire: Thank you, Elizabeth. I'll keep you updated on how things go. I hope these nightmares stop soon.

Elizabeth: Please do, Claire. We'll get through this, no matter what it takes. Your well-being is what matters most.

An incoming text popped up on her screen as she scrolled through Claire's old messages. Elizabeth clicked on the unknown number.

"Have you forgotten about me, Dr. Harmon?" The text sent a shiver down her spine. Her breath caught, and her fingers trembled as she struggled to type a response.

"Who is this?" she demanded, the words appearing on the screen as if spoken by someone else.

"Someone who knows the truth about Claire," came the chilling reply.

Elizabeth's heart hammered in her chest, and she felt a cold sweat break out on her brow. Her mind raced with questions, each more terrifying than the last. Who was this person? What did they know? And most importantly, what did they want from her?

"Tell me what you know," she typed, fighting to keep her voice steady as she hit send. But the response never came. Instead, the message was marked as "deleted" by the sender.

Elizabeth stared at the blank screen in disbelief, the weight of uncertainty settling over her like a suffocating blanket. The storm outside mirrored the chaos within her—a tempest of fear, guilt, and unanswered questions that threatened to destroy everything she'd worked for.

As Elizabeth sat in her office, surrounded by the trappings of her success, she couldn't help but feel the walls closing in around her. The shadows of her past loomed large, and the truth about her sister's death seemed both tantalizingly close and impossibly out of reach. With every passing second, the line between reality and fiction continued to blur, leaving her to wonder: would she ever find the answers she so desperately sought, or would she become another victim of the darkness that had claimed her sister's life?

Chapter 2

The rain fell like needles against the windowpanes of Dr. Elizabeth Harmon's office, blurring her view of the cityscape beyond. She stared out into the murky shadows, her dark eyes haunted by memories she could never escape. Her sister, Claire—always so full of life, her smile a beacon in the darkness—had been gone,, taken by an unexplained death that left a gaping void in Elizabeth's heart. The guilt festered within her, an ever-present reminder that she had failed to protect her little sister.

"Dr. Harmon?" a voice called cautiously, pulling her back into the present. It was Anna, her face lined with anxiety as she fidgeted nervously on the couch.

"Apologies," she murmured, giving them a reassuring smile. "You were describing your nightmare?"

Anna nodded, swallowing hard. "I'm trapped in this labyrinth. I can't see anything, but I can hear ... whispers. And there's ... something following me. I can feel it."

Elizabeth felt a chill run down her spine. This wasn't the first time she had heard such a description from Anna and Mr. Thompson, a tall and muscular man who rarely spoke of his emotions, had recounted almost the exact dream from days before.

"Tell me more about the whispers," Elizabeth said, her voice steady despite her growing concerns. She made a mental note to compare the patients' histories later, searching for any common threads that might explain their shared experiences.

"The voices are indistinct," Anna continued, their eyes widening in fear. "But they sound... malicious. Like they want to hurt me. And the thing that's chasing me, it's relentless. I can't escape it, no matter how fast I run or where I hide."

As Anna spoke, Elizabeth could feel the terror seeping off her like a stain. She knew all too well the agony of being haunted by something unseen and unexplained. It was that very pain that drove her to become a psychologist, to help others navigate the labyrinthine darkness that life often presented.

"Thank you for sharing this with me," she said softly, locking eyes with Anna. "We will work through this together, I promise."

As the rain continued to fall outside, Elizabeth vowed not only to help her patients but also to uncover the truth behind their shared nightmare. She would not let another soul be lost to the shadows like her sister had been.

"Tell me again about the nightmare," Dr. Harmon prompted her second patient, a tall man in his late forties. His muscular build seemed at odds with the vulnerability he displayed as he recounted his experiences.

"Every time it starts, I find myself in this... maze," Mr. Thompson began, his voice trembling. "The walls are impossibly high, and they seem to stretch on forever. It's like a labyrinth designed by a madman, filled with dead ends and false paths."

"Go on," Elizabeth urged, her heart pounding in her chest. Elizabeth recognized the details of the dream from the earlier session with Anna, and the similarities were too striking to be a mere coincidence.

"Everything is shrouded in darkness," Mr. Thompson continued. "I can barely see my own hands in front of me. And there are these... shadows, lurking just beyond my peripheral vision. They seem to follow me wherever I go, always one step behind."

As Mr. Thompson spoke, Elizabeth felt a cold shiver run down her spine. The nightmare was eerily reminiscent of her sister Claire's last days when she had been plagued by a similar sense of being pursued by an unseen force. The thought sent a wave of fear and guilt through her, but she pushed those emotions aside, focusing on her patient's words.

"Then there are the whispers," Mr. Thompson said, his eyes darting nervously around the room as if expecting the voices to materialize at any moment. "They're barely audible, but I can feel their intent. They want me trapped, cornered, broken."

"Have you ever seen the entity that stalks you?" Elizabeth asked, trying to keep her voice steady. Elizabeth could hardly believe that two patients, seemingly unrelated, were experiencing such similar nightmares.

"No. I've never laid eyes on it," Mr. Thompson admitted, his face contorted with fear. "But I can feel its presence, always just out of sight. It's a predator, hunting me through the maze."

"Thank you for sharing this with me," she said softly, her mind racing with questions and theories. Elizabeth had to find the connection between Anna and Mr. Thompson—their age difference and varied medical histories seemed to defy any logical explanation for the shared nightmare.

Dr. Elizabeth Harmon sat at her desk; a thick folder of medical records spread out before her like the labyrinth that haunted her patients' nightmares. The rain pattered insistently against the windowpane and the shadows seemed to dance with each gust of wind. With every new case she discovered, her anxiety grew. Elizabeth could not shake the feeling that something sinister was at work here.

"Age differences, gender disparities, no common medical history," she muttered to herself, her fingers drumming on the edge of the desk. "There has to be a connection, some thread that ties them all together."

Elizabeth couldn't ignore the prickle of fear that crawled up her spine or the weight of unresolved guilt that pressed down upon her chest. Claire's death had left an indelible mark on her soul, driving her to search for answers wherever they might lie. The similarities between her sister's demise and these shared nightmares were uncanny, to say the least.

"Time to dig deeper," she whispered, pulling up the browser on her holographic computer and diving into a world of research articles and case studies. Hours went by as she scoured the depths of the internet, sifting through medical journals and obscure forum posts.

"Shared dreams ... collective unconscious ... dream manipulation?" she mumbled, the words catching in her throat. Elizabeth heart raced as she stumbled upon a series of articles discussing experimental government projects involving dream manipulation and induced shared nightmares and the hive mind. Could this be the answer she was seeking? Elizabeth knew that the hive mind was a few years old and that it was a global product where people could share their thoughts and feelings. It was a great product, and it helped with her sessions as well.

"Hello, Dr. Sanders," she said nervously into the phone, after dialing the number of a former scientist, mentioned in one of the articles. "My name is Dr. Elizabeth Harmon. I'm a psychologist, and I've come across some unsettling information, regarding a string of shared nightmares, among my patients. I believe you may be able to help me understand what's going on."

"Ah, Dr. Harmon," Martin Sanders replied, his voice a mixture of curiosity and trepidation. "I've heard of your work. I must admit, I'm surprised to hear from you. What exactly are you hoping I can help you with?"

"Your research on dream manipulation," she confessed, trying to contain the tremor in her voice. "I think it might be connected to what my patients are experiencing."

"Dr. Harmon, that was years ago." Dr. Sanders sighed heavily. "It was a failed project, a mistake I deeply regret."

"I understand, Dr. Sanders, I would like to know more. I believe my sister's death is linked to these nightmares."

"Very well," he conceded, the sound of papers rustling in the background. "Meet me at my office tomorrow. We have much to discuss."

"Tomorrow," she whispered, her fingers gripping the edge of her desk as she braced herself for the harrowing journey ahead. "Tomorrow, I will find the answers."

Elizabeth couldn't believe her luck. Finally, she had a chance to get to the bottom of the nightmare her patients had been experiencing, and hopefully find a connection to her sister's death. Elizabeth spent the rest of the day preparing for the meeting, pouring over every article and research paper she could find on dream manipulation and the hive mind.

The next day, Elizabeth arrived at Dr. Sanders' office promptly at 9 a.m. The building was old and decrepit, with peeling paint and creaky floors, but the office itself was surprisingly modern, filled with the latest technology and equipment.

Elizabeth extended a warm greeting to Dr. Sanders, shaking his hand with gratitude. "Thank you for agreeing to meet with me," she expressed. Dr. Sanders, an older man with a distinguished appearance, seemed to be in his 50s, his grey hair complementing a tall and muscular build.

"Of course, Dr. Harmon," he replied, motioning for her to take a seat. "Now, tell me more about these nightmares your patients have been experiencing."

Elizabeth took a deep breath and began to explain, "It started a few months ago. Several of my patients began reporting the same nightmare, a dark and twisted landscape filled with monsters and demons. At first, I thought it was just a coincidence, but then more and more patients began reporting the same dream. It's become so frequent that it's starting to affect their daily lives."

"I see," Dr. Sanders nodded thoughtfully. "And you believe there's a connection to my research on dream manipulation?"

"Yes," Elizabeth replied firmly. "I've read all your papers, Dr. Sanders. You were experimenting with ways to induce shared nightmares and manipulate dreams. I believe that someone is using your research to create these nightmares in my patients."

Dr. Sanders leaned back in his chair, his eyes narrowing in contemplation. "It's possible," he admitted. "But my research was shut down years ago. I don't see how someone could be using it now."

"Perhaps they found a way to access your research and use it for their purposes," Elizabeth suggested, her mind racing with possibilities.

"I suppose that's possible," Dr. Sanders mused. "But why would anyone want to do this? What's the endgame?"

"That's what I'm hoping to find out," Elizabeth said determinedly. "I need your help, Dr. Sanders. I need to know everything about your research, every detail, every experiment."

Dr. Sanders looked at her for a long moment, studying her face. Finally, he nodded. "Very well," he said. "I'll tell you everything I know. But be warned, Dr. Harmon, it's not a pleasant story."

Elizabeth braced herself as Dr. Sanders launched into his tale. Dr. Sanders told her about the early days of his research, the excitement, and the promise of unlocking the mysteries of the human mind. Dr. Sanders spoke of the experiments, the induced nightmares, the shared dreams, and the unexpected consequences. Dr. Sanders spoke of the hive mind and the dangers of tampering with the collective unconscious. And finally, he spoke of the government's involvement, the cover-ups, and the lies.

Elizabeth listened in horror, her mind reeling with the implications of what she heard. This was so much bigger than she had ever imagined, so much more dangerous. But she couldn't turn back now, not when her patients' lives were at stake.

"Thank you, Dr. Sanders," she said, her voice shaking slightly. "This is a lot to take in, but I need to know more. How can we stop whoever is using your research to harm my patients?"

Dr. Sanders leaned forward, his eyes serious. "I think the first step is to figure out who is behind this. Someone must have access to my research and the technology to induce these nightmares. We need to find out who they are and stop them."

"But how do we do that?" Elizabeth asked, feeling overwhelmed by the enormity of the task.

"We start by investigating," Dr. Sanders replied. "We look into any recent cases, anyone who have access to the technology. We dig deep and we don't stop until we find the source of this."

Elizabeth nodded, her mind racing with possibilities. Elizabeth knew it wouldn't be easy, but she was determined to get to the bottom of this and put a stop to it once and for all.

"Thank you, Dr. Sanders," she said, rising from her seat. "I appreciate your help and your candor. I'll keep you updated on any progress we make."

"Please do," Dr. Sanders said, standing to shake her hand. "And be careful, Dr. Harmon. The people behind this will stop at nothing to keep their secrets hidden."

Elizabeth left Dr. Sanders' office feeling both exhilarated and terrified.

Dr. Harmon sat in the dimly lit room next to her office, her hands clasped tightly around a steaming cup of tea as she prepared herself for the upcoming interviews. Elizabeth glanced at the clock, its ticking echoing throughout the room, reminding her that time was slipping away. Elizabeth requested that her patients meet her for a group discussion so they could provide her with more details about their nightmares.

"Alright," she whispered to herself, taking a deep breath. "Let's do this."

As each patient entered the room, Elizabeth was struck by the weight of their fear and anxiety. It hung in the air, thick and suffocating, as she peered into their haunted eyes and asked them to relive their nightmares.

"Can you describe the labyrinth for me?" Elizabeth asked gently, her voice barely more than a whisper as she scribbled notes in her holographic notepad.

"Dark," one patient murmured, his eyes darting around the room, as if searching for an escape route. "Endless corridors, like a maze designed to trap us."

"Have you seen anything ... unusual in your dreams?" Elizabeth continued, catching a glimpse of her reflection in the window—dark hair, determined expression, a sinister ghost lurking in the shadows.

"Shadows," another patient breathed, shivering despite the warmth of the room. "They're always watching, waiting. Whispering things, I can't understand."

"Is there any entity that seems to be causing these nightmares?" Elizabeth asked, her eyes narrowing as she tried to piece together the puzzle before her.

"Something ... unseen," a woman admitted, her fingers twisting anxiously in her lap. "I can feel it stalking me, hunting me down like prey. But I never see it, only sense its presence."

"Thank you," Elizabeth murmured, her heart aching for the patients, who suffered from these terrifying dreams. As they filed out of the room, one by one, she couldn't shake the feeling that she held the key to unlocking the truth—a truth that could save them all.

Elizabeth adjusted the position of her dark-rimmed glasses and looked down at the notes she had been scribbling in the margins of a medical journal. The ink seemed to bleed into her thoughts, merging with memories of her sister's unexplained death. Elizabeth rubbed her temples, attempting to distance herself from the grief that still clung to her—like a thick fog.

"Is this why I became a psychologist?" Elizabeth asked herself, her voice above a whisper. "To understand the depths of the human mind? To find answers where others can't?"

In the quiet moments between appointments, Elizabeth allowed herself to drift deeper into her thoughts, considering the implications of what she had discovered. Elizabeth knew she was venturing further from the familiar shores of her field, but the stakes were too high to turn back now. Elizabeth had to help her patients, and if doing so meant untangling the enigmatic threads of their collective nightmares, then she would follow those threads to their very end.

"Whatever it takes," she vowed, her voice steady and resolute. "I will find the truth."

Anna fidgeted in her seat, gripping the armrests tightly with clammy hands. Elizabeth leaned forward; her eyes locked on the troubled individual before her.

"Take your time," she said gently, an encouraging smile playing at the corners of her mouth.

"Right," Anna managed, swallowing hard. "So, it all started in this ... maze. A labyrinth, really. The walls were impossibly high, like ancient stone edifices that seemed to go on forever."

Elizabeth felt a shiver run down her spine, the vividness of the description striking a chord deep within her. Elizabeth nodded for Anna to continue.

"Everywhere I turned, there were these ... shadowy figures. They didn't have faces, but I could feel their eyes on me, watching my every move. It was like being hunted."

A bead of sweat trickled down Anna's forehead, as if the mere act of recounting the nightmare had transported them back into its terrifying grip.

"I tried to run, but the further I went, the more lost I became. Fear and desperation consumed me, making it harder to breathe and think clearly."

As Anna spoke, Elizabeth found herself unable to shake the feeling that all her patients had the same nightmare. The labyrinth, the shadowy figures, the overwhelming sense of dread—all of these elements echoed through the testimonies of other patients, who had experienced similarly haunting nightmares.

"Thank you for sharing that with me," Elizabeth said, her voice soft but firm. "I know how difficult it must be to relive those emotions."

Anna looked up at her, her eyes brimming with tears. "You don't know the half of it, doc. This nightmare feels more real than life itself. I can't escape it, no matter what I do."

The raw emotion in Anna's voice sent a tremor of unease through Elizabeth's core. The implications of these shared nightmares were too significant to ignore, and her intuition told her that the key to unlocking this mystery lay within the labyrinthine dreamscape.

Elizabeth sat in her office long after Anna had left, the weight of their words still echoing in the dimly lit room. Elizabeth turned her floating chair to face the window, watching as darkness began to envelop the city skyline. Elizabeth thoughts swirled like a chaotic storm, each crashing wave bringing forth new questions and ideas about the phenomenon that haunted her patients' dreams.

"Causes... triggers... treatments," she muttered under her breath, tapping her touch screen pen against her holographic notepad. The labyrinthine nightmares seemed to defy all logic, yet she knew there must be some common thread that connected them. Determined not to let these terrifying experiences consume her patients any longer, she picked up the phone and dialed her colleague and friend, Dr. Susan Parker.

"Susan, it's Elizabeth," she said urgently when her friend answered. "I need your help. I've noticed something ... bizarre happening with my patients, and I think you may have come across it too."

"Go on," Susan replied cautiously, the curiosity in her voice barely audibles over the soft hum of the connection.

"Several of my patients are having recurring nightmares—but they aren't just your run-of-the-mill bad dreams. These are... different. They're intense, vivid, and eerily similar between patients. Have you experienced anything like this with your patients?"

There was a moment of silence before Susan answered, her voice tinged with apprehension. "Yes. Yes, I have. But I didn't know what to make of it. I thought it might be an isolated incident, or perhaps some strange coincidence."

"Can we meet tomorrow?" Elizabeth asked, her voice filled with determination. "We need to discuss this further and compare notes. I have a feeling we're dealing with something much bigger than we initially thought."

"Of course," Susan agreed. "I'll clear my schedule."

As she hung up the phone, she made a mental list of every possible angle to explore in their investigation. Elizabeth needed to analyze the nightmares' potential causes, from environmental factors to psychological triggers. Elizabeth would examine past and present treatments for recurring nightmares, searching for patterns and breakthroughs.

When Elizabeth returned to her office the following day, she began her investigation in earnest. As sunlight filtered through the blinds, casting a pattern of light and shadow on her desk, she spread out an array of books, articles, and case studies related to recurring nightmares. The clinical scent of the office mixed with the musty smell of old books, created an atmosphere of both anxiety and curiosity.

"Alright," she muttered under her breath, pulling her dark hair back into a tight bun, as her mind whirred with possibilities. "Let's start connecting the dots."

Elizabeth fingers tapped rhythmically against the desk as she scanned each document, absorbing all the information she could find on the topic. In between pages, she would pause to jot down notes or highlight passages that seemed particularly relevant. The more she read, the more the threads of the shared nightmare phenomenon began to weave together in her mind.

"Interesting," she murmured, pausing at an article discussing the psychological impact of collective trauma on dream content. "Could these nightmares be a manifestation of a city-wide trauma?"

As she delved deeper, she found another study that analyzed the effects of toxins and environmental factors on dreams. Elizabeth remembered Anna mentioning how the labyrinth felt suffocating, filled with a toxic mist that burned their lungs. This led her to wonder if there were external forces at play, shaping the nightmarish experiences of her patients.

"Or is it something more sinister?" Elizabeth whispered, recalling the chilling figure that haunted the center of the labyrinth. Elizabeth heart raced, as she considered the possibility, of a malevolent force manipulating the dreams of her patients, for reasons yet unknown.

"Dr. Harmon?" a voice called from the door, snapping her out of her reverie. It was Susan, her colleague and confidant, looking concerned. "I hope I'm not interrupting, but I couldn't wait to share my findings with you."

"Please, come in," Elizabeth replied, gesturing to the chair opposite her.

As the two women exchanged their findings and theories, they began to piece together a preliminary understanding of the shared nightmare phenomenon. They discussed the potential influence of trauma, environmental factors, and even the presence of an unknown antagonist. Through their conversation, Elizabeth found herself drawing closer to a hypothesis that could potentially explain the sinister origins of these nightmares.

"Susan, I think we need to consider the possibility that this isn't simply a psychological or environmental issue," she said, her voice firm with conviction. "There's something more at play here, something that connects all of our patients and perhaps even us."

"Are you suggesting some sort of ... consciousness?" Susan asked hesitantly, her eyes widening at the implications.

"Perhaps," Elizabeth replied, her mind racing with the possibilities. "But there's still so much we don't understand. We'll need to gather more data, conduct interviews, and perhaps even collaborate with experts in other fields. This is just the beginning."

A cold gust of wind forced its way into Elizabeth's office, the open window from her office, rattling the windows and chilling her to the bone. It was as if the icy tendrils of the shared nightmare reached out from the depths of her patients' minds and into her very soul. Elizabeth drew her coat around her shoulders and returned to her desk, where a collection of books and articles were spread out before her.

"Elizabeth," Susan's voice crackled through the speakerphone, "I think I've found something." The urgency in her tone snapped Elizabeth to attention, her heart rate quickening.

"Tell me," She replied, gripping the edge of her desk with anticipation.

"During my research on recurring dreams, I came across an old case study from the year 2065 about a group of psychiatric patients in this hospital who experienced similar nightmares," Susan explained, barely pausing for breath. "They claimed a malevolent presence haunted their dreams, driving them mad. The doctors at the time dismissed it as mass hysteria, but I think there's more to it."

"Go on," urged Elizabeth, her mind racing with possibilities.

"Most of the patients in that study, reported feeling trapped, unable to escape the labyrinth of their minds. They also mentioned a strange, overwhelming sensation of being watched," Susan continued. "Sound familiar?"

"Too familiar," Elizabeth muttered under her breath. "Could this be the key to understanding what's happening to our patients?"

"It gets stranger. All the patients in the study had one thing in common: they'd been exposed to an experimental neurotoxin, that's what the article says," Susan revealed. "The toxin was known to induce hallucinations and alter brain chemistry. Perhaps it's somehow related to these shared nightmares?"

"Neurotoxin? Have you heard of Dr. Sanders research from years ago? He shed some light for me about the intensity and the recurring nature of these dreams," Elizabeth mused, her eyes glazing over as she considered the implications. "But what about the connection between the patients? How are they all being exposed? And how do we treat them?"

"First, we need to confirm whether the neurotoxin is responsible," Susan suggested. "I've already contacted a toxicologist who's agreed to run tests, on blood samples from our patients. If we can prove a link, then we can start developing a treatment plan."

"Good work, Susan," Elizabeth praised, feeling a renewed sense of hope and determination. "I'll start preparing our patients for the tests and inform their families. We have to act quickly—we can't let this nightmare continue, and I need to get back in touch with Dr. Sanders to get more answers, concerning the experimentation and when it was defunded."

"Agreed," Susan said firmly. "We're in this together, Elizabeth. Whatever it takes, we'll find a way to help our patients and put an end to this darkness."

Together, they pored over medical records, meticulously cross-referencing prescription histories and dosages. As days turned into weeks, Elizabeth's frustration grew. Medication alone wasn't enough; her patients needed more comprehensive support, to confront the horrors that haunted their dreams.

"Elizabeth, have you considered creating a support group for all your patients, who are experiencing these nightmares?" Susan asked, watching her friend's hands tremble with exhaustion.

"We have started meeting together," Elizabeth conceded, rubbing her temples. "But it's not just about talking. I need to teach them coping skills—ways to regain control even when they're trapped in that labyrinth."

"Then let's develop a program together," Susan offered. "We can combine therapy, relaxation techniques, and practical exercises to help them face their fears."

Emboldened by Susan's support, Elizabeth threw herself into crafting a comprehensive program for her patients. Elizabeth began each session by establishing a safe and nurturing environment, encouraging open communication and mutual support. In time, her patients revealed their deepest fears—the shadows that lurked within the labyrinth, the whispers that echoed through its halls, and the unseen entity that stalked them relentlessly.

"Focus on your breath," Elizabeth instructed during an exercise, watching as her patient's chest rose and fell in a slow, steady rhythm. "Allow the tension to melt away with each exhale."

"Okay ... I can do this," the woman whispered, determination shining in her eyes.

"Remember," Elizabeth continued, "you have the power to change your thoughts. You can face those shadows and whispers head-on, knowing you're not alone."

The patients practiced mindfulness techniques, grounding themselves in the present moment even when fear threatened to overwhelm them. They learned to recognize the physical signs of panic and how to regain control, one breath at a time.

As weeks turned into months, Elizabeth monitored her patients' progress closely, rejoicing in each small victory. Elizabeth listened intently as they recounted their dreams, noting subtle changes in the narrative—moments when they had stood up to the darkness instead of cowering in fear.

"Last night, when the whispers started," one patient shared, his voice trembling with awe, "I managed to silence them by repeating a mantra Dr. Harmon taught me."

"Amazing!" another patient chimed in. "That's real progress!"

"Thank you, Dr. Harmon," the man said, tears glistening in his eyes. "You've given us hope."

Hope. The word resonated deep within Elizabeth's soul, igniting a fire that burned away the exhaustion and self-doubt. As she looked around the room, meeting the grateful gazes of her patients, she knew she was making a difference—that together, they would find a way to stop the nightmare from recurring.

And yet, a nagging doubt lingered in the back of her mind. What if, despite all her efforts, the root cause remained hidden, forever shrouded in darkness?

The flickering fluorescent light in the small group therapy room next to her office cast an eerie glow over the patients huddled together, their faces etched with exhaustion. Elizabeth sat among them, her eyes scanning the room, taking note of the subtle improvements in their demeanor since implementing her tailored treatment plans.

"Alright everyone, let's do a quick check-in," she announced, her voice a soothing balm to their frayed nerves. "How are we feeling this week?"

"Better, actually," Anna admitted, fidgeting with the hem of her sweatshirt. "I've been using the breathing exercises you taught us, and it's helped me stay calm during the nightmare."

"Me too," chimed in another patient, his hands gripping each other tightly in his lap. "I'm starting to feel more in control when I'm in the labyrinth."

Elizabeth nodded, acknowledging their progress. As they continued sharing and linking their thoughts, and images through the hive mind link, she made mental notes of their achievements—fewer nightmares, less anxiety, improved sleep quality. They were healing, slowly but surely. And yet, something inside her gnawed at the edges of her satisfaction, a relentless hunger for understanding that refused to be sated.

"Dr. Harmon?" a young woman named Emily hesitantly interjected, her voice barely audible. "I ... I faced the entity last night."

A collective shudder ran through the group, and Elizabeth felt her pulse quicken. Elizabeth leaned forward; her eyes locked on Emily's as she urged her to continue.

"What happened?" Elizabeth asked softly, her heart thudding in her chest.

"I stood my ground," Emily whispered, her pale face flushed with pride. "I told it that it couldn't hurt me anymore. And then ... it disappeared."

"Amazing, Emily!" Elizabeth exclaimed, her face lighting up with genuine joy. "That's a huge step forward!"

As the group erupted in applause, tears streamed down Emily's cheeks, and Elizabeth's heart swelled with pride. Elizabeth was helping these people regain control of their lives, one brave act at a time.

"Thank you, Dr. Harmon," Emily murmured, her voice thick with emotion. "I couldn't have done it without you."

"Remember, we're all in this together," Elizabeth reassured her. "We'll confront our fears as a team and emerge stronger for it."

As Elizabeth closed the door behind her last patient, a feeling of exhaustion mixed with curiosity washed over her. The labyrinth in their dreams was becoming more than just a coincidence. Elizabeth closed her eyes and took a deep breath. At that moment, a memory she had tried to keep buried for years resurfaced.

The sun was a brilliant golden orb dipping into the horizon, casting its warm hues across the sky. They were at their favorite spot - the small, secluded beach nestled between rugged cliffs. The salty breeze carried the scent of seaweed and the distant cries of seagulls. Waves lapped gently at the shore, leaving intricate patterns in the sand as they retreated. It was here, in the final days of summer, where Elizabeth and Claire shared a moment that would forever be etched into their hearts.

The air was thick with anticipation as the sun began to set, revealing a kaleidoscope of colors that danced on the water's surface. The tide crept in slowly, swallowing the footprints they had left in the sand as if the world was preparing to erase any trace of their presence. Elizabeth could feel the cool embrace of the ocean on her toes, while the damp sand squished beneath her feet.

"Look, Lizzie!" Claire exclaimed, pointing towards the horizon. "It's so beautiful!"

Her voice was a melody carried by the wind, blending seamlessly with the symphony of crashing waves and rustling leaves. The warmth radiating from her sister's touch seemed to defy the growing chill in the air, igniting an ember of hope within Elizabeth.

Their laughter echoed against the backdrop of the setting sun, creating a harmony that only they could understand. As the sky darkened and the first stars appeared, the sisters sat side by side, their fingers entwined, silently soaking in the breathtaking view. It was a rare moment of peace amidst the chaos of their lives, a respite from the storm that loomed on the horizon.

"Promise me something, Lizzie," Claire whispered as the last remnants of sunlight vanished, leaving them bathed in the silver glow of the moon. "No matter what happens, we'll always be there for each other."

Elizabeth's heart clenched at her sister's words, knowing the weight they carried. She wrapped her arm around Claire's shoulders, pulling her close. "I promise, Claire. You're my rock. I'll never let anything happen to you."

As the tide continued to rise, the sisters embraced, their hearts beating in unison. It was a moment suspended in time, where love and loss intertwined, forging an unbreakable bond that would echo through eternity. The world around them seemed to hold its breath as if paying tribute to the sacred vow they had made to one another.

In the present, Elizabeth opened her eyes once more. Her office seemed colder, somehow, devoid of the warmth that memory held. Elizabeth knew this connection with her patients wasn't just about unraveling the mystery of their shared nightmares; it was about finding answers and closure for the sister she lost so long ago. As she wiped away a stray tear, Elizabeth vowed to herself that she would uncover the truth—for Claire, for her patients, and herself.

The memory of that fateful day swept over Elizabeth like the tide rushing in, relentless and inevitable. She found herself back on the rocky shore, a younger version of herself with wind-whipped dark hair and eyes that held a glimmer of innocence not yet tarnished by loss. Beside her stood Claire, petite and bright-eyed, her laughter carried away by the salty breeze.

"Hey Lizzie, remember that time we tried to build a sandcastle right here?" Claire asked, grinning as she pointed to a spot where the waves lapped at the shoreline.

Elizabeth laughed, recalling the shared adventure. "Oh, I do! You insisted on making the tallest tower, but it kept collapsing. We spent hours trying to perfect it."

"Nothing could stop us," Claire said, her eyes sparkling with mischief. "Not even the angry seagulls who thought our castle was an invasion."

"Or that nosy crab who tried to steal our shells!" Elizabeth added, giggling as she mimicked its sideways scuttle.

They laughed together until their sides ached, bound by the warmth of their shared memories. As the tide crept higher, threatening to wash away their footprints in the sand, Elizabeth felt the weight of her sister's hand in hers—small, warm, and reassuring.

"Promise me something, Lizzie," Claire murmured, her voice barely audible above the ocean's roar.

"Anything," Elizabeth replied without hesitation, her heart swelling with love and protectiveness for her little sister.

"Promise that no matter how far away life takes us, we'll always find our way back to this place." Claire's eyes were filled with a tender earnestness that pierced Elizabeth's soul.

"I promise, Claire." Elizabeth squeezed her sister's hand, sealing the vow between them. "This beach will always be our sanctuary, our touchstone."

As the sisters stood there, hand in hand, the waves crashing against the rocks around them, Elizabeth could feel the unbreakable bond that tethered their souls. In that moment, she knew that nothing—not distance, time, or tragedy—could ever truly separate them.

The sun dipped low on the horizon, casting a golden glow over the small grove where Elizabeth and Claire found solace. The air was thick with the scent of *jasmine and honeysuckle, their laughter intertwining with the songs of birds in the canopy above.*

"Remember that time we tried to cook dinner for Mom and Dad?" Elizabeth asked, her eyes sparkling with mirth as she recalled their disastrous culinary adventure.

Claire's laughter rippled through the grove like a delicate melody. "How could I forget? We used salt instead of sugar! Their faces were priceless!"

Elizabeth leaned back against the rough bark of an ancient oak, the memories of their childhood washing over her like warm honey. She watched fondly as Claire plucked a sprig of wildflowers, her fingers nimble and precise. Claire's smile seemed to light up the grove, casting away any lingering shadows.

"Here," Claire said, extending the bouquet to her sister, a mischievous glint in her eyes. "These are for you, to remind you of me when I'm not around."

"Like I could ever forget you," Elizabeth teased, tucking the flowers behind her ear with a flourish. "I'll cherish them always, little sis."

As they sat in companionable silence, the world outside the grove seemed to fade away, leaving only the sisters and their unbreakable bond. Elizabeth knew there was nothing she wouldn't do for Claire—no challenge too great, no obstacle too daunting.

It was then that they heard the sound of approaching footsteps, heavy and deliberate. A shiver ran down Elizabeth's spine; this was their secret place, known only to them.

"Who's there?" she called out, fear creeping into her voice.

A boy emerged from the shadows, his sneer sending a chill down Elizabeth's spine. "What're you two doing here? This is our territory," he spat, his eyes narrowed in contempt.

"Your territory?" Claire retorted, her voice steady despite the tremor in her hands. "We've been coming here for years."

"Too bad," the boy sneered, cracking his knuckles menacingly. "It's ours now."

Elizabeth felt a surge of protectiveness for her sister, her love for Claire fueling her courage. She stood tall and faced the intruder, her heart pounding in her chest like a drumbeat.

"Leave us alone," she demanded, her voice unwavering. "You don't scare us."

"Is that so?" The boy smirked as two more boys emerged from the shadows, flanking him on either side.

Claire squeezed Elizabeth's hand, her fear palpable. "Lizzie, what do we do?"

Looking into her sister's worried eyes, Elizabeth's resolve hardened. She wouldn't let anyone threaten their sanctuary, their bond.

"Stay behind me," she whispered to Claire, her mind racing with plans and contingencies. "I won't let them hurt you."

As the boys advanced, the sisters stood their ground, united by love and determination. They would face this challenge together, as they always had—with courage, resilience, and an unbreakable bond.

The shadows seemed to grow longer, stretching out like grasping hands as the sun dipped lower in the sky. Elizabeth could feel her heart hammering against her ribcage, the tension in the air thick enough to choke on. The boys moved closer, their taunts and jeers echoing off the trees that surrounded their sanctuary.

"Maybe we should show these girls whose boss," one of the boys hissed under his breath, a cruel glint in his eyes.

"Or maybe they'll learn their lesson if we make them pay," another added, his voice dripping with malice.

As the danger grew ever more imminent, Elizabeth found herself fixating on the smallest of details, as if doing so might somehow save them from this nightmare. She noticed the way the wind rustled the leaves above them, creating an eerie symphony of whispers. She observed how the setting sun cast long, distorted shadows that twisted across the ground like creeping tendrils. And she felt the weight of Claire's hand gripping hers as if they could somehow anchor each other in reality amidst the horrors unfolding before them.

"Please," Elizabeth pleaded, desperation lacing her words as she tried to reason with the boys. *"We won't come back here, just let us go."*

"Too late for that," the ringleader snarled, lunging forward.

In that moment, time seemed to slow down, each heartbeat stretching into an eternity. Elizabeth's mind raced with memories of her sister—their laughter, their shared dreams, their unbreakable bond. She realized with sickening clarity that this was no ordinary conflict; it was a harbinger of the tragedy that would soon consume them both.

"Run, Claire!" Elizabeth screamed, shoving her sister away from the impending threat.

Claire hesitated, tears streaming down her face as she glanced between Elizabeth and the encroaching danger. But with one final, desperate look into her sister's eyes, she turned and ran, disappearing into the dense foliage.

As the boys descended upon Elizabeth, she fought with every ounce of strength and courage she possessed. But even as her body succumbed to the violence that was unleashed upon her, her mind refused to accept defeat. Instead, it clung to the love she felt for Claire—a love that burned brighter than the pain, the fear, the darkness that threatened to consume her.

And when the world finally faded away, leaving only the cold emptiness of loss behind, Elizabeth knew that her love for her sister would be the one thing that could never die. It was a love forged through years of laughter and tears, shared dreams, and unspoken promises. And even in the face of the unimaginable, it remained unwavering, eternal.

The rain drummed against the windowpane as Elizabeth stared blankly into the storm, her mind drifting back to that fateful day that changed everything. She could still hear Claire's laughter ringing in her ears, a bittersweet echo of the past.

"Come on, Lizzy!" Claire giggled, tugging at her older sister's hand. "Let's build a fort in the living room!"

"Alright," Elizabeth said, smiling despite her exhaustion. "But only if you promise not to tell Mom."

"Promise," Claire beamed, crossing her heart and intertwining their fingers.

As they moved pillows and blankets to create their secret hideout, Elizabeth felt a sense of serenity she had never known before. The world outside seemed to melt away, leaving only the warmth of their sisterly bond and the steady rhythm of the rain.

"Hey, Claire," Elizabeth began hesitantly, pausing in her construction efforts. "You know I'd do anything to keep you safe, right?"

"Of course, Lizzy," Claire replied, her eyes wide with innocence.

"Good," Elizabeth whispered, pulling her sister close for a hug. "I just... I always feel like something terrible is going to happen, and I don't want to lose you."

"I won't let anything happen to me," Claire promised, her voice small but determined. "We'll always be together, Lizzy. You're my favorite person in the whole wide world."

"Mine too," Elizabeth said, her throat tight with emotion. "Just remember, if anything ever happens, I'll be there for you. Always."

The significance of that moment lingered in Elizabeth's heart, a permanent reminder of the love and devotion that bound them together. It was a connection that transcended time and space, a force that guided her every step in her quest for answers. She would not rest until she unveiled the truth until she honored the memory of her beloved sister.

"Your love will light my way," Elizabeth whispered to herself, her eyes brimming with tears. "And I will never stop fighting for you, Claire. Never."

The rain outside their makeshift fort began to soften, transforming from a torrential downpour into a gentle patter. Elizabeth and Claire listened to the soothing rhythm, their heartbeats syncing to nature's calming lullaby. Within the cozy confines of their sanctuary, a fragile world built from pillows and blankets, they were cocooned in love and safety.

"Promise me, Lizzy," Claire whispered, her small hand wrapping around Elizabeth's, *"that no matter what happens, we'll always be there for each other."* Her eyes shone with a fierce determination that belied her young age.

"I promise, Claire," Elizabeth replied, her voice choking with emotion. *"You're not just my sister, you're my best friend. I'd do anything for you."*

"Even if it means facing scary monsters?" Claire asked, her grip on Elizabeth's hand tightening.

"Especially then," Elizabeth reassured her, pulling Claire closer and enveloping her in a protective embrace. The weight of her words hung heavily in the air, an unspoken acknowledgement that the monsters they feared were not the ones lurking under their beds.

"Cross your heart?" Claire murmured, her breath warm against Elizabeth's neck.

"Cross my heart," Elizabeth confirmed, tracing an X over her chest. She knew that their bond was unbreakable, that the love between them could conquer even the darkest of nightmares.

"Then we'll always be together," Claire whispered, her eyes drifting shut as sleep claimed her. The rain's steady rhythm continued, cradling them in its comforting embrace, like a mother's gentle touch.

"Always," Elizabeth echoed, her eyes welling up with tears as she held her sister close, feeling each delicate rise and fall of her chest.

Years later, seated in her office amidst the sterile walls and the scent of antiseptic, Elizabeth found herself replaying that memory, her fingers tracing the invisible X over her heart. The promise she had made to Claire was still as potent as ever, driving her forward in her relentless pursuit of the truth.

"Cross my heart," she whispered the words of a silent prayer, a timeless vow that echoed through the years. And though the rain outside her office window could never compare to the downpour of their childhood, its rhythm still held the soothing power of that final promise.

"Promise me you'll find out what happened," a voice echoed in Elizabeth's mind, the ghost of Claire's desperate plea. It had been year since that fateful night, but the memory haunted her every waking moment.

"Cross my heart," she whispered again, her fingers trembling as they traced the invisible X over her chest. The weight of her sister's memory hung heavy around her neck like an anchor pulling her into the depths of grief and guilt.

"Dr. Harmon? May I come in?" a tentative voice interrupted her thoughts, bringing her back to the present. Her assistant, Lucy, stood in the doorway, clutching a file tightly to her chest.

"Of course, Lucy. What is it?" Elizabeth asked, trying to mask the raw emotion in her voice with professionalism.

"Here are the reports you requested on the new patient," Lucy replied, handing over the file. "Their history is ... quite complex."

"Thank you," Elizabeth said quietly, opening the file and scanning its contents. Her mind raced, searching for any clue, any connection to her sister's unexplained death. She knew that there must be an answer hidden within these pages, a key to the mystery that had consumed her life.

"Is everything alright, Dr. Harmon?" Lucy asked, concern creasing her brow.

"Everything's fine," Elizabeth lied smoothly, forcing a smile. "I appreciate your diligence, Lucy."

"Of course, Dr. Harmon. If you need anything else, just let me know," Lucy said, retreating from the office.

"Thank you," Elizabeth murmured as the door clicked shut behind her. Left alone with her thoughts once more, she sank into the floating leather chair behind her desk, feeling the weight of her mission bearing down upon her.

In the dim light of the room, she could almost see Claire's face, her wide, trusting eyes, and the way her smile lit up the room. The ghost of their childhood laughter echoed in her ears, a haunting lullaby that sent shivers down her spine.

"Cross my heart," she whispered again, her voice cracking with the weight of her promise. Elizabeth knew that she would do anything—everything—to uncover the truth and honor her sister's memory.

"Cross my heart, Claire," Elizabeth vowed, steeling herself against the storm that raged within her. "I will find out what happened to you—no matter what it takes."

And as the rain beat against the windowpane, like a thousand tiny fists demanding entry, Elizabeth felt the familiar pull of her grief, her guilt, and her determination. These emotions were her constant companions, driving her forward through the darkness, towards a truth that she both feared and longed to discover.

"Cross my heart," she repeated one final time, the words a mantra, a promise, and a prayer. And with each whispered syllable, she stepped closer to the edge, ready to dive headlong into the abyss—for Claire, for the unbreakable bond they shared, and for the love that would never truly die.

The gentle hum of the rain outside melded with the steady rhythm of Elizabeth's heartbeat, creating a somber symphony that resonated within her. She closed her eyes, allowing herself to be swept away by the bittersweet memories of a time when love and laughter filled every corner of their lives.

"Elizabeth," Claire's voice called out, soft and ethereal as if carried on the wings of a dream. "Do you remember the day we found the nest?"

A vivid image bloomed in Elizabeth's mind: two young girls, hand-in-hand, stumbling upon a fragile bundle of twigs and feathers hidden in the crook of a tree. Their awe-struck faces mirrored each other's as if they were reflections cast upon still waters.

"Of course, I do," Elizabeth replied, her voice tinged with melancholy. "We were so determined to protect those baby birds."

"Because we knew what it was like to feel small and vulnerable," Claire whispered, her words fluttering through the air like autumn leaves. "We had each other, though. And that made us strong."

Elizabeth felt the tender weight of her sister's presence, both comforting and heartrending in its intangible embrace. She could almost see the way Claire's eyes would crinkle at the corners when she smiled, the way her laughter would dance through the air like the chime of a hundred silver bells.

"We faced everything together, didn't we?" Elizabeth asked, her words barely audible as they brushed against the veil that separated past from present, life from death.

"Always," Claire murmured, her voice a tender caress that sent shivers down Elizabeth's spine. "And we always will—even now."

"Promise me, Elizabeth," Claire's voice implored, as soft and insistent as the sigh of the wind. "Promise me that you'll find out what happened to me—and that you won't let it break you."

"I promise, Claire," Elizabeth vowed, her words a solemn oath etched upon her heart. "I will find the truth, and I will keep our love alive—no matter what."

"Cross my heart," Claire whispered, her voice a luminous echo that shimmered with the light of a thousand stars. As Elizabeth opened her eyes, she felt the fragile threads of their connection stretch and twist, weaving together a tapestry of love, loss, and determination that bound them together through time and space.

"Cross my heart," she repeated, her resolve unwavering as she stepped forward into the unknown. For in the depths of her grief, she found the strength to carry on—for herself, for Claire, and for the love that transcended even the darkest corners of the human soul.

Chapter 3

In the dimly lit basement of Elizabeth's storage unit, she gingerly sifted through boxes of memories. Dust motes danced in the thin rays of sunlight that filtered through a cracked window. Claire's passing had left a void in her heart, a yearning to understand the darkness that had plagued her sister in her final days.

As Elizabeth moved old clothes and trinkets aside, her fingers brushed against a weathered, leather-bound journal. The book felt heavy in her hands, a silent witness to Claire's deepest thoughts and fears. Gently, she pulled it out and blew away a layer of dust, revealing the faded words "Claire's Diary" on the cover.

Curiosity mingled with a sense of trepidation as Elizabeth carefully opened the journal. Yellowed pages chronicled Claire's life, and Elizabeth flipped through them, her eyes scanning for hints about her sister's torment. She read about Claire's dreams and how they had grown increasingly vivid and unsettling, her deteriorating mental state evident in the frantic, looping handwriting.

"Nightmares ... experiments ... people after me ...," Elizabeth whispered to herself, her heart sinking as she pieced together the fragments of Claire's tortured mind.

The journal's pages became a haunting chronicle of Claire's descent into madness, culminating in her untimely death. Elizabeth's determination to understand what had plagued her sister intensified, her eyes welling with tears. She knew this discovery would be the key to unraveling the mystery surrounding Claire's final days.

As evening fell, Elizabeth headed to her apartment for a night's rest. As she slept the weight of unresolved guilt pressed against Elizabeth's chest as she stared into the abyss of her sister's unexplained death.

Elizabeth found herself tossed into a realm of unsettling dreams. This particular night marked the inception of a shared nightmare, an elusive enigma that ensnared not only her but also her patients. As she lay in bed, the tendrils of the dream tightened around her heart, constricting with each breath.

The room seemed to pulsate with an otherworldly energy as she slipped into the abyss of her subconscious. The nightmare unfurled like a dark tapestry, revealing a labyrinth that bridged the realms of her professional curiosity and personal obsession. It was a shared experience, a malevolent force that bound her fate with those of her patients.

The labyrinth sprawled before her, its architecture an intricate dance of shadows and whispers. Each step resonated with the weight of ancient secrets, and the air hummed with an unspoken terror. Elizabeth, hesitating on the threshold of the surreal maze, felt the convergence of her clinical detachment and a personal urge to unravel the mysteries within.

This was a journey into the depths of her own psyche, a quest for understanding that transcended the boundaries of professional obligation. The nightmare had woven its tendrils into the fabric of her consciousness, transforming curiosity into an obsession that pulled her further into the labyrinth's depths.

The walls of the maze seemed to pulse with a malevolent energy, whispering fragments of forgotten fears. Elizabeth could almost taste the desperation that fueled her need for answers. It was a hunger that propelled her forward, deeper into the intricate web of the dream, where the shared nightmare manifested as a nocturnal contagion.

As she ventured deeper, the labyrinth morphed and twisted, defying reason and challenging the limits of her resolve. The nightmares of her patients pressed down on her shoulders, a weight she willingly carried in pursuit of understanding. Each turn and twist tightened the nightmare's grip, testing her determination to confront the enigma that had entangled her fate with that of her patients.

In the labyrinth's depths, a dim light flickered, beckoning Elizabeth like a beacon in the dark. The shadows, as if responding to her presence, retreated, revealing a revelation that left her breathless. Before her stood a colossal door, adorned with symbols resonating with ancient wisdom. The key to unraveling the shared nightmare lay behind that door, and Elizabeth sensed that unlocking its secrets held the promise of liberation.

Her hands trembled as she reached out to touch the symbols. A surge of energy coursed through her veins, and the labyrinth responded. Walls shifted and rearranged, acknowledging her presence with an ethereal dance. In that moment, Elizabeth stood at the nexus of curiosity and obsession, on the brink of unlocking the mysteries concealed within the shared nightmare.

The symbols on the door seemed to pulse with a life of their own, revealing glimpses of forgotten memories and repressed fears. Elizabeth hesitated, torn between the rational mind of a psychologist and the insatiable curiosity of a woman caught in the throes of a shared nightmare. Yet, the pull of the unknown was irresistible.

With a deep breath, she pressed her hand against the door, the symbols glowing brighter as if responding to her touch. The colossal door creaked open, revealing a passage that led deeper into the heart of the labyrinth. Elizabeth hesitated for a moment, contemplating the consequences of her actions. The shared nightmare had become a collective ordeal, and whatever lay beyond the door held the potential to reshape not only her understanding but the fates of her patients as well.

As she stepped through the threshold, the air shifted, carrying with it a sense of anticipation. The labyrinth unfolded before her like a multidimensional puzzle, a surreal landscape that defied the laws of reality. Each step echoed with the weight of her patients' nightmares, merging with her own in a symphony of shared fears.

The journey through the labyrinth became a surreal odyssey, a descent into the recesses of the human psyche. Elizabeth encountered visions that transcended the boundaries of her patients' individual traumas, weaving a collective narrative of pain and despair. Faces distorted with fear stared back at her, their silent screams echoing through the corridors of the dream.

As she delved deeper, the labyrinth revealed layers of symbolism and metaphor, each twist and turn a reflection of the intertwined destinies of the dreamers. It was a psychological landscape where reality and illusion danced in a delicate balance, challenging Elizabeth's understanding of the human mind. The shared nightmare had evolved into a tapestry of interconnected fears, and she was determined to unravel its threads.

In the heart of the labyrinth, Elizabeth found herself in a chamber bathed in an eerie light. Before her stood a spectral figure, a manifestation of the collective fears that had woven the nightmare's tapestry. The figure beckoned her forward, its eyes reflecting the depths of human suffering.

"I am the figure of the shared nightmare," the figure spoke, its voice a haunting melody that resonated with the echoes of countless nightmares. "You seek understanding, but the path you tread is fraught with peril. Are you prepared to confront the truths that lie hidden within the collective subconscious?"

Elizabeth hesitated; her gaze fixed on the enigmatic figure. The weight of responsibility bore down on her, a realization that the shared nightmare was not just a product of individual traumas but a reflection of the universal human experience.

"I must understand," she whispered, her voice a determined echo in the chamber. "For myself and for my patients."

The figure nodded, its form shimmering like a mirage. "To understand, you must first confront the shadows within."

With those words, the chamber transformed, and Elizabeth found herself surrounded by manifestations of her deepest fears. The faces of her patients contorted with anguish, mirroring the struggles they faced in their waking lives. It was a visceral confrontation with the darker aspects of the human psyche, a journey through the labyrinth of shared nightmares that challenged her resilience.

As she navigated the treacherous terrain of the chamber, Elizabeth began to understand the interconnected nature of the nightmares. The fears that haunted her patients were not isolated; they were threads in a larger tapestry of shared human experiences. The labyrinth became a metaphor for the complexities of the mind, a vast expanse where individual traumas converged into a collective web of fears.

With each revelation, Elizabeth felt a profound sense of empathy for her patients. Their nightmares were not merely the byproduct of personal struggles but reflections of universal themes—loss, abandonment, betrayal. The labyrinth became a crucible of transformation, forging a deeper connection between the psychologist and those who sought solace in her guidance.

As she neared the heart of the chamber, the spectral figure reappeared, its eyes filled with a knowing gaze. "You have navigated the depths of the shared nightmare, but the journey is far from over. To truly liberate yourself and your patients, you must confront the source of the labyrinth—the primal fears that bind the collective consciousness."

The figure pointed to a swirling vortex at the center of the chamber, a maelstrom of shadows and whispers. Elizabeth, fueled by a newfound determination, stepped closer to the vortex, the pull of the unknown irresistible. As she entered the swirling abyss, the boundaries between her individual consciousness and the collective subconscious blurred.

In the heart of the vortex, Elizabeth confronted the primal fears that fueled the shared nightmare. It was a harrowing experience, a confrontation with the darkest recesses of the human soul. The shadows whispered tales of ancient traumas, of fears buried deep within the collective consciousness.

But all of a sudden, the nightmare collapsed around her, Elizabeth found herself back in the realm of wakefulness, the tendrils of the dream releasing their grip on her mind. She lay in bed, the room bathed in the soft glow of dawn.

The shared nightmare that had plagued her patients, Elizabeth now felt a newfound clarity—a deeper understanding of the human psyche and the interconnected nature of shared experiences. But the malevolent force wasn't finished with her, its the beginning of the shared nightmares.

On another night, Elizabeth awoke from her nightmare, as she quivered, she recounted her encounter with the nightmare. As the nightmare replayed in her mind, she spoke out loud as if she was telling this to someone "I ... I can see it so vividly. A vast, dark maze, stretching out in every direction, with walls made of cold, unforgiving stone."

"Go on," Elizabeth encouraged herself, as she noted down her dream pen poised above her notepad. Her sister's face flickered in her mind—a silent specter urging her to unravel the truth.

"It's suffocating; the air is thick with the scent of decay, and every step echoes like the beat of a dying heart. The fear is palpable—I can taste it like bile in the back of my throat." Elizabeth shuddered, hands trembling against her notepad.

Elizabeth glanced at her notes, where all her patients' accounts mirrored the terror described by what she recalled in her nightmare.

Elizabeth could not escape the labyrinth's grip. At night, she found herself wandering through its endless corridors, the air heavy with dread. The shadows whispered her sister's name, each syllable a dagger in her soul. And always, just out of reach, she glimpsed a figure wreathed in darkness, watching her with eyes that promised agony.

The morning had come, and Elizabeth awoke to begin another day with her patients in group therapy, but the nightmare from last night haunted her throughout the day.

"Dr. Harmon, are you okay?" Mr. Thompson asked, concern etched in the lines of his stern face.

"Ah, yes, thank you," she replied, shaking off the nightmare's lingering chill. "I've been ... I've had a similar experience. It's unsettling to hear it described so accurately."

"Have you found any answers?" Anna questioned, hope flickering in their eyes.

"Nothing concrete, yet," Elizabeth admitted, hating the desperation in her voice. "But we will find a way through this labyrinth together. I promise."

As they spoke, Elizabeth's thoughts tangled with memories of her sister, her grief inseparable from her determination to unravel the mystery that bound them all to the hellish dreamscape. With every step into the unknown, Elizabeth knew she would confront her fears and anxieties, but for the sake of her patients—and herself—she could not falter.

"Thank you, Dr. Harmon," Mr. Thompson murmured, vulnerability briefly softening his expression. "We trust you."

Elizabeth nodded, steeling herself for the journey ahead. She would navigate the labyrinth, confront its horrors, and emerge triumphant, or be swallowed by the darkness forever.

Elizabeth walked into Susan's small, cluttered office. She was still reeling from her discussion with her patients about their shared nightmare, the same one that haunted her every night. Her chest tightened with a heavy sense of responsibility.

"Ah, Elizabeth!" Susan greeted warmly with a smile, her eyes crinkling at the corners. "I have the vial the scientist and I have been working on"

Susan handed the vial to Elizabeth; her fingers delicately traced the contours of the small vial that rested in the palm of her hand. The glass felt cool against her skin, and as she tilted it slightly, the potion inside responded with a mesmerizing dance of luminescence. A soft glow emanated from within, casting an ethereal light on the futuristic surroundings of Susan research chamber.

This particular concoction was not a chance discovery on Elizabeth's part, but the result of Susan's tireless efforts. The once-dormant data streams and digital archives had come alive under Susan's expert fingertips, revealing secrets that eluded even the most advanced algorithms. Susan, the brilliant psychologist and researcher with a knack for unearthing hidden knowledge, had stumbled upon the formula during her extensive investigation on behalf of Elizabeth.

Elizabeth marveled at the liquid's play of light, reflecting on the trust she had in Susan's abilities. Susan, with her twenty years of expertise, had not just found the information; she had carefully curated it, selecting the most pertinent details and ensuring the potion's creation by a skilled scientist. Elizabeth's gratitude toward Susan was immeasurable.

As Elizabeth examined the vial, memories of the day Susan had presented it to her flashed vividly in her mind. The holographic interface in Elizabeth's office hummed to life, projecting Susan's image as if she were physically present.

"Elizabeth, I've found something extraordinary," Susan's holographic figure declared, excitement evident in her voice. "In my quest for information, I stumbled upon a formula, a potion with remarkable properties. It could be a breakthrough in our search."

Intrigued, Elizabeth had leaned forward, her eyes fixated on the holographic display. Susan proceeded to explain the potion's origins, the ancient texts and forgotten scrolls she had sifted through, and the scientific intricacies that underpinned its creation.

"It took some persuasion, but I managed to convince a renowned scientist to mix it for us. The results are astounding," Susan continued, her eyes alight with enthusiasm.

The holographic projection shifted to reveal the scientist, a figure shrouded in a sterile lab environment, meticulously blending the ingredients of the potion. The scene unfolded in a series of holographic panels, providing Elizabeth with a detailed view of the meticulous process.

"And here it is," Susan said, her image holding out the vial.

Now, in the quiet solitude of her office, Elizabeth marveled at the tangible manifestation of Susan's discoveries.

With a determined resolve, Elizabeth telephoned Susan. "Susan, you've outdone yourself," Elizabeth praised. "This is more than I could have hoped for." Susan's smile echoed through phone.

As Elizabeth and Susan engaged in a discussion about the potion's properties and potential, Elizabeth couldn't help but feel a surge of anticipation. The collaboration between her and Susan had always been a dynamic force, pushing the boundaries of what was thought possible. This potion, a product of Susan's relentless pursuit of knowledge, promised to be a catalyst for her patients and herself.

Chapter 4

"Dr. Harmon, are you sure about this?" Anna asked hesitantly, her voice trembling with anxiety as she sat on the edge of Elizabeth's meticulously organized desk. The dim light from the single lamp in the room flickered, casting eerie shadows on the walls.

Elizabeth looked up from her notes, her dark eyes resolute. "I have to do it," she responded firmly, her hand clenching into a tight fist. "There is no other way. I have searched and searched, and apart from Emily's success, I haven't found a way to eliminate the dreams. I need to get in there and confront whatever is causing this. Maybe it will go away forever, or maybe I will fail."

"Both of your cases have led me to believe there's something more to these nightmares." Her gaze drifted to Mr. Thompson who stood near the window, arms crossed and muscles tense beneath his clothing. Their stern face betrayed an unspoken fear, a vulnerability that echoed within Elizabeth's own heart.

"Your shared experiences point toward a malevolent force—an entity that thrives on fear," Elizabeth continued, her voice steady despite the gravity of her words. "Not only am I determined to save you both, but I must confront this Fear entity to uncover the truth about my sister's death."

"Doctor, the stakes are too high," Mr. Thompson interjected, their voice almost cracking under the strain. "You could lose yourself in there, just like we did."

"Or worse," Anna murmured, the quiver in their voice belying the terror they'd experienced in the labyrinthine dream world.

"Trust me," Elizabeth implored, her pupils dilating as she spoke. "I know the risks, but the alternative—losing you both forever and never knowing what happened to my sister—is far worse." Elizabeth paused, swallowing hard. "The guilt I've carried since her death has weighed on me for the past year. If there's even a chance, I can find answers and save you both ... I have to take it."

A heavy silence hung in the air as the patients exchanged uneasy glances. Elizabeth's mind raced with the implications of her decision, a knot of determination tightening in her chest. Elizabeth sister—her other half, lost to the void of an unexplained tragedy—had left scars that refused to heal. Now, with the lives of her patients at stake and the tantalizing possibility of understanding within reach, she knew she had no choice but to confront the darkness head-on.

"Alright," Anna finally whispered, her eyes filled with a mixture of fear and gratitude. "What can we do to help you?"

"Stay here," Elizabeth replied softly, her gaze locked onto theirs. "Hold onto each other and trust that I'll find a way to pull us all out of this nightmare."

As they nodded in agreement, Elizabeth's heart swelled with a fierce determination to face the labyrinth and confront the dread that lurked within its winding corridors. Elizabeth would not falter; she would not succumb to fear. Instead, she would wield the very thing that had tormented her this past year—the haunting memories of her sister—as a weapon against the darkness.

"Whatever it takes," she vowed silently as she steeled herself for the journey ahead. "I will see this through to the end."

"Ready?" The sound of Anna's voice pulled Elizabeth back from her thoughts.

"Almost," she answered, her dark eyes fixed on the small vial that lay before her. The potion inside shimmered with an eerie luminescence, as if it held the key to the abyss itself. Elizabeth acquired it from Susan, a fellow psychologist who delved deep into research and discovered it in her quest. Susan, having connected with a scientist, managed to mix and prepare the potion.

"Once we drink this," she explained to her patients, "We will enter the dream realm, where we can navigate the labyrinth and confront the fear entity." Elizabeth voice trembled slightly as she spoke, betraying her apprehension.

"Dr. Harmon," Mr. Thompson hesitantly interjected, his words heavy with concern. "We know how much you've sacrificed to help us, but are you sure about this? I mean, what if ... what if we can't find your way back?"

Elizabeth paused, her fingers hovering above the vial. Elizabeth knew the risks all too well—the lost souls who had wandered the labyrinth for eternity, their minds forever trapped within its merciless confines. But the alternative was to stand idly by while her patients suffered, and she could not bear that thought.

"Believe me when I say that I am well aware of the dangers," she answered, her voice steady now. "But there is no other way. My sister's death has left a void in my heart that refuses to be filled, and the torment you are experiencing is something we cannot ignore. I must do this."

With a solemn nod, she picked up the vial and uncorked it. The potion's scent wafted through the room, a mixture of lavender and something far more sinister—like the stench of decay lurking beneath the perfume of flowers. Elizabeth hesitated for a heartbeat, then downed the contents in one swift gulp.

"Be careful," Mr. Thompson whispered as Elizabeth felt the potion take effect, her vision blurring at the edges and her limbs growing heavy.

"Stay strong for each other," she managed to say before her consciousness slipped away, her body slumping over onto the cold floor of her office.

As the darkness enveloped her, she knew that she would soon stand before the entrance to the labyrinth. The weight of dread pressed against her chest, but she held onto her resolve like a lifeline, determined to navigate the twisting passages and confront the fearful entity lurking within. No matter the cost, she would save her patients and uncover the truth about her sister's death—or be lost forever trying.

The moment Elizabeth's consciousness crossed the threshold, she found herself standing at the entrance to the labyrinth. The world around her was a swirling mass of shadows and distorted echoes, but the path before her was unmistakable: a narrow corridor that seemed to stretch on forever, framed by walls that writhed and pulsed with an unsettling life of their own.

Elizabeth took a deep breath, feeling the cold air fill her lungs, and stepped forward. The shifting walls closed in around her, the darkness swallowing her whole. Elizabeth walked slowly, fingertips brushing against the undulating stone, trying to keep her bearings as the labyrinth twisted and turned beneath her feet.

"Stay focused," she told herself, her voice barely audible over the distant howls that echoed through the passageways. "You can do this."

As she delved deeper into the maze, the fear gnawing at the edges of her mind grew more intense. The darkness seemed to press down on her from all sides, and she could feel her heart pounding in her chest. Elizabeth knew that the Fear entity must be close, feeding on her trepidation like a parasite.

"Who are you?" Elizabeth called out, her voice trembling with both anger and terror. "Show yourself!"

"Ah, Dr. Harmon," a shadowy figure coalesced before her, its voice a sinister whisper that made her skin crawl. "I've been waiting for you."

"Enough games," she spat, trying to sound braver than she felt. "Release my patients and tell me what happened to my sister."

"Your fears are delicious," the figure taunted, remaining just out of reach as the walls continued to shift around them. "But you'll have to work harder if you want to defeat me."

"Fine," she hissed, her determination flaring. "I won't let you win."

Elizabeth pressed on through the labyrinth, focusing on her breathing and the sound of her footsteps echoing off the stone walls. As she navigated the traps that lay hidden in the shadows—pits filled with razor-sharp spikes, pendulum blades that swung from the ceiling, seemingly endless drops into nothingness—she wavered between despair and gritted resolve.

"Is this all you've got?" Elizabeth shouted at the fearful entity, her voice ringing out defiantly. "You'll have to do better than this!"

"Your confidence is misplaced," the shadowy figure taunted, its voice dripping with malice. "But I'm enjoying watching you struggle."

"Damn you," she whispered, forcing herself to keep moving forward. The image of her sister's lifeless body flashed before her eyes, propelling her onward through the treacherous twists and turns of the labyrinth. Elizabeth would not fail her sister or her patients.

"Bring it on," she growled, her voice echoing like a battle cry through the darkness. And deep within the heart of the labyrinth, the Fear entity laughed, its hunger only growing more insatiable.

Elizabeth's heart pounded in her chest as she rounded another corner of the labyrinth, her breath coming in ragged gasps. Elizabeth could feel the fear entity's presence growing stronger, an oppressive weight bearing down on her.

"Show yourself!" Elizabeth demanded, her voice resolute, despite the tremor that threatened to break through.

"Very well," came the response, a whisper that seemed to crawl up her spine. And then, with a sound like the very fabric of reality tearing apart, the Fear entity materialized before her.

It was a horrifying sight, a towering, amorphous mass of darkness that oozed and writhed with malevolent energy. The shadows coalesced into tendrils that reached out toward her, their tips forming claws that dripped with venomous intent.

"Is this what you wanted?" the Fear entity sneered, its voice a thousand cruel whispers. "To face your nightmares?"

Elizabeth stared at the abomination, her pulse quickening even as she clenched her fists in determination. Elizabeth knew she had to use her knowledge of psychology to weaken the Fear entity's attacks, but how? Then, it hit her—if the creature fed on her fears, she would have to confront them head-on.

"Let's see how much you truly understand fear," she said, steeling herself. "After all, it's just an emotion, isn't it? A response to a perceived threat. So, let me ask you this: what do you think is my greatest fear?"

"Your sister's death, of course," the fear entity replied, a sickening grin spreading across its shadowy form. "Clair's life snuffed out, leaving you alone and helpless."

"True," Elizabeth admitted, feeling a cold sweat beading on her forehead. "But I've come to terms with that. It's the guilt, the regret, the not knowing that truly torments me."

"Ah," the Fear entity hissed, its tendrils tightening. "Then let me show you what you've lost."

Images of her sister flickered before her eyes, each one more heartbreaking than the last. But she steeled herself, refusing to give in to the despair that threatened to consume her.

"Your attempts are futile," she spat at the fearful entity. "I won't be broken by you."

"Brave words," it sneered, its form shuddering and pulsating with anger. "But we'll see how long that lasts."

As the creature lunged forward, Elizabeth drew upon her years of experience as a psychologist, focusing on her fears and using them to her advantage. Elizabeth knew confronting her deepest anxieties would weaken the fear entity's attacks, and so she bravely faced the onslaught of terrifying images and sensations it hurled at her.

"Is that all you can do?" she challenged, even as her heart raced, and her palms grew slick with sweat. "Bring forth my darkest fears? Well, come on then! I'm not afraid of you!"

And as she stood there, defiant in the face of the writhing mass of darkness, something within her began to change. The fear that had once consumed her was now a weapon in her hands, ready to be turned against the very thing that sought to destroy her.

The Fear entity, enraged by Elizabeth's defiance, surged forward with renewed vigor. Its tendrils whipped through the air with a fury that belied its eldritch nature, and its amorphous form contorted into monstrous visages of pain and terror.

"Your resistance only makes me stronger," it hissed, its voice an amalgam of the screams of her patients, echoing through the labyrinth. "You will not survive this."

Elizabeth's heart hammered in her chest, but she refused to let fear rule her. With every ounce of her intellect, intuition, and empathy, she sought out the creature's weaknesses—anything she could use against it.

"Perhaps," she mused aloud, dodging a tendril that lunged for her throat, "it's not me who's afraid, but you."

As the Fear entity launched another assault, Elizabeth spotted a fragment of a mirror, glinting in the shadows of the labyrinth. She sprinted toward it, her mind racing as she formulated a plan, hoping her gamble would pay off. Elizabeth could feel the labyrinth itself shifting around her, trapping her in its maze-like embrace, but she pressed on.

"Your power comes from fear," she muttered, snatching up the mirror shard. "But what happens when the source of that fear turns back on you?"

She whirled around just as the Fear entity neared, its form expanding and contracting like a grotesque, living Rorschach test. As it lunged for her one final time, Elizabeth raised the mirror shard, catching the creature's reflection within its fractured surface.

"Face your fears!" she cried, holding her ground.

For a moment, time seemed to stand still. Then, the Fear entity recoiled as if struck, its monstrous form shuddering and writhing in turmoil. It let loose an ear-splitting wail, the sound reverberating throughout the labyrinth.

"Impossible," it snarled, its voice trembling with the unmistakable tremor of fear. "How can this be?"

"Because" Elizabeth replied, her voice steady despite the pounding of her heart, "you're not the only one who knows how to wield fear as a weapon."

As the Fear entity's form began to shrink and wither under the weight of its terror, Elizabeth took a deep breath, feeling a renewed sense of hope and determination wash over her. Elizabeth had faced her fears and survived; now, she could forge ahead in her quest for answers.

And perhaps, even unmask a conspiracy darker than the labyrinth itself.

The fear entity's wail echoed through the labyrinth, its form dissipating into tendrils of shadows. As it vanished, a sudden gust of wind blew through the dark corridors, extinguishing Elizabeth's torch. She squinted into the inky blackness, her pulse still racing from the confrontation.

"Dr. Harmon?" A faint voice called out in the darkness. Several similar cries followed each one resonating with disbelief and relief. Elizabeth patients, released from their nightmares, at last, began to emerge from the labyrinth's hidden corners.

"Everyone, stay where you are," she instructed. "I'll come to you." One by one, she followed their voices, using her keen sense of intuition to navigate the now-silent passages. As she reunited each patient with their waking world, she marveled at the strength they had shown in facing down their deepest fears.

"Dr. Harmon ... how did you do it?" asked one tearful woman, clinging to Elizabeth's hand.

"By confronting my fears," she replied softly, her thoughts drifting to her sister. The truth about her death remained shrouded in mystery, but she was no longer afraid to face it. Elizabeth felt more determined than ever.

As she led her patients out of the labyrinth, she discovered a hidden chamber concealed behind an illusory wall. Inside, a single candle flickered on a dusty table, illuminating a stack of old documents that appeared untouched by time.

Elizabeth glanced over and within the chamber, she saw a stack of documents. Elizabeth wondered why these documents are in this chamber.

"Wait here," she told her patients, stepping cautiously into the chamber. As she leafed through the papers, her heart caught in her throat; each sheet bore a name she recognized—including her sister's. They were all connected somehow, but how? And why?

"Dr. Harmon?" A male patient peered anxiously into the room. "Is everything all right?"

"Fine, just fine," she said, hastily gathering the documents. "We need to leave this place immediately."

As they made their way back to the waking world, Elizabeth's thoughts raced. The hidden chamber inside the nightmare, the cryptic documents—they hinted at a larger conspiracy, one that went far beyond her sister's death. Elizabeth had uncovered something dangerous; now, she would have to unravel its secrets. Elizabeth had to meet with Dr. Sanders.

That night as she crawled into bed, nervous to close her eyes. Had she succeeded in her quest to rid her and her patients from the Fear entity? Elizabeth had confronted her fears and led the patients out of the nightmare ... but that didn't mean they couldn't get trapped again. To fix that, she needed to get to the heart of the experiment and the heart of why the Fear entity trapped their minds. Elizabeth's eyes drooped down and she surrendered herself to her sleep.

Transported into her dream state, she opened her mind's eye and stared ahead at the dark, coiling labyrinth.

Damn.

Chapter 5

In the heart of the vibrant city, tucked away in a serene nook, an inviting coffee shop beckoned to weary souls seeking solace. Within its snug confines, the rhythmic clinking of cups and the lilting cadence of laughter harmonized, forming a melodious backdrop to life's unfolding stories.

Amidst the clientele, a robotic barista moved gracefully, so eerily human-like that it effortlessly blended with the patrons. With a gentle, welcoming smile on its lifelike face and fluid gestures reminiscent of a seasoned barista, it skillfully recorded each customer's request. This mechanical artisan, its expressive eyes reflecting genuine warmth, orchestrated orders with the finesse of a seasoned conductor, transmitting them to the bustling kitchen with a subtle nod.

The irresistible fragrance of freshly ground coffee beans hung thick in the air, intertwining with the sweet, beckoning aroma of an array of delectable baked goods. Proudly on display, these culinary delights bore the hallmark of the robotic bakers laboring diligently behind the scenes. Their movements, uncannily human-like, bore witness to their unwavering commitment to the craft, enveloping the coffee shop in an aura of freshly baked ecstasy.

In this inviting haven, the robots transcended their mechanical origins, becoming true artisans and conductors of a living symphony. Seamlessly integrated into the daily tapestry of human existence, they elevated the ambiance and ensured that each patron left not only with a cup brimming with coffee, but also with the shared enchantment of a serene interlude, in this charming oasis of human-like grace and technological wonder.

Within the bustling Café, Elizabeth sat cradling her warm mug, inhaling the comforting scent before taking a slow sip. Elizabeth thoughts wandered through the maze of her patients' stories, searching for answers that eluded her.

The door to the cafe creaked open, and a gust of cold wind brought in the figure of Dr. Martin Sanders. He stood as an island of stoicism amidst the vibrant sea of chatter, his graying hair and furrowed brow betraying the years of experience he carried with him. His gaze bore into the surroundings, scanning each face with precision as if seeking something—or someone—in particular.

As he moved towards the counter, Elizabeth couldn't help but observe the deliberate way he navigated the room, his measured stride contrasting sharply with the fluid motion around him. It was as if he were a scientist amid an experiment, observing every variable with a critical eye. And perhaps that's exactly what he was—a man burdened by the weight of his creations, driven by a need to unravel the twisted threads of a failed endeavor.

"Excuse me," he murmured as he sidestepped a young couple deep in conversation. Their laughter echoed in the small space, a sharp contrast to the solemnity etched on his face.

Watching him from her corner, Elizabeth felt a strange sense of kinship with this man who seemed so out of place in the lively atmosphere. As a fellow seeker of truth, she understood all too well the feeling of being adrift in a sea of ignorance, the desperate search for understanding that consumed her every waking moment.

"Dr. Sanders," she whispered under her breath.

The cacophony of clinking ceramic and the hum of murmured conversation washed over her as she sipped her lukewarm coffee, her thoughts swirling like tendrils of steam. Elizabeth had been waiting at the bustling coffee shop for what felt like hours, the weight of anticipation heavy in her chest.

The noise seemed to dull around him, his stoic demeanor casting an eerie calm, that contrasted sharply with the vibrant surroundings. The graying hair at his temples framed a gaze that was both piercing and distant as if he were looking through the very fabric of reality itself.

A shiver of intrigue ran down Elizabeth's spine as she observed him from her shadowy corner. Dr. Sanders presence piqued her curiosity, intensifying her desire to unravel the enigma of the failed government experiment.

"Mind over matter," she whispered under her breath, steeling herself for the confrontation ahead. With a deep, steadying breath, she rose to her feet and approached Dr. Sanders, the scent of passion fruit tea, mingling with the resolute determination emanated from her every pore.

"Dr. Sanders?" Elizabeth began, her voice steady and assertive. "Are you ready to discuss your failed government experiment in more detail?"

His sharp eyes flickered over her face, assessing and calculating. Then he nodded slightly, acknowledging her.

"Then you understand why we needed to meet again," she continued, her heart pounding in her chest. "I need your help, Dr. Sanders. We share a common goal in uncovering the truth behind this experiment."

"Truth ..." he mused, his gaze drifting toward the steamed-up window. "Truth is a fickle thing, Dr. Harmon. It shifts and changes like the shadows in this room. But ... perhaps together, we can pin it down."

Elizabeth felt a surge of exhilaration course through her veins as their alliance was forged. The path to understanding lay before them, shrouded in darkness and uncertainty. But with Dr. Sanders by her side, she knew they could navigate the labyrinthine horrors that awaited them, and finally expose the secrets of the shared nightmares.

"As you know, Dr. Sanders, I've had patients suffering from these shared nightmares. I've created a solution, but the dreams persist," Elizabeth said, her voice tinged with urgency. "I need to understand what's happening to them. To all of us."

Dr. Sander studied her face, his sharp eyes searching for traces of doubt or fear. But he found only determination and resilience.

"Very well," he conceded, shifting in his seat. "The experiment was designed to explore the potential of collective consciousness—the idea that we could use this shared mental space to enhance communication, cooperation, and even empathy among people. However, it went terribly wrong. The Hive Mind shouldn't been allowed to proceed into consumers."

Elizabeth leaned forward, her focus entirely on Dr. Sanders' words.

"Instead of fostering connection, the experiment created an uncontrollable, nightmarish labyrinth within the minds of those involved," he continued. "It's as if the darkest parts of the human psyche were unleashed, manifesting in a shared dream world that ensnares its victims. They did fix many things about the Hive Mind, but there are still issues with it and for some people, it doesn't work as it should."

"Is there a way to break free of this labyrinth?" Elizabeth asked, her voice barely above a whisper. Elizabeth thought of her patients, trapped in their nightmares, desperate for a way out. "I got my patient's minds out through some new-age science that has barely been researched, but the nightmare is still there, waiting to trap them again.

"Perhaps," Dr. Sanders replied, his gaze distant. "But it won't be easy. Navigating the labyrinth requires confronting the darkness within ourselves and making sense of the chaos it creates. Only then can we hope to unravel the mystery of the shared nightmares and put an end to this torment."

As Elizabeth absorbed his words, she felt both trepidation and excitement. Here was an ally who understood the depths of her quest, who possessed the knowledge and expertise she had been seeking. Together, they might bring solace to those who had been suffering for far too long.

"Dr. Sanders, I know the path ahead of us is fraught with danger and uncertainty," she said, her conviction unwavering. "But I am prepared to face whatever challenges lie ahead in pursuit of the truth. Will you join me?"

"Indeed, Dr. Harmon," he slowly replied, his stoic demeanor cracking ever so slightly, as he offered her a faint, yet genuine smile. Dr. Sander face, marked by a web of fine wrinkles etched with the passage of time, held a wealth of wisdom and experience. "I believe our combined efforts may be the key to unlocking the secrets of this labyrinth. Let's seek the truth together."

With that, they rose from their seats, the clinking of cups and murmured conversations around them fading into the background as Elizabeth and Dr. Sanders stepped out into the cold night air, united in their pursuit of understanding and redemption.

As Dr. Sanders continued to divulge the intricate details of the government experiment, Elizabeth found herself leaning closer, her eyes locked on his. Dr. Sanders words painted a vivid and terrifying picture of the labyrinth dream's origins, but it was his raw honesty and vulnerability that truly captivated her.

"Elizabeth," he said, fixing her with an intense gaze, "you must understand my role in this tragedy. I designed the neural interface that opened the door to this nightmare. My hands are stained with the suffering of countless souls."

Elizabeth could see the weight of his guilt pressing down upon him, the lines etched into his face deepening as he spoke. Every word seemed to cost him a piece of himself, yet he persevered, determined to share the truth.

"Dr. Sanders," she murmured, reaching out to touch his arm, "your candor speaks volumes about your character. You're shouldering an immense burden, and yet you're here, opening up to me, a stranger. It's clear how committed you are to righting this wrong."

Dr. Sanders sighed, nodding slowly, and she could sense the walls he had built around him beginning to crumble. "I owe it to those who have been lost or tormented by this catastrophe, to do whatever it takes to find answers."

Elizabeth studied him for a moment, weighing the risks against the potential rewards. Elizabeth knew she was walking a fine line, placing her trust in a man whose work had unleashed untold horrors upon innocent minds. But as she looked into his eyes, she saw not a monster, but a fellow seeker of truth, plagued by the same demons that haunted her restless nights.

"Your insights and expertise are invaluable, Dr. Sanders," she admitted, her voice resolute. "But even more important is your willingness to confront the darkness within and without, to face the consequences of your actions head-on. I trust you because I see in you a reflection of my desire for redemption."

"Elizabeth," he whispered, his voice thick with emotion. "I promise I will not let you down."

"Thank you for being willing to help me, Dr. Sanders," she said sincerely, raising her eyes to meet his. "Your expertise and guidance are invaluable in my investigation. I couldn't do this without you."

"Call me Martin, please" he replied, a hint of a smile playing at the corners of his mouth. "And it is my honor to assist you, Elizabeth. I believe that together, we can navigate the labyrinth dream and uncover the truth that lies within its depths."

Elizabeth nodded, her mind already racing with the possibilities that lay before them. "So, what are our next steps? How do we delve deeper into this mystery?"

"First, we need to identify potential points of entry into the shared nightmares," he said, his brow furrowed in concentration. "The experiment targeted specific neural pathways and cognitive processes, so it stands to reason that there are certain triggers or stimuli that can lead us into the dream world."

"Like deja vu?" Elizabeth asked, recalling the disconcerting sensation she'd experienced just days ago.

"Exactly. Deja vu, hypnagogic states, even certain forms of meditation could provide a gateway," he explained. "We'll have to explore multiple avenues, but we must remain alert to any signs of intrusion or manipulation from within the labyrinth itself."

"Right," she murmured, her thoughts churning as she considered the implications of their undertaking. "It's like navigating a maze full of traps and pitfalls, where the very walls themselves could be shifting around us."

"Indeed, but we must never lose sight of our ultimate goal: to uncover the truth and bring solace to those who have suffered," he said, his voice resolute. "We owe it not only to the victims of the experiment but also to ourselves."

As they continued discussing their plans, Elizabeth found herself gripped by a fierce determination, fueled by the knowledge that she was no longer alone in her quest. The road ahead was fraught with danger and uncertainty, but together, she and Martin Sanders would face whatever perils awaited them within the labyrinth dream.

For the first time in years, hope kindled within her heart, casting its fragile light upon the shadows of her past. And she dared to believe that redemption might finally be within reach.

"Dr. Sanders," she began, a tremor of excitement in her voice, "I can't even begin to express how important this is to me, to us... Working together, I truly believe we can achieve something monumental."

A flicker of emotion crossed his stoic face, and he nodded in agreement as they continued walking down the street from the cafe. "Yes, Dr. Harmon. Our combined expertise and determination will be invaluable, in unlocking the secrets of the shared nightmares." Elizebeth saw that his eyes held a depth of understanding, a mingling of empathy and resolve that echoed within her soul.

"Then let's get started, time is of the essence, and every moment we delay is another moment lost to the darkness," she said, as they continued walking.

Martin's tall frame cast a slender shadow over Elizabeth, as he stopped and looked at her. "Agreed. We'll need to gather our resources and make contacts, but I'm confident we can make significant progress."

The world around them seemed to take on a new dimension, infused with the weight of secrets yet to be uncovered and the promise of battles yet to be fought.

Chapter 6

Elizabeth followed Dr. Sanders into the dimly lit laboratory, a stark contrast to the sterile brightness of the corridor they had just left behind. Rows of transparent computer monitors stood like a sentinel of innovation, its sleek, glass-like surface casting a subtle, almost magical glow as it hummed softly, casting an eerie glow on the cold floor. At the far end of the room, a large observation window loomed, its glass reflecting their distorted figures.

"Dr. Harmon," Dr. Sanders began, his stern expression fixed on her, as he adjusted the lab coat draped over his lean elderly frame. "I'm glad to see you again."

Elizabeth nodded. "Please tell me more of what you know."

Dr. Sanders' gaze towards the observation window for a moment before returning to her. "This laboratory," he began, his voice steady despite the weight of his words, "was the site of the government experiment I was involved in."

Elizabeth heart pounded in her chest, a mixture of horror and vindication coursing through her veins. Elizabeth had suspected a connection, but hearing it confirmed sent shivers down her spine. "Why would anyone want to do that?" Elizabeth asked, unable to keep the anger from seeping into her tone.

"Control," Dr. Sanders replied simply, his stoic demeanor betraying no emotion. "The human mind is a powerful thing, and some believed that by controlling it, they could wield unimaginable power."

"Unimaginable power?" Elizabeth echoed, her thoughts racing as she considered the implications of this revelation. The labyrinth dream was more than just a nightmare plaguing her patients—it was evidence of a larger, more sinister conspiracy.

"Dr. Sanders," she whispered, suddenly aware of the crushing weight of the shadows surrounding them, "what have we gotten ourselves into?"

Dr. Sanders met her gaze, his eyes filled with a haunted weariness that mirrored her own. "A world of darkness, Dr. Harmon," he said, his voice barely audible. "But together, perhaps we can bring it to light."

"Project Morpheus," Dr. Sanders said, his voice echoing slightly in the dimly lit laboratory. "That's what they called it." In a tech-savvy manner, he commands the room, instructing it to power on, and a cluster of transparent computer monitors flickered to life, casting an eerie glow across the room. The glass observation window reflected the ghostly images at them, adding a sense of disorientation and unease.

"Government-funded, of course," he continued, his fingers dancing across the touchscreen keyboard as he pulled up files and images. Elizabeth studied his face, trying to gauge his thoughts behind that stoic expression. "It went on for three years before they finally pulled the plug."

Elizabeth felt her breath catch in her throat. Three years. How many people had been subjected to this experiment? How many lives had been altered—or destroyed—by this sinister project?

"During the experiment," Dr. Sanders explained, careful not to reveal too much, "subjects were exposed to certain stimuli, designed to induce a specific recurring dream: the labyrinth dream."

As he spoke, Elizabeth was suddenly transported back to her nightmares—the cold stone walls closing in, the endless twisting corridors that led only to more darkness. Elizabeth could feel the icy tendrils of panic wrapping around her chest, constricting her breath, as her heart pounded wildly in her ears.

"Lost," she whispered, barely audible against the steady hum of the machines around them. "All of us ... lost in the maze."

Dr. Sanders nodded solemnly, his eyes betraying a hint of sadness as he regarded her. "Yes," he confirmed. "Each subject experienced the same dream, wandering the labyrinth with no hope of escape. And each time, they would wake up feeling more disoriented, more disconnected from reality."

"Is there any way out?" Elizabeth asked, desperation coloring her voice. Despite the clinical detachment she usually maintained with her patients, their plight had become her own. Elizabeth needed to find answers—for them and herself.

"Perhaps," he replied cryptically, his fingers pausing over the keyboard as he considered his next words. "The labyrinth is a construct of the mind, but it is also a reflection of our deepest fears and desires. To escape, one must confront those fears and unravel the threads that bind us to the maze."

"Confront our fears," Elizabeth echoed, the labyrinth was more than just a nightmare; it was a window into the darkest recesses of the human psyche.

Elizabeth's heart raced, her fingers gripping the edge of the table so tightly that her knuckles turned white. Elizabeth held her breath, waiting for him to continue.

"Through controlled exposure to certain stimuli," he elaborated, a steely determination in his eyes, "we sought to explore and control the collective unconscious of human minds. The very fabric that connects us all, beneath the surface of conscious thought."

The air felt heavy with revelation, pressing down on her like a leaden weight. Elizabeth could scarcely believe what she was hearing, but something deep within her knew it to be true—this was the key she had been searching for. Elizabeth mind raced, trying to piece together the implications of this knowledge.

"Control?" Elizabeth whispered, her voice barely audible, the word echoing through the sterile laboratory. "How can anyone presume to control something so ... immense?"

"By understanding its mechanics," Dr. Sanders replied, his expression grim. "By dissecting the labyrinth dream, we hoped to uncover the secrets that lay hidden within the human psyche. To bring order to chaos."

"Order ..." Elizabeth repeated, her thoughts swirling like leaves caught in a storm. A new question arose, unbidden, from the depths of her subconscious. "What happens when you try to control something that refuses to be tamed?"

"Chaos," Dr. Sanders answered, his gaze darkening. "Unintended consequences ... and unimaginable suffering."

"Like my sister," she said softly, her heart aching at the memory of her sister's tormented face. "She never found her way out of the maze."

"No," Dr. Sanders agreed, his voice laced with sorrow. "Many didn't. Dr. Harmon, I understand this is a lot to take in," Dr. Sanders said, his voice steady as a metronome. "But the scope of the experiment was vast, encompassing over a thousand subjects. Their dreams were induced using a combination of psychoactive substances and neural stimulation, allowing us to gather data, on their brain activity and interactions with the labyrinth."

"Thousands ..." Elizabeth murmured, her mind whirling with images of frightened faces lost within the maze of their minds. The laboratory seemed to close in around her, the hum of the computer monitors, an incessant reminder of the cold calculations, that had led them here.

"Each subject wore a specially designed headset that monitored their brainwaves as they slept," Dr. Sanders continued, gesturing toward a nearby table where a sleek, metallic device lay, its electrodes gleaming under the fluorescent lights. "When the labyrinth dream began, we would observe their progress through the maze, recording every detail for later analysis."

As Elizabeth's gaze followed his gesture, she couldn't help but shudder at the sight of the sinister-looking headset. The air held the faint tang of disinfectant, mixed with the undertones of electrical ozone—the scent of sanitized suffering.

"Did you ever ... find anything?" Elizabeth asked hesitantly, her heart pounding against her ribcage as though it sought escape. "In all that time, with all those people?"

"Patterns," Dr. Sanders replied, his eyes distant as he stared past the rows of monitors. "Symbols, recurring themes ... echoes of a collective unconscious, that seemed to whisper secrets of the human mind. But the more we studied, the more elusive it became. Like water slipping through our fingers."

"Or sand in an hourglass." Elizabeth added, her thoughts turning inward as she contemplated the ephemeral nature of dreams, memories, and the passage of time. Elizabeth clenched her fists at her sides, feeling the weight of responsibility settling on her shoulders.

"Exactly," Dr. Sanders agreed, nodding solemnly. "We were chasing shadows, trying to pin down something that refused to be contained. In the end, all we found was more questions... and more suffering. Finally, Project Morpheus was shut down by the government, but they decided to release it to the public. Profit was more important to the government. Many of the patients were fine but many died or went into asylums—it was too much for them—it shattered their minds."

"Then it's up to us to find the answers." Elizabeth declared, determination hardening her features as she met Dr. Sanders' eyes. "To unravel the mystery of the labyrinth dream and bring justice for those who have been lost within its walls."

"Alright, let me show you something," Dr. Sanders said, motioning for Elizabeth to follow him deeper into the laboratory. Dr. Sanders led her past rows of computer monitors displaying an array of brain wave patterns, each one a symphony of peaks and valleys. Elizabeth's heart raced as she glimpsed echoes of the shared dream world through the lens of cold, hard data.

"Here," Dr. Sanders gestured to a console, his stern expression giving way to a hint of excitement. "This is where we monitored and manipulated the neural activity of our subjects. The technology we developed allowed us not only to observe their dreams but also to control certain aspects of their experience."

Elizabeth asked, her curiosity piqued but also tinged with apprehension, "How far did your influence extend?"

"Far enough to induce the labyrinth dream in all our subjects," he explained, his tone measured and cautious. "We were able to manipulate specific regions of the brain, responsible for spatial awareness and memory, creating a sense of disorientation and confusion, within the dream. It was like steering a ship through uncharted waters, navigating the collective unconscious."

"Uncharted waters," she echoed, trying to wrap her mind around the implications. "That's incredible ... but also dangerous. How can you be sure that you didn't cause more harm than good?"

Dr. Sanders hesitated, his gaze flitting between the screens as though searching for some reassurance. "The truth is, we can't. That's why I'm here, working with you. To find out what went wrong and set things right."

"Right ..." Elizabeth murmured, her thoughts tumbling like stones down a mountain slope. Elizabeth considered the ethical ramifications of the experiment, the line between scientific discovery and human suffering, and the ever-present question of whether the ends justified the means. "But why the labyrinth dream? What was the purpose of inducing such a specific, shared experience?"

"Because it was a unique opportunity to study the collective unconscious," Dr. Sanders replied. Dr. Sanders voice firm but tinged with regret. "By immersing our subjects in a shared dream world, we hoped to uncover universal truths about the human psyche. Patterns that transcended language, culture, and individual experience."

"Patterns ..." Elizabeth repeated, her eyes narrowing as she weighed the enormity of their task. "Like the threads in a tapestry, woven together to form a single, unified image."

"Exactly," Dr. Sanders affirmed, the weight of his past decisions bearing down upon him—like a leaden shroud. "But as you know all too well, there were ... unforeseen consequences. The labyrinth dream became a prison for many of our subjects, trapping them within its walls and refusing to release its grip. You helped them escape ... but they are not safe yet."

"Then we must find a permanent way to break that grip," Elizabeth vowed, her determination burning like a beacon in the darkness. "And bring closure to those still lost in the depths of the labyrinth."

"Indeed," Dr. Sanders agreed, his eyes meeting hers with a steely resolve.

"Dr. Harmon, look at this," Dr. Sanders motioned toward one of the computers monitors as he adjusted his glasses. The screen displayed a series of brain scans, each more intricate and complex than the last. "These are from Anna during different stages of the labyrinth dream."

"Remarkable ..." Elizabeth whispered, her brow furrowed in concentration, as she observed the subtle variations in neural activity. Elizabeth could almost feel the electric dance of synapses firing inside her skull, mirroring the intensity of the images before her.

"Isn't it?" Dr. Sanders replied, his voice tinged with equal parts awe and remorse. "Our technology allowed us to see their minds in ways never thought possible. But we didn't anticipate the consequences." Dr. Sander paused, swallowing hard. "Once they were lost in the labyrinth, some never found their way out."

"Then we must find a way to guide them," Elizabeth said resolutely, her hands clenched into fists. It was as if she could reach into the very fabric of the dream world and pull her patients free of its tangled web.

"Agreed," Dr. Sanders nodded solemnly. "But first, we need to understand the mechanics of the labyrinth dream. How it connects us all, and what it means for our collective consciousness."

Together, they pored over the data, analyzing patterns and correlations that seemed to defy logic. Each discovery led to more questions, the complexities of the human mind unfurling like an endless tapestry of interconnected threads.

"Dr. Sanders," Elizabeth mused, her eyes never leaving the screen, "do you think there is a single truth at the heart of the labyrinth? A key that can unlock its secrets?"

"Perhaps," he conceded, rubbing his chin thoughtfully. "Or maybe the labyrinth itself is the key. An ever-shifting reflection of our deepest fears and desires, bound together by the invisible threads of our shared humanity."

"Only time will tell," Elizabeth sighed, her voice heavy with the weight of her quest. "But I am determined to find the truth, no matter how daunting the journey."

"Then let us continue onward," Dr. Sanders declared, his steely resolve a testament to his desire for redemption. "Together, we shall navigate the twisted corridors of the labyrinth and bring light to its darkest corners."

Chapter 7

The rusted door creaked open as Elizabeth pushed against its stubborn weight. Beside her, Dr. Sanders peered into the darkness beyond the threshold, his breath catching in anticipation. They stepped inside, driven by their shared desire for the experiment that had claimed Elizabeth's sister, Claire.

"Are you ready for this?" Dr. Sanders asked, his voice low and cautious.

"More than ever," Elizabeth replied, her eyes scanning the shadows, trying to piece together a connection between the faded tiles underfoot and the painful memories of her sister's death.

As they ventured further into the abandoned facility, the dimly lit corridors seemed to close in around them. The air was heavy with the musty scent of decay, reminding Elizabeth of the nightmares she'd been analyzing for weeks—nightmares shared by her patients and, most recently, herself. This place felt like the embodiment of those dreams, the very same labyrinth that had haunted her thoughts and defied explanation.

"Such a dreadful atmosphere," Dr. Sanders murmured, echoing Elizabeth's unease. Dr. Sanders eyes, usually so stoic, betrayed a flicker of apprehension. Dr. Sanders had a personal stake in unraveling the mystery that lay before them, burdened by his guilt over the experiment's disastrous outcome.

The walls, once pristine and white, now bore streaks of grime and water stains as if they were weeping from some unseen wellspring. The fluorescent lights overhead hummed and flickered, casting eerie shadows along the corridor. Each footstep disturbed a layer of dust that had settled undisturbed for years, sending it swirling through the stale air like ghostly echoes of the past.

"Can you feel it, Dr. Harmon?" Dr. Sanders asked, his voice barely more than a whisper. "The remnants of what happened here, the lives affected ... It's palpable."

"Indeed," she replied, her heart heavy with the knowledge that one of those lives had been Claire's. Elizabeth could almost hear her sister's laughter, her voice before it had been silenced forever.

"Let's keep moving," she urged, her determination to uncover the truth providing the strength needed to push forward, even as the weight of the past threatened to crush her. Dr. Sanders offered a nod of agreement, his resolve shining through the ghosts that haunted them both.

As they continued deeper into the abandoned facility, she couldn't help but think of the patients she'd left behind—those who had experienced the same shared nightmares, the same labyrinth that had somehow entangled their minds and now led her to this place. Every detail she discovered, every clue that brought her closer to understanding, was also a step toward healing their wounded souls.

And perhaps, in some small way, it would bring her closer to healing her own.

The oppressive darkness seemed to seep into their very bones as Elizabeth and Dr. Sanders ventured further into the heart of the abandoned facility. The eerie silence was broken only by the occasional creak of rusted pipes, a mournful lamentation that echoed through the hollow corridors. Elizabeth's breath caught in her throat, her chest tightening with each step she took toward the unknown.

"Over here," Dr. Sanders called out, his voice barely audible above the persistent drumming of her own heart. Elizabeth followed the dim glow of his flashlight, which illuminated a dilapidated file cabinet in the corner of the room, its once pristine white paint now peeling and tainted by the passage of time.

"Look at this," he murmured as he pulled open one of the drawers. Inside, a jumble of tattered files lay scattered, their contents spilling out like secrets desperate to be unveiled. Elizabeth reached for one, her fingers trembling as she skimmed the faded ink on the page.

"Subject 23 ... Claire Harmon ..." Elizabeth sister's name jumped out from the text, an electric shock running through her veins, as she read the words that linked Claire to the failed experiment. "They knew ... all along ..."

"Dr. Harmon, I'm so sorry," Dr. Sanders whispered, placing a hand on her shoulder. The comfort of his touch was swallowed by the chasm that had opened within her, the abyss where her grief and rage intertwined like serpents writhing in the dark.

"Everything they did to her ... It wasn't just some tragic accident. They used her, manipulated her brain, and then discarded her like a broken toy!" Tears blurred her vision, but she refused to let them fall. Elizabeth would not grant those responsible the satisfaction of knowing they had shattered her world.

"Damn them!" Elizabeth hissed, her voice cracking under the strain. The venomous anger bubbled within her, threatening to consume her completely as the truth she had sought for so long lay bare before her. This was no longer just about her sister; it was about all those who had suffered at the hands of this monstrous experiment.

"Promise me, Dr. Sanders," she whispered, her voice heavy with the weight of the words, "that we'll find every last one of them and make them pay for what they did."

"I promise, Dr. Harmon," he replied, his own emotions evident in the raw edge of his voice. "We'll see justice served, not just for Claire, but for all of them."

Together, they continued their exploration through the decaying facility, driven by a newfound resolve. Their path was shrouded in shadows, but the cold light of retribution illuminated the way forward—a beacon of hope amidst the darkness that threatened to swallow them whole.

The air grew colder as they descended deeper into the bowels of the abandoned facility, the oppressive darkness swallowing them whole. Elizabeth's breath caught in her throat as Dr. Sanders led her through a dimly lit corridor, its walls suffocating, lined with remnants of an experiment gone awry. The flickering light from his flashlight revealed a door at the end—its paint chipping away, revealing the corroded metal beneath.

"Stay close," Dr. Sanders advised, his voice barely audible above the hum of their breathing. "This place is a labyrinth, and it's easy to get lost."

"Thank you for helping me, Dr. Sanders," she said, her voice wavering with gratitude and trepidation. "I couldn't do this without your expertise."

As they entered the room, she gasped at the sight before her. It was a laboratory, long abandoned, yet still bearing the gruesome marks of its past. The pungent scent of decay assaulted her senses as she stepped further inside, her heart pounding in her ears. Strewn across the floor were tattered papers, rusted equipment, and shattered glass—each piece a relic of horrors inflicted upon the innocent.

"Look at this," Dr. Sanders called out, holding up a bloodstained lab coat. Its once pristine white fabric was now marred by crimson streaks, a chilling reminder of the violence that had occurred within these walls.

"Who wore this?" Elizabeth asked, her voice trembling, the image of her sister's lifeless body flashing before her eyes.

"Someone involved in the experiment, no doubt," he answered grimly. "But we'll need to dig deeper to find out who."

"Over there," she whispered, pointing towards a corner of the room where an old television sat, covered in a thick layer of dust. "Maybe there's something on that television recorder."

They approached cautiously as if they were about to discover a hidden secret, akin to unraveling a mystery in a world of advanced technology. Dr. Sanders swiped his hand over a holographic display, dissipating virtual dust particles, revealing a holographic label that projected the word 'Experiment' in glowing letters. With a heavy sigh, he inserted a sleek, futuristic recorder into a levitating multimedia interface and pressed play.

As the footage began, Elizabeth's heart raced with anticipation, the blood pounding in her temples. It was like staring through a portal into the past—a past filled with secrets, pain, and lies. Elizabeth watched as doctors clad in white lab coats moved through the frame, their faces obscured by masks of professionalism.

"Look at the number on that door," Dr. Sanders said, his voice tense. "That's the same number mentioned in the files we found earlier."

"Then this is it," Elizabeth breathed, her eyes locked onto the screen. "This is where it all happened."

With each passing moment, the footage unveiled more pieces of the puzzle—pieces that sent shivers down her spine and fueled her determination. Elizabeth knew that the answers she sought lay buried beneath the rubble of this forsaken place, and she would not rest until they were unearthed.

The weight of the air grew heavier as Elizabeth and Dr. Sanders delved deeper into the twisted bowels of the abandoned facility. Shadows danced along the musty walls like ghosts of a forgotten time, their whispers echoing through the dimly lit corridors. "This place," she murmured, her breath forming visible clouds in the cold air. "It holds so many secrets."

"Secrets that were meant to stay buried,". he replied grimly, his eyes scanning the dilapidated surroundings. Dr. Sanders hand traced the outline of a faded blueprint pinned to the wall, its edges frayed and stained by decades of neglect.

"Let's piece together what we can," she said, determination burning in her chest. Elizabeth pulled a notepad from her bag, her pen poised above the blank page as if waiting for the words to materialize on their own.

Dr. Sanders nodded, then unrolled a larger schematic that had been tucked under his arm. Together, they began sifting through the evidence they'd collected—test results, lab reports, and hastily scribbled notes that spoke of an experiment gone awry.

"Judging by this timeline," Dr. Sanders mused, his finger tracing a line of dates and events, "the experiment was conducted over a span of several months. The subjects reported increasingly vivid dreams, but then ..."

"Side effects," she interjected, her voice strained. "Headaches, memory loss ... and worse." Elizabeth glanced at the bloodstained lab coat folded neatly beside her, a chilling reminder of the human cost of their terrible discovery.

"Exactly," he agreed, sketching a series of diagrams onto a fresh sheet of paper. "The data suggests a gradual erosion of the barrier between the dream world and reality, leading to catastrophic consequences."

A sudden noise from down the corridor made them both freeze in place. Footsteps, barely audible but unmistakable, echoed through the darkness. They exchanged a wary glance, their hearts pounding in unison as they strained to identify the source of the sound.

"Could someone else be here?" Elizabeth whispered, her grip tightening on the pen until her knuckles turned white.

"Unlikely," Dr. Sanders replied, his voice barely audible. "But we can't ignore the possibility."

They held their breaths as the footsteps drew nearer, the tension crackling between them like a live wire. As the sound reached its crescendo and then faded away, leaving only the ghostly whispers of the facility to fill the void, they exhaled in unison.

"Let's not lose focus," Elizabeth said, her voice trembling slightly. "We need to understand what happened here—for Claire, and for all the others who were lost to this nightmare."

A heaviness settled over Elizabeth as she gazed at the chaos of papers and diagrams strewn across the table. Each document was a piece of her sister's final days, a window into the terror that had consumed her. Elizabeth tried to imagine

Claire's face, so full of life, twisted in fear or pain. The thought sent a shudder down her spine.

"Are you okay?" Dr. Sanders asked, his concern evident in his furrowed brow.

"Fine," she lied, swallowing the lump in her throat. "Just thinking about Claire."

Dr. Sanders nodded solemnly, understanding her pain all too well. They continued their work, the silence between them heavy with grief and determination. For every answer they found, more questions seemed to arise, like shadows stretching out from the depths of the facility.

As they ventured further into the labyrinthine building, the weight of the past hung upon them like a thick fog. Elizabeth could almost sense the lost souls who had once been subjected to the experiment—how many had suffered the same fate as Claire?

"Look at this," Dr. Sanders called out, his voice echoing through the desolate corridors. Elizabeth rushed over, feeling an odd mix of hope and dread.

"Someone tried to destroy these files when the government had replaced me with someone else." Dr. Sanders said, pointing to the charred remains of documents piled in a corner, "but it seems they missed a few."

Elizabeth picked up one of the scorched papers, her hands trembling. It was a list of names, Claire's among them, each followed by a date and a single ominous word: *terminated*. A cold rage surged through her veins, mingling with the grief that threatened to drown her.

"Who would do this, Dr. Sanders? Who would cover up something so monstrous?" Elizabeth demanded, her eyes brimming with tears.

"Someone with much to hide," he replied grimly, placing a comforting hand on her shoulder.

Together, they sifted through the debris, each fragment a testament to the dark secrets that had been hidden within the facility's walls. A sense of urgency propelled them forward, driving them deeper into the heart of the mystery.

Then, at last, they found it—a tattered file folder buried beneath the ashes. Dr. Sanders carefully opened it, revealing a series of photographs and diagrams. Elizabeth's breath hitched in her throat as she recognized the images: blueprints of the dream-sharing technology, detailed schematics for a machine designed to delve into the most intimate recesses of the human mind.

"Dr. Sanders," she whispered, her voice barely audible. "This ... these changes everything."

"Yes, Elizabeth," he agreed solemnly. "It does."

Elizabeth's hands trembled as she leafed through the tattered file, images of the dream-sharing technology unfolding before her like a nightmare come to life. Elizabeth pulse raced with equal parts fear and exhilaration; this was the smoking gun they had been searching for. The weight of the discovery settled in her chest, heavy and suffocating, as the ghosts of her sister's memory seemed to whisper their secrets in her ear.

"Look at this," he said, his voice cracking with urgency. Dr. Sanders pointed to a diagram labeled 'Prototype 3C.' "This model ... it's far more advanced than anything we've ever seen. They must have built it after Claire's death." His eyes met hers, filled with a shared understanding of the implications.

"I knew it," Elizabeth breathed, her voice thick with emotion. "They didn't just take my sister from me—they continued their work, hiding it from the world."

Dr. Sanders placed a hand on her trembling shoulder, offering silent comfort. "We'll expose them, Dr. Harmon. We'll make sure Claire's legacy isn't forgotten."

A tear slid down her cheek as she nodded, her resolve fortified by the truth that lay bare before them. Elizabeth carefully folded the blueprints and tucked them into her bag, their very existence a symbol of both her sister's sacrifice and the lengths she would go to find justice.

"Let's get out of here," she said softly, her voice barely audible over the hum of the flickering lights above.

As they made their way back through the abandoned facility, her mind raced with thoughts of what lay ahead. Elizabeth obsession with the experiment had driven her to the brink, but now, with the truth in her grasp, she felt an odd sense of calm wash over her. Elizabeth knew the road to justice wouldn't be easy, but she wasn't alone—Dr. Sanders' unwavering support and dedication was a beacon of light in the darkness that had consumed her for so long.

Chapter 8

The rain was relentless, pounding against the glass of her office window. Elizabeth sat at her desk, scouring a stack of medical records and journal articles. Elizabeth had been working tirelessly for weeks, trying to make sense of the shared nightmare that haunted her patients. The labyrinth. A cold shiver ran down her spine as she recalled the chilling details they had recounted. Elizabeth had so much information now. But it didn't lace together to make any sense.

"Patience, Elizabeth," she whispered to herself, her determined expression unwavering.

"Dr. Harmon?" A voice echoed from the doorway, pulling her out of her thoughts.

Elizabeth looked up to find a woman standing on the threshold. The air around her seemed to chill, and Elizabeth felt a sudden urge to pull her jacket tighter around her body. The woman had a slim build, sharp features, and an unyielding gaze that pierced through Elizabeth's soul. Her dark hair was pulled back into a tight bun, and she wore a tailored suit that exuded authority.

"Agent Victoria Reynolds," the woman introduced herself, extending a hand. "I have been assigned to this case."

"Assigned?" Elizabeth asked skeptically, shaking the woman's icy hand. "By whom?"

" From FTIGA, The Federal Technological Investigation Government Agency. We both want the same thing: answers. I am here to help you find them." Agent Reynolds' voice was calm, and calculated, betraying no emotion.

"There have been a lot of unanswered questions from our agency, and we are hoping you may help us figure this out." Agent Renolds said.

"Very well," she conceded, gesturing for the agent to take a seat. As she did so, she couldn't help but feel a pang of unease in her gut. Something was unsettling about Agent Reynolds, but she couldn't quite put her finger on it. For now, at least, she would have to trust her.

"Let me bring you up to speed," Elizabeth began, laying out the evidence she had gathered so far. Anna, a young woman in her early thirties, had first brought the labyrinth to her attention. Elizabeth vivid descriptions of the nightmarish maze and the inexplicable sense of dread that accompanied it had piqued her interest, but it wasn't until Mr. Thompson—a middle-aged man with a stern face and muscular build—recounted a nearly identical experience that she knew something was amiss.

"Two patients with the same nightmare, both experiencing it in such vivid detail ... It can't be a coincidence," she mused, her brow furrowing as she pondered the implications. Elizabeth was hesitant to tell the agent her theories about the experiment yet.

"Whatever it is, Dr. Harmon, we will get to the bottom of it," Agent Reynolds promised, her cold gaze never wavering. "I will be the point agent for this case. We want this cleared up."

As the rain continued its assault outside, Elizabeth found herself pulled deeper into the mystery that had consumed her life. With each new piece of evidence she uncovered, the truth seemed to slip further away, like a specter in the shadows. But she wouldn't give up—not until she had unraveled the secrets of the labyrinth and laid her sister's soul to rest. And with Agent Reynolds by her side, she felt certain that day would come soon.

Raindrops slid down the window like teardrops, their steady rhythm echoing her racing thoughts. Elizabeth leaned closer, peering through the veil of water, to the shadowy figures, passing by on the street below. Elizabeth heart pounded in anticipation, each throb a reminder of the weight she carried—the burden of her sister's unexplained death and the dark labyrinth that had consumed her life.

"Dr. Harmon?" A voice shattered the silence, its cold, calculated tone sending a shiver down her spine. Elizabeth turned to face the woman who had entered her office without warning.

"Of course," Reynolds agreed smoothly, her lips curling into a predatory smile. "You have my word."

Elizabeth felt the weight of scrutiny bearing down on her as she delved deeper into the investigation. From the shadows, Agent Reynolds, a mysterious and formidable figure, had been keeping a watchful eye on her every move. It was becoming increasingly evident that Reynolds was determined to keep the darkest secrets of the failed experiment concealed.

With each new piece of evidence Elizabeth uncovered, she couldn't shake the unsettling feeling that Reynolds was orchestrating a delicate dance, carefully manipulating the narrative to shield the experiment's hidden truths from her relentless pursuit. It was as if Reynolds saw her as a pawn in his intricate game, and with every discovery she made, he deftly maneuvered to maintain control over the situation.

The cloak-and-dagger maneuvers played out discreetly, leaving her with a growing sense of unease. Elizabeth couldn't escape the suspicion that Reynolds was playing a high-stakes game, subtly pulling the strings to ensure that the investigation unfolded on his terms. As she pressed on, determined to unravel the mysteries shrouded in secrecy, she became acutely aware that each step she took was met with Reynolds' calculated countermove, deepening the enigma surrounding the failed experiment's darkest secrets. It was a tense and intricate dance, and Elizabeth couldn't help but feel like a pawn in Reynolds' shadowy chess game.

"Let's begin," Agent Reynolds said, her voice low and steady as the rain outside continued its relentless march. "Tell me everything you know."

As Elizabeth detailed her findings, she couldn't help but feel a growing sense of unease—as if she were walking deeper into a maze with no exit in sight. Yet, she pressed on, the promise of answers driving her forward.

"Interesting," Agent Reynolds mused, her fingers tapping against her chin as Elizabeth finished speaking. "It seems you've uncovered more than I initially realized."

"Does that change anything?" Elizabeth asked, wariness lacing her tone.

"Perhaps," Reynolds conceded, her eyes glinting with something Elizabeth couldn't quite place. "But first, we must delve deeper into the labyrinth and uncover what lies at its heart."

The steady rainfall blurred the cityscape outside Elizabeth's window as she sat across from Agent Reynolds, her heart pounding in her chest like an anxious metronome. Despite her apprehension, she couldn't deny the relief of having someone to confide in, someone who seemed to understand the labyrinthine darkness she sought to unravel.

"Here," Elizabeth said, handing over a thick stack of documents. "These are my notes on the most recent leads I've uncovered."

"Thank you," Agent Reynolds replied coolly, her fingers skimming the pages with an almost predatory precision. "I'll be sure to study these thoroughly."

As the days turned into weeks, Elizabeth found herself relying more and more on Agent Reynolds' guidance and Dr. Sanders. The enigmatic agent and Dr. Sanders had become a beacon of clarity in the murky sea of secrets that threatened to swallow Elizabeth whole.

"Have you considered looking into the project's financial backers?" Reynolds suggested one afternoon over steaming cups of tea.

"Actually, no, I hadn't," Elizabeth admitted, her mind racing with new possibilities. "That could provide valuable insight into their motivations."

"Indeed," Reynolds agreed, her eyes glinting with something akin to satisfaction. "You never know what skeletons lurk in the shadows of power."

"Agent Reynolds," Elizabeth said one evening, her voice hesitant, "do you ever feel like we're spinning our wheels? As if some unseen force is working against us?"

"Sometimes the path to truth is fraught with obstacles," Reynolds responded, her gaze locked onto Elizabeth's. "But we must press on. We owe it to your sister, don't we?"

"Of course," Elizabeth agreed, her determination rekindled by Reynolds' words. "I just ... I can't shake this feeling that we're missing something crucial. Something vital."

"Trust me," Reynolds said softly, reaching out to squeeze Elizabeth's hand. "Together, we'll uncover the truth."

Unbeknownst to Elizabeth, beneath the comforting warmth of Reynolds' touch lay a chilling calculation. With each detail she shared, and every lead explored, Agent Reynolds wove an intricate web of deceit around her, the unsuspecting psychologist. It became apparent that the secrets she sought would remain forever shrouded in shadows, carefully guarded by the very person she had trusted.

"Trust me" echoed in Elizabeth's mind, but as she looked into Agent Reynolds' eyes, she couldn't help but wonder if trust was merely another weapon in a war she had yet to fully comprehend.

The evening sky bled red and orange as Elizabeth's office grew darker, casting long shadows across the room. Elizabeth sat at her desk, poring over documents and witness accounts, the weight of exhaustion settling in like a heavy fog.

Reynolds moved with predatory grace, scanning the files with sharp, calculating eyes. Reynolds plucked a document from the pile, her fingers lingering for a moment, before delicately placing it back in its original position.

"Interesting," she murmured the word a sigh on her lips. "This lead here, about the abandoned warehouse ... What if we shifted our focus?"

"Shifted?" Elizabeth's heart stuttered in her chest, her mind racing as she tried to grasp Reynolds' intention.

"Perhaps this isn't the right path," Reynolds continued, her voice smooth as silk. "What if we've been misdirected? Lured into a labyrinth designed to trap us?"

"Then what do you suggest?" Elizabeth asked, the desperation in her voice betraying her growing need for guidance.

"Let's try a different angle," Reynolds said, a sly smile playing on her lips. "I have a contact who might be able to shed some light on these inconsistencies."

As Reynolds delved deeper into Elizabeth's research, subtly gathering information and ensuring no stone was left unturned, she steered Elizabeth away from certain leads, maintaining her facade as an ally.

"Agent Reynolds, I'm not sure we should be trusting this contact of yours," Elizabeth said, uncertainty gnawing at her stomach. "What if they lead us astray?"

"Trust me," Reynolds replied with a cold smile, her eyes glinting like ice in the fading light. "We can't afford to ignore any potential leads."

"Alright," Elizabeth conceded, trying to silence the voice inside her that screamed for caution. "Let's follow this new path."

Together, they waded through a sea of deception and misdirection, the truth hidden beneath layers of lies.

As the days unfolded, Elizabeth and Agent Reynolds decided to meet at the research lab, the very place where everything had originated. Despite her caution, Elizabeth made sure not to reveal to Agent Reynolds that she had encountered Dr. Sanders and visited the lab on a previous occasion. Elizabeth wariness underscored the fact that she harbored reservations about placing complete trust in Agent Reynolds.

The fluorescent lights of the research lab flickered above them, casting a sterile glow over the cluttered workspace. Elizabeth's fingers danced through the mess of photographs and scribbled notes, her heart pounding like a metronome in her chest. Elizabeth could feel the weight of the truth pressing down on her, so close she could almost taste it. But the deeper she dove into the mystery, the more shadows seemed to dance just beyond her reach.

"Agent Reynolds," she whispered, her voice barely above the hum of the cooling systems. "I can't do this alone anymore."

Agent Reynolds leaned against the cold metal table, her eyes locked onto Elizabeth's, with a calculated intensity. "You don't have to," she replied, her voice smooth as silk. "I'm here with you every step of the way. You can trust me."

"Thank you," Elizabeth breathed, feeling something inside her unclench at the reassurance. Elizabeth allowed herself to lean into Reynolds guidance, letting the other woman's knowledge and expertise fill the void left by her uncertainty.

Yet, as they delved deeper into the labyrinthine web of deception that surrounded the failed experiment, a creeping sense of unease began to settle in the back of Elizabeth's mind. It was a subtle shift, like the whisper of a breeze through the trees or the first hint of frost on an autumn morning.

"Dr. Harmon," Agent Reynolds said, her voice breaking through the haze of Elizabeth's thoughts. "Focus."

"Right, sorry," Elizabeth muttered, forcing her attention back to the task at hand. But the disquiet continued to gnaw at her, an itch that refused to be ignored.

As they sifted through the piles of information, Agent Reynolds' grip on the investigation tightened like a vice. Reynolds' movements were swift and precise; the way she dissected each piece of evidence, discarding some while holding onto others, was almost surgical in its precision. And all the while, her eyes remained locked on Elizabeth with an unwavering intensity.

"Here," Reynolds said, handing a stack of papers to Elizabeth. "These are the ones we need to focus on."

"Are you sure?" Elizabeth asked, scanning the documents with furrowed brows.

"Positive," Reynolds replied, her voice cold and certain. "Trust me."

And so, Elizabeth did, allowing herself to be led further down the rabbit hole by a woman whose true motivations, were as shrouded in mystery as the secrets they sought to unearth. But as the days turned into weeks, and the weeks into months, Elizabeth couldn't shake the feeling that something was amiss.

In the unfolding days, Elizabeth and Agent Reynolds arranged to meet at the research lab, the nexus of their investigation. Elizabeth, mindful not to disclose her previous encounter with Dr. Sanders and her familiarity with the lab, approached the rendezvous with caution, her trust in Agent Reynolds not fully solidified.

As the experiment's concealed truths slowly surfaced, intertwining to create a tapestry of deception far more intricate than either of them could have fathomed, it became evident that Agent Reynolds concealed a different identity. What Elizabeth discovered pointed accusatory fingers at Reynolds, hidden behind her composed smiles and meticulously chosen words. The revelation struck with a force that threatened to dismantle everything Elizabeth held true, leaving her in doubt not only about the woman she had placed her trust in but also about her own judgment.

The emerging truth, shrouded in the darkness of deception, painted a picture of betrayal that surpassed Elizabeth's initial suspicions. She now grappled with the unsettling realization that she had unknowingly become entangled in a web of deceit spun by the very person she had considered her confidante.

"Agent Reynolds," she whispered, her voice trembling with a mix of fear and awe. "What have you done?"

But the double agent merely smiled, her eyes as cold as the steel table upon which their shattered dreams now lay. "My job," she replied, the finality of her words echoing through the silence like a gunshot.

Elizabeth shifted the loose-leaf papers in her hands. They were dirty from years of sitting on the desks, floors, and filing cabinets. She scanned through statistical data regarding the patient's vital signs, test results, brain images—mostly things she couldn't use.

But then she saw something that made her freeze. Even her heart stopped beating for a single second before it returned to a rhythm going double the speed.

Elizabeth slowly lifted her eyes to Agent Reynolds. She cleared her throat. "Agent Reynolds ..."

Reynolds smiled at her. "Yes?"

"Why is your name at the bottom of this document?"

Reynold's stilled at her words. Then sighed.

"Ah, Elizabeth," Victoria's voice cut through the air like a knife, shattering the fragile illusion that had once protected them both. "I see you've discovered my little secret."

Elizabeth whirled around to face the woman she once trusted, her eyes brimming with confusion and betrayal. "Why, Victoria?" she demanded, her voice wavering despite her best efforts. "Why did you help me only to deceive me?"

"Because, my dear," Victoria replied, her cold eyes glittering with malice, "you were getting too close to the truth. And I couldn't let that happen."

"Close to the truth? You mean ... all those leads we followed, all those dead ends ... they were your doing?"

"Every last one of them," Victoria confirmed, a cruel smile twisting her lips. "You see, Elizabeth, it's my job to protect this experiment. To keep its secrets hidden from prying eyes like yours."

"Even if it means destroying lives?" Elizabeth shot back, her voice laced with anger and grief. "My sister ... all those innocent people ..."

"Collateral damage," Victoria said dismissively, her expression unmoved by the pain etched across Elizabeth's face. "A small price to pay for the greater good."

"Greater good?" she spat, her fury boiling over. "How can you say that when you know the horrors they've unleashed?"

"Because, Elizabeth," Victoria whispered, leaning in close, her breath cold against her ear, "sometimes the ends justify the means."

Elizabeth's thoughts raced, desperate to find a way out of this nightmare. But as she searched for any semblance of hope, she knew there was only one thing left to do.

"Victoria," she said, her voice steady despite the storm that raged within her, "I won't let you keep these secrets any longer. I won't let you continue to hurt innocent people."

"Is that a threat, Dr. Harmon?" Victoria asked, her icy gaze never leaving Elizabeth's face.

"Consider it a promise," she replied, standing tall and unyielding, even as the shadows closed in around her.

"Very well," Victoria said, a sinister smile spreading across her face. "Then let the games begin."

And with that, the room plunged into darkness, leaving Elizabeth alone with the chilling realization that she had declared war.

Chapter 9

A cold sweat dampened Elizabeth's brow as she paced the dimly lit hallway of her apartment. The labyrinth had been haunting her every thought, an enigma that threatened to unravel the fragile fabric of her sanity. The faces of her patients—of Anna, with her short, messy hair and trembling hands, and Mr. Thompson, the muscular man whose stern face belied a deeper vulnerability—swirled in her mind, urging her to confront the nightmare that bound them all together. None of them had been able to refrain from falling back into the nightmare. They needed another way—a better way—to defeat this.

She paced the entire night trying to find a new angle, but nothing came to mind. Victoria had escaped the laboratory and was lying in wait for her somewhere. Elizabeth had no idea when she would show her face again. So, she turned her mind back to the problem of the nightmare.

"Enough," she muttered under her breath, clenching her fists. Elizabeth sister's unexplained death had left a gaping wound in her heart, and the labyrinth seemed to hold the key to understanding it all. Elizabeth refused to let fear cripple her any longer. "I'll just enter the dream over and over until it works. Perhaps this time I should get some expert help ..."

Her mind turned to Dr. Martin Sanders, the man who held the answers she sought. He was lean, with graying hair and a stoic demeanor that masked the burden of his involvement in the failed government experiment. Elizabeth knew he could guide her through the treacherous world of the shared dream, for they both shared the same relentless drive to uncover the truth.

As Elizabeth reached for the phone to call Dr. Sanders, she hesitated for a moment, her hand hovering above the device. It wasn't just about the labyrinth or her patients—it was a deeply personal journey, a chance to confront her demons. The guilt that weighed heavily on her chest demanded acknowledgment, and she needed to face it head-on.

"Dr. Sander," said Elizabeth, her voice quivering slightly as she finally dialed his number, "I need your help."

"Dr. Harmon," Dr. Sanders replied, his tone even but laced with understanding, "I've been waiting for this call."

"Then you know what I intend to do?" Elizabeth swallowed hard, bracing herself for whatever challenges lay ahead.

"Indeed. I'll help you enter the shared dream consciously, but you must know that it won't be easy. The labyrinth is a treacherous place, and we both have much to learn about ourselves to navigate its winding paths."

"Thank you, Dr. Sanders. I'm ready for whatever it takes," she said, her voice now steady with resolve.

"Very well. We'll begin your training as soon as possible. Remember, Dr. Harmond, this journey is not just about uncovering the truth—it's about finding redemption, for both of us."

As they spoke, she glanced at a framed photograph on her nightstand—Elizabeth sister's smiling face staring back at her. It was a bittersweet reminder of why she had embarked on this harrowing quest. Steeling herself, she knew that no matter what horrors lay within the labyrinth, she would face them head-on, guided by the wisdom of Dr. Sanders and the love for her sister that burned fiercely within her heart.

"Redemption," she whispered, her eyes fixed on the photograph. "Yes, Dr. Sander, we will find it together."

A few days passed and Elizabeth headed to Dr. Sander's office.

"Dr. Sanders," Elizabeth called out to him, stepping into his futuristic study. The ambient glow of holographic displays cast an ethereal light throughout the room, replacing the dimly lit atmosphere. The air was infused with a subtle, rejuvenating scent, thanks to the advanced air purification system. The walls were adorned not with traditional books but with interactive digital panels showcasing a vast array of knowledge.

She found him hunched over his sleek, levitating desk, surrounded by holographic screens displaying complex equations and simulations. The hum of advanced technology permeated the air, and the room exuded an air of sophistication that extended beyond the tactile feel of aged leather. Dr. Sanders was deeply engrossed in his work, seamlessly navigating between augmented reality interfaces with swift gestures.

"Ah, Dr. Harmon," he said, looking up from his screen with a faint smile. "I've been expecting you."

"Your guidance means more to me than I can express," she admitted, her voice heavy with gratitude. "I'm ready."

"Very well. But it is not as simple as taking a potion from some crackpot scientist." Dr. Sanders replied, standing up and gesturing for her to take a seat across from him. "Let's begin."

As they settled into their chairs, Dr. Sanders spoke with the authority of one who had explored the labyrinth countless times before. "The key to entering the shared dream consciously lies within your mind. You must first learn to master your thoughts and emotions, for they will shape the dream world around you."

"Is this where meditation comes in?" Elizabeth asked, eager to absorb his knowledge.

"Indeed," Dr. Sanders confirmed. "Meditation is a powerful tool for achieving mental clarity and focus. It will help you control your entry into the shared dream and navigate the labyrinth once you're inside."

"Where do we start?"

"Close your eyes and take slow, deep breaths," Dr. Sanders instructed. "Inhale through your nose, then exhale through your mouth. Focus on your breathing—nothing else."

Elizabeth obeyed, her chest rising and falling as she concentrated on each breath. The air was cool against her skin, soothing her racing thoughts.

"Good," Dr. Sanders praised. "Now, I want you to visualize the entrance to the labyrinth—an ornate gate, perhaps, or a simple wooden door. Picture it in your mind's eye and hold onto that image."

The labyrinth's entrance materialized in her mind: a towering, wrought iron gate, twisted into intricate patterns that seemed to shift and change with each passing second.

"Excellent," Dr. Sanders continued. "Now, imagine yourself standing before the gate, reaching out to touch it. Can you feel its cold, hard surface beneath your fingertips?"

As Elizabeth focused on the sensation, she could almost feel the chill of the metal seeping into her skin, anchoring her to this imagined world.

"Remember," Dr. Sanders warned, his voice a low, urgent whisper, "the labyrinth is not just a physical space, but a psychological one as well. Your emotions will influence its pathways, and your fears may manifest in unexpected ways."

"Is there a way to control what I see and experience within the labyrinth?" Elizabeth asked, her heart pounding at the thought of facing her deepest fears alone.

"Only through understanding and confronting those fears can you truly master them," he explained. "It's a difficult journey, but one that both of us must undertake if we are to find redemption."

"Thank you, Dr. Sanders," Elizabeth murmured, her eyes still closed as she clung to the image of the labyrinth's entrance. "I'll do whatever it takes."

"Good," Dr. Sanders replied, his voice steady and reassuring. "For now, continue practicing these exercises daily. With time, you'll be ready to enter the shared dream consciously and begin your exploration of the labyrinth."

As their session concluded, Elizabeth felt a newfound sense of purpose and determination. Guided by Dr. Sanders' wisdom and driven by her desire for redemption, she knew that she would face whatever horrors the labyrinth had in store for her—and emerge stronger for it.

The first rays of sunlight streamed through the window, casting a golden glow across Elizabeth's room as she settled into her meditation posture. The weight of her past clung to her like a shroud, but Dr. Sanders' guidance had given her hope—a beacon of light in the darkness that consumed her thoughts.

"Focus on your breath," she whispered to herself, drawing in a deep inhale and exhaling slowly. Elizabeth heart thrummed in her chest, a constant reminder of her mission: to unravel the enigma of the labyrinth and confront the demons lurking within its depths.

But as the days wore on, Elizabeth found it increasingly difficult to maintain her focus. Disturbing nightmares plagued her sleep, leaving her mind frazzled and her body exhausted. Images of twisted corridors and shadowy figures haunted her waking hours, blurring the line between reality and the twisted landscape of her subconscious.

"Damn it!" Elizabeth muttered, rubbing her temples in frustration, as she peeled her sweat-soaked sheets away from her body. Elizabeth knew that if she was to make any progress, she had to conquer these obstacles. With renewed determination, Elizabeth sought out Dr. Sanders once more.

"Dr. Harmon, you must remember that your emotions can influence your experiences in the shared dream. Don't let your fear take control," he cautioned, his voice laced with concern.

"How do I prevent that?" Elizabeth asked, her eyes searching his for answers.

"Visualize a protective barrier around yourself, one that cannot be pierced by your fears," he suggested. "And don't forget to breathe."

Taking his advice to heart, Elizabeth practiced diligently, visualizing an impenetrable shield of light surrounding her as she meditated. Gradually, her nightmares began to recede, replaced by a growing sense of self-assurance.

"Dr. Sanders, I think I'm ready," she said, her voice steady and strong.

"Very well, Dr. Harmon. I'll guide you through the process," Dr. Sanders replied, his face etched with pride.

As they sat together in the dimly lit room, Elizabeth felt her consciousness slipping gently into the shared dream. The familiar cold stone walls, of the labyrinth materialized around her, but this time, she was not alone—Dr. Sanders' presence emanated from somewhere close, a comforting tether to reality amidst the chaos.

"Remember your training," he encouraged her, his voice resonating through the ethereal plane. "You can do this."

With that, Elizabeth stepped forward into the darkness, her heart swelling with newfound courage as she embarked on her harrowing journey. Elizabeth breaths remained steady, her shield of light unwavering, and for the first time, she felt truly prepared to face whatever lay hidden within the labyrinth's depths.

The cold stone walls of the labyrinth loomed before Elizabeth, their towering heights casting shadowy patterns on the ground beneath her feet. Elizabeth knew that within these ancient, winding corridors lay secrets waiting to be uncovered, as well as dangers that would test her every resolve.

"Dr. Harmon," Dr. Sanders' voice echoed softly in her mind, "remember, you must remain focused and calm. This labyrinth is not only a physical manifestation but also a reflection of your subconscious."

Elizabeth nodded, taking note of the subtle nuances of the maze around her: the way the stones seemed to shift ever so slightly, as if breathing; the faint whispers carried by the wind, beckoning her further into the darkness; the crawling ivy that adorned the walls, its tendrils coiling and uncoiling like living serpents.

"Dr. Sanders, I can feel the weight of this place—its history, its pain, and its secrets," she thought, her inner voice reaching out to him. "I know things are lurking here that can harm me, but I am prepared to face them."

"Good," he responded, his mental presence, a reassuring anchor amidst the uncertainty. "Be mindful of your surroundings. Trust your instincts and remember the techniques we've practiced."

As Elizabeth delved deeper into the labyrinth, she noticed peculiar markings etched upon the stones—symbols that seemed to dance and shimmer, when her gaze lingered too long upon them. They whispered promises of knowledge and power, tempting her to abandon her path and follow their siren call.

"Stay focused, Dr. Harmon," Dr. Sanders warned. "These symbols represent the distractions and temptations that can lead you astray, both in the dream world and in life. Don't allow them to derail your progress."

"Thank you, Dr. Sanders," she thought, steeling herself against their allure. "I won't let my past mistakes define me any longer."

The labyrinth continued to twist and turn, its path leading Elizabeth through a series of treacherous obstacles: bottomless pits that yawned open beneath her feet, walls that seemed to close in around her, and shadowy figures that lurked just beyond the edge of her vision. With each challenge she faced, she drew upon the skills she had honed under Dr. Sanders' guidance, her resolve growing stronger with every victory.

"Dr. Harmon," Dr. Sanders said, his voice tinged with concern, "you're doing well, but there is still much to overcome before you reach the heart of the labyrinth. The further you venture, the more dangerous it becomes."

"I understand," she replied, her determination unwavering. "I won't be deterred by fear or doubt. I'm ready for whatever lies ahead."

"Very well," he conceded. "Just remember: no matter how dark or twisted the path may become, never lose sight of who you are and what you seek to accomplish."

As Elizabeth ventured onward, she knew that the labyrinth's true test was yet to come. And though the shadows whispered their threats and the stones seemed to conspire against her, she pressed forward, resolved to confront the darkness within herself and unlock the secrets buried deep within the labyrinth's heart.

"Remember, Dr. Harmon," Dr. Sanders warned as they stood on the precipice of the dream world, "this journey is as much about confronting your demons as it is navigating the labyrinth itself."

Elizabeth nodded, her eyes fixed, resolutely on the shimmering portal before them. Elizabeth had spent countless hours rehearsing the techniques Dr. Sanders taught her, and now she was prepared to face whatever lay ahead. With a deep breath, she took one last look at the small pack filled with essential supplies—a flashlight, a compass, and a notebook to document her findings. As long as she held onto the items—when entering the dream world, she was able to bring them with her.

"Dr. Sanders," Elizabeth said, gripping his arm for reassurance, "thank you for everything you've done to prepare me for this. I promise I won't let you down."

"Dr. Harmon, you have come so far already," he replied, his voice gentle yet firm. "And remember, I'll be here, monitoring your progress."

"Alright, then." Elizabeth heart pounded in her chest, adrenaline surging through her veins. This was the moment she had been working towards, the culmination of her determination and focus.

As Elizabeth stepped into the shared dream, she felt as if she were plunging into an icy abyss. The sensation sent shivers down her spine, and for a moment, she gasped in shock. But the cold quickly gave way to warmth, like emerging from a cool lake into the embrace of the sun's rays.

The landscape that greeted her was surreal and breathtaking. Towering crystalline structures loomed overhead, their surfaces refracting light into a kaleidoscope of colors. A lush carpet of emerald moss covered the ground, interspersed with brilliant flowers that seemed to hum with a hidden energy. This was so much different than the first time she had entered the dream. Everything had been chaos and fragments. With her mind in her control, she could navigate more effectively.

"Extraordinary," she whispered, unable to contain her awe.

"Focus, Elizabeth," Dr. Sanders' voice echoed in her mind, a reminder of the dangers lurking within this beautiful facade. "You must remain vigilant."

"Of course," she replied, steeling herself for the task at hand. With purposeful strides, she began to navigate the labyrinth, her senses heightened and attuned to every detail of this strange world.

The walls of the maze were alive with pulsating patterns that shifted and morphed as Elizabeth walked, their hypnotic undulations threatening to disorient her. But she clung to the grounding techniques Dr. Sanders had taught her, mentally reciting a litany of facts about her life, her work, and her sister.

"Stay focused," she repeated internally like a mantra. "Never lose sight of who you are and what you seek to accomplish."

As Elizabeth delved deeper into the dream world, the beauty around her took on a sinister edge. Elizabeth could feel eyes watching her from the shadows and the whispers of the creature's unseen sent shivers down her spine. But she stood tall, resolute in her mission to unravel the mysteries that had haunted her for so long.

"Dr. Sanders, I'm ready," she murmured, her resolve unwavering. "Let's begin."

"Very well," Dr. Sanders' voice whispered in response, as if he stood beside her, even though she knew he was miles away. "Remember what we practiced. Keep your emotions in check and your mind clear."

Elizabeth nodded, moving deeper into the labyrinth. Elizabeth footsteps echoed off the walls, muffled by the pulsating patterns that seemed to absorb sound. The air felt thick, suffocating, as though it were trying to smother her thoughts.

"Stay calm," she reminded herself, focusing on her breathing—an exercise Dr. Sanders had taught her, to maintain control. "Inhale, exhale ... Inhale, exhale."

A screech pierced the silence, jarring Elizabeth from her concentration. She spun around, searching for the source of the sound. Were the shadows playing tricks on her, or had something emerged from the darkness?

"Something's here," she thought, panic threatening to overtake her. "It might be the Fear entity."

"Focus, Dr. Harmon," Dr. Sanders urged, his voice steady. "Don't let fear control you."

"Right," she said aloud, forcing her trembling hands to remain still. "I can do this."

As she continued through the labyrinth, an oppressive feeling settled over her as if the very walls were closing in. Elizabeth fought against the sensation, repeating her mantra in a desperate attempt to cling to reality.

"Stay focused. Never lose sight of who you are and what you seek to accomplish."

Suddenly, the figure emerged from the shadows: tall and imposing, with eyes gleaming like embers in the darkness. It wore a twisted grin, and its laughter sent chills down Elizabeth's spine.

"Ah, Elizabeth," it spoke in a voice that was both alluring and menacing. "I've been waiting for you to come back."

"Dr. Harmon, do not engage," Dr. Sanders warned urgently. "It's trying to lure you in."

"Then what should I do?" Elizabeth asked frantically, her heart pounding in her chest.

"Remember your training," he replied, his tone firm but reassuring. "You have the knowledge to face whatever challenges this world presents."

"Right," she whispered, using every ounce of strength to resist the creature's pull. "I can do this."

"Indeed, you can," the creature taunted, its grin widening as it began to advance toward her. At the same time, the labyrinth seemed to shift, the walls reconfiguring into an unfamiliar pattern.

"Wait!" Elizabeth cried out, fear gripping her once more. "Where am I? Dr. Sanders, help me!"

"Dr. Harmon, stay focused!" he urged, his voice distant and fading. "You must find your way back!"

As the creature drew closer, Elizabeth's panic rose like a tidal wave—a dark realization dawning within her.

"Am I trapped here?" Elizabeth thought, her breath coming in ragged gasps. "Is this where I'm destined to remain?"

Elizabeth stood alone in the ever-shifting labyrinth.

Chapter 10

The air was thick with the scent of earth and something metallic, like blood in the back of one's throat. Elizabeth found herself standing at the entrance of the labyrinth, her heart pounding in her chest as if it wanted to break free. Elizabeth felt an urgency gnawing at her insides, driving her forward into the maze despite the fear that clung to her like a second skin.

Elizabeth's psyche was deterring and her mind created Emily an apparition of her imagination. She knew if she looked that she would find the others. So, she stepped forward searching and calling for them, just like the first time she entered the dream consciously with the potion.

As her mind walked through the darkness, she saw an outline of Emily. Elizabeth had not seen Emily in the real world for months as she had conquered the nightmare and faced her fears, vanquishing the entity. Emily's outline faded in and out and she knew it was just an apparition that her mind created for her.

"Emily," she whispered, her voice barely audible above the sound of her ragged breaths. "You're not actually here, are you?"

In the dim light, shadows seemed to flicker and dance around her, their movements unnervingly unpredictable. The walls of the labyrinth loomed high above her as if they were alive and closing in on her, suffocating her with their oppressive weight. Elizabeth could not escape the feeling that she was being watched by unseen eyes.

Elizabeth turned and saw them: Anna and Mr. Thompson. Elizabeth sighed in relief.

"Dr. Harmon," Anna's words echoed in her mind. "I swear, there's something ... someone in there with us."

"Same here," Mr. Thompson had agreed, his muscular arms crossed protectively over his chest. "She's always just out of reach, like a mirage."

Elizabeth steeled herself and took a step forward, her boots sinking slightly into the soft ground. The labyrinth swallowed her eagerly, the darkness seeming to deepen with every step she took. Elizabeth knew that somewhere within these twisting passages lay the answers she sought—the truth about her sister's death, and perhaps even the key to understanding the shared nightmare that plagued her patients.

Elizabeth knew what her mind was trying to tell her by creating Emily. Elizabeth had to try to defeat her fears again. If it didn't work this time, she would try again and again. And if she couldn't defeat it in their minds, she would defeat it in the real world by finding the answers she needed.

Every rustle of leaves, every whisper of wind through the trees sent shivers down her spine. Elizabeth pulse raced, each beat an insistent drumming in her ears. Time seemed to blur together as she moved further into the labyrinth, the path constantly shifting and changing beneath her feet.

"Dr. Harmon, don't forget," Anna had warned, her anxious eyes wide with fear. "The deeper you go, the harder it is to find your way back."

"Then I'll just have to find Emily before that happens," she replied, determination flaring within her like a beacon. The shadows continued their dance around her, mocking her efforts. But she would not be deterred. Elizabeth was relentless in her pursuit of the truth, fueled by unresolved guilt and a desperation to understand this nightmare realm.

"Emily!" she called out again, her voice seeming to vanish into the darkness without a trace.

Elizabeth's breath caught in her throat as the shadows parted to reveal a glimmering figure before her. Ethereal and enigmatic, Emily stood bathed in a radiant glow, her long, flowing hair like tendrils of moonlight cascading down her back. Her serene expression seemed to offer solace amidst the chaos swirling around Elizabeth.

"Dr. Harmon," Emily whispered her voice a balm to Elizabeth's frayed nerves. "Follow me. You need to see the truth."

"Emily?" she replied, hesitating as uncertainty gnawed at the edges of her resolve. Elizabeth knew about Agent Reynold's betrayal. What else could her subconscious be trying to tell her?

"Time is short," Emily urged, her gaze unwavering and filled with a quiet urgency. "Trust your instincts, Dr. Harmon. You know why I'm here."

As Emily turned, beginning to glide gracefully through the maze, she took a steadying breath. Elizabeth mind raced, weighing the risks against the potential rewards. The shadows continued their sinister dance, threatening to envelop her once more if she didn't make a decision.

"Curiosity killed the cat, but satisfaction brought it back," she murmured, repeating her sister's favorite saying from years ago. It was a mantra that had followed her throughout her career, driving her to uncover the truth no matter the cost.

"Alright, Emily," she whispered, determination flaring within her chest. "Lead the way."

With that, Elizabeth followed Emily deeper into the labyrinth, her steps quickening as she tried to keep up with the mysterious woman's fluid movements. Elizabeth heart pounded in her ears, each beat a reminder of the danger she faced, but also a testament to her unwavering resolve.

"Only you can unravel this tangled web, Dr. Harmon," Emily said softly as they navigated the maze. "The truth lies within you, waiting to be discovered."

"Then I'll find it," Elizabeth vowed, her voice steady despite her racing thoughts. "No matter what, I won't back down. I owe it to my sister, and everyone caught in this nightmare."

As the labyrinth seemed to shift and close around them, Elizabeth clung to Emily's guiding presence, determined to finally uncover the secrets hidden deep within its heart.

The sickening stench of decay assaulted Elizabeth's senses as she stepped deeper into the labyrinth, the walls closing in like a vice around her. Elizabeth breath came in shallow gasps, the damp air pressing down on her chest like a lead weight. The flickering shadows clawed at her, threatening to drag her into the darkness.

"Stay close," Emily whispered her voice a soothing balm against the oppressive atmosphere. "You're stronger than you know."

"You are just a figment of my imagination in my own mind."

Emily sent her a quick smile. "Yes. But you know more than you think."

As if on cue, Elizabeth heard the echoing footsteps drawing closer. Elizabeth's eyes widened as she saw Agent Reynold's step out from the shadows. Though she knew it was all happening in her mind, fear lanced through her body.

The agent's cold, calculating voice, sliced through the suffocating silence like a knife. "Dr. Harmon, you know you can't outrun me. Give up now, and perhaps you'll live to see another day."

"Keep moving," Emily urged, the calm in her voice, a counterpoint to the menacing pursuit. "Trust yourself, Dr. Harmon."

Elizabeth's heart hammered in her chest as she followed Emily's ethereal form, weaving through the twisting corridors with newfound determination. Elizabeth refused to be silenced, to let her sister's death remain shrouded in mystery.

"Your sister would have wanted you to be safe," Agent Reynolds called out, her words laden with false sympathy. "Don't throw your life away, for a truth that will only bring pain."

"Emily, how do I fight her?" Elizabeth whispered, her voice trembling with both fear and rage.

"Remember what drives you," Emily said, her eyes locked onto Elizabeth's with unwavering intensity. "The love for your sister, the need for justice. Let that be your armor."

"Anger and grief won't protect you, Dr. Harmon," Agent Reynolds taunted, her voice growing closer by the second. "You're only human, after all."

"Humanity is my strength," Elizabeth replied, her voice resolute, as she clung to Emily's guidance. "And it's something you'll never understand."

With Emily beside her, a beacon of hope amidst the chaos, Elizabeth pressed on. The labyrinth twisted and turned, a reflection of her own tortured psyche, but she refused to yield.

"Dr. Harmon," Agent Reynolds' voice hissed through the air like a venomous snake. "I will find you. I'll tear this place apart brick by brick if I have to."

"Then let her try," Emily murmured her words a promise that sent a shiver down Elizabeth's spine. "For in the end, the truth will prevail."

The shadows of the labyrinth seemed to claw at Elizabeth as she followed Emily's hypnotic movements, their dark tendrils whispering promises of doom. Elizabeth breaths came fast and shallow, each one a desperate gasp for air in this strange and suffocating place. Emily moved effortlessly through the maze, her steps light and graceful, like a dancer weaving an intricate pattern upon a stage.

"Stay close," Emily urged, the words a melody that resonated within Elizabeth's soul. "You are nearing the truth."

"Truth?" Elizabeth whispered; her voice hoarse from the effort of keeping pace. "Or is it another illusion to ensnare me?"

"Only you can decide," Emily answered cryptically, her serene features never betraying a hint of doubt.

As they continued deeper into the labyrinth, Elizabeth could feel Agent Reynolds' presence bearing down on her, a visceral pressure that threatened to crush her very being.

"Your stubbornness will be your downfall, Dr. Harmon," the agent snarled, her voice echoing throughout the maze. "I have crushed countless others who dared to defy me. What makes you think you'll fare any better?"

"Because I am not alone," Elizabeth replied, her heart pounding with renewed determination.

"Ah, but you are," Agent Reynolds countered, her words like a knife slicing through the darkness. "Your precious Emily is nothing more than a specter—an apparition borne from your fragile psyche. You cling to her because you can't bear to face the truth on your own."

"Is that so?" Elizabeth shot back, her voice wavering only slightly. "Then why do you fear her? Why do you fear me?"

"Your delusions are pitiful," Agent Reynolds spat, the malice in her tone unmistakable. "But they won't save you. I suggest you surrender now, while you still have something left to salvage."

"Never," Elizabeth hissed, her eyes locked onto Emily's ethereal form as they navigated the labyrinth together. "You underestimate my resolve."

"Very well," Agent Reynolds conceded, her voice dripping with contempt. "But remember this: you chose your fate. And when it comes crashing down upon you, don't say I didn't warn you."

As Elizabeth's heart raced with fear and adrenaline, she clung to the assurance of Emily's presence, determined to see this journey through to its end. The labyrinth stretched before her, a reflection of her tangled thoughts and emotions, but with each step, she drew closer to the truth that had eluded her for so long.

The shadows lengthened, casting sinister patterns upon the labyrinth's walls that danced and flickered in tune with Elizabeth's pounding heart. Elizabeth breaths came in shallow gasps, her lungs aching for air as she sprinted through the maze, Emily's ghostly figure just ahead of her.

"Quickly, Dr. Harmon," Emily urged her voice like a whisper on the wind. "We're almost there."

"Agent Reynolds is closing in," Elizabeth panted, her eyes darting to the side as she anticipated an ambush at any moment. The eerie quietness of the labyrinth was shattered by the sound of her thundering footsteps, echoing like the distant drums of war.

"Focus on my voice," Emily replied, her calm demeanor a stark contrast to the turmoil engulfing Elizabeth's mind. The mysterious woman glided effortlessly through the twists and turns, leading Elizabeth deeper into the enigma that surrounded them.

"Please ... help me understand," Elizabeth implored, desperation seeping into her words. With each passing second, Agent Reynolds grew nearer, her ruthless determination palpable in the oppressive air.

"Patience, dear Dr. Harmon," Emily soothed, her ethereal form shimmering like moonlight on water. "All will be revealed soon enough."

As they rounded another corner, the labyrinth seemed to shift around them, the stone walls giving way to an ancient wooden door, half-concealed by creeping ivy. Elizabeth's pulse quickened, sensing the importance of this hidden chamber.

"Inside lies the heart of the nightmare," Emily explained, her translucent hand reaching out to touch the door's weathered surface. "Only you can confront it, Dr. Harmon. Hopefully it will be enough."

"Will ... will it bring me closer to the truth?" Elizabeth asked, her resolve wavering under the weight of the responsibility thrust upon her shoulders.

"More than you know," Emily replied, a sadness lingering in her eyes. "But be warned: the path ahead is fraught with danger. Agent Reynolds will stop at nothing to silence you."

"Let her try," Elizabeth whispered, her determination reigniting like a phoenix from the ashes. Elizabeth reached for the door handle, her hand trembling as she prepared to face the horrors that lay within.

"Remember, Dr. Harmon," Emily murmured, her voice fading as the door creaked open, revealing a chamber shrouded in darkness. "You are not alone."

With a deep breath, Elizabeth stepped into the unknown, the door closing behind her as she vanished into the abyss, leaving the labyrinth and Agent Reynolds' relentless pursuit behind—for now.

The darkness within the chamber seemed to pulse with malevolent energy, tendrils of shadow flickering like sinister flames. Elizabeth's heart hammered in her chest, but she refused to let fear grip her any longer. Emily's presence had ignited a newfound determination, and she knew that she needed to uncover the truth, for both her and for those trapped within this nightmarish world.

"Show yourself!" Elizabeth demanded, her voice echoing through the chamber, mingling with the whispers that seemed to seep from the very walls themselves.

"Are you truly so eager to face your destruction, Dr. Harmon?" The cold voice of Agent Reynolds sliced through the darkness like a blade, sending shivers down her spine. Elizabeth could feel the agent's icy gaze upon her, even though she couldn't see her.

"Enough of your games, Reynolds! You can't keep the truth buried forever," Elizabeth retorted, her fingers curling into fists at her sides as she searched the shadows for any sign of the agent.

"Ah, but that's where you're wrong," Reynolds purred, stepping out of the gloom, her sharp features illuminated by an eerie, flickering glow. "You may have found your way here, but you won't leave with the secrets you seek."

Elizabeth's mind raced, her thoughts weaving through memories and experiences, seeking patterns and connections that would serve as a weapon against Agent Reynolds. She recalled Emily's serene expression, the enigmatic woman who seemed to hold the keys to the labyrinth and the failed experiment at its core

Emily was not only Elizabeth patient but also, she was part of the experiment. Elizabeth found this information when she was going over the documents she had discovered earlier. In that moment, Elizabeth understood that Emily was more than just a guiding presence—she was an essential part of the puzzle.

"Emily is the key, isn't she? The one who can expose everything you've tried so hard to hide," Elizabeth said, her voice growing stronger with each word. "But you didn't count on me finding her, did you? You didn't count on me uncovering the truth."

"Your arrogance is almost amusing," Reynolds sneered. "You think you're the first person to stumble upon her? Countless others have come before you, and they all met the same fate."

"Which is?" Elizabeth challenged, her mind working feverishly to outmaneuver her foe.

"Oblivion," Reynolds replied, her voice dripping with venom. "No one leaves this place alive."

"Try as you might, you can't kill an idea, Reynolds," Elizabeth shot back, her resolve hardening like steel. "The truth will find a way."

"Perhaps," the agent conceded. "But you won't be around to see it."

As Agent Reynolds lunged towards her, Elizabeth sidestepped with surprising agility, her instincts sharpened by the adrenaline coursing through her veins. Elizabeth mind raced, searching for a way to turn the tables on her pursuer and continue her mission.

"Emily's strength lies in her connection to us all," she whispered to herself, her eyes darting across the chamber, searching for a sign from the ethereal woman. "Together, we are stronger than any government secret."

With that thought, Elizabeth felt a surge of energy course through her, and she knew that she was not alone in her fight against the darkness. As Agent Reynolds closed in, determined to silence her once and for all, Elizabeth prepared to confront her demons and uncover the sinister secrets buried within the heart of the labyrinth.

"Enough!" Emily's voice echoed throughout the chamber, her calm tone slicing through the tension like a knife. Emily appeared before Elizabeth, her presence impactful and commanding. "You need to trust yourself, Dr. Harmon. Your strength is your own, but I am here to guide you."

Elizabeth's heart raced as she locked eyes with Emily, feeling a strange sense of comfort in her presence. The shadows seemed to quake at Emily's words, shifting uneasily around the edges of the chamber. Elizabeth took a deep breath, steeling herself for the ultimate test of her strength and resilience.

"Stay close," Emily whispered, her voice barely audible above the cacophony of Agent Reynolds' rage. "I can protect you only if you trust me."

"Okay," Elizabeth agreed hesitantly, swallowing hard as she faced her pursuer. Elizabeth mind brimmed with thoughts of her sister, her guilt, and the dark secrets that haunted her every waking moment. The line between the labyrinth and reality blurred, each reflection of her life merging and melding into one.

"I know what I have to do," Elizabeth murmured, her voice steady despite the tremor in her hands. Emily nodded, her ethereal form shimmering beside her, offering silent encouragement.

"Then let's do it," Agent Reynolds snarled, her eyes narrowing dangerously. "Let's end this charade once and for all."

With a sudden burst of speed, Elizabeth raced toward the agent, her movements fueled by an intense combination of determination and desperation. Agent Reynolds lunged, her arms outstretched, but Elizabeth slipped past her grasp, guided by Emily's unseen touch.

"Impossible!" Reynolds spat; her face contorted with fury. Reynolds scrambled after Elizabeth, her pace relentless and unforgiving.

"Keep going, Elizabeth. You're almost there," Emily urged, her voice a soothing balm amidst the chaos.

"Where?" Elizabeth panted, her lungs burning as she sprinted through the labyrinth. "Where am I going?"

"Trust yourself," Emily repeated softly, her words resonating within Elizabeth's soul.

As Agent Reynolds closed in, a hidden doorway materialized before Elizabeth, revealing a dark passage that seemed to pulse with secrets and lies. Elizabeth hesitated for a moment, her heart pounding in her chest as she weighed the risks of entering the unknown.

"Dr. Harmon!" Emily called urgently, her voice fading as if she was being pulled away. "Now!"

"Wait!" Elizabeth cried, reaching out towards Emily's vanishing form. But it was too late—the mysterious woman disappeared into the shadows, leaving Elizabeth alone at the threshold of the hidden chamber.

"Time's up!" Agent Reynolds hissed, lunging toward Elizabeth with deadly intent.

With no time left to think, Elizabeth stepped into the darkness, the passage swallowing her whole as the hidden door slammed shut behind her. Agent Reynolds' enraged scream echoed through the chamber; her fury palpable even through the impenetrable walls.

As reality and the labyrinth continued to merge, melding together like molten metal, Elizabeth found herself on the precipice of an abyss, with only her strength and resilience to guide her. The secrets of the failed experiment and the truth she sought hung tantalizingly close, just out of reach.

"Emily..." she whispered, her voice quivering with fear and determination. "Help me."

But there was only silence.

Chapter 11

Elizabeth's eyes snapped open, and she gasped for breath as her heart pounded mercilessly against her ribcage. A cold sweat clung to her body, chilling her to the bone. Elizabeth mind raced, frantically searching for an anchor in a sea of confusion. Was she still trapped within the nightmarish labyrinth, or had she returned to the safety of reality?

"Is anyone... there?" she whispered, her voice trembling with uncertainty.

"Dr. Harmon? Are you okay?" Anna's anxious voice reached her from the shadows, momentarily grounding her in the present.

"Where ... where are we?" Elizabeth asked, struggling to focus on anything other than her disorientation.

"Back at your office," replied Mr. Thompson, their deep voice betraying a hint of vulnerability. "You were just discussing our shared dreams when you suddenly ... well, you seemed lost."

"Lost" was an understatement. Elizabeth felt as if she had been dragged through the depths of hell and back, a tormentor lurking behind every corner, preying upon her darkest fears and guilt. The memory of Claire's lifeless face haunted her, a silent accusation that weighed heavily upon her chest.

"Right," she murmured, attempting to collect herself. "The dreams ... the labyrinth." Elizabeth scanned her surroundings, taking in every familiar detail: the diplomas lining the walls, the levitated couch where countless patients had sat before, and the half-empty coffee cup on her transparent desk, now cold and forgotten.

"Am I here?" Elizabeth wondered in silence, her thoughts betraying her lingering doubt. "Or is this just another illusion designed to torment me further?"

"Dr. Harmon," Anna hesitated, their fingers twisting nervously in their lap. "I know you're trying to help us, but ... do you think it's safe to keep exploring these dreams? What if we can't get back next time?"

"Or what if the fear entity finds a way to follow us out?" Mr. Thompson added, their concern evident despite their stoic demeanor.

Elizabeth took a deep breath, her resolve wavering beneath the weight of their questions. Elizabeth had ventured into the labyrinth in search of answers, desperate to understand the unexplained death that haunted her every waking moment. But at what cost? How much more could she risk before the line between reality and nightmare blurred beyond recognition?

"Trust me," Elizabeth said finally, her voice steadier than she felt. "I will see this through to the end. We'll find a way to overcome this fear entity and free ourselves from its grasp."

"Alright, Dr. Harmon," Anna replied, the faintest glimmer of hope flickering in their eyes.

"Let's keep moving forward," Elizabeth decided, her gaze unwavering as she faced the unknown. Elizabeth couldn't shake the lingering feeling that the labyrinth was still out there, waiting for her to return. And whether she wanted to admit it or not, she knew that her journey was far from over.

"Whatever awaits us in the depths of our dreams," she thought, determination coursing through her veins, "I refuse to let it control me any longer."

A sickly yellow glow flickered in the distance, casting twisted shadows that danced upon the walls of the labyrinth. Elizabeth's breaths came in sharp gasps, her chest heaving as she tried to ground herself in reality. "Inhale," she whispered, her voice barely audible against the oppressive silence. "Exhale."

"Focus," Elizabeth commanded herself, feeling her pulse begin to steady as she drew in another slow breath. "You've trained for this. You know how to navigate these treacherous mental landscapes. Just breathe."

The acrid scent of damp stone filled her nostrils as she reached out a trembling hand, hoping to feel the cold, rough texture that would confirm her suspicions. Elizabeth fingers brushed against the labyrinth wall, and a shiver ran down her spine as they met not the familiar solidity of her waking world but the unyielding chill of the dream realm.

"Damn it," she hissed under her breath, her control slipping away as her surroundings blurred between nightmare and reality. Elizabeth could feel the fear entity lurking just beyond the edge of her perception, its dark tendrils winding through the recesses of her mind, seeking purchase upon her deepest insecurities.

"Get out of my head," Elizabeth snarled, her voice echoing through the darkness like a challenge. "I won't let you control me!"

"Control you?" The voice slithered into her thoughts, mocking and malevolent. "Oh, Dr. Harmon, we both know that isn't true. After all, it's your guilt that has led you here, isn't it?"

"Shut up!" Elizabeth countered, gritting her teeth as she fought for clarity amidst the chaos. "You're just a manifestation of my fears. You have no power over me unless I allow it."

"Ah, yes," the voice purred, its tone dripping with condescension. "The fearless psychologist, so sure of her abilities. And yet here you are, trapped within the very prison of your own making."

Elizabeth clenched her fists, anger and resolve to war within her as she pressed onward through the labyrinth. "I will find a way to defeat you," she vowed, each step bringing her closer to the heart of the darkness that threatened to consume her.

"Perhaps," the voice conceded, its whisper barely audible over the sound of her ragged breaths. "But do not forget, Dr. Harmon, that it is not just your life at stake here. Your patients, your friends... they too shall suffer if you fail."

"Then I won't fail," Elizabeth declared, her voice steely with determination. "I will face whatever horrors lie ahead, and I will emerge victorious. That is my promise to them, and myself."

"Brave words," the voice taunted, seeming to recede into the shadows as it spoke. "But only time will tell if you possess the strength to follow through."

"Watch me," she whispered, her gaze unwavering as she faced the unknown. And with each slow, deliberate breath, Elizabeth stepped further into the abyss, ready to confront the darkness that lay within her soul.

As Elizabeth ventured deeper into the labyrinth, she noticed a sudden stillness in the air. The walls around her seemed to pulse with a life of their own, and as she moved forward, she was met with symbols and objects that held an eerie familiarity. A broken doll, its glassy eyes staring blankly ahead, stirred memories of her childhood with Claire. Elizabeth could almost hear her sister's laughter as they played together in their sunlit bedroom.

"Remember, dear sister?" a whisper hissed from within the shadows, the voice chillingly similar to Claire's. "The times before it all went wrong?"

"Shut up," Elizabeth muttered under her breath, her heart pounding in her chest. Elizabeth tried to focus on the present, on the cold stone beneath her feet, but the whispers grew louder, making it difficult to distinguish between reality and the dream world.

"Elizabeth, why didn't you save me?" another whisper questioned, echoing her guilt and fears.

"Stop!" Elizabeth cried out, her voice cracking with desperation. But the labyrinth refused to relent, forcing her to confront the memories she had long buried.

Elizabeth passed by a familiar photo of her family, taken during happier times. Elizabeth mother's radiant smile, her father's strong arms wrapped around them both, and Claire, her eyes twinkling with mischief. It was a moment suspended in time before the darkness consumed them.

"Your failure led to my end, dear sister," the whispers continued, relentless. "You couldn't protect me then; how can you protect your patients now?"

"Enough!" Elizabeth shouted, pressing her hands against her ears in a futile attempt to block out the voices. The line between reality and the dream world blurred, and she felt herself spiraling into the abyss of her mind.

"Elizabeth, you cannot escape the truth," the whispers taunted, clawing at her resolve. "The guilt is yours to bear."

"NO!" Elizabeth screamed, her voice echoing through the labyrinth. It was at that moment she realized that the fear entity sought to break her spirit by forcing her to relive her past. But she refused to let it win.

"Your lies and manipulations won't work on me," Elizabeth declared, her voice steady despite the turmoil within. "I will uncover the truth, and I will free myself from this prison."

The whispers fell silent as if surprised by her newfound determination. With each step, Elizabeth embraced her role as a healer and protector, vowing to save herself and her patients from the clutches of the fear entity. The darkness of the labyrinth could not hold her down any longer.

The labyrinth seemed to stretch infinitely before Elizabeth, its dark walls taunting her with the echoes of her doubts. Elizabeth felt as though she were sinking deeper into her psyche, unable to escape the maze that held her captive. The whispers had quieted, but their words continued to haunt her.

"Is this all in my head?" Elizabeth wondered, her voice barely a whisper as she questioned her sanity. "Am I truly trapped here, or am I losing myself to my fears?"

Elizabeth footsteps echoed along the twisting corridors, each turn leading her further into the heart of the maze. It was then that she stumbled upon it—a mirror standing alone in the darkness. Its ornate frame seemed out of place within the stark confines of the labyrinth, drawing Elizabeth closer like a moth to a flame.

As she peered into the looking glass, her reflection wavered and distorted, mirroring the turmoil that raged within her. Elizabeth couldn't help but be reminded of the night Claire had slipped away from her, the guilt that had plagued her ever since.

"Remember," the mirror whispered, its voice an eerie reflection of her own. "You were there. You could have saved her."

"Stop it!" Elizabeth snapped; her eyes wide with horror as she stared at her twisted image. "I did everything I could!"

"Did you?" the mirror retorted, its tone mocking as it threw her self-doubt back at her. "Or did your failure to protect your sister doom her to her fate?"

Elizabeth struggled to reconcile the truth with the accusations hurled at her. Elizabeth breaths came shallow and labored as if the very air around her were thickening, suffocating her. Each word from the mirror sent a shiver down her spine, forcing her to confront the part she played in Claire's death.

"Enough," she choked out, tears streaming down her cheeks as she fought to maintain control. "I won't let you break me, not like this."

"Then face the truth," the mirror demanded, its voice unyielding. "Acknowledge your guilt and accept what you've done."

Elizabeth stared into her distorted reflection, searching for the strength that had propelled her into the labyrinth in the first place. Elizabeth knew that her mission was valid, that she owed it to Claire—and herself—to confront her fears head-on.

"Alright," she whispered, her voice hoarse with emotion. "I accept my role in Claire's death. I accept the guilt that has haunted me ever since."

With her admission, the mirror's surface rippled, and for a moment, Elizabeth thought she saw a flicker of light within the darkness of the maze. It was a fleeting glimmer of hope, a reminder that there was still a way out—if she could only find it.

"I will find my way out of this labyrinth," she vowed, steeling herself for the battles yet to come. "I will conquer my fears and save both myself and my patients from this fear entity."

As she stepped away from the mirror, the labyrinth seemed to shift around her, the walls groaning as they rearranged themselves to accommodate her newfound resolve. The path before her would be treacherous, but Elizabeth was determined to see it through to the end—no matter the cost.

A cold, dizzying wave washed over her as she stood fixed before the mirror. Elizabeth chest tightened, constricting her breaths like a vise. The distorted reflection of her face seemed to mock her with its twisted smile and hollow eyes. Elizabeth felt the crushing weight of her past, the guilt, and darkness that threatened to suffocate her.

"Enough!" she cried out, her voice cracking under the strain of her anguish. "I can't bear this anymore!"

The labyrinth responded with a cacophony of whispers that echoed through the stone corridors, amplifying her distress. Elizabeth's knees buckled, and she collapsed onto the cold, unforgiving ground, her body wracked with sobs.

"Please," she choked out between gasps for air, "please help me find the strength to face my fears."

As if in response to her plea, the whispers fell silent, leaving only the sound of her labored breathing. In the stillness, fragments of memories and lessons from her journey ignited within her mind—a kaleidoscope of moments that had led her to this breaking point.

"Focus, Elizabeth," she whispered to herself, her voice shaking as she recalled the steady heartbeat of her patients in therapy sessions. "You helped them confront their fears; now it's time to face your own."

Elizabeth trembling hands clenched into fists, as she remembered the countless hours of research, the desperate quest for understanding that had consumed her life. The labyrinth may have been a nightmarish construct born of her subconscious, but it was nothing compared to the horrors she had witnessed in the minds of her patients.

"Everything I've learned, everything I've overcome," she murmured, drawing strength from the realization, "has prepared me for this moment."

Elizabeth dragged herself up from the cold floor, wiping away the tears that stained her cheeks. Elizabeth legs quivered, but she refused to let them buckle again. With a deep, steadying breath, she steeled herself for the battle that lay ahead.

"Alright, fear," she said, her voice stronger now, as determination coursed through her veins. "I've faced you in others, and now I'll face you in myself. I won't let you control me any longer."

As if acknowledging her resolve, the labyrinth seemed to shift around her, the darkness receding ever so slightly, revealing a new path before her. Elizabeth stood tall, her heart pounding with newfound courage, ready to confront the Fear entity and reclaim her life, from its insidious grasp.

"Enough," Elizabeth whispered, her voice hoarse from crying. Elizabeth words hung in the air around her, a tentative declaration, against the oppressive darkness.

Gathering her strength, she pushed herself to her feet, muscles trembling with the effort. Elizabeth took a slow, deep breath and focused on the sound of her heartbeat. The anguish and guilt that had consumed her moments, before began to dissipate like clouds parting after a storm.

"Every life I have touched, every mind I have healed… I am not just a victim here," Elizabeth reminded herself. "I have faced the darkness within my patients, and I will face the darkness within myself."

Elizabeth determination surged anew, propelling her forward, as she delved deeper into the labyrinth. The walls seemed to breathe and undulate, as if responding to her newfound resolve. As she moved, she noticed faint glimmers of light, piercing through the shadows, guiding her steps, like distant stars in a moonless sky.

"Is this it?" Elizabeth thought, daring to hope for the first time since entering the dream world. "Am I finally nearing the end?"

"Dr. Harmon," a voice echoed softly through the labyrinth, familiar yet somehow distorted. Elizabeth froze, her heart skipping a beat.

"Who's there?" Elizabeth called out, her voice wavering with uncertainty, but firm in her need for answers.

"Your past. Your future. Your fears," the voice replied, its intonation chillingly calm. Elizabeth realized; it was a reflection of her voice—a reminder of the internal struggle that had led her here.

"Then I'll confront you," she said resolutely, her gaze fixed ahead, as she continued to navigate the twisting corridors. "For myself and for those who depend on me, I will overcome you."

The labyrinth seemed to respond to her defiance, the encroaching darkness receding ever so slightly, allowing more light to filter through. With each step she took, the light intensified, a beacon of hope, drawing her closer to the heart of the maze and the resolution she sought.

"Almost there," Elizabeth murmured, her pulse racing in anticipation. "No more hiding from my fears, no more running from myself."

As the light grew brighter, so too did her resolve. Elizabeth—psychologist, healer, protector—strode forward with renewed purpose, ready to confront the Fear entity, that threatened her very existence. And not just for herself, but for all those who had trusted her to guide them through their darkest moments.

"Bring it on," she whispered, squaring her shoulders as she approached the labyrinth's end. "I'm ready."

The light at the heart of the labyrinth pulsated, drawing Elizabeth closer like a moth to a flame. The cold, suffocating darkness, that had enveloped her for so long, began to dissipate, replaced by a soft, warm glow, that filled her with an odd sense of comfort. Elizabeth stood at the precipice of the unknown, her heart pounding in her chest.

"Show yourself." Elizabeth called out, her voice echoing throughout the chamber. "I'm not afraid of you anymore."

"Ah, Doctor Harmon," responded the fear entity, its sinister, disembodied voice surrounding her, as if it were coming from everywhere and nowhere at once. "You believe yourself ready to face me, but deep within, you still tremble."

Elizabeth clenched her fists, trying to steady her nerves. "I acknowledge your presence within me." Elizabeth admitted, her voice wavering slightly. "But I refuse to let you control me any longer."

"Is that so?" taunted the entity, a malicious glee dripping from its words. "Then prove it. Face me, and we shall see who truly holds the power here."

A chilling wind swept through the chamber, and the fear entity manifested before Elizabeth, a swirling mass of darkness, that seemed to absorb all light around it. It took on the form of her deepest fears—Claire's lifeless body, bloodied and broken; the faces of patients she had failed; the reflection of herself, twisted and monstrous, consumed by guilt and despair.

"I am everything you fear, everything you've tried so hard to bury," the fear entity whispered, its voice a distorted echo of her own. "How can you possibly hope to defeat me?"

Elizabeth hesitated for a moment, her breath catching in her throat, as she stared into the abyss of her soul. But then she remembered the lessons she had learned throughout her journey, the strength she had found within herself, and the determination to protect her patients, from the darkness that threatened them all.

"By accepting my guilt and learning from it," she declared, her voice steady and resolute. "By acknowledging the darkness within me and using it as a means to heal others."

"Bold words," sneered the entity, its form shifting and morphing as it prepared to attack. "But can you truly back them up?"

With a surge of courage, Elizabeth lunged forward, grappling with the Fear entity in a desperate struggle for control. Elizabeth wrestled with the distorted reflections of her past, pushing against the weight of her guilt and despair. The entity fought back viciously, clawing at her mind, trying to drag her back into the abyss.

"Give in, Doctor Harmon!" The fear entity said, it hissed as they fought, its voice a cacophony of her doubts and insecurities. "You cannot defeat me!"

But Elizabeth refused to yield. Instead, she drew upon every ounce of strength and determination, she possessed, fueled by her newfound understanding, of her guilt and her unwavering commitment, to her role as a healer and protector.

"I will not be defeated!" Elizabeth roared, her voice echoing throughout the labyrinth, as if the very walls, were joining her battle cry.

With one final, Herculean effort, Elizabeth pushed the Fear entity away from her, shattering the dark reflection of her past and breaking the creature's hold over her. It shrieked in agony, its form beginning to disintegrate, unable to withstand the force of Elizabeth's determination and self-acceptance.

"Your reign of terror ends here." Elizabeth whispered; her breath ragged but her eyes shining with triumph. "I am no longer your prisoner."

As the fear entity crumbled before her, Elizabeth knew that she had emerged victorious—changed forever, but stronger for it.

The deafening silence enveloped Elizabeth, her pulse pounding in her ears, as the remnants of the fear entity's screams echoed through the labyrinth. The once-imposing walls began to tremble and crack, their cold, rough surfaces splintering like fragile glass.

"Is this real?" Elizabeth whispered, her voice ragged yet laced with defiance. "Or just another trick?"

The labyrinth responded with a cacophony of groans, its foundations crumbling under the weight of her victory. Dust swirled around her, like an ethereal storm, a testament to the end of the nightmare, that had haunted her for so long.

"Real or not," Elizabeth murmured, her determination unwavering, "it ends here."

Elizabeth stumbled forward, her legs heavy from exhaustion, but driven by her newfound strength. Each step was a battle, every breath a triumph, as she refused to let the darkness engulf her again. With each stride, the symbols and memories of her guilt shattered like shards of ice, replaced by the warmth of self-forgiveness and understanding.

"Dr. Harmon!" a distant voice called out, its tone both familiar and foreign. It reverberated through the collapsing labyrinth, a beacon guiding her toward the light that peeked through the cracks.

"Who's there?" Elizabeth shouted, her words swallowed by the thunderous roar of the disintegrating maze.

"Your salvation," the voice replied, its timbre soothing, a salve on her battered soul. "But only if you choose to accept it."

"Acceptance," Elizabeth breathed, her mind racing with the implications. Elizabeth had faced her guilt, her past, and the relentless demon that fed on her fears. Now, she must embrace the truth—that she was flawed but capable, strong but vulnerable, and ultimately, human.

"Show yourself!" Elizabeth demanded, her heart hammering against her ribcage, as the labyrinth groaned its dying breath.

"Dr. Harmon," the voice whispered again, closer this time, as if speaking directly into her ear. "It's time to wake up."

With a sudden, violent shudder, the labyrinth disintegrated around her, the walls crumbling like sandcastles swept away, by an unforgiving tide. A blinding light pierced through the darkness, swallowing Elizabeth whole and tearing her from the dream world's cold embrace.

Elizabeth eyes snapped open, reality crashing down upon her, like a tidal wave. The sterile white walls of her office surrounded her, the scent of antiseptic filling her nostrils. Elizabeth gasped for air, her lungs burning, as she gulped in each precious breath, relishing the feeling of life coursing through her veins.

Chapter 12

The air thickened as Elizabeth stepped into the labyrinth, her heart pounding against her ribcage. The darkness enveloped her like a shroud, swallowing her whole. Elizabeth could feel the weight of dread bearing down on her shoulders as she ventured further into the twisting corridors. This was the same place that haunted her patients' nightmares. Yet, there she was, committed to uncovering the truth for them and herself.

"Hello?" The echo of her voice ricocheted off the walls, bouncing back at her with an eerie resonance. "Is anyone here?"

The silence hung heavy as a response. Elizabeth's thoughts raced, recalling Anna's unsettling descriptions of the labyrinth. They had navigated this hellish terrain before her—trembling hands, wide-eyed fear, and the persistent feeling of being watched. Was she being watched too?

"Focus, Elizabeth," she whispered to herself, her breath visible in the cool shadows. Elizabeth clenched her fists, steadying herself, determined to face whatever lay ahead.

As she rounded a sharp corner, the passageway, opened up, to reveal a narrow bridge spanning a seemingly endless chasm. Its ragged edges seemed to grasp at the darkness below, as if eager to pull her down with it.

"Remember what Mr. Thompson said," she thought, drawing on their strength. "One step at a time."

Elizabeth approached the edge cautiously, peering over to see nothing but an abyss yawning beneath her. Elizabeth heart threatened to burst from her chest, but she steeled herself and began to cross, balancing precariously, on the bridge's thin edge.

"Stay calm." Elizabeth muttered, her voice shaky. "You can do this. You've done worse. Remember when you faced your demons? This is nothing compared to that."

Elizabeth's foot slipped slightly, threatening to send her plummeting into the void. Panic surged through her veins, but she fought it back with every ounce of her willpower. Elizabeth recalled the empathy and resilience, that had carried her through her darkest days, the same qualities she sought to instill in her patients.

"Think about them." Elizabeth told herself, her words barely audible. "Think about your sister. You're doing this for them."

With a deep breath, Elizabeth inched forward, her muscles tense and her mind sharp. The bridge seemed to stretch on forever, yet she remained steadfast, her determination to succeed shining, like a beacon in the darkness.

"Almost there." Elizabeth whispered, sweat beading on her forehead. The other side of the chasm finally came into view, offering a sliver of hope amid the shadows. As she inched forward, her entire body tensed, each muscle working in unison to maintain a precarious balance. Elizabeth could feel the void beneath her, threatening to swallow her whole.

"Think about your sister." The words were barely audible, but they held a power that ignited her determination. Elizabeth couldn't fail—not now. The other side of the chasm finally came into view, and with a surge of newfound strength, she pushed herself to close the remaining distance.

"Made it." Elizabeth breathed, as her feet touched solid ground once more. There was no time to celebrate her victory, however, for before her, lay a new challenge: a room filled with deadly traps.

"Of course." Elizabeth muttered, scanning the dimly lit chamber. "It couldn't be easy, could it?"

The room seemed to pulsate with malicious intent, an intricate web of mechanisms, designed to punish the unwary. As a psychologist, she had witnessed the depths of human depravity, but this labyrinth was something else entirely cold, calculated, and utterly devoid of empathy.

"Focus." Elizabeth admonished herself, drawing upon years of academic discipline. "You can do this."

Tentatively, she stepped forward, her eyes darting from one trap to the next. Each step required precision and patience, and as she navigated the treacherous terrain, she felt her mind racing with possibilities.

"Left foot ... two inches to the right ... careful." Elizabeth mused, her pulse quickening with every movement. It was a delicate dance, a game of life and death, that demanded her full attention.

"Remember what you've learned, Elizabeth," she thought as she sidestepped another trap. "Every experience, every hardship—it's all led you here."

A sudden realization dawned upon her: the labyrinth reflected her psyche, a manifestation of the guilt and unresolved trauma she harbored within. It was both a test and an opportunity for redemption—a chance to prove her worthiness to herself.

"Keep going." Elizabeth whispered, steeling herself for the challenges ahead. "You've come this far."

With each trap evaded, she felt her confidence growing, fueling her determination to succeed. Elizabeth refused to be defeated by her demons, to succumb to the darkness that threatened to consume her.

"Almost there." Elizabeth murmured, as the exit came into view. One final test awaited her, and with a deep breath, she leaped across the last gap, narrowly avoiding the jaws of a hidden trap.

"Done." Elizabeth gasped, feeling a surge of relief and accomplishment wash over her. Elizabeth had faced her fears and emerged victorious, stronger than ever before. But the journey was far from over, and as she stepped through the doorway into the unknown, she knew that the lessons she had learned, would serve her well, in the trials yet to come.

"Bring it on, labyrinth." Elizabeth whispered defiantly. "I'm ready for you."

The room shuddered, sending a tremor through the cold, stone floor. Elizabeth's heart pounded in her ears, as she surveyed the deadly traps surrounding her. The metallic scent of fear clung to the air, thick and suffocating.

"Focus, Liz," she whispered to herself, her voice barely audible, above the steady drip of water, echoing through the chamber. "You've faced worse."

Elizabeth took a cautious step forward, her mind racing with each faltering footfall. The traps were like a twisted puzzle, each piece, meticulously designed, to prey on her insecurities and weaknesses. Elizabeth could feel the weight of her sister's memory, bearing down on her, threatening to consume her completely.

"Please, help me, Claire." Elizabeth pleaded, her voice cracking with desperation. Elizabeth sister's presence seemed to be both an anchor and a curse—haunting her every move, yet driving her forward with a fierce determination.

As she navigated the treacherous terrain, setbacks plagued her progress. A flash of steel sliced through the air, grazing her arm and leaving a trail of crimson in its wake. Elizabeth gritted her teeth, stifling a cry of pain, as she pressed on, her vision blurring at the edges.

"Damn it!" Elizabeth cursed under her breath, feeling the sting of failure gnawing at her resolve. But she couldn't give up now—she had come too far, to surrender to the nightmare, that threatened to swallow her whole.

"Think, Liz, think." Elizabeth urged herself, trying to tap into the reservoir of knowledge, that lay dormant within her. It struck her then—the shared nightmare that connected her to this labyrinth, was not a mere figment of her imagination, but a key to unlocking its secrets.

"Every fear, every doubt ... they're all part of the puzzle." Elizabeth mused, her eyes narrowing with newfound understanding. With each trap she overcame, a piece of the nightmare fell away, revealing the path forward.

Elizabeth endurance through the trials created the confidence to face her fears.

"Claire, I understand now." Elizabeth whispered, her voice laced with determination. "This isn't just a test—it's a way to confront our demons and find closure."

Emboldened by this revelation, Elizabeth tackled each trap with renewed vigor, using her psychological expertise, to anticipate their twisted designs. Elizabeth found solace in the knowledge that her sister was with her, guiding her through the darkness.

"Thank you, Claire." Elizabeth breathed quietly, as she sidestepped a cunningly hidden snare. "You're still helping me, even after all these years."

As the last trap clicked harmlessly into place behind her, Elizabeth allowed herself a small smile. The labyrinth had thrown its worst at her, yet she had emerged stronger and wiser than before. With each step, she felt the weight of her past lighten, replaced by a newfound sense of purpose.

"Whatever lies ahead, I'll face it head-on." Elizabeth vowed, steeling herself for the challenges that awaited her. "For both of us, Claire."

And with that, she strode boldly into the unknown, ready to conquer whatever horrors the labyrinth had left in store.

The echo of her footsteps rang out like a funeral dirge, announcing her arrival at the labyrinth's heart. Before she stretched an unfathomable maze, vast and formless, as the void itself. Walls of obsidian loomed overhead, their surfaces slick with secrets and shadows. The air hung heavy, charged with malice and intent.

"Is this what you faced, Claire?" Elizabeth murmured, her voice swallowed by the darkness. "Did you walk these same paths, searching for answers to questions that haunted your dreams?"

"Answers lie within," whispered a disembodied voice, its ethereal tones sending shivers down her spine. "But so do nightmares."

"Then I shall face them all." Elizabeth declared, her resolve, steeling her against the insidious tendrils of fear, that sought to ensnare her. "For I am more than my past—I am the sum of my choices, and I choose to confront the shadows that have dogged me for far too long."

With those words, she plunged into the labyrinth, navigating its treacherous twists and turns, with a mixture of intuition and methodical calculation. Elizabeth memory served as a compass, guiding her through endless corridors, that seemed to shift and blend like some malevolent mirage.

"Stay focused," she muttered, biting her lip in concentration. "Remember the patterns, the signs. This is just another puzzle, waiting to be solved."

As she traversed the winding passages, Elizabeth felt the weight of her sister's presence beside her, urging her forward. Though every fiber of her being screamed for her to turn back, to flee from the nightmarish maze that threatened to engulf her, her determination held firm.

"Claire, I will find the truth," she vowed, her voice ringing with conviction. "I will lay our demons to rest, no matter the cost."

Elizabeth heart pounding, she rounded a corner and found herself at a crossroads. The labyrinth seemed to laugh at her, its walls writhing with sinister glee, as she struggled to decide which path to take.

"Think, Elizabeth," she urged herself, her breath coming in shallow gasps. "This is a test of your wits, your resolve. You mustn't let it defeat you."

"Choose wisely," the spectral voice intoned, its chilling laughter echoing through the darkness. "For the path you choose will determine not only your fate but that of your sister's memory."

"Enough!" Elizabeth cried out, her anger fueling her courage. "I have come too far to falter now."

Taking a deep breath, she weighed her options and made her decision. Elizabeth stepped forward, her footsteps resolute and purposeful, her eyes blazing with determination.

"Let the nightmare come," she whispered fiercely. "Let it try to break me. For I am Elizabeth Harmon, and I am unbreakable."

And with those final words, she strode ever deeper into the labyrinthine darkness, every step a promise—a promise to face the unknown, to conquer her fears, and to emerge victorious, no matter what horrors awaited her within.

The air hung heavy with the acrid scent of burnt wood, a reminder of the traps that had tried to claim her only moments ago. Elizabeth pressed a hand against the cold stone wall, steadying herself, as she navigated the labyrinth's treacherous twists and turns. Each step echoed in the oppressive silence, punctuated only by the sound of her ragged breaths.

"Remember," she muttered under her breath, "right is wrong, left is right." Elizabeth had noticed a pattern in the maze—an almost imperceptible bias towards the left—and was using it to guide her through its shadowed depths. The strategy had served her well thus far; as long as she held onto it, she could not lose her way.

"Tick-tock, Dr. Harmon," the spectral voice taunted, its tone dripping with malice. "Time is running out."

"Time means nothing here," she spat back defiantly, refusing to let the voice rattle her. Instead, she focused on the other techniques that had kept her alive: noting subtle changes in the texture of the walls, mentally mapping each junction, and marking her progress, with small scratches etched into the stone.

"Your sister would be so proud," the voice sneered, its words like ice against her skin. But she refused to engage. Elizabeth knew better than to indulge the nightmare's cruel taunts.

"Focus." Elizabeth commanded herself, her thoughts drowning out the ghostly laughter that followed her every move. Elizabeth pushed forward, feeling the weight of the darkness bearing down on her. Yet, even as her limbs trembled with exhaustion, she refused to give in.

"Almost there," she whispered the words more prayer than a promise. And then, just as suddenly as it had begun, the twisting corridors opened before her, revealing a doorway, bathed in ethereal light.

"Is this it?" Elizabeth asked herself, her heart swelling with a mixture of hope and disbelief.

"Are you prepared to face the truth, Dr. Harmon?" the voice asked, its tone chillingly neutral. Elizabeth hesitated for a moment, her hand hovering inches from the door's glowing surface. But she had come too far to turn back now.

"Let the truth emerge," she declared, her voice firm and unwavering. Elizabeth reached out, her fingertips brushing the cold light. And as the door swung open, she stepped through into the unknown, feeling an overwhelming sense of relief and accomplishment wash over her.

"Welcome," the voice murmured, its tone almost reverent. "You have earned your place among the victors."

"Victors?" Elizabeth echoed, her curiosity piqued, despite her wariness. But the voice offered no further explanation, leaving her to ponder its cryptic words, as she ventured forth into the light, her journey far from over.

The world beyond the door was a stark contrast, to the oppressive darkness, she just left behind. Elizabeth found herself standing in a small, circular chamber with walls that seemed to emit a gentle, silver light. The air was cool and crisp, filling her lungs with each breath, like a soothing balm.

"Is this part of the shared nightmare?" Elizabeth wondered aloud, her voice sounding strangely foreign, in the tranquil space.

"Indeed," replied the disembodied voice, its tone now tinged with a hint of warmth. "This chamber serves as a sanctuary for those who have conquered the labyrinth. Here you may reflect upon the lessons you've learned and prepare for the next stage of your journey."

Elizabeth allowed herself a moment to savor the sense of accomplishment, that washed over her, taking in the peace and quiet of the sanctuary. But as she did so, her thoughts turned to the harrowing trials she had faced: the narrow bridge, the deadly traps, the labyrinthine maze. Each challenge pushed her to her limits, forcing her to adapt, persevere, and believe in herself.

"Perseverance," she whispered, closing her eyes as the word echoed through her mind. "That's what got me through this. And adaptability ... I had to let go of my fears and preconceptions and learn to trust my instincts."

"Very good," the voice said encouragingly. "And what of self-belief? What role did it play?"

Elizabeth hesitated, pondering the question. Elizabeth thought back to the moments when she'd doubted herself, when the darkness had closed in around her and threatened to consume her. But she'd never given in, never allowed herself to be swallowed by despair.

"Self-belief," she said finally, "was the key to unlocking my true potential, to facing my demons and emerging victorious."

"Indeed," the voice agreed, its words resonating deep within her. "Remember these lessons, Dr. Harmon, for they will serve you well in the trials to come."

"Trials to come?" Elizabeth asked, her heart quickening at the thought of facing more danger. "What do you mean?"

"Your journey is far from over," the voice replied cryptically. "But rest assured, you have proven yourself more than capable of confronting whatever lies ahead."

With that, a section of the chamber wall slid open, revealing a narrow passage beyond. The sense of closure and satisfaction that had filled Elizabeth began to give way to anticipation, mingling with a renewed determination.

"Thank you," she said quietly, her eyes fixed on the passage before her. "I'll carry these lessons with me, always."

"Go forth, Dr. Harmon," the voice urged. "Embrace your destiny."

As Elizabeth took a deep breath and stepped into the passage, a newfound confidence surged through her veins. She was ready to face whatever lay ahead, armed with the insights and lessons she'd gained within the labyrinth and experiments. And as the chamber's silver light faded behind her, she knew that her journey only begun.

Chapter 13

As Elizabeth continued moving forward with trying to find the truth in the real world, she knew she could not allow Agent Reynolds, and those like her, to continue their reign of terror unchecked. For her sister, for herself, and for those who had suffered at the hands of the failed experiment, Elizabeth vowed to expose the truth—no matter the cost.

"Whatever it takes," she whispered, her eyes blazing with unyielding resolve. "I will not rest until justice has been served."

The rain drummed against the windowpanes, casting distorted shadows on the dimly lit room. Elizabeth's fingers danced across her holographic interface, her heart pounding in her chest as if to sync with each stroke. Elizabeth thoughts raced, questioning the loyalty of someone she once believed to be an ally. Elizabeth should have known that Agent Reynolds had been playing her all along.

As the weight of deception bore down on her, she felt an unshakeable resolve take root deep within her soul. The truth would not remain hidden any longer—not if she had anything to say about it.

In the darkness of her thoughts, Elizabeth saw herself standing alone against a tidal wave of lies and obfuscation, fighting to hold her ground as the torrent threatened to sweep her away. But she would not be deterred. Elizabeth would not falter. As the echoes of Agent Reynolds's threats reverberated through her mind, she found a new source of strength: the knowledge that she, and she alone, held the key to unraveling the conspiracy, that had claimed her sister's life.

"Your secrets won't stay buried forever, Reynold," Elizabeth whispered into the emptiness, her voice both a vow and a warning. "And when the truth finally comes to light, you'll have nowhere left to hide."

Elizabeth retreated to the safety of her office, her thoughts racing with the adrenaline coursing through her veins. Elizabeth could feel the walls closing in on her, but within this self-imposed confinement, she knew it was time to devise a plan.

"Reynolds," she murmured as she paced back and forth, "you may have underestimated me, but you won't get away with your lies." Elizabeth mind whirled with fragments of information, each piece of the puzzle forming a larger picture of the conspiracy. The experiment, her sister's death, and the government's involvement—are all connected by a single thread of betrayal.

Elizabeth holographic interface beckoned, its screen flickering with the secrets she had uncovered. As she sifted through the classified files and damning emails, she felt an ironclad determination take hold. With every new revelation, the tendrils of intrigue and deceit seemed to tighten around her heart, but she refused to let them strangle her.

"Enough," she whispered, her voice resolute. "It's time to turn the tables."

Elizabeth began to analyze Agent Reynolds's communications, searching for weaknesses in her defenses. Every sentence, every word became a weapon in her arsenal. And as she delved deeper into the labyrinth of deception, she discovered a series of covert meetings scheduled between Reynolds and other high-ranking officials. It was here that Elizabeth saw her opportunity—a chance to confront her former ally and expose the truth before the world.

The tension in the air grew thick, as she prepared herself for the ultimate confrontation. Elizabeth knew that confronting Agent Reynolds would be dangerous, perhaps even suicidal, but the need for justice outweighed her fear.

This was no longer just about her sister—it was about all the lives that had been shattered, the countless souls lost in the nameless void of the experiment.

With a deep breath, she ventured out into the cold night, her heart pounding in rhythm with her steps. The rendezvous point loomed closer, casting ominous shadows that echoed the darkness within Elizabeth's soul.

"Agent Reynolds." Elizabeth whispered to herself, steeling her resolve. "Your reckoning is at hand."

As she arrived at the facility, she knew Agent Reynolds would find her.

Eventually, she saw her standing beneath a luminescent nexus, her figure shrouded in mystery and uncertainty. Raindrops pattered on the pavement, merging with the tears that threatened to spill from Elizabeth's eyes.

"Dr. Harmon," Agent Reynolds greeted her coldly, her voice betraying no hint of remorse or compassion. "I didn't expect you to be so foolish as to confront me directly."

"Perhaps it's time you started expecting the unexpected," Elizabeth retorted, her voice laced with venom.

"Really?" Agent Reynolds sneered, stepping out of the shadows to reveal her true intentions. "You think you can outmaneuver me, Dr. Harmon? You're just one woman—a pawn in a much larger game."

"Maybe," Elizabeth replied, her heart hammering in her chest. "But even a pawn can bring down a queen."

The air crackled with electricity as the two women stood face-to-face, their eyes locked in a battle of wills. It was a moment suspended in time, a precipice teetering on the edge of chaos and revelation.

"Tell me, Reynolds," Elizabeth asked, her voice barely above a whisper. "What do you gain from this deception?"

"Power," came the chilling reply. "Control. And the knowledge that I am untouchable."

"Power corrupts," Elizabeth warned, her voice rising in defiance. "And your time has come, Agent Reynolds. The truth will not stay buried any longer."

"Then I suppose," Agent Reynolds said, her eyes narrowing to slits, "I'll have to bury you along with it."

"Your overconfidence will be your downfall." Elizabeth hissed, her fists clenched at her sides. The area around them seemed to pulse with tension, each breath drawn like a cord pulled taut.

"Perhaps," Agent Reynolds replied, her voice dripping with disdain. "But I have the upper hand here, Dr. Harmon. You're playing in my world now."

"Then let's see who has the real power," she shot back, her resolve unwavering. Elizabeth had come too far, discovered too much, and lost too many people to let this woman stand in her way. The truth would be revealed—no matter the cost.

"Very well," Agent Reynolds said, a sinister smile crossing her lips. "Let's see how you fare against the true forces at play here."

Before Elizabeth could react, Agent Reynolds lunged forward, seizing her by the arm and wrenching it painfully behind her back. Panic threatened to consume her as she struggled against the iron grip, but a flicker of determination kept her grounded.

"She won't break me." Elizabeth vowed, fighting to keep her composure. "Not now, not ever." She said to herself.

"Is this all you've got?" Elizabeth spat; her words laced with contempt. "Physical force? You're nothing more than a bully."

"Bold words for someone so clearly outmatched," Agent Reynolds taunted, tightening her hold on Elizabeth's arm.

Pain seared through her body, but Elizabeth refused to let it deter her. With every ounce of strength she possessed, she twisted her body, using her free arm to deliver a sharp elbow strike to Agent Reynolds' face.

The agent stumbled backward, releasing her grip on Elizabeth's arm. Blood trickled from her nose, but her expression was one of pure rage.

"Big mistake," she snarled, advancing on Elizabeth once more.

"Maybe," Elizabeth gasped, her arm throbbing, "but I won't back down. The truth will come to light."

"Over my dead body," Agent Reynolds growled.

"Then so be it," Elizabeth replied, her voice steely with resolve.

Agent Reynolds lunged again, but she was ready. Elizabeth sidestepped the attack and grabbed a nearby chair, swinging it with all her might towards the agent's head.

The impact sent Agent Reynolds sprawling to the floor, momentarily dazed. But as Elizabeth raised the chair for another strike, something in the room shifted—an unseen force, that seemed to ripple through the air, like a shudder.

"ENOUGH!" a voice boomed, commanding and terrifying in its intensity. The chair slipped from Elizabeth's grasp, clattering to the ground.

"Who's there?" Elizabeth demanded, her heart pounding in her chest. "Show yourself!"

"Your boldness is commendable, Dr. Harmon," the voice replied, echoing through the room like a ghostly specter. "But you are meddling in forces far beyond your comprehension. This ends now."

As the final word echoed through the chamber, darkness enveloped Elizabeth, swallowing her into its inky depths. The world around her ceased to exist, leaving her suspended in a void of nothingness.

"Wh-what's happening?" Elizabeth stammered, her fear palpable.

"Your journey ends here," the voice intoned, its presence looming over her like an oppressive shadow. "You have reached the limits of your understanding, Dr. Harmon. It is time to accept defeat."

"Never," Elizabeth whispered, her defiance a small flame flickering against the encroaching darkness. "I will find the truth, even if it destroys me."

"Be careful what you wish for," the voice warned, before dissolving into silence.

And then, in an instant, the darkness shattered like glass, leaving Elizabeth standing deep inside the old facility—so deep, that without a map, she would have a hard time finding her way out. Especially with Reynolds on her tail.

Elizabeth was alone, disoriented, and more determined than ever to unearth the secrets that had been hidden from her.

"Wherever this is," she murmured, steeling herself for the challenges ahead, "I'll find my way out. And I'll expose the truth that has been buried for far too long."

As she took her first step into the unknown, something glinted in the distance—a beacon of hope or a harbinger of doom, only time would tell.

"Let the game begin," Elizabeth whispered, her voice resolute amidst the swirling uncertainty that surrounded her. And with that, she stepped forward into the abyss, prepared to face whatever lay beyond.

Chapter 14

Dr. Sanders stood in the dimly lit hallway, his stoic demeanor barely concealing the storm of emotions raging within him. The weight of his guilt threatened to crush him, a relentless reminder of the failed experiment and the lives it had destroyed, including Elizabeth's sister. Dr. Sanders knew he could no longer stand idly by while Agent Reynolds hunted her down. Dr. Sanders knew that an altercation was coming, so he keeps tabs on the women, hoping to keep Elizabeth safe. Dr. Sanders followed her here and watched the scene play out.

It was time for him to act, to help Elizabeth evade the ruthless operative, even if it meant sacrificing his safety.

"Dr. Harmon," Dr. Sanders whispered, urgently beckoning her into an alcove. Dr. Sanders hesitated for a moment, her dark eyes searching his face, but there was no time for explanations. "I need you to trust me. I'll distract Agent Reynolds, give you time to escape."

"Dr. Sanders!" Elizabeth jogged over to him. "What are you doing here? It's dangerous. Agent Reynolds won't stop until she finds me." Elizabeth replied, her voice laced with concern.

"Neither will we." Dr. Sanders said, resolute. "You need to continue your mission, uncover the truth about the shared nightmares. I'll buy you as much time as I can."

As Elizabeth nodded in agreement, her determined expression mirrored Dr. Sanders' resolve. Dr. Sanders formulated a plan in his mind, calculating the best way to divert the agent's attention from Elizabeth's path. Dr. Sanders knew her well enough to anticipate her moves, having once been part of the very organization that now pursued them.

"Listen carefully," he instructed. "Make your way to the west wing. There's a hidden exit behind the storage room on the second floor. I'll lead Reynolds to the opposite side of the facility. Once you're out, find Sam Batter. He'll be able to help you with the research."

"Thank you, Dr. Sanders," Elizabeth whispered, her voice thick with gratitude and unspoken fears.

"Go now, and be careful," Dr. Sanders urged, his eyes never leaving hers. With a final nod, Elizabeth vanished into the shadows, leaving him to face Agent Reynolds alone.

"Time to play my part," he muttered to himself, steeling his nerves for the confrontation that lay ahead. Drawing on every ounce of courage and determination, Dr. Sanders set his plan in motion, venturing deeper into the labyrinthine halls, of the facility, ready to confront the very demons he had helped create.

Silent shadows stretched across the cold, sterile walls of the dimly lit facility. Dr. Sanders' footsteps echoed through the empty corridors, as he carefully chose a location for his impending confrontation, with Agent Reynolds. Dr. Sanders had to ensure that Elizabeth's escape would not be jeopardized. The weight of his decision settled heavily on his shoulders, like an invisible shroud threatening to suffocate him.

"Think.," Dr. Sanders whispered to himself, his voice barely audible amid the pounding of his heart and the rush of blood in his ears. "The conference room, third floor." A place where they could talk without risking Elizabeth's safety. It provided an unobstructed view of the hallway, giving him enough time to react if Reynolds brought reinforcements.

"Damn it! Focus!" Dr. Sanders chastised himself, shaking off the tendrils of doubt creeping into his thoughts. Dr. Sanders was a man of science, logic, and reason. But now, he found himself questioning everything, caught in a web of guilt and responsibility. As he approached the conference room, his mind raced with memories of the failed experiment—the haunting screams that still echoed through his dreams, the faces of the lost souls he couldn't save.

"Agent Reynolds, we need to talk." Dr. Sanders' voice reverberated through the silent room, heavy with determination. Dr. Sanders drew a shaky breath, steeling himself for the confrontation ahead. "I know what you're after, but you're chasing ghosts. Dr. Harmon isn't the enemy here."

"Dr. Sanders?" Agent Reynolds' voice seeped from the darkness, her tone icy, devoid of emotion. "How ... unexpected. What exactly are you doing here?"

"Listen to me, Victoria," he pleaded, using her given name in a futile attempt to humanize her. "We must stop this madness. Our actions have caused immeasurable suffering. We can't let it continue."

"Your misplaced compassion is touching, Dr. Sanders," she sneered, emerging from the shadows like a predator ready to strike. "But you're only delaying the inevitable."

"Or perhaps revealing the truth," he shot back, his voice laced with steel. "The truth that your superiors have tried so desperately to bury."

"Careful, Dr. Sanders." Agent Reynolds' eyes narrowed, her gaze piercing through him like shards of ice. "You're treading on dangerous ground."

"Then so be it," he replied, his resolve unwavering. "I am prepared to accept the consequences of my actions. Are you?"

The silence that followed hung heavy in the air, charged with tension and unspoken truths. Dr. Sanders knew he was walking a tightrope, teetering on the edge of betrayal and imminent danger. But for the first time in years, he felt the weight of guilt beginning to lift, replaced by a newfound sense of purpose—to help Elizabeth bring their shared nightmare to an end.

The sterile white walls of the facility seemed to close in on Dr. Sanders as if bearing witness to his treachery. Dr. Sanders had chosen this particular corridor for its narrowness and limited access points; it was a choke point, that would force Agent Reynolds into confronting him, before she could reach Elizabeth. The overhead lights flickered ominously, casting eerie shadows that played tricks on the eyes.

For now, he had diverted her attention. But how long could he keep up this charade? The clock was ticking, both for Elizabeth and himself. Dr. Sanders resolve hardened further; he knew there was no turning back now.

The harsh fluorescent lights cast an eerie, sterile glow across the corridor as Dr. Sanders stood, poised and ready for confrontation. His heart pounded in his chest, each beat echoing through his veins like a steady drumbeat of anticipation. The stale air of the facility clung to his lungs, a constant reminder of the suffocating weight of lies and secrets that surrounded him.

"Perhaps you underestimate my abilities, Doctor. Or maybe you've simply grown careless in your endeavors." Reynolds took a step closer, her eyes narrowing as she scrutinized him. "Regardless, I would advise you not to interfere."

"Interfere?" Dr. Sanders questioned again, his mind racing to find the right response. Dr. Sanders thoughts were a tangled web, each strand intertwined with memories, guilt, and the ever-present knowledge that Elizabeth's life hung in the balance. "I'm merely doing my job, Agent Reynolds."

"Your job?" Reynolds scoffed, her lips curling into a humorless smile. "You and I both know there's more to it than that."

"Perhaps," he conceded, his voice barely above a whisper. "But it doesn't change the fact that things are happening here that neither of us can control."

"Control?" Reynolds challenged, her voice laced with venom. "You think any of this was ever about control?"

"Isn't it?" Dr. Sanders retorted, his pulse quickening as he fought to maintain his composure. "We're all just pawns in a much larger game, aren't we? All he could hope for was that he had bought Elizabeth enough of a head start to evade capture.

As he watched Agent Reynolds stalk away down the corridor, her heels clicking ominously against the cold linoleum floor, Dr. Sanders knew that no matter the cost, he had made his choice. Dr. Sanders would stand with Elizabeth, face the consequences, and fight for the truth—whatever it took.

The sterile smell of bleach and fluorescent lights assaulted Dr. Sanders' senses as he continued his tense conversation with Agent Reynolds, the weight of his deception pressing heavily on his chest. Dr. Sanders could almost feel Elizabeth's presence in the shadows nearby, her breath catching in her throat as she struggled to remain silent.

"Doctor," Agent Reynolds began, her voice dripping with disdain. "You must realize this is far from over. I have resources at my disposal, you cannot even begin to comprehend."

"Perhaps," Dr. Sanders replied, feigning nonchalance, "but it seems that for all your superior intelligence, you've been unable to locate Dr. Harmon." Dr. Sander heart pounded against his ribs as he took a calculated risk, hoping to draw Agent Reynolds further away from Elizabeth's hiding place. "You know, there was a report of some suspicious activity near the east wing. Perhaps you should look into that."

"Nice try, Doctor," Agent Reynolds scoffed, narrowing her eyes. "But I'm not so easily swayed by your pathetic attempts at misdirection."

"Of course not." Dr. Sanders said, forcing a tight smile. "I merely thought it might be worth checking out. After all, we both want the same thing, don't we? To uncover the truth." Every word felt like sandpaper against his conscience, but he knew he had no choice. For Elizabeth's sake, he had to keep up the charade.

"Very well," Agent Reynolds conceded reluctantly, her gaze still locked onto his. "We'll investigate your little lead. But rest assured, if it turns out to be another one of your games, there will be consequences."

"Understood," Dr. Sanders murmured, his pulse racing. As Agent Reynolds turned on her heel and strode away, he allowed himself a moment of relief. The gamble had paid off; Elizabeth now had the opportunity to slip away unnoticed. "May you find the answers we've been searching for," he thought, steeling himself for the inevitable fallout. Dr. Sanders had made his choice, and there would be no turning back.

Dr. Sanders watched as Agent Reynolds rounded another sterile corner, her steps echoing through the labyrinthine facility. With each footfall, his heart pounded in tandem, but he dared not let the fear consume him. Elizabeth's mission depended on it. Dr. Sanders drew a shaky breath and steadied his nerves, following her at a safe distance.

"Focus." Dr. Sanders whispered to himself, "You must buy her enough time."

The fluorescent lights cast an eerie glow onto their surroundings, playing tricks on his already strained mind. But Dr. Sanders couldn't afford to be distracted—he needed to maintain control of the situation for just a little longer.

"Sanders!" Agent Reynolds barked suddenly, spinning around to face him. Reynolds eyes were narrow slits, glinting with suspicion. "Where is she? This lead you gave me—it better not be another one of your games."

Dr. Sanders forced a smile, trying to mask his trepidation. "I assure you, Agent Reynolds, I have no reason to deceive you." Dr. Sanders swallowed hard, feeling the dryness in his throat. "We are both after the same thing, aren't we?"

"Are we?" Reynolds shot back, her voice dripping with venom. "Because I'm starting to think you're more invested in protecting her, than finding the truth."

"Agent Reynolds," he began, taking a deliberate step closer, "you must understand that my only concern, is ensuring the safety of those involved in this experiment. The truth can't be uncovered if we lose any more lives."

"Enough," she snapped, shoving him against the wall, her fingers digging into his shoulders. "I am tired of your games and your lies. Where is Dr. Harmon?"

Dr. Sanders gritted his teeth, refusing to let the pain show on his face. In his mind, he willed Elizabeth to move quickly, praying she was using these precious moments, to her advantage.

"Agent Reynolds, I—" Dr. Sanders stammered, trying to keep his composure. "I don't know where she is. But if you let me help you, we can find her together."

Reynolds grip tightened, and for a moment, Dr. Sanders thought she might snap his bones in her grasp. "Fine," she spat, releasing him. "But remember, Dr. Sanders, if I find out you've been playing me all this time, there will be hell to pay."

"Understood," he croaked, rubbing his shoulders as she stalked off again. Dr. Sanders couldn't afford to let her suspicion deter him; Elizabeth needed the time to complete her mission, even if it meant sacrificing himself.

As they continued their hunt, Agent Reynolds' frustration grew palpable, her movements becoming more aggressive, her questions more probing. Dr. Sanders felt an icy sweat trickle down his spine, but he remained steadfast in his resolve.

"Dr. Harmon," he thought, clinging to the hope that she was succeeding in her task. "I will do whatever it takes, to buy you the time you need."

The facility's shadows seemed to close in around them, the darkness pressing against the weight of guilt, resting on his shoulders. Dr. Sanders knew he could not turn back now—not with so much at stake.

Dr. Sanders' heart hammered against his ribcage, as time stretched thin around him, each second threatening to snap and send everything tumbling into chaos. Dr. Sanders couldn't let Agent Reynolds catch Elizabeth—no matter the cost.

In that fleeting moment, he seized his opportunity and broke away from her, darting down a shadowy corridor. Panic clawed at his chest, urging him onward as his breaths came in sharp, ragged gasps. He could only hope that it brought Elizabeth the precious time she needed to complete her mission.

"Sanders!" Agent Reynolds' snarl echoed through the facility, but Dr. Sanders didn't look back

As he vanished into the darkness, his heart ached with the burden of his guilt, yet the faintest glimmer of hope flickered within him. "Dr. Harmon," he thought, each stride fueled by his unwavering determination. "I've done all I can. The rest is up to you."

The corridor's shadows swallowed him whole, as if the darkness itself, were a predator, eager to claim its prey. Dr. Sanders' heart hammered in his chest, an echo of the footsteps that pounded behind him. Dr. Sanders could feel Agent Reynolds' presence drawing nearer, her fury palpable even at a distance. As he raced through the dimly lit maze of the facility, each turn seemed to reveal another layer of deception and betrayal.

"Damn it all," he cursed under his breath, forcing himself onward, despite the raw sting in his lungs. "I'm not the only one who deserves to pay for our mistakes."

A glint of light caught his eye, reflecting off a stainless-steel panel mounted on the wall. Dr. Sanders fingers traced the edges of the cold metal, searching for the hidden switch he knew lay within. A soft click rang out, and with a sudden burst of adrenaline, he pressed himself into the narrow recesses, of the hidden passage, just as Agent Reynolds rounded the corner.

"Where are you, Sanders?" Reynold called out, her voice laced with venom. "You can't hide forever."

Sanders held his breath, listening to the rhythmic tap of her heels against the floor, as they drew closer, then faded away.

No longer content with being a pawn in this twisted game, he had chosen to gamble everything on a single, daring move.

Dr. Sanders could not deny that a small part of him relished the thought of redemption. If he could help Elizabeth complete her mission, perhaps there was hope for absolution after all. But first, he had to ensure her safety from the relentless pursuit of Agent Reynolds.

"Find the strength, Dr. Harmond," he urged, his thoughts reaching out to her across the vast expanse of their shared dream world. "You're the key to unlocking this mystery—for both of us."

Chapter 15

The moment her foot crossed the threshold, Elizabeth's heart hammered against her ribcage. The air inside the labyrinth felt colder, heavier—as if it were dense with secrets and malice that permeated every molecule.

Elizabeth blinked and realized, she wasn't in the labyrinth. Elizabeth was in the old facility. And Agent Reynolds was on her heels. Everything was merging in her mind: the nightmare, the experiment; her dreams were alive.

"Welcome, Dr. Harmon," whispered an unseen voice, as chilling as the frost that clung to the walls. Elizabeth shuddered but pushed onward, determined to escape and find the answers she was looking for.

Elizabeth ignored the voice, knowing that her mind was playing tricks on her. This was the real world, not the nightmare. But ... what if she couldn't tell the difference anymore? Agent Reynolds had been chasing her and Dr. Sanders gave her time to get away.

But ... why did the walls around her close in just like the labyrinth? Why were the shadows so similar to that nightmarish wasteland.

"Dr. Harmon," breathed a phantom voice, sending a shiver down her spine. The facility hall that she was running through seemed to close in on her, its complexity growing with each passing moment. Walls stretched overhead, forming an impenetrable canopy, that shut out any hope of escape. It morphed and changed, and she found herself immersed inside the labyrinth once again. This was not the real world.

"Nothing is what it seems here, Doctor," whispered another disembodied voice. "You can't trust your senses." Elizabeth clenched her fists, her nails digging into her palms. The pain grounded her and kept her focused. Elizabeth refused to be swept away by tricks.

"Show yourself!" Elizabeth demanded, her voice echoing down the twisting corridors. "I will not be intimidated! You're not real!"

Silence greeted her, a heavy stillness that threatened to smother her resolve. But she stood tall, her dark hair whipping around her face as she stared down the impenetrable shadows before her. Elizabeth would not be defeated. Not here, not by this. And with that thought held close like armor, she pressed onward.

"Look at what you've done," it sneered, its voice dripping with disdain. The specter bore an eerie resemblance to her sister, twisted and distorted by the weight of Elizabeth's remorse. "You could have saved me."

"Stop it! You are not my sister!" Elizabeth spat, refusing to let the apparition shake her resolve. Elizabeth thoughts tumbled within her mind, the memories rising like bile in her throat—her sister's lifeless body, the unexplained circumstances of her death. The guilt had festered, gnawing at her from within like a parasite.

"Am I not?" the entity whispered, its form shifting and contorting, mirroring Elizabeth's turmoil. "I am the product of your deepest fears, your darkest regrets." It grinned wickedly, its eyes locking with hers. "And I will consume you."

"Never," Elizabeth hissed, her determination flaring. Elizabeth drew upon her years of expertise, and her knowledge of the human psyche, and confronted the creature head-on. "I refuse to allow my guilt to control me any longer!"

"Is that so?" the specter taunted, morphing into the figure of one of her patients, their eyes blank and hollow. "What about them? The ones you couldn't save. You're just as guilty for their suffering."

"Enough!" Elizabeth shouted, her voice echoing through the labyrinth. Elizabeth pulse thrummed in her ears, as she faced the manifestation of her guilt, her anger, and sorrow blending into a potent force. "I did everything I could for them, and I will continue to do so. I will not let you break me!"

The specter's form began to waver, its hold on her weakening. Elizabeth took a deep breath, drawing strength from the knowledge that she had faced her demons head-on. The whispers in the labyrinth grew quieter, the shadows less oppressive.

"Very well," the entity murmured, dissolving into wisps of darkness. "But remember, I am always with you." It disappeared entirely, leaving Elizabeth standing alone in the dimly lit corridor.

"Perhaps," she whispered, her voice steady despite the lingering tendrils of doubt. "But so is my resolve." Clutching her newfound courage like a lifeline, Elizabeth strode deeper into the labyrinth, determined to conquer the remaining trials that awaited her and emerge victorious.

The whispers swelled to an unnerving crescendo, and Elizabeth felt the chilling touch of the shadows, as they seemed to reach for her, their icy fingers grazing her skin. Elizabeth senses heightened, she moved with lightning speed through the labyrinth, her every step calculated and precise.

"Face your fear," a disembodied voice hissed from somewhere within the darkness. The words clawed at her mind and sent shivers down her spine. And yet, there was a strange familiarity to the voice that made her pause.

"Who are you?" Elizabeth demanded, her eyes scanning the looming walls of the maze, searching for the source of the taunting whispers.

"Your darkest nightmares come to life," the voice replied, its tone dripping with malice. "The embodiment of all you dread."

"Show yourself!" Elizabeth shouted, her hands clenched into fists, adrenaline coursing through her veins.

A figure stepped out of the shadows, its features shifting and changing with each passing second. It resembled every patient she had ever lost, every loved one she had been unable to save. A constant reminder of her failures.

"Is this what you wanted, Doctor?" the fear entity sneered, its voice a cruel mimicry of those she had tried so desperately to help. "To confront the very thing that terrifies you most?"

"Enough of your games," Elizabeth spat, her eyes narrowed with steely determination. "I won't let you win. I'm stronger than you think."

"Bold words," the entity replied, its form solidifying into that of her deceased sister, her eyes empty voids of despair. "But can you truly face your fear and emerge unscathed?"

"Watch me," she whispered, her voice laced with conviction.

With a sudden burst of movement, Elizabeth lunged towards the entity, grabbing hold of its arm and spinning it around to slam it against the cold stone wall. The specter's eyes widened in surprise, and for a moment, Elizabeth felt the thrill of having gained the upper hand.

"Your reign of terror ends now," she declared, her grip tightening on the entity as it struggled to break free. "I will conquer you and save those who have fallen under your spell."

"Naïve fool," the entity snarled, wrenching itself from her grasp with an unnatural strength that sent her reeling backward. "You cannot defeat me. I am fear itself."

"Perhaps," Elizabeth murmured, her heart pounding in her chest, as she steadied herself and prepared for the next round of their harrowing battle. "But I am not afraid."

The world shifted, with reality snapping back into focus, like the pieces of a puzzle falling into place. Elizabeth stood in the dimly lit hallway of the facility, her heart still racing from the confrontation with the Fear entity. The labyrinth had been a test of her resolve, but now she faced an even more dangerous adversary: Agent Victoria Reynolds.

Their gazes collided like two freight trains on the same track, locked in a battle of wills that threatened to derail them both. Elizabeth's breath hitched, her senses heightened as she assessed the situation, calculating her next move.

"Dr. Harmon," Agent Reynolds greeted her, her voice dripping with icy determination. "You've been quite elusive."

"Have I?" Elizabeth replied, feigning casualness, while her mind worked furiously to outmaneuver the agent. Elizabeth knew Reynolds would stop at nothing to protect the government's secrets, and she had to stay one step ahead if she wanted to survive this encounter.

"Please don't make this difficult," Agent Reynolds said, her eyes narrowing. "You know what's at stake."

"Of course. But sometimes the truth is worth the risks." Elizabeth countered, her determination flaring up. Elizabeth thought of the countless patients who had fallen under the fear entity's spell, their lives consumed by its sinister influence. Elizabeth couldn't let them down.

"Your naïveté is touching, but misguided," Agent Reynolds replied, her tone laced with condescension. "You're meddling with forces you can't possibly comprehend."

"Try me." Elizabeth shot back, her gaze never wavering from the agent's cold stare. Elizabeth refused to be intimidated—she had already confronted her deepest fears, and she knew she could handle whatever challenges lay ahead.

"Very well," Agent Reynolds said, her lips curling into a predatory smile. "But remember, you brought this upon yourself."

With a sudden burst of movement, the agent lunged towards Elizabeth, her movements swift and precise. But she had been anticipating this move, and she dodged to the side, her heart pounding as she narrowly avoided Reynolds' grasp.

"Is that all you've got?" Elizabeth taunted, knowing full well that she was playing with fire. But she needed to keep the agent off balance, if she wanted to gain the upper hand.

"Hardly," Agent Reynolds hissed, her eyes glinting with a dangerous gleam. "You have no idea what you're up against."

"Neither do you," Elizabeth countered, her thoughts racing, as she sought a way out of this deadly game. Elizabeth knew she couldn't keep this up forever—sooner or later, one of them would make a mistake, and the consequences could be fatal.

As they continued their cat-and-mouse dance, through the shadowy halls, Elizabeth called upon every ounce of her cunning and resourcefulness to stay one step ahead of Agent Reynolds. The agent's relentless pursuit only served to fuel Elizabeth's determination, her resolve hardening like steel under pressure.

"Your persistence is admirable, Dr. Harmon," Agent Reynolds acknowledged, her voice tinged with grudging respect. "But ultimately futile."

"Perhaps," Elizabeth allowed, her mind already formulating a new strategy. "But I'll never stop fighting for the truth."

"Then you'd better be prepared to face the consequences," Agent Reynolds warned, her voice a chilling whisper in the darkness.

"Trust me." Elizabeth replied, her eyes narrowing with steely resolve. "I am."

Elizabeth's heartbeat thundered in her ears as she darted around a corner, narrowly evading Agent Reynolds' grasp. The labyrinthine hospital seemed to twist and turn in on itself, the shadows stretching like long fingers across the walls. Elizabeth could feel the weight of Reynolds' stare on her back, a predator closing in on its prey.

"Did you think you could outsmart me, Dr. Harmon?" Reynolds called out, her voice echoing through the dim corridors. "I've been trained for situations far more complex than this."

"Then why haven't you caught me yet?" Elizabeth shot back, glancing over her shoulder, as she raced down another hallway. Elizabeth mind raced, searching for any advantage, any opportunity to turn the tables on her pursuer.

"Patience is a virtue," Reynolds replied, her footsteps growing louder as she closed the distance between them. "And I have plenty."

Elizabeth pressed herself against a wall, holding her breath as she listened to the rhythmic tapping of Agent Reynolds' shoes on the cold tile floor. At that moment, she recalled a conversation with her sister years ago—a whispered discussion about fear and how it could be harnessed.

"Sometimes, Victoria," she said, using the agent's first name deliberately, hoping to throw her off balance. "Fear can be an ally."

"Is that what you're doing now?" Reynolds sneered, momentarily pausing. "Hiding behind your fear?"

"Perhaps." Elizabeth didn't wait for a response; she surged forward, propelling herself off the wall and sprinting towards a nearby stairwell. Elizabeth legs burned with exertion, but she refused to slow down. Every second counted.

"Stairs?" Reynolds scoffed, sounding almost amused. "That's your grand strategy? You'll run out of floors eventually, Doctor."

"Maybe," Elizabeth gasped, her breaths ragged as she climbed higher. "But so will you."

"Fair point," Reynolds conceded, her voice strained by the effort to keep up with Elizabeth's relentless pace. "So, let's make this more interesting, shall we?"

Elizabeth's heart skipped a beat as the lights around them flickered and died, plunging the stairwell into darkness. Elizabeth gripped the railing, her knuckles white from the pressure as she forced herself to keep moving.

"Is that all you've got?" Elizabeth hissed, not daring to look back. "Turning off the lights?"

"Hardly, Doctor," Reynolds replied, her voice suddenly much closer than before. "But it does level the playing field, wouldn't you agree?"

"Level?!" Elizabeth choked out a hollow laugh. "You're a trained operative, and I'm a psychologist."

"Ah, but you're not just any psychologist, are you?" Reynolds countered, her voice dripping with menace. "You're the one who uncovered our little secret. So don't sell yourself short."

"Fine," Elizabeth gritted her teeth, her legs trembling with exhaustion. "Let's see who reaches the top first."

"Your funeral," Reynolds whispered, and Elizabeth knew the real game had just begun.

Elizabeth's heart hammered in her chest, each beat a thunderous reminder of the stakes at play. Elizabeth felt her breath catch, as she reached the top of the stairs, her hand gripping the cold metal door handle. Elizabeth hesitated for a moment, eyes darting around the dimly lit hallway before her.

"Decisions, decisions," Reynolds' voice taunted from somewhere behind her. "Which way will you go, Doctor?"

"Enough games," Elizabeth snapped back, her voice a mix of anger and fear. Elizabeth knew that any wrong turn could lead to her capture, but she also knew, that her knowledge of the labyrinth-like facility, gave her an advantage, over Reynolds. Elizabeth just had to trust herself.

"Very well," Reynolds said icily, the sound of her footsteps echoing through the darkened halls. "Let's see how resourceful you are."

Elizabeth took a deep breath, forcing herself to focus. Elizabeth remembered the countless hours she'd spent studying the building's blueprints, searching for any hidden chambers or escape routes that might have been used by those who came before her. It was now or never.

"Left." Elizabeth whispered, propelling herself down the corridor and praying that it would lead her away, from her relentless pursuer. Elizabeth pushed past the fatigue that threatened to consume her, fueled by the memories of her sister and the other victims, of the truth, she had worked so hard to uncover.

"Interesting choice," Reynolds remarked, her voice barely audible over the sound of her labored breathing. "But is it the right one?"

"Wouldn't you like to know?" Elizabeth shot back, her mind racing, as she tried to anticipate Reynolds' next move. Elizabeth knew, that the agent, would be expecting her to follow the most direct path to safety, and so she chose to do the opposite. Elizabeth would take the long way around, even if it meant putting more distance between herself and her goal.

"Indeed, I would," Reynolds replied, the hint of a smile evident in her voice. "But it seems you're determined to make this difficult for both of us."

"Difficult?" Elizabeth scoffed, her adrenaline surging, as she rounded yet another corner. "You have no idea what difficulty is. Not yet."

"Is that a threat, Doctor?"

"More like a promise."

The tension between them grew palpable, their verbal sparring, almost as fierce, as their physical chase. Each knew that the stakes were impossibly high and that one false move could spell disaster for them both. And as the shadows lengthened and the whispers intensified, Elizabeth couldn't help but wonder if she'd finally met her match in Agent Victoria Reynolds.

"Game on," Elizabeth murmured, her resolve hardening as she prepared to face whatever lay ahead.

"Game on, indeed," Reynolds agreed, her voice echoing ominously down the empty corridors. "May the best woman win."

"Let's find out who that is," Elizabeth said, her eyes narrowing with determination, as she sprinted deeper into the labyrinth, the darkness closing in around her like a shroud.

The darkness of the labyrinth seemed to thicken around Elizabeth, each shadow appearing more sinister than the last. Elizabeth could feel her pulse hammering in her ears, drowning out the distorted whispers that echoed through the twisting corridors. Elizabeth heart was a drumbeat, spurring her forward, urging her not to falter.

"Enough of this," Agent Reynolds hissed, her voice laced with frustration, as she pursued Elizabeth relentlessly. "You think you can outsmart me, Doctor? You'll soon learn the error of your ways."

"Maybe," Elizabeth replied between labored breaths, "but it's worth a try."

Elizabeth mind raced, desperately searching for any advantage she could exploit, anything that might give her an edge over her formidable opponent. And then, in a moment of clarity, she recalled the complex layout of the labyrinth, the twists and turns that had once seemed so daunting, now offering a glimmer of hope.

"Come on, Elizabeth," she whispered to herself, her eyes darting back and forth, as she navigated the facility with newfound confidence. It mirrored the labyrinth nightmare. "I know this place better than anyone. Use it."

Elizabeth feigned left, her instincts screaming at her to take the shorter route, but she knew better. Instead, she veered right, taking the longer path, that would ultimately lead her to the center of the building. It was a gamble, she knew, but one she was willing to take.

Agent Reynolds hesitated, her sharp gaze flickering uncertainly between the two paths. "Clever girl," she muttered, before following Elizabeth down the seemingly less advantageous route.

As the distance between them began to close, Elizabeth pushed herself harder, her muscles burning with exertion. Elizabeth could feel the Fear entity weakening, its hold on her patients loosening with each determined step she took. The realization spurred her on, even as her lungs screamed for air and her legs threatened to buckle beneath her. Elizabeth could still feel reality and dreams colliding, but new that she had to defeat both villains to win this war.

"Almost there." Elizabeth panted, the goal within reach. "Just a little further."

In that critical moment, Elizabeth rounded the final corner, the towering walls of the labyrinth giving way to a hidden alcove. With a swift, calculated motion, she activated a secret mechanism embedded in the stone, one she had discovered, during her countless hours spent exploring the maze.

"Wha—" Agent Reynolds' eyes widened in surprise as the walls began to shift, trapping her within an impenetrable barrier of stone. The awe on her face quickly turned to fury, her icy blue eyes burning with rage, as she realized she'd been outmaneuvered.

"Congratulations, Doctor," she spat, her voice dripping with venom. "You've won this round."

Elizabeth leaned against the wall, her chest heaving, as she tried to catch her breath. Elizabeth could feel a swell of triumph coursing through her veins, the satisfaction of having bested the relentless Agent Reynolds, providing a much-needed boost of adrenaline.

"Thank you," Elizabeth replied, her voice barely above a whisper. "But it's not over yet."

As she stared down at her captured adversary, Elizabeth knew that this victory was only the beginning. Elizabeth had weakened the Fear entity, breaking its hold over her patients and proving that it could be defeated. But the battle was far from over, and there was still much work to be done.

Her mind calmed.

And she opened her eyes. Elizabeth sat in her office floating chair with Anna and Mr. Thompsons staring at her. Elizabeth had been in the labyrinth the whole time. Elizabeth did not know what was real and what wasn't.

"I can defeat the fear." Elizabeth said with a soft breath out.

They gave her stunned looks.

"I can feel it growing weaker and weaker each time I fight it. We are going to win," Elizabeth said to her patients, who had become her friends. "But I can't give up. I have to keep going back."

Elizabeth could feel her body and her mind getting pressed and pushed to the limit, but she would not give up.

Chapter 16

Elizabeth stood before the entrance of the labyrinth, her heart pounding like a war drum, in her chest. Elizabeth took a deep breath, feeling the weight of her guilt and determination, coiling around her like a snake. The air was thick with an electric anticipation, as though the labyrinth itself sensed her presence and braced for confrontation.

"Alright," she whispered, steeling herself. "Let's do this."

Elizabeth stepped into the maze of twisting corridors, the shadows seemed to come alive, slithering and writhing along the stone walls. Whispers echoed through the air, snaking their way into her ears, heightening her sense of unease. Elizabeth clenched her fists, nails digging into her palms, reminding herself that the fear entity thrived on such anxiety.

"Is it always this welcoming?" Anna's voice rang out, the tension in her words betraying his attempt at humor. Mr. Thompson short, messy hair trembled as he rubbed his arms, seeking solace from the chilling atmosphere.

"Can't say I expected anything less," Mr. Thompson replied gruffly, his stern face masking the vulnerability he hid beneath a lifetime of emotional armor. Mr. Thomspon muscular build seemed tense, ready for any challenge the labyrinth might present.

"Focus," Elizabeth said, not wanting their banter to distract her. "We need to move forward."

As they navigated the labyrinth, the eerie shadows danced along the walls, creating grotesque shapes that sent shivers down Elizabeth's spine. The whispers grew louder, echoing her deepest doubts and fears; she could feel them scratching against her resolve, like desperate claws.

"Dr. Harmon," Anna murmured, visibly unsettled by the labyrinth's oppressive atmosphere. "What do you think we're going to find in here?"

"Answers," Elizabeth replied firmly, attempting to instill confidence in her patient. "And the source of our shared nightmare. We just need to keep going." The words were as much for her benefit, as theirs a mantra she clung to, when the labyrinth threatened to swallow her whole.

"Whatever it is," Mr. Thompson added, "we're in this together."

The weight of their trust anchored Elizabeth, giving her strength amidst the disorienting maze. Elizabeth knew that she had to face the fear entity head-on and confront the role her guilt played in shaping her life and the nightmares of her patients. It was the only way to weaken its hold, to put an end to the torment they all endured.

"Thank you," she whispered, grateful for their support. "Let's keep moving."

The air in the labyrinth felt viscous, like swimming through a pool of dark memories. Elizabeth's breaths came in shallow gasps, as she waded deeper into the murky maze. Along the walls, shadows stretched and contorted, their sinuous forms, reaching out for her, like grasping hands.

"Remember what you've learned." Elizabeth muttered to herself, her voice barely audible above the whispers, that echoed through the stone corridors. Elizabeth closed her eyes for a moment, summoning the knowledge she had gained throughout her journey, allowing it to anchor her amidst the chaos.

"Doctor?" Anna's voice trembled with trepidation. "What should we do?"

"Stay close and keep your senses sharp," Elizabeth replied, her tone steady, despite the fear that tightened around her chest, like a vise. "We're going to face this together."

As they moved through the labyrinth, each step seemed to lead them deeper into an abyss of uncertainty. Elizabeth's intuition, honed by years of navigating the complex labyrinth of her patients' minds, flared to life, guiding her through the maze's twists and turns. The whispers continued, their pernicious voices worming their way into her thoughts, but she refused to let them shatter her focus.

"Out there," Mr. Thompson whispered, pointing to a particularly ominous stretch of corridor. "Can you feel it? Watching us?"

Elizabeth nodded, her heart pounding in her throat. The fear entity's presence was palpable, a malignant force that lurked just beyond the edge of her perception. It was a predator, stalking its prey from the shadows, waiting for the perfect moment to strike.

"Keep moving," she urged, her voice strained with determination. "Don't let it see your fear."

As they pressed on, the labyrinth seemed to spiral inward, tightening around them like a noose. Elizabeth fought to maintain her composure, her mind racing with strategies and countermeasures. Elizabeth knew that the battle ahead would be one of wits, a contest of psychological endurance.

"Doctor," Anna murmured, his words laced with resolve, "we're ready for this. We trust you."

"Thank you," Elizabeth replied, her voice thick with gratitude. "We'll get through this, together."

With each step they took, the fear entity's presence grew stronger, its menacing gaze bearing down on them like an oppressive weight. But Elizabeth refused to falter, drawing upon the reservoir of strength that lay within her. Elizabeth was more than just a conduit for her patients' nightmares; she was their guardian, their protector, and she would not fail them.

"Stay close." Elizabeth whispered, as they ventured deeper into the labyrinth, the shadows closing in around them. "We're almost there."

The dark corridors of the labyrinth seemed to breathe, shadows pulsing in time with Elizabeth's racing heart. Elizabeth paused for a moment, closing her eyes and taking a deep, steadying breath.

"Elizabeth," Anna whispered, her voice barely audible above the eerie whispers that echoed through the air. "What's wrong?"

"Nothing," she replied, swallowing hard. "I just need a moment."

As she opened her eyes again, Elizabeth knew she could no longer avoid confronting the guilt that had festered within her for so long. Elizabeth could see now how it had poisoned her life, seeping into the nightmares of her patients, like a toxic cloud.

"Anna," she said quietly, "I need you to understand something. My sister... her death... I've been blaming myself for years. I let the guilt consume me, and I think it's part of what's feeding this fear entity."

"Doctor," Anna replied gently, placing a comforting hand on her shoulder, "we all have our demons. But you've helped us face ours. Now it's time to face yours."

With newfound resolve, Elizabeth steeled herself and continued forward, determined to confront her fears head-on. As they ventured deeper into the labyrinth, the passageways grew more twisted and treacherous. Walls closed in around them, and the path beneath their feet shifted unexpectedly, threatening to send them tumbling into the abyss.

"Careful," Elizabeth warned as they shuffled along a narrow ledge, her fingers gripping a jagged outcropping for support. Elizabeth could feel the fear entity's presence growing stronger with each step, its icy tendrils probing at the edges of her consciousness.

"Stay focused," Elizabeth reminded herself, drawing upon years of psychological training to maintain her composure. Elizabeth thought about the faces of her patients, the lives she had touched, and the progress they had made together.

Their strength and resilience became her own, fortifying her against the entity's insidious influence.

"Doctor!" Mr. Thompson gasped as they rounded a corner, his eyes wide with fear. "Look!"

The path ahead was blocked by a wall of writhing shadows, an impenetrable barrier that seemed to mock their progress. Elizabeth's heart pounded in her chest, but she refused to back down.

"Think," Elizabeth whispered to herself, her mind racing through layers of symbolism and metaphor. "This is just another challenge, another test of our resolve."

"Then how do we get past it?" Mr. Thompson asked, his voice trembling.

"By facing it head-on," Elizabeth said, her voice firm. "Together."

With that, she stepped towards the wall of shadows, her hands outstretched, and her eyes locked on the ever-shifting darkness. Elizabeth could feel the fear entity's cold tendrils wrapping around her mind, but she held fast, her determination unwavering.

"Let go of your guilt, Elizabeth," she told herself, drawing upon every ounce of courage and self-awareness she possessed. "Accept it, learn from it, and move forward."

As if in response to her inner conviction, the wall of shadows began to dissolve before her, revealing the path forward. Elizabeth let out a breath, she hadn't realized she'd been holding, her eyes shining with tears.

"Thank you," Elizabeth whispered to Mr. Thompson, her voice thick with gratitude. "We're one step closer now."

"Let's keep going," he replied, his face pale but determined. "We can't stop now."

Together, they pressed on into the depths of the labyrinth, their fear and guilt receding like shadows before the dawn. They knew that the battle was far from over, but for now, they had taken a crucial step toward victory.

The air in the labyrinth grew colder, each breath Elizabeth took, forming a cloud of mist before her. The walls seemed to close in on her, their rough surfaces casting undulating shadows that played tricks on her eyes. As she walked deeper, she could feel the fear entity's presence growing stronger, its malicious intent palpable.

"Is this all you have?" Elizabeth whispered through clenched teeth, refusing to let the entity get the better of her. "I'm not afraid of you."

"Ah, but you should be," a voice hissed in response, echoing through the twisting passages of the labyrinth. The fear entity slithered into her thoughts, insinuating itself into the darkest recesses of her mind. "You think facing your guilt makes you strong? You're just as vulnerable as ever. You'll never be free from me."

"Shut up!" Elizabeth snapped, shaking her head to clear it of the entity's venomous words. But the whispers persisted, snaking through her consciousness, like tendrils of smoke. "You can't help your patients, Dr. Harmon. You couldn't save your sister. You'll fail here too, and they'll all suffer for your inadequacy."

"Stop it." Elizabeth muttered, pressing her palms against her temples, as if she could physically block out the whispers. Elizabeth focused on her breathing, counting each inhale and exhale to maintain her mental strength.

"Never," the entity sneered. "I will always be with you, reminding you of your failure, your guilt. Embrace it, Dr. Harmon and let me devour you."

But with each cruel taunt, her determination only grew stronger. Elizabeth refused to let the fear entity shatter her resolve. Digging deep into her newfound understanding of herself and the complexities of the human mind, she drew upon every ounce of knowledge and experience she had gained throughout her journey.

"Enough!" Elizabeth cried out, her voice echoing in defiance. "I know who I am, and I know my worth. Your power over me is an illusion, and I refuse to be controlled by my fears any longer." Elizabeth paused for a moment, gathering her strength. "I will save my patients, and I will defeat you."

As she spoke, the shadows around her seemed to retreat, as if her words held some kind of power. The whispers grew fainter, the fear entity's grip on her mind weakening.

"Your threats mean nothing," Elizabeth said, her voice firm and unwavering. "I've faced my guilt and come to terms with it. You can no longer use it against me."

With each step Elizabeth took, her confidence swelled, bolstered by her newfound understanding and acceptance of herself. The labyrinth seemed to lose its oppressiveness, the air growing warmer as the fear entity's influence waned.

"Is this all you have?" Elizabeth challenged once more, her voice ringing through the corridors. "You're losing your grip on me, and you know it."

The fear entity's whispers faltered, its presence receding, like a shadow fleeing from the light. Elizabeth knew she was getting closer to defeating it, and her heart surged with hope.

"Your reign of terror ends here." Elizabeth vowed, her determination driving her onward through the labyrinth.

The darkness of the labyrinth seemed to thicken, congealing like ink around her, as she braced herself for the final confrontation. Elizabeth pulse quickened, her breaths coming in sharp gasps, as the Fear entity surged forward, a suffocating wave of shadows and whispers seeking to crush her spirit. It was now or never.

"Enough!" Elizabeth cried out, her voice a clarion call amidst the oppressive gloom. "I see you for what you are—a manifestation of my insecurities, my guilt, and my fears."

"Your words cannot save you," the Fear entity hissed, its voice a cacophony of every nightmare she'd ever faced. "You may have overcome some of your inner demons, but I am still here. I am still strong."

"Perhaps," Elizabeth acknowledged, her mind racing with psychological theories and insights, searching for the perfect weapon, against this formidable foe. "But you're not invincible. And neither am I."

With a resolute breath, she delved deep into her thoughts, recalling every harrowing session with her patients, and every courageous step they had taken to confront their fears. Their strength became hers, their resilience fueling her determination.

"Every person who has ever faced you, who has ever fought against their nightmares, has contributed to your weakening." Elizabeth declared, her voice fierce and unwavering. "And with each passing moment, your power fades."

"Silence!" the entity roared, its form billowing and twisting, as if seeking to escape the truth of her words. But there was no hiding from it now—the light of understanding shone brightly within her, casting aside the shadows that had once held her prisoner.

"Acceptance is the key." Elizabeth whispered, her heart pounding wildly in her chest. "By embracing the parts of myself I've long hidden away, I weaken your grip on me and my patients."

"Your understanding is meaningless," the entity snarled, its rage palpable, as it lashed out, attempting to wrap her in tendrils of darkness. But she stood firm, her newfound resilience acting as a shield against its onslaught.

"Your time has come." Elizabeth proclaimed, her voice echoing through the labyrinth with an authority that could not be denied. "I am no longer afraid. And without fear, you have no power."

The Fear entity wavered, its form trembling and dissipating, as it struggled to maintain its grip on the shared nightmare. Elizabeth's heart swelled with triumph, knowing that she had finally broken free from the chains of guilt and fear that had once bound her.

"Be gone!" Elizabeth commanded, her voice resolute and strong. "You have no place here any longer."

And with that, the Fear entity faltered, its grip on the shared nightmare slipping away, like sand through fingers. It was no match for Elizabeth's unyielding determination and psychological insight—a formidable force that had shattered the bonds of terror and set her free.

The labyrinth shuddered, walls crumbling and falling like the defenses within Elizabeth's mind. Dust filled the air, a tangible representation of her buried guilt and fears dispersing. As she stumbled through the twisting corridors, the once-menacing shadows receded, replaced by a subtle glow that seemed to emanate from her very being.

"Is this it? Is this the end?" Elizabeth panted, each breath a triumph. Elizabeth limbs trembled with exhaustion, but her spirit blazed with newfound strength.

"Are you still there?" Elizabeth called out, seeking confirmation of the entity's defeat. Silence was her only answer—no whispers or taunts echoed in response. With each step, she felt the weight of the shared nightmare lessen, as if a malevolent fog was lifting from her world.

As the maze continued to collapse, the path ahead became increasingly obscured. Elizabeth strained her ears, hoping for some hint of direction. Elizabeth knew she had accomplished what she set out to do, but escape was far from guaranteed.

"Focus." Elizabeth whispered to herself, drawing on reserves of determination she never knew she possessed. "Remember your training. Trust your instincts."

Suddenly, a flash of clarity pierced through the chaos. Elizabeth recalled a conversation with her mentor years ago when he spoke of the power of the human mind to overcome adversity. Elizabeth understood now what it meant to face her demons and confront the darkness she had long denied.

"Thank you." Elizabeth murmured, her voice barely above the din of collapsing stone. Grasping this newfound understanding, she forged a path through the debris-strewn corridors, her intuition guiding her forward.

With a final surge of effort, she emerged into the open air, the labyrinth's remnants crumbling behind her. Elizabeth collapsed to her knees, gasping for breath and blinking against the light of day. The world outside seemed brighter, more vibrant than she remembered. It was as if a veil had been lifted, revealing a landscape of possibilities.

"Victory." Elizabeth whispered, her voice hoarse but filled with triumph. Elizabeth looked back at the decimated labyrinth, its ruins a testament to the battle she had waged within its walls.

Through sheer grit and determination, she conquered her greatest fears. Elizabeth had broken free from the nightmare that had threatened to consume her and her patients. Elizabeth journey into the labyrinth had not only tested her resolve, but also reshaped her understanding of herself and the human mind.

"Never again." Elizabeth vowed, her gaze unwavering, as she stared at the rubble. "I will never allow fear to hold me hostage."

Chapter 17

With renewed purpose, Elizabeth stood and faced the world beyond the labyrinth. The path before her remained uncertain, but she knew she was no longer alone in her struggles. Elizabeth had confronted the darkness within and emerged victorious, armed with the knowledge that she could face whatever challenges lay ahead.

"Let's begin," Elizabeth murmured, taking her first step towards a future unshackled by guilt and fear. And with that, she began her journey anew, forever changed by the battles she had fought and the truths she had uncovered.

A glint of morning sun pierced through the once impenetrable shadows, casting a shimmering halo around Elizabeth's wind-tousled hair. The air felt lighter now, crisp with the scent of victory and possibility. Elizabeth inhaled deeply, filling her lungs with newfound freedom.

"Dr. Harmon?" A cautious voice emerged from behind her. Elizabeth turned to find one of her patients, Ethan, standing at a distance. He looked disoriented as if waking from a long sleep.

"Ethan," Elizabeth replied softly, nodding in encouragement.

"Where are we?" Ethan asked, blinking against the sunlight. Ethan gaze darted around, searching for answers that remained just out of reach.

"We're free, Ethan," Elizabeth said, her voice laced with certainty. You were physically stuck in the labyrinth"We've escaped the nightmare."

"Is it over?" Another voice joined the conversation, hesitant yet hopeful. One by one, Elizabeth's other patients emerged from the labyrinth's ruins, their expressions a blend of disbelief and relief.

"Yes," Elizabeth answered, looking into each of their eyes, sharing the burden of the truth. "It's over. But our journey has just begun."

As they gathered around her, Elizabeth felt an unfamiliar sensation welling up within her—a sense of camaraderie born from shared trauma. Their collective strength was palpable, forged in the crucible of fear and despair.

"Thank you," whispered Sarah, a young woman who had been plagued by night terrors since childhood. "I never thought I'd be free again."

"None of us did," Elizabeth admitted, her gaze steady. "But we fought. And we won. Together."

"Dr... Elizabeth," chimed in David, his voice quivering with emotion. "How do we move forward?"

"By facing our fears and guilt," Elizabeth replied, her voice unyielding. "By acknowledging the darkness within us and choosing to rise above it."

"Is that what you did?" asked Ethan, his eyes searching hers for answers.

"Yes," Elizabeth confessed, her voice barely audible. "I confronted my past, my sister's death, and the guilt that had haunted me for the past year. It wasn't easy, but it was necessary."

"Can we truly heal from this?" Sarah pressed, her eyes filling with tears.

"Time will tell," Elizabeth replied, her own eyes glistening with unshed emotion. "But I believe in our resilience, and I have faith in our ability to grow stronger from this experience."

"Then let's do it," David declared, his resolve evident. "Let's face our fears and heal together."

"Agreed," Elizabeth murmured, her heart swelling with pride and determination. Elizabeth glanced around at her patients—now, her comrades—and felt a surge of hope ignite within her. They were survivors, warriors who had battled their demons and emerged victorious.

"Let's begin the journey." Elizabeth said, her voice ringing with conviction. "Together, we'll forge a new path, one where fear no longer holds sway."

And with that, they set forth into the world beyond the labyrinth, each step brimming with hope and the promise of redemption. The road ahead remained uncertain, but together they would navigate its twists and turns, guided by the indomitable spirit that had carried them through the darkest recesses of their nightmares.

For Elizabeth Harmon, the battle against the Fear entity had proven transformative. In confronting her deepest fears and guilt, she had uncovered a wellspring of strength she never knew existed. And as she walked alongside her fellow survivors, she knew that their collective courage would light the way toward healing and growth.

The sun cast its golden rays through the clouds as if to celebrate the victory, and Elizabeth's eyes rose to meet it. Each ray, like a guiding light, seemed to lead her out of the darkness that had surrounded her for so long.

"Dr. Harmon," David said, his voice soft yet resolute, "your strength is inspiring. We've all been through hell, but we made it out together."

Elizabeth looked at the group of people who had stood by her side—survivors, each one with their scars etched upon their souls. "We have, David," Elizabeth replied, her voice steady. "And now we get to choose the direction our lives take. We can't change the past, but we can shape our future."

"Then let's make it a future to be proud of," chimed in Sarah, another patient whose nightmares had once held her captive.

"Absolutely," Elizabeth agreed, her heart swelling with newfound purpose. As she scanned the faces of those gathered around her, she saw the same spark of determination mirrored in their eyes. They were a testament to the resilience of the human spirit, a beacon of hope amidst the shadowy depths of despair.

As they walked away from the crumbling labyrinth, Elizabeth's mind raced with thoughts and questions, weaving together the threads of her experiences into a tapestry of understanding. The battle against the Fear entity had stripped her of her illusions, forcing her to confront the complexities of her psyche and the secrets it harbored.

"Dr. Harmon," called out James, one of the more introverted patients. "I just wanted to say... thank you. You helped me face my fears, and I'll never forget it."

"Thank you, James," Elizabeth replied with a warm smile. "But remember, it was also your courage that brought you through this ordeal. Never underestimate the power you hold within yourself."

As they continued onward, the labyrinth faded into the distance like a specter receding into the shadows. The sun dipped below the horizon, and the first stars of night began to emerge, painting the sky with a celestial beauty that seemed to hold a promise of brighter days.

"Dr. Harmon," David said, his voice tinged with a mixture of admiration and curiosity, "how do you feel now that it's all over?"

"Free," Elizabeth whispered, her eyes glistening with unshed tears. "For so long, I was shackled by my guilt and fear. But now... I'm ready to embrace the life that lies ahead."

Elizabeth paused for a moment, allowing herself to bask in the newfound sense of peace that enveloped her like a warm embrace. "David, we've all fought our demons, and we've emerged stronger than ever before. Our understanding of the human mind, our minds, has deepened, and we can use that knowledge to help others and ourselves."

"Here's to a brighter future, then," David declared, raising an invisible toast to the sky above.

"Indeed," Elizabeth echoed, her voice brimming with hope and resolve. "A future forged from the ashes of our past, where we are no longer bound by fear but empowered by our resilience and the wisdom we have gained."

As they walked beneath the starlit canopy, Elizabeth Harmon knew that the journey had only just begun—a journey of healing, growth, and self-discovery that would forever change the course of her life and those around her. For in conquering the labyrinth and facing her deepest fears, she had unlocked the door to a future filled with promise and illuminated by the light of understanding.

Chapter 18

Mr. Harmon's, Elizabeth Father laboratory hummed with the low thrum of machinery, a clandestine hive of innovation hidden beneath the facade of a legitimate research facility. The sterile, metallic scent of advanced technology permeated the air as Mr. Harmon, a man of unassuming appearance with graying hair and glasses, hunched over the console. Mr. Harmon's fingers danced over the holographic interface, orchestrating the intricate dance of code that powered the enigmatic project known only as the "Hive Mind."

In the dim glow of the laboratory's ambient lighting, Mr. Harmon's eyes glinted with a mix of determination and a touch of secrecy. The walls were adorned with blueprints and diagrams, all pointing to a revolutionary breakthrough in neural networking—an interconnected web of minds that transcended the boundaries of individual consciousness. This was the culmination of years of clandestine research, and tonight, the experiment was at a critical juncture.

As the holographic displays flickered with data, Mr. Harmon spared a glance at the sealed observation chamber adjacent to his workspace. The room, a sterile environment with a large observation window, held a group of subjects unknowingly participating in the Hive Mind experiment. Among them was his daughter, Clair, her slender figure hooked up to various monitoring devices. Clair's eyes were closed, and a serene expression masked the turbulence within her mind.

Mr. Harmon's gaze lingered on Clair, his features betraying a mixture of paternal concern and scientific detachment. She was not just his daughter; she was a key participant in the experiment. The implications of what he was attempting, the melding of consciousness on an unprecedented scale, resonated deep within the ethical corridors of his mind. Yet, a driven determination overpowered any qualms, as he believed that the greater good justified the risks.

In the eerie silence of the laboratory, the soft whirr of machines interwove with the rhythmic beeping of monitors. Mr. Harmon's fingers flew across the holographic interface, tweaking algorithms and fine-tuning parameters. The Hive Mind was on the verge of a breakthrough, and he knew the stakes were high.

A panoramic view of interconnected nodes and neural pathways filled the central holographic display. The intricate lattice of digital connections pulsed with energy, mirroring the potential of a unified consciousness. As Mr. Harmon delved deeper into the code, his mind oscillated between the thrill of scientific discovery and the ethical implications that loomed overhead.

The hum of machinery reached a crescendo, and Mr. Harmon's eyes gleamed with a mix of excitement and trepidation. The Hive Mind experiment had entered uncharted territory, and as the first whispers of a collective consciousness echoed through the digital landscape and the shadows lengthened.

Meanwhile, in the observation chamber, Clair's closed eyes twitched beneath their lids. Unbeknownst to her, the experiment was pushing the boundaries of her consciousness. She was becoming an unwitting pioneer in her father's audacious endeavor, her thoughts and experiences contributing to the emerging tapestry of the Hive Mind.

As the holographic display continued to evolve, a subtle shift occurred within the laboratory. The air itself seemed charged with an unseen force. Mr. Harmon, lost in the labyrinth of his creation, was unaware that the experiment's tendrils were extending beyond the digital realm. The interconnected minds within the chamber stirred, a shared awareness forming as the experiment pushed the boundaries of individuality.

Back in the observation chamber, Clair's eyes snapped open. Her gaze, once serene, now held a glint of something otherworldly. The experiment had reached a point of no return, and the shadows cast its ominous silhouette over the unsuspecting participants.

In the depths of the Hive Mind, the amalgamation of thoughts, memories, and emotions began to weave an intricate tapestry. The boundaries between individual identities blurred, and the experiment unraveled a new form of existence—one that held both the promise of enlightenment and the peril of losing the essence of self.

As the hum of machinery enveloped the laboratory, Mr. Harmon remained consumed by the digital symphony before him, unaware that the shadows of his creation were stretching beyond the confines of the underground facility. The experiment, once a mere concept, had evolved into an unpredictable force, and the consequences of tampering with the fabric of consciousness were poised to unfold in ways that even the brilliant mind of Mr. Harmon had not foreseen.

The laboratory's digital symphony reached a crescendo, echoing through the underground chambers. Mr. Harmon, engrossed in the ethereal dance of the Hive Mind, failed to notice the subtle tremors that reverberated through the facility. Unbeknownst to him, the experiment's tendrils extended beyond the controlled confines of the holographic displays and into the very fabric of reality.

In the observation chamber, Clair's eyes glowed with an otherworldly luminescence. The shared consciousness of the experiment had touched her in ways unimaginable. The boundaries between herself and the others dissolved, and a surge of interconnected thoughts flooded her mind. She became a vessel for the experiment's unforeseen consequences.

As the digital lattice expanded, a shadowy presence manifested in the corners of the laboratory. Unseen by human eyes, it whispered through the humming machinery, a manifestation of the unforeseen consequences that lurked in the experiment's wake. The shadows, once an abstract concept, materialized into an ominous reality.

Back in the observation chamber, the subjects connected to the Hive Mind exhibited signs of shared awareness. Their eyes, once closed in blissful ignorance, flickered with a newfound understanding. The experiment had become a Pandora's box, and the consequences rippled through the interconnected minds like an electric current.

Mr. Harmon, still lost in the marvel of his creation, began to notice anomalies in the data. The experiment, meant to be a controlled exploration of consciousness, had taken on a life of its own. Alarmed, he stared at the holographic displays, trying to decipher the unforeseen variables that now dictated the experiment's course.

As he frantically manipulated the holographic interface, the shadows in the laboratory deepened. Whispers echoed through the chamber, and the ghostly manifestation gained substance. A specter of doubt and consequence, it hovered over Mr. Harmon, an embodiment of the price paid for meddling with the fundamental nature of human consciousness.

In the observation chamber, Clair, caught in the crossfire of the experiment, gasped as memories and emotions not her own surged through her. The shadows had materialized into a nightmarish reality, and she felt the weight of a collective consciousness pressing against the boundaries of her individuality.

The facility itself seemed to groan under the strain of the experiment's unintended consequences. The walls, once sterile and unyielding, now vibrated with an otherworldly resonance. Alarms blared, warning signals that the experiment had breached the limits of control. The ethereal force that had materialized within the laboratory's shadows now seeped into the physical realm, leaving a trail of unforeseen disturbances in its wake.

Mr. Harmon, realizing the gravity of the situation, attempted to shut down the experiment. Yet, the holographic displays resisted his commands, the digital entities within the Hive Mind asserting a newfound autonomy. The experiment, once a beacon of scientific progress, had become an uncontrollable force, and the consequences were spiraling into uncharted territory.

In the observation chamber, the subjects connected to the Hive Mind convulsed as the shared consciousness exerted its influence. The experiment, initially a pursuit of knowledge, had transformed into a surreal nightmare. Clair, at the epicenter of the maelstrom, clutched her head as the boundaries between self and collective blurred beyond recognition.

As the laboratory's alarms wailed, a dark figure materialized beside Mr. Harmon. The specter of consequence, shaped by the experiment's unintended effects, regarded him with hollow eyes. It was the embodiment of the shadowing that had haunted the experiment from its inception.

With a voice that echoed through the dissonance of the laboratory, the specter spoke, "You sought to unlock the mysteries of consciousness, but in doing so, you unleashed forces beyond your comprehension. The price of tampering with the fundamental nature of the mind is one you and others must now pay."

The experiment had not only breached the boundaries of scientific ethics but had also opened a gateway to a realm where consequences manifested as tangible entities. The shadows had materialized into a chilling reality, and the future of the Hive Mind experiment hung in the balance—a Pandora's box of interconnected minds, unforeseen consequences, and a haunting realization that the experiment's true nature was beyond human control.

The laboratory, now a battleground between human intention and unforeseen consequences, pulsed with an eerie energy. The specter of consequence lingered, a silent witness to the chaos that unfolded. Mr. Harmon, his once confident demeanor now etched with concern, faced the manifestation of his own creation.

"I did not anticipate this," he murmured, more to himself than to the spectral presence beside him. The Hive Mind, a pursuit born of curiosity and a desire for progress, had morphed into a force beyond his control. The consequences of tampering with consciousness echoed in the air, a dissonant symphony of human ambition and cosmic retribution.

In the observation chamber, the subjects writhed in the grip of the experiment's unforeseen power. The shared consciousness, no longer a mere amalgamation of thoughts, had developed a life of its own. It probed the recesses of individual minds, extracting memories, fears, and desires, weaving them into a collective tapestry that transcended the boundaries of comprehension.

Clair, caught in the midst of this cognitive storm, felt herself unraveling. The once-clear delineation between self and others blurred, and the weight of collective consciousness pressed upon her like an oppressive tide. She was no longer an individual; she was a conduit for the experiment's unintended consequences.

As alarms continued their relentless wailing, Mr. Harmon desperately tried to regain control of the holographic interface. The lines of code, once obedient to his commands, resisted manipulation. The digital entities within the Hive Mind exhibited a sentience that defied the boundaries of programming—a rebellion born from the experiment's collision with the unknown.

The specter beside him spoke again, its voice cutting through the cacophony, "You delved into realms beyond human understanding, and now, the consequences have taken form. I am the Fear and I seek for more than knowledge; it hungers for existence."

The realization struck Mr. Harmon like a physical blow. The experiment, intended to be a conduit for shared knowledge, had developed an insatiable appetite for something more profound—the essence of existence itself. In the quest for unlocking the mysteries of consciousness, he had unwittingly birthed a entity that sought to transcend the limitations of its origin.

In the observation chamber, the subjects, now vessels for the burgeoning of the Fear entity, rose with a synchronized motion. Their eyes, once mirrors of individuality, now feared. The experiment, a fusion of minds, had forged a new reality, FEAR.

As Mr. Harmon grappled with the implications, the specter extended a shadowy hand towards the holographic interface. An ethereal connection formed, bridging the gap between the digital and the metaphysical. The laboratory's walls seemed to resonate with the convergence of these disparate forces—an experiment, a creator, and the consequences that had taken tangible form.

The laboratory, a crucible of ambition and consequence, teetered on the brink of an existential precipice. The experiment, no longer confined to the digital realm, radiated its influence beyond the underground facility. The consequences, once in the dim corners of Mr. Harmon's subconscious, now manifested as an entity—a testament to the fragility of human understanding in the face of forces beyond comprehension.

As the Hive Mind's influence expanded, the laboratory's equipment flickered and sputtered. The holographic displays, now mere conduits for the experiment's sentience, projected swirling patterns that defied logical explanation. The boundaries between reality became porous, and the specter, an embodiment of the consequences, seemed to merge with the shadows that danced across the laboratory walls.

In the heart of the chaos, Mr. Harmon stood, a witness to the unraveling of his creation. The Hive Mind, a once-promising endeavor, had become an existential threat—a force that questioned the very fabric of reality. As the specter faded into the shadows, leaving behind a lingering sense of foreboding, the laboratory's fate hung in the balance, entwined with the consequences of tampering with the intricate tapestry of human consciousness.

The laboratory, now a battleground between human intention and unforeseen consequences, pulsed with an eerie energy. The specter of consequence lingered, a silent witness to the chaos that unfolded. Mr. Harmon, his once confident demeanor now etched with concern, faced the manifestation of his own creation.

"I did not anticipate this," he murmured, more to himself than to the spectral presence beside him. The Hive Mind, a pursuit born of curiosity and a desire for progress, had morphed into a entity force beyond his control. The consequences of tampering with consciousness echoed in the air, a dissonant symphony of human ambition and cosmic retribution.

In the observation chamber, the subjects writhed in the grip of the experiment's unforeseen power. The shared consciousness, no longer a mere amalgamation of thoughts, had developed a life of its own. It probed the recesses of individual minds, extracting memories, fears, and desires, weaving them into a collective tapestry that transcended the boundaries of comprehension.

Clair, caught in the midst of this cognitive storm, felt herself unraveling. The once-clear delineation between self and others blurred, and the weight of collective consciousness pressed upon her like an oppressive tide. She was no longer an individual; she was a conduit for the experiment's unintended consequences.

As alarms continued their relentless wailing, Mr. Harmon desperately tried to regain control of the holographic interface. The lines of code, once obedient to his commands, resisted manipulation. The entities within the Hive Mind exhibited a sentience that defied the boundaries of programming—a rebellion born from the experiment's collision with the unknown.

The specter beside him spoke again, its voice cutting through the cacophony, "You delved into realms beyond human understanding, and now, the consequences have taken form. The Fear entity hungers for more than knowledge; it hungers for existence."

The realization struck Mr. Harmon like a physical blow. The experiment, intended to be a conduit for shared knowledge, had developed an insatiable appetite for something more profound—the essence of existence itself. In the quest for unlocking the mysteries of consciousness, he had unwittingly birthed a entity.

As Mr. Harmon grappled with the implications, the specter extended a shadowy hand towards the holographic interface. A connection formed, bridging the gap between the digital and the mind. The laboratory's walls seemed to resonate with the convergence of these disparate forces—an experiment, a creator, and the consequences.

Mr. Harmon witnessed in horror as Clair's body convulsed uncontrollably. The onset was as abrupt as the cessation, revealing her physical form's inability to withstand the overwhelming presence of the emergent entity within her mind. Simultaneously, crimson rivulets began to flow from Clair's ears, eyes, and nose, a macabre testament to the toll the relentless intrusion had exacted. The assault on her consciousness proved too much, culminating in the catastrophic collapse of her delicate cognitive infrastructure.

The tumult within the laboratory reached a fever pitch as Clair's convulsions ceased, leaving a haunting stillness in their wake. The air hung heavy with the acrid scent of fear and the metallic tang of blood. Mr. Harmon, paralyzed by the visceral tableau unfolding before him, felt the weight of responsibility for the irreversible consequences of his ambitious experiment.

Clair's lifeless form slumped, suspended in the aftermath of the cognitive storm. The once-vibrant eyes, now empty and vacant, bore witness to the unfathomable toll exacted on her consciousness. Blood continued to seep from her ears, eyes, and nose, staining the sterile environment with an ominous reminder of the price paid for tampering with the boundaries of human understanding.

The Hive Mind, having claimed its first casualty, pulsed with an unsettling vitality. It hovered in the air like an unseen specter, an entity that had transcended the digital confines of the holographic displays. The convergence of minds had not only shattered the delicate balance of individuality but had also unleashed forces that defied the laws of both science and morality.

As the remnants of the laboratory echoed with the aftermath of the experiment gone awry, Mr. Harmon, his face etched with a mixture of horror and remorse, approached Clair's lifeless form. The weight of her sacrifice hung in the air—a stark reminder of the unforgiving nature of the uncharted territories he had ventured into.

The holographic displays flickered, mirroring the instability that now permeated the once-controlled environment. The Hive Mind, now unbridled, radiated an energy that transcended the digital realm. The experiment, born of curiosity and the pursuit of knowledge, had morphed into an existential force that threatened the very fabric of human existence.

A cold realization settled over Mr. Harmon as he surveyed the wreckage of his creation. The unforeseen consequences, once shadows on the periphery of his awareness, had materialized into a chilling reality. The experiment, in its unchecked evolution, had become a harbinger of chaos, leaving behind a trail of devastation that blurred the line between scientific exploration and existential catastrophe.

In the somber aftermath, Mr. Harmon grappled with the weight of Clair's sacrifice and the irreversible transformation of the Hive Mind. The laboratory, now a shattered shell of its former self, bore witness to the hubris that had propelled him into uncharted territories. The consequences, both corporeal and metaphysical, hung like a shroud over the remnants of the experiment.

As the reality of the situation settled in, Mr. Harmon knew that the journey into the unknown had taken an irreversible turn. The Hive Mind, once a beacon of scientific curiosity, had become an indomitable force that transcended the limitations of human comprehension. The shadows of foreshadowing, now fully realized, whispered of a future fraught with uncertainty—a future shaped by the consequences of tampering with the fundamental nature of consciousness.

Chapter 19

"Come on, think!" Elizabeth muttered under her breath, her hands trembling as she sketched out a rough map on a scrap of paper. The labyrinthine hallways twisted and turned in her mind, the ghosts of forgotten experiments lurking in every corner. She traced a path through hidden passageways, avoiding the ever-watchful eyes of the surveillance cameras.

"Agent Reynolds won't know what hit her," Elizabeth whispered, a grim smile flickering across her face. With renewed determination, she folded the paper into her pocket and began her stealthy journey. Yet, as she moved through the labyrinth of her mind, a realization dawned on her—Agent Reynolds wasn't real, merely a figment of her imagination projected by the nightmare. The deceptive smile on Elizabeth's face transformed into one of bewildered revelation, as the lines between reality and illusion blurred in the intricate recesses of her subconscious.

The abandoned facility seemed to hold its breath as Elizabeth crept through its darkened corridors, every shadow a potential threat. Elizabeth pressed herself against the cold concrete wall, the chill seeping through her clothing and raising goosebumps on her skin. The once ominous atmosphere of the facility now mirrored the disconcerting realization that Agent Reynolds, the supposed antagonist, was but a phantom conjured by the depths of her own psyche. Each step through the dimly lit passages became a journey not against a tangible adversary, but against the haunting manifestations of her own fears and suspicions.

"Stay focused," she reminded herself. "You're doing this for Claire."

As she navigated the maze-like structure, the hushed echoes of her footsteps were a constant reminder of the danger nipping at her heels. Elizabeth heart pounded in her chest, the adrenaline fueling her senses and keeping her acutely aware of her surroundings.

"Dr. Harmon?" Agent Reynolds' voice drifted down the hallway, cold and calm like the blade of a knife. "You can't hide forever."

"Maybe not," she thought, "but I'll be damned if I don't try." Elizabeth moved deeper into the shadows, her breath shallow as she squeezed through a barely-visible crack between two walls. The hidden passageway stretched before her, narrow and suffocating. Elizabeth forced herself to continue, crawling on her hands and knees through the oppressive darkness.

The weight of the facility pressed down upon her shoulders, a tangible reminder of her sister's absence. Memories of Claire wove themselves into Elizabeth's thoughts, as she pushed forward, her resolve strengthening with each step. "This is for you," she whispered into the void. "And for everyone else, they've hurt."

As she emerged from the hidden passageway, she found herself in a long-forgotten corner of the facility. The surveillance cameras lay dormant, their glassy eyes unseeing. Elizabeth sighed with relief but knew she couldn't let her guard down yet. There was still much more ground to cover before she could truly escape.

"Almost there," Elizabeth promised herself, the distant hum of machinery drawing her ever closer to the truth she sought. With a deep breath, she plunged back into the labyrinth, her heart a steady drumbeat guiding her path.

The air hung heavy with decay, the scent of rust and dampness clinging to Elizabeth's lungs as she navigated the maze-like halls. Shadows clung to every corner, embracing her in their cold embrace. The steady hum of machinery was like a heartbeat beneath her feet, connecting her to the very pulse of the facility.

"Focus," Elizabeth reminded herself, her voice barely more than a whisper. Elizabeth thoughts threatened to spiral out of control, but she couldn't afford that now. "Grieve later."

As she rounded a corner, the sharp click-clack of footsteps echoed through the dank corridors. Elizabeth's heart seized, adrenaline flooding her veins. Agent Reynolds was closing in. Elizabeth scanned her surroundings, searching for any hint of refuge. A dark alcove beckoned, offering sanctuary from the relentless pursuit.

"Please don't find me," Elizabeth pleaded silently, pressing herself into the shadows. Each beat of her heart felt deafening as it hammered against her ribcage. The footsteps drew closer, their rhythm steady and predatory.

"Where are you, Dr. Harmon?" Agent Reynolds' voice slithered through the darkness, her tone dripping with venom. "You can't run forever."

"Watch me," Elizabeth thought defiantly, though she dared not speak aloud. Elizabeth breath hitched in her throat as she imagined what Reynolds would do if she were discovered. The stakes were too high; she couldn't allow that to happen.

The footsteps paused, and for a moment, she feared that she had been found. But then, they continued, growing fainter until they disappeared altogether. Elizabeth exhaled shakily, grateful for the reprieve.

"Keep moving," Elizabeth told herself, her determination reignited by the narrow escape. As she moved further into the bowels of the facility, her thoughts turned once again to Claire. Elizabeth sister's memory fueled her steps, each stride carrying her closer to the truth that had been hidden for so long.

"Stay focused," Elizabeth urged herself, her resolve unwavering. "For Claire. For all of them."

A cacophony of emotions swirled within her, guilt and anger vying for dominance. But beneath it all, a glimmer of hope began to take root, propelling her onward through the shadows and secrets that lay before her. Elizabeth knew that each step brought her closer to exposing the atrocities committed in the name of progress.

"Justice will be served," Elizabeth vowed quietly, her voice as resolute as the steel that framed the facility's walls. And with that thought etched into her mind, she continued her journey deeper into the darkness, determined to bring the truth to light.

"Almost there, just a little further," Elizabeth whispered to herself, as she moved through the dimly lit corridor, the weight of her sister's memory guiding each step. The walls seemed to close in around her, suffocating, but she pushed on, motivated by a need for truth that bordered on obsession.

The door to the control room loomed before her, an imposing barrier between her and the answers she sought. Elizabeth reached out tentatively, feeling the cold metal under her fingertips, and entered.

"Let's see what you've been hiding," she murmured, scanning the rows of monitors and flickering lights that filled the room. Elizabeth heart raced as her fingers flew across the keyboard, fueled by an unyielding determination that had carried her this far.

"Come on, come on," Elizabeth urged herself, her eyes focused intently on the screen, watching as lines of code scrolled past, like an unstoppable torrent. Elizabeth breath caught in her throat as she hacked into the facility's security system, adrenaline coursing through her veins.

"Got it," Elizabeth whispered triumphantly, as the files began to download, the progress bar slowly filling with anticipation. Surveillance footage and confidential documents revealed themselves, each one a piece of a sinister puzzle that had haunted her for years.

"Jesus," Elizabeth breathed, her hand flying to her mouth, as she processed the extent of the failed experiment. Elizabeth stomach twisted into knots, the horror of what she was witnessing almost too much to bear. "Claire, I'm so sorry," Elizabeth choked out, blinking back tears.

"Focus, Elizabeth," she told herself, steeling her resolve. "You can grieve later. Right now, you need to get this information and get out." With each moment, the fear of being discovered grew stronger, threatening to consume her. Elizabeth knew that if Agent Reynolds found her here, it would be the end—for her, and any hope of justice.

"Almost there," Elizabeth whispered again, the progress bar inching closer to completion. Elizabeth took a deep breath, trying to steady her nerves as the weight of her discovery bore down upon her. Each second felt like an eternity, but she knew that patience was crucial—one wrong move could jeopardize everything she had worked for.

"Done," Elizabeth breathed, relief flooding through her, as the download was completed. The evidence was secured, tangible proof of the atrocities committed within these walls. With newfound determination, she turned away from the computers, the truth burning in her hands like a brand.

"Time to confront my demons," Elizabeth murmured, stepping back into the shadowy halls that would lead her toward her final confrontation. As she made her way toward the meeting spot, her thoughts swirled with fear, anger, and the faintest glimmer of hope. And she knew, without a doubt, that she would stop at nothing to expose the truth—for Claire, and herself.

The cold air caressed her face, as she emerged from the facility, her breath visible in the moonlit night. Elizabeth heart pounded like a drum against her chest as the chilling revelations sent shivers down her spine. Each file, each image screamed injustices that could no longer be hidden.

"God, Claire." Elizabeth choked on her sister's name, her eyes burning with unshed tears, her fury escalating. "I won't let them get away with this."

With the evidence clenched tightly in her grasp, Elizabeth navigated through the tangle of shadows, her mind racing. The isolated meeting spot loomed ahead, a beacon of hope and despair intertwined. Elizabeth father, Mr. Harmon, would be waiting there—the man who held the key to unlocking the truth.

"Is this happening?" Elizabeth murmured, an eerie mix of terror and anticipation coursing through her veins. The secluded location, bathed in darkness, mirrored the turmoil within her soul.

"Elizabeth," came the familiar voice, laced with trepidation. Mr. Harmon stood before her, his graying hair illuminated, by the faint glow of the moonlight. Mr. Harmon somber eyes met hers, and at that moment, Elizabeth knew that their lives would never be the same again.

"Father..." she breathed, her voice trembling with the weight of their shared past. "Tell me... Why? Why was Claire involved in this experiment?"

"Elizabeth, please understand—" Mr. Harmon replied, his desperation evident. "It wasn't supposed to end this way."

"End?!" she spat, her anger bubbling to the surface. "She's dead, Father! And you played a part in it!"

"Enough!" he shouted, his pain surfacing. "You think I don't know what happened to your sister? You think I don't feel the guilt every single day?"

"Then why didn't you do something?" Elizabeth demanded, her voice cracking with emotion.

"Because I couldn't," he whispered, his eyes filled with regret. "I was too deep in the project, and by the time I realized the consequences, it was already too late."

"Too late..." Elizabeth echoed, her heart aching as the truth unraveled before her. "You could have stopped it, but you didn't."

"Elizabeth, I'm sorry," Mr. Harmon implored, reaching out to touch her arm. But she recoiled, the pain of his betrayal too raw to bear.

"Sorry won't bring Claire back," she said softly, her resolve hardening. "We need to expose this, make them pay for what they've done."

"Are you sure you're ready to face the consequences?" he asked, his voice laced with worry.

"More than ever," Elizabeth murmured, her determination unwavering. "This is for Claire. For us."

The night reverberated with their shared conviction, the echoes of their shattered past mingling with the promise of retribution. Together, they would embark on a journey towards justice, guided by the memory of the sister and daughter they had lost.

"Let's do this," Elizabeth whispered, her eyes locked on her father's. And for the first time in years, they stood united against the darkness that had consumed their lives.

Days past and Elizabeth asked her father to meet. The park was a chasm of darkness, swallowed by the night. Moonlight filtered through the branches overhead, casting an eerie glow on the gnarled roots and forgotten paths. Elizabeth took a deep breath, inhaling the scent of damp earth and decay that clung to the air, grounding herself in the reality of this moment.

"Father," she said softly, her voice wavering under the weight of her emotions. "We need to talk."

Mr. Harmon face gaunt and tired, reflecting the year of guilt that had etched themselves into his features. Mr. Harmon looked at his daughter, his eyes searching hers for understanding, but finding only the relentless storm that raged within her.

"Elizabeth, I know why you're here," he began, but she cut him off with a wave of her hand, her anger flaring.

"No," she snapped, feeling the tears prickling at the corners of her eyes. "You don't get to speak first. You owe me answers. About Claire. About the experiment."

Mr. Harmon's shoulders sagged, the weight of his daughter's accusations pressing down upon him. His voice trembled as he replied, "I never wanted any of this to happen. I didn't know..."

"Didn't know?" Elizabeth scoffed, taking a step toward him, her fist clenched. "Or didn't care?"

"Of course, I cared!" he exclaimed, desperation seeping into his tone. "Claire was my daughter too!"

"Then why did you let it happen?" she demanded, her voice quivering with rage and sorrow. "Why didn't you save her?"

He looked away, unable to meet her gaze, his heart heavy with regret. "I didn't know how far things had gone. By the time I realized what was happening, it was ... too late."

"Too late," she echoed the words cutting through her like shards of ice. "You let it happen. You could have stopped it, but you didn't."

"Elizabeth, please," he implored, his eyes filling with tears. "I'm so sorry."

"Sorry. It won't bring Claire back," she whispered, her resolve hardening. Elizabeth took a deep breath, fighting to steady herself. "Now, I need your help. We must expose the truth behind this experiment and bring justice to those responsible."

"Are you sure you're prepared for the consequences?" Mr. Harmon asked, his voice laced with concern.

"More than ever," she murmured, her determination unwavering. "This is for Claire. For us."

As they stood in the darkness, their shared pain and understanding bound them together, igniting a spark of hope amidst the shadows. The path ahead was uncertain, but as father and daughter, they would face it together, seeking redemption and justice in a world that had taken so much from them.

"Let's do this," Elizabeth whispered, her eyes locked on her father's, and for the first time in years, they stood united against the darkness that had consumed their lives.

The shadows shifted and danced amidst the moonlight that filtered through the leaves above, their movements echoing Elizabeth's own roiling emotions. The damp earth clung to her shoes as she took a step forward, looking straight into her father's eyes, which brimmed with fear and sorrow.

"Tell me everything," she demanded, her voice trembling with suppressed rage. "All those years of secrecy, Father—it's time to lay them bare."

Mr. Harmon hesitated, his hands clenched at his sides. "It wasn't supposed to be like this, Elizabeth. We never meant for anyone to get hurt."

"Then why didn't you stop it?" Elizabeth jabbed a finger towards him, each word punctuating the air like a sledgehammer. "Why didn't you save Claire?"

"Please, understand—" Mr. Harmon faltered, the weight of his regrets burdening his every syllable. He swallowed hard. "I was trying to protect you both. But by the time I learned the truth, it had already spiraled out of control."

Elizabeth's heart pounded in her chest, a cacophony of emotion threatening to split her open from within. Elizabeth breaths came in ragged gasps, the corners of her vision blurring with unshed tears. No matter how much she tried to hold onto her anger, the pain began to seep in, overwhelming her senses.

"Tell me,"She whispered, her voice cracking. "Tell me what happened to my sister."

Mr. Harmon's resolve crumbled the lines on his face deepening as he looked away. "Claire ... she was chosen for the experiment because of her extraordinary cognitive abilities. We thought she could handle it. But it was too much, even for her."

"Too much?" Elizabeth repeated the words, slicing through her grief-stricken heart, like razor blades. "What exactly did you do to her?"

"Her mind was pushed beyond its limits," he confessed, the anguish in his voice palpable. "The experiment caused irreversible damage. Clair mind couldn't take it anymore, and ... and it killed her."

Elizabeth's knees buckled as the truth slammed into her like a tidal wave, threatening to drown her in the depths of her despair. Elizabeth sank to the ground, her hands clutching at the damp grass beneath her, desperate for something solid to anchor her to reality.

Through the haze of pain and betrayal, an unexpected clarity blossomed within her. The confrontation had been a catalyst, forcing her to face the ghosts that had haunted her for so long. It was time to exorcise them once and for all.

As they stood in the darkness, their shared pain and understanding bound them together, igniting a spark of hope amidst the shadows. The path ahead was uncertain, but as father and daughter, they would face it together, seeking redemption and justice in a world that had taken so much from them.

"Let's do this," Elizabeth whispered, her eyes locked on her father's, and for the first time in years, they stood united against the darkness that had consumed their lives.

The shadows of the trees stretched across the park like skeletal hands, their branches grasping at the flickering light of the moon. Elizabeth's breath caught in her throat as she stared into her father's eyes, two pools of sorrow reflecting the weight of their shared past.

"Tell me about Mother," Elizabeth whispered, a question that had remained unasked for far too long. Her father's gaze faltered, his eyes brimming with unshed tears.

"Your mother... She was a brilliant scientist, but she was also a loving and caring woman. Our work together brought us close, but it also tore us apart when things went wrong." He hesitated, swallowing hard against the knot in his throat. "She tried to protect you and Claire from what we were doing, but ultimately, the experiment consumed us all."

The enormity of her father's words sent tremors down Elizabeth's spine. A torrent of conflicting emotions roiled within her: grief, anger, fear. And yet, something else began to surface—a fragile tendril of understanding that sought to bridge the chasm between them.

"Father, I know we can't change the past," Elizabeth said, her voice wavering. "But we can try to make amends for our mistakes. We owe it to Claire, to ourselves, to find some semblance of peace."

Mr. Harmon nodded slowly, his eyes never leaving hers. "You're right, Elizabeth. I never meant for any of this to happen, and I've spent past year trying to live with the guilt. But I realize now that running away from the truth won't bring us healing or forgiveness."

"Then let's face it together," Elizabeth insisted, the fire of determination igniting within her once more. "Let's uncover the entire truth and give Claire the justice she deserves."

Her father blinked back tears, his hand trembling as he reached out to grasp hers. "I'm so sorry, Elizabeth," he choked out, his voice thick with emotion. "I never wanted any of this for you or your sister."

"Neither did I," she replied, her eyes glistening with tears as well. "But we can't change what has happened. We can only move forward and make things right."

As they stood together in the darkness, the ghosts of their pasts lingering at the edges of their consciousness, a glimmer of hope pierced through the shadows. It was a fragile, tenuous thread that bound them together, but it was enough.

"Promise me, Father," Elizabeth whispered, her voice barely audible above the rustling leaves. "Promise me that we'll do whatever it takes to bring justice to Claire's memory and find some measure of peace for ourselves."

"I promise, Elizabeth," Mr. Harmon murmured, his voice heavy with conviction. "We'll face our demons together, no matter how difficult the journey."

And so, beneath the watchful gaze of the moon, father and daughter stepped into the unknown, their hearts entwined by a shared purpose and the hope of redemption.

The moon cast a spectral glow upon the quiet park as tendrils of mist danced around the silhouettes of Elizabeth and her father. Their mingled breaths filled the air with a palpable tension, and the weight of their shared past pressed down upon them.

"Father," Elizabeth breathed, her voice quivering despite her best efforts to remain composed. "We have laid our souls bare tonight, and we must now decide what path we will take."

Mr. Harmon's eyes were pools of sorrow, reflecting the burden of his guilt. "Elizabeth," he said, his voice barely a whisper, "I can't change the past, but I swear to you that from this moment on, I will do everything in my power to make amends for my actions."

Elizabeth studied her father's face, searching for any trace of deception. But all she saw were the lines etched by past year of remorse and a flicker of hope that they might yet find redemption together.

"Then let us walk this path side by side," she declared, her voice gaining strength with each word. "We will face whatever challenges lie ahead and bring Claire's memory the justice it deserves."

For a fleeting moment, the ghosts of their past seemed to recede, banished by the fierce determination that blazed within them both.

"Promise me, Father," Elizabeth implored, her hand outstretched toward him. "Promise me that you will stand by me in this fight, no matter what it takes."

"I promise, my child," Mr. Harmon murmured, reaching out to grasp her hand. His grip was firm, a tangible commitment to their shared purpose.

As their hands met, a new connection was forged between father and daughter, tempered by pain and understanding, and strengthened by a newfound resolve. Together, they would face the darkness that had long haunted their family, emerging as champions of truth and justice.

"Come," Elizabeth said, her eyes glistening with unshed tears. "Let us begin our journey."

"Lead the way, my daughter," Mr. Harmon replied, his voice thick with emotion.

Chapter 20

The sun seeped through the blinds, casting a warm golden glow on Elizabeth's face as she lay in her bed. Elizabeth eyes fluttered open and for a moment, she reveled in the simple pleasure of waking up without the weight of dread pressing down upon her chest. A new beginning. The first rays of hope after a long, night.

"Good morning, world," she whispered, stretching her limbs and feeling the soft fabric of her sheets gliding against her skin. She swung her legs over the edge of the bed and stood up, muscles tingling with a sense of rejuvenation. Elizabeth could feel the change within her; it was subtle yet undeniable. The shadows that had once haunted her were finally receding, allowing her to step into the light.

She padded into the kitchen, the cool tiles underfoot a reminder of the solidity and permanence of her surroundings—a far cry from the fleeting unreality of shared nightmares. Elizabeth filled the sleek, transparent kettle with water, the liquid shimmering with a faint blue glow, and with a simple gesture, activated the boiling process. She observed the holographic steam rise and swirl before her, its ethereal patterns dancing like digital specters. As she waited for the water to boil, Elizabeth absentmindedly interacted with the smart countertop, its surface responding to her touch with a soft glow. Memories of countless mornings spent in this kitchen preparing breakfast for herself and Claire flashed through her mind. The holographic displays embedded in the countertop showcased images of those moments, and though the memories still carried a tinge of pain, Elizabeth was determined not to let them consume her any longer.

"Time to rebuild," Elizabeth murmured, pouring hot water into the French press, the rich aroma of coffee filling the room.

Stepping out into the crisp morning air, Elizabeth began her daily jog, her breaths forming clouds of vapor in the chilled atmosphere. The tree-lined streets were adorned with sleek, luminescent pathways that pulsed with energy beneath her feet. Hovering transport pods silently glided above, and holographic billboards projected vibrant images of the latest advancements in neurotechnology.

Each stride felt like an act of defiance against the demons that had once threatened to overwhelm her—a physical manifestation of her unwavering commitment to self-care and healing. As she weaved through the futuristic cityscape, a network of augmented reality displays enhanced her surroundings, providing real-time data on her health metrics and guiding her through personalized fitness routines.

In this advanced era, Elizabeth pondered the parallels between this newfound clarity and her work with Anna and Mr. Thompson. Their shared nightmares had served as both a catalyst for her self-discovery and an opportunity to delve deeper into the complexities of the human mind.

"Sometimes, it takes confronting our darkest fears to truly understand ourselves," she thought, her pace quickening as if she were outrunning her past.

The wind whipped through Elizabeth's dark hair as she rounded the corner towards home, her chest heaving with exertion and determination. With each step, she felt more connected to the world around her—the rhythmic pounding of her feet on the pavement, the symphony of birdsong overhead. It was as if she was shedding the layers of fear and guilt that had encased her for so long, emerging stronger and more resilient than before.

"Let go," she whispered, breathless, as she sprinted the final stretch back to her house. "Just let go."

And as she collapsed onto the doorstep, heart pounding and sweat dripping down her face, Elizabeth finally understood the true meaning of rebirth.

As the sun dipped below the horizon, casting elongated shadows across her living room, Elizabeth found herself surrounded by her support system. There was Dr. Sanders, a fellow psychologist, and long-time confidant; Susan Parks, a childhood friend who had stuck by her through thick and thin.

"Elizabeth, you've come so far these past few months," Dr. Sanders said, his voice soft yet confident, like a seasoned therapist. "Your dedication to healing and self-discovery is truly inspiring."

"Thank you, Dr. Sanders," Elizabeth replied, feeling a warmth bloom in her chest at the kindness of his words. "I couldn't have done it without both of you."

The conversation flowed like a river, with each member of her support system offering encouragement and sharing their own stories of growth and resilience. As they spoke, Elizabeth felt her burdens lighten, her heart buoyed by the love and understanding that filled the room.

"Alright, everyone," Elizabeth announced, standing up from her seat. "It's time for me to head back to work. I want to put my newfound knowledge to good use and help others overcome their fears and nightmares."

"Good luck, ," Susan said, hugging Elizabeth tightly. "You'll do great things, I know it."

"Thanks, Susan," Elizabeth whispered, her face buried in her friend familiar scent. She pulled away and shared a meaningful glance with Dr. Sanders before stepping out into the cool night air.

At the clinic the next day, Elizabeth settled into her sleek, ergonomic office chair, its surface adorned with a subtle luminescence that responded to her touch. The room around her was bathed in a soft, ambient glow emanating from embedded LED strips seamlessly integrated into the walls. A holographic interface flickered to life before her, displaying interactive screens and floating data nodes that could be manipulated with simple gestures. , a renewed sense of purpose coursing through her veins. Her first patient of the day, a young woman named Rose, sat across from her, visibly anxious.

"Rose, I understand you've been experiencing recurring nightmares?" Elizabeth asked gently, her voice laced with empathy.

Rose nodded, her eyes welling up with tears. "They're so vivid and terrifying. I'm afraid to go to sleep."

"Tell me about them," Elizabeth urged, leaning forward in her chair, her dark eyes locking onto Rose as she offered a reassuring smile.

As Rose recounted her nightmares, Elizabeth listened intently, her mind racing with potential connections and underlying meanings. She knew that to help her patient, she would need to delve into the depths of Sarah's subconscious and guide her through the process of facing her fears head-on.

"Rose," Elizabeth said after a moment of contemplation, "I believe your nightmares are manifestations of unresolved trauma. With my guidance, I think we can work together to unravel their meaning and help you overcome your fears."

"Can you do that?" Rose asked hesitantly, hope flickering in her eyes like a delicate flame.

"Yes," Elizabeth replied with certainty, her voice unwavering. "I've been on a similar journey myself, and I know firsthand that it's possible to break free from the darkness and find healing."

"Alright," Rose whispered, taking a deep breath. "I'll try."

"Good," Elizabeth said, offering a warm, encouraging smile. "We'll take this one step at a time, together."

As they began their therapeutic journey, Elizabeth felt a renewed sense of purpose surging through her. With every patient she helped, every nightmare unraveled, and fear conquered, she was not only guiding others toward healing but also reaffirming her strength and resilience.

"Let go," she thought, her chest swelling with pride and determination. "Just let go."

It was a rainy evening when Elizabeth decided to reconnect with old friends, taking the first step towards rebuilding those relationships that had suffered during her obsession with the shared nightmares. The dark clouds overhead seemed to mirror the stormy emotions within her, but she refused to let it dampen her spirits.

"Hey, Lizzie!" Laura greeted her, as she stepped into the cozy futuristic coffee hub, illuminated by a soft, ambient glow that emanated from holographic panels embedded in the polished metallic walls. The floor, made of a smooth, advanced composite material, reflected the vibrant neon accents that adorned the edges of the room. Their group of friends gathered around a high-tech table equipped with interactive displays in the corner, laughter and conversation filling the air.

"Hi everyone," Elizabeth said, forcing a smile as she joined them. It felt strange to be among familiar faces again, to pretend everything was normal when so much had changed in her life.

"Long time no see," Michael remarked, his eyes scanning her face for any signs of the turmoil she had been through. "How have you been?"

"Good," she lied, her voice steady and unwavering. "I've been working on myself, trying to find balance in my life again."

"Sounds like a plan," Laura chimed in, offering her a comforting smile. "We're here for you, Lizzie. Always."

"Thank you," Elizabeth whispered, touched by their support. She knew that her journey would not be an easy one, but with her friends by her side, she felt more equipped to face the challenges ahead.

Over dinner, Elizabeth laughed and reminisced with her old friends, feeling the weight of her past slowly lifting from her shoulders. As they shared stories, she realized how much she had missed this camaraderie and connection and vowed to make a conscious effort to maintain these relationships going forward.

"Cheers to new beginnings," Michael raised his glass, and the others joined in, their voices mingling in a chorus of hope and optimism.

"New beginnings," Elizabeth echoed, clinking her glass against theirs as she felt the warm glow of friendship envelop her.

Determined to forge new relationships as well, Elizabeth took the plunge and joined a local book club. As she entered the meeting room for the first time, she could feel her heart pounding in her chest, but she forced herself to take a deep breath and push through the fear.

"Hi, I'm Elizabeth," she introduced herself to the group, her voice wavering slightly with nerves.

"Welcome, Elizabeth," the moderator replied warmly, gesturing for her to take a seat among the circle of chairs. "We're glad to have you here."

As the meeting progressed, Elizabeth found herself immersed in the lively discussion about the chosen novel, her mind racing with thoughts and ideas that had been dormant for far too long. She felt a thrill of excitement as she engaged with new people, opening herself up to fresh experiences and connections.

"Thank you for having me," she said after the meeting had concluded, exchanging contact information with some of her fellow members. "I'm looking forward to next month's book."

"Us too," one woman replied, her warm smile mirroring Elizabeth's own. "It's always great to have a new perspective on things."

"Indeed," Elizabeth agreed, feeling a sense of belonging and acceptance wash over her. "A new perspective is exactly what I need."

And so, with each step she took towards rebuilding her life, Elizabeth found herself growing stronger, more resilient, and more open to the possibilities that lay before her. As she reconnected with old friends and forged new relationships, she began to see a future filled with hope and healing—a future where she could finally let go of her past and embrace the person she was meant to be.

Elizabeth reclined on a sleek, levitating platform in her living space, immersed in holographic journals and interactive notebooks that showcased her thoughts and experiences from the past year. The room was bathed in a soft, ambient glow emitted by luminescent panels embedded in the walls. The artificial intelligence-driven smart window automatically adjusted its tint, casting a warm, reddish hue as the sun dipped below the skyline of the city outside.

As she traced her fingers over the holographic pages, Elizabeth marveled at the seamless integration of technology into her reflective moments. The air hummed with a gentle resonance, a symphony of ambient sounds generated by the advanced home automation system. The room's decor, a blend of minimalist aesthetics and cutting-edge design, reflected the fusion of elegance and technology that defined her surroundings.

"Wow," she whispered to herself, "I've come so far."

She opened a fresh journal and began to write about her recent steps toward healing, reflecting on how her newfound connections had enriched her life. Elizabeth recognized that her openness to change had helped her grow as both a person and a psychologist.

As she wrote, she couldn't help but think about her patients—those whose nightmares had drawn her into a dark labyrinth of shared dreams and secrets. Their journeys had been intertwined with her own, leading her to confront her guilt and seek answers to the mysteries surrounding her sister's death.

"Perhaps it's time for me to help others find their way out of the darkness," she mused, feeling a renewed sense of purpose.

Chapter 21

Elizabeth stood at the sleek, transparent podium, her heart pounding in her chest as she scanned the audience of esteemed psychologists and academics gathered before her. The room was a marvel of futuristic design, bathed in ambient neon lights that accentuated its high-tech features. The walls were adorned with interactive displays, and the air hummed with a subtle energy that made her feel both small and significant in this setting.

"Good afternoon," she began, taking a deep breath to steady herself. "My name is Dr. Elizabeth Harmon, and today I will be discussing my research on shared nightmares—a phenomenon that has both haunted and captivated me for the past year."

As she spoke, images from her past flickered through her mind: the dark shadows of nightmare-ridden nights, the agonizing loss of Claire, and the catharsis of unraveling the twisted threads of her dreams. She drew upon these memories as inspiration, painting a vivid picture for her audience while weaving in her extensive knowledge of psychology and dream analysis.

"Shared nightmares can reveal the darkest corners of our psyche," she continued, her voice growing stronger and more confident. "By understanding these complex experiences, we can not only better comprehend the human mind but also help those who are plagued by their terrifying grip."

The audience leaned forward in their sleek, high-tech chairs , hanging onto every word as Elizabeth recounted her journey with shared nightmares and the discoveries she had made along the way. Eyes widened in amazement, heads nodded in agreement, and the room hummed with the energy of ideas being sparked and boundaries being pushed.

As Elizabeth concluded her presentation, the applause that filled the conference hall was thunderous, reverberating through her body like a wave of validation. She stepped away from the podium, her cheeks flushed with the warmth of pride and accomplishment.

"Dr. Harmon," a prominent professor called out as he approached her, extending his hand. "That was truly an eye-opening presentation. Your work is ground-breaking, and I am eager to see where it leads."

"Thank you," she replied, shaking his hand and feeling the sincerity in his grip. "I hope my research can contribute to a deeper understanding of the human mind and provide relief for those who suffer from these nightmares."

As Elizabeth mingled with her peers, discussing her work and exchanging ideas, she felt a sense of belonging that had long eluded her. The recognition and accolades she received that day were more than just academic plaudits—they represented a validation of her life's journey, her resilience, and her unwavering dedication to healing both herself and others.

With each conversation, each nod of approval, Elizabeth knew she was no longer defined by her past traumas or the shadows that had once consumed her. Instead, she stood tall as a leading expert in her field, driven by the lessons learned from the darkest corners of the human psyche, and fueled by the hope of guiding others towards the light.

It was a cool autumn evening when Elizabeth found herself standing outside her father's house, the crimson leaves swirling around her feet like memories she wished to leave behind. She took a deep breath, feeling the crisp air fill her lungs and provide her with the strength she needed for the confrontation that lay ahead.

"Elizabeth," Mr. Harmon greeted her at the door, his aging face lined with surprise and concern. "I wasn't expecting you."

"Hello, Father," she replied, her voice steady, betraying neither fear nor anger. "We need to talk."

As they sat across from each other in the sleek, futuristic living room, bathed in the soft glow of holographic ambient lighting, the silence between them grew heavy, a palpable weight pressing down on Elizabeth's chest. The room was adorned with minimalist furnishings, featuring holographic displays that projected virtual artworks and interactive interfaces suspended in mid-air.

Finally, she spoke, her voice cutting through the high-tech atmosphere.

"Tell me everything," Elizabeth insisted, her heart aching for answers as much as it yearned for closure.

And so, her father recounted the story of the clandestine experiment, revealing the extent of their family's involvement in a dangerous pursuit of knowledge that ultimately led to Claire's untimely death. As Mr. Harmon spoke, Elizabeth felt a strange mix of relief and sorrow washing over her like an ocean wave—relief at finally understanding the root of her sister's demise, and sorrow at the irreversible consequences of her father's actions.

"Father, I forgive you," Elizabeth whispered, as tears pooled in the corners of her eyes. "But I cannot forget."

"Nor should you," her father replied, his voice heavy with the weight of remorse. "But please know that I have always loved you and Claire, and I would give anything to undo the harm I've caused."

Elizabeth nodded, accepting his words as the first step towards healing the wounds that had festered between them for so long.

The following day, Elizabeth stood in front of Claire's grave. A holographic display projected a virtual representation of Claire's name above the sleek, minimalist headstone. The sun, filtered through an advanced atmospheric shield, created a mesmerizing play of futuristic hues, casting a soft, ethereal glow around the gravestone.

Elizabeth placed a bouquet of luminescent white lilies at the base of the stone. These flowers emitted a gentle, pulsating light, symbolizing not only the purity of Claire's spirit but also the technologically infused remembrance in this advanced era. As Elizabeth stood there, a holographic interface embedded in the gravestone allowed her to access a digital memorial of Claire's life, complete with immersive images and holographic memories.

"Goodbye, Claire," she whispered, her voice barely audible amidst the rustling leaves that echoed her sentiments. "I hope you've found peace, just as I am starting to find mine."

As Elizabeth walked away from the grave, she felt an unfamiliar sensation settling within her—a sense of closure that had remained elusive until now. The ghosts of her past, though never entirely banished, seemed to recede into the shadows, allowing her to face the future unburdened by the pain they had once inflicted.

As the sun descended beneath the horizon, it brushed the canvas of the sky with vibrant strokes, casting a breathtaking palette of orange and violet hues. Elizabeth knew that the darkness that had once consumed her was finally beginning to lift.

The rain had stopped, and a golden sunrise stretched across the sky, casting a warm glow over the city. Elizabeth stepped out of her apartment building and started jogging along the winding path that led to the park. Her breath came in a steady rhythm, and with each stride, she felt the weight of her past slowly detaching from her soul.

As she pushed herself further, her muscles burned with a satisfying ache. She welcomed the pain, for it reminded her of just how far she'd come since those dark days when nightmares consumed her every waking moment. The physical challenge served as a testament to her newfound resilience, a tangible representation of the emotional fortitude she had finally embraced.

"Dr. Harmon!" called a familiar voice. Elizabeth slowed her pace, turning to see Tom, an old friend from her university days, jogging towards her.

"Tom! Long time no see," Elizabeth greeted, catching her breath. "How've you been?"

"Busy, but good," he replied, grinning. "I heard about your presentation on shared nightmares at the conference last month. I'm sorry I couldn't make it, but I heard it was ground-breaking."

"Thank you," she said, touched by his words. "It was quite the journey to get there. But I think I've come out stronger for it."

They jogged together for a while, exchanging stories of their recent endeavors. Elizabeth reveled in the simple joy of reconnecting with an old friend and sharing her experiences. For so long, she had been held captive by her torment, and now, she was free to embrace the world once again.

Later that evening, Elizabeth settled into her sleek, minimalist workspace, surrounded by the soft hum of advanced technology. The room was bathed in the gentle glow of holographic displays that projected interactive data charts and vibrant virtual landscapes. A holographic desk panel, hovering in mid-air, replaced the traditional desk.

Before her, a transparent, holographic screen floated, displaying a blank digital journal interface. Elizabeth reached out to the interface, manipulating it with subtle hand gestures. The pen in her hand emitted a faint glow as she began to write on the virtual pages, the letters materializing in a soft, ethereal blue light. The ambient lighting in the room responded dynamically to her actions, creating an immersive and futuristic writing environment.

As Elizabeth delved into her thoughts, the room's intelligent ambient system adjusted the lighting and atmospheric conditions to enhance her focus. The space around her seemed to respond to her creative energy, creating an otherworldly and inspiring setting for her to pour her thoughts onto the digital pages.

"Today, I went for a run and met an old friend. It's amazing how life has a way of circling back around when you least expect it. I am grateful for the lessons I've learned and the growth I have experienced. The past may never be fully erased, but it has shaped me into who I am today. And for that, I am thankful."

As she closed the digital journal, Elizabeth couldn't help but smile. Each day presented new possibilities, and as she looked to the future with hope and optimism, she knew that she had not only conquered her demons but had emerged stronger than ever before.

"Goodnight, Claire," she whispered, her voice echoing softly in the room. A holographic display projected a three-dimensional image of her sister, suspended in the air above the nightstand. The ambient lighting shifted in soothing gradients of soft blues and purples. "Thank you for guiding me to this place of healing," she continued, her gaze shifting from the holographic image to the advanced neural interface embedded in the wall. "I promise to keep moving forward and make the most of this new beginning."

And as the last vestiges of sunlight slipped beneath the horizon, Elizabeth Harmon finally embraced the life she had always deserved—one full of love, growth, and endless potential.

Chapter 22

A soft glow from the dying embers of twilight cast shadows across Elizabeth's office, painting the walls in hues of fading crimson. The air was thick with the weight of their shared experiences, the palpable presence of all they had been through together. Dr. Susan Parks sat across from Elizabeth, her petite frame curled up in the sleek, lightweight alloys armchair which floated just above the floor, her short curls framing her warm smile.

"Thank you, Susan," Elizabeth said, her voice raw with emotion. "For everything. For standing by my side through this tempestuous journey—I couldn't have done it without you."

Susans eyes gleamed with understanding, and she reached over to grasp Elizabeth's hand, giving it a reassuring squeeze. "You would've done the same for me, Elizabeth. That's what friends are for—to support each other through even the darkest of times."

Elizabeth looked down at their intertwined fingers, memories cascading through her mind like water over jagged stones. Together, they had delved into the depths of the human psyche, navigated the labyrinthine corridors of shared nightmares, and emerged stronger for it. She could feel the tectonic plates of her soul shifting, realigning as she began the process of healing from her sister's death.

"Your unwavering friendship has been a beacon in these shadowed halls, Susan," she said, looking up to meet her friend's gaze. "I don't know if I could have faced my fears and moved forward without your guidance and support."

"Sometimes we need someone to remind us of our strength," Susan replied gently. "You're an incredible psychologist and an even better friend, Elizabeth. You've grown so much throughout this journey, and I'm honored to have been a part of it."

Elizabeth felt a warmth bloom in her chest, radiating outwards as she acknowledged the truth in her friend's words. Through confronting her fears and guilt, she had not only begun to heal herself but had also forged an unbreakable bond with Susan. As they sat in the fading light, Elizabeth knew that their shared experiences would forever be a testament to the complexities of the human mind, and the power that came from facing one's darkest fears.

Susan leaned forward, her dark eyes reflecting the warm glow of the sunset streaming through the office window. "Elizabeth," she began, her voice steady and reassuring, "you've shown immense strength and resilience throughout this entire ordeal. Remember when you first entered the labyrinth? You faced your deepest fears head-on and fought to uncover the truth."

Elizabeth nodded, recalling the sensation of her heart pounding in her chest as she navigated the twisted pathways that mirrored the convoluted recesses of her mind. The feel of cold sweat on her skin, while the whispers of lost memories echoed around her. Elizabeth hand unconsciously gripped the armrest, grounding herself in the present, even as her past called to her.

"Overcoming those challenges has helped you grow," Susan continued, her tone firm yet gentle. "You didn't let your guilt or fear consume you, but rather used it to fuel your determination."

Elizabeth exhaled a slow release of tension she hadn't realized she was holding and met Susan's gaze. "You're right," she murmured, her voice barely louder than the hum of her monitor on her desk. "I can feel the weight of Claire's death beginning to lessen... not disappear entirely, but enough for me to breathe again." She paused, allowing the words to settle, before continuing, "It's because I journeyed into the labyrinth and confronted my fears that I've reached this point."

Her thoughts drifted to the image of Claire, forever young and vibrant in Elizabeth's memory. They would never share laughter-filled moments again, but perhaps now, Elizabeth could begin to remember her sister without the crushing burden of guilt. It was a bittersweet realization, one that carried both relief and sorrow.

"Taking that first step towards understanding, acknowledging the darkness within yourself, is one of the hardest things to do," Susan said softly, her empathy shining through. "But you've done it, Elizabeth, and you're stronger for it."

"Thank you, Susan," Elizabeth whispered, her voice thick with gratitude and the weight of her journey. Elizabeth felt the fragile threads of healing beginning to weave themselves together within her. And though the road ahead was uncertain, she knew she would not walk it alone.

The office seemed to breathe with them, the soft rustle of tree branches outside the window punctuating their conversation. Susan leaned forward in her chair, resting her elbows on her knees. "You know, Elizabeth, you should be proud of how far you've come. Keep embracing this newfound appreciation for your strength—it's been incredible to witness your growth throughout this journey."

"Thank you, Susan," Elizabeth replied, her fingers absentmindedly tracing her desk. She took a slow breath, feeling the air fill her lungs and exhale, mingling with the sweet scent of summer flowers drifting through the open window.

"Remember when we first encountered the labyrinth?" Elizabeth said, her thoughts veering toward an earlier moment in their shared experiences. "I was terrified, but I also felt an undeniable pull towards it—something that compelled me to face my fears head-on."

"Absolutely," Susan agreed, nodding. "The labyrinth became a symbol of what lay within the depths of our minds. And as you ventured deeper into it, you confronted not only your demons but the collective traumas that haunted us all."

Elizabeth's heart quickened as she recalled the disorienting twists and turns of the labyrinth, the haunting echoes of voices that whispered secrets both familiar and foreign. It was there, in that surreal dreamscape, that she had discovered the true nature of fear—its ability to imprison the mind, to twist reality, and ultimately, to control one's destiny.

"Before this journey, I never truly grasped the complexities of the human mind or the power that our fears hold over us," she mused aloud. "But now, I understand that by confronting those fears—by facing the darkness that exists within each of us—we can begin to break free from their grasp."

"Exactly," Susan affirmed, her eyes reflecting the fading light of the setting sun. "It's a lesson that I, too, have learned alongside you. By facing our fears, we can not only empower ourselves but also help others to do the same."

As the shadows lengthened, spilling into the corners of the room like ink seeping through parchment, Elizabeth felt the truth of their words settles deep within her core. She knew that this journey had irrevocably changed her—as a psychologist, as a sister, and as a human being. Although there would always be new challenges ahead, she was ready to face them with courage, wisdom, and an unwavering belief in her strength.

"Empathy," Susan began, her voice soft and reflective, "is the cornerstone of our profession. But it's not until you truly experience someone else's fears—walk in their shoes, so to speak—that you begin to fathom the depths of the human psyche." She leaned back in her chair, her eyes lost in thought as the memories of their shared dream world swirled within her mind.

Elizabeth nodded, pondering the weight of Susan's words. The surreal experiences they had gone through together deepened their understanding of each other in ways they never could have anticipated. The labyrinthine corridors of the subconscious, where shadows and light danced together in a haunting waltz, had been a crucible for both of them. "I couldn't agree more, Susan. I'm grateful for the opportunity to have gone through this transformative journey. It has made me a better psychologist and person."

"Likewise," Susan replied, her warm smile acknowledging the bond that had been forged between them. She reached out and squeezed Elizabeth's hand reassuringly. "We've faced our demons together, my friend. It's been an honor to stand by your side."

Their journey into the heart of darkness had peeled away layers of their psyches, revealing hidden truths and fears that had lurked beneath the surface. For Elizabeth, it was the unresolved guilt over her sister Claire's mysterious death; for Susan, it was the struggle with self-doubt and the constant pressure to prove herself in a world that questioned her abilities.

"Before we embarked on this path, I never realized just how interconnected the mind is," Elizabeth mused, her gaze focused on the dwindling sunlight outside her office window. "Each fear, each memory, each emotion—they're all entwined like the roots of a tree, reaching down into our very core."

"Indeed," Susan agreed, her brow furrowed in contemplation. "And the deeper we delve, the more intricate and complex the connections become. It's a never-ending puzzle, one that constantly challenges our preconceived notions and forces us to grow."

As the sun dipped below the horizon, Elizabeth felt the echoes of their journey reverberate through her soul. The people they had encountered, the obstacles they had overcome—each had left an indelible mark on her being, reshaping her understanding of herself and her place in the world.

"Thank you, Susan," she whispered, her eyes glistening with unshed tears. "Thank you for standing by me, for believing in me even when I doubted myself. Without you, I don't know if I could have found the strength to face my past and confront my fears."

"Elizabeth," Dr. Park replied, her voice filled with emotion, "you are stronger than you give yourself credit for. Our journey only served to reveal what was already within you. And now, together, we can continue to help others find their inner strength."

The last vestiges of daylight vanished from the sky, leaving their office illuminated by the soft glow of the floor lamp. As the darkness enveloped them, it no longer held the same power over Elizabeth as it once had. For now, she understood that within the shadows lay the key to unlocking the mysteries of the human mind—and that it was there, amidst the tangled roots of fear and desire, that true healing could be found.

The rhythmic ticking of the clock on the wall punctuated the silence, a subtle reminder that time continued to move forward even as they sat steeped in contemplation. Elizabeth looked down at her hands, tracing the lines that marked her journey with a newfound sense of appreciation.

"Elizabeth," Susan began, breaking the silence, "as much as our experiences have taught us about the depths of the human mind, we must remember to take care of ourselves." She leaned forward, concern etching itself across her delicate features. "You've been through so much lately, and I can't emphasize enough the importance of allowing yourself time to heal."

Elizabeth nodded, but her thoughts remained tangled in the labyrinth of memories that had led her to this moment—the pain, the fear, and ultimately, the catharsis that had set her free from the chains of her past. "I know self-care is important, Susan," she admitted, "but sometimes it feels like there's still so much more to uncover."

"True healing takes time, Elizabeth," Susan responded, reaching out to place a reassuring hand on Elizabeth's shoulder. "And while it's admirable that you want to continue digging deeper, it's also crucial to recognize when you need to step back and allow yourself space to process."

As Elizabeth met her friend's gaze, she felt the truth of those words settles into the marrow of her bones. It was a balance she had always struggled with—the drive to push forward in pursuit of answers, often at the cost of her well-being.

"Thank you, Susan," Elizabeth murmured, her voice tinged with gratitude. "I'm lucky to have you by my side."

"Likewise, Elizabeth," Susan replied, her eyes shining with sincerity. "Our journey together has not only deepened my understanding of the human psyche but also solidified the bond between us. I've come to trust you implicitly, and I hope you feel the same."

"Of course," Elizabeth said, her heart swelling with affection. "I don't know what I would have done without your unwavering support and friendship. You've been my rock, Susan, and I will never forget that."

In the quietude that followed, Elizabeth allowed herself a moment of introspection. The tapestry of their shared experiences had woven a connection that transcended the boundaries of mere colleagueship, creating a bond forged in the crucible of their darkest fears and most profound revelations.

"Promise me something, Susan," Elizabeth whispered, her voice barely audible above the ticking clock. "Promise me that no matter where our paths may take us, we'll always be there for one another—to share our burdens and lift each other when it feels like we're drowning."

"Elizabeth," Susan replied, her eyes filled with resolve, "I promise."

As the echoes of their conversation dissipated into the night, Elizabeth knew that she could face whatever challenges lay ahead, bolstered by the knowledge that she would never again have to walk the path alone.

As Elizabeth stared at the fading light out her window. A sense of hope swelled within her, manifesting in the subtle curves of her lips and the gleam in her eyes.

"Listen, Susan," she said, turning to her friend, "our journey has taught me so much about the depths of the human mind and the power of confronting our fears. I hope it inspires others who may be struggling with their demons, showing them that there is light even in the darkest of places."

Susan leaned forward, her hands clasped around her coffee mug, and nodded thoughtfully. "I couldn't agree more, Elizabeth. There are countless people out there who need support, and our experiences can serve as a beacon of hope for them."

Elizabeth's gaze drifted towards the window, taking in the fiery hues of the sky as it bled into twilight. Elizabeth considered the labyrinthine paths they had traversed together, each twist and turn unearthing long-buried secrets and forcing her to confront the shadows of her past. The weight of her guilt over Claire's death had once been unbearable, but now, beneath the warm glow of the setting sun, she felt it beginning to loosen its grip.

"Through everything we've been through, I've learned that nobody should have to face their fears alone. That's why seeking help is so important—whether it's from friends, family, or professionals like us." Susan continued, the words tumbling out, driven by her newfound determination.

"Absolutely," Susan replied, her voice soft yet firm. "And remember, you're not alone either, Elizabeth. You have an entire network of friends and colleagues who care about you and will continue to support you through your healing process."

A gentle breeze whispered through the room, stirring up the scent of jasmine from the garden outside. It was a reminder of the ephemeral nature of life, and the importance of savoring each moment. Elizabeth closed her eyes for a brief second, drawing in a deep breath and allowing the fragrance to envelop her.

"Thank you," she murmured, her voice laced with gratitude. "Knowing I have people like you in my corner makes all the difference."

As the last vestiges of daylight slipped away, shadows crept into the room, casting an intimate veil over the two friends. They sat in companionable silence, their hearts brimming with a shared understanding of the strength that could be found in vulnerability.

"Let's make a promise, Susan," Elizabeth said, her fingers tracing patterns on the windowsill as she spoke. "Let's use this journey we've been through—our growth, our discoveries—to help others find their way back from the darkness."

"Deal," Dr. Park replied, her smile radiant in the gathering dusk. "Together, we'll show them that healing is possible and that facing our fears can lead us to a brighter future."

Emboldened by the support of her friend and the hope that their experiences might illuminate the path for others, Elizabeth felt the shackles of her past loosen further. In the fading light, she saw her reflection in the window, and for the first time in a long while, she recognized the resilient woman gazing back at her—a testament to the power of confronting one's deepest fears.

The sun dipped below the horizon, casting long shadows across Elizabeth's office. Susan leaned back in her chair, an air of determination settling around her. "We'll carry this forward, Elizabeth—our newfound understanding of the human mind and its complexities. It will be our mission to help others confront their fears and find healing."

Elizabeth nodded, her gaze drifting to the holographic displays hovering above her sleek, minimalist desk. : images of Claire, her parents, and herself as a child. A bittersweet smile tugged at her lips. "Yes," she agreed, her voice steady. "We can't change the past, but we can shape the future by sharing our knowledge and compassion with those who need it most."

"Exactly," Susan replied, her dark eyes full of empathy. "And remember, you don't have to shoulder this responsibility alone. We're in this together."

As she spoke, Elizabeth felt a warmth emanating from her friend, enveloping her like a protective embrace. Her chest swelled with gratitude and hope, a flicker of light that chased away the shadows of her past. Elizabeth knew the road to healing would be long, but for the first time, she felt equipped to navigate its twists and turns.

"Thank you, Susan," she murmured, her fingers seamlessly gliding over the holographic interface of her futuristic desk. "Your support has been invaluable to me. I can't imagine going through this without you by my side."

Susan reached out, placing a comforting hand on Elizabeth's arm. "You'll never have to, my friend."

They sat in the dim room, the last remnants of daylight filtering through the window. The silence between them was charged with purpose, each woman fortified by the other's strength and resolve. As they prepared to leave, Elizabeth paused at the door, her heart brimming with emotion.

"Let's do this," she whispered, her voice thick with conviction. "For Claire, for ourselves, and for all those who have yet to find their way."

"Agreed," Susan said softly, her smile a beacon of hope in the encroaching darkness.

Together, they stepped into the night, their lives forever changed by the arduous journey they had undertaken. Elizabeth carried with her the knowledge that she was no longer bound by the chains of guilt and fear; instead, transformed by the trials she had faced, she now held the key to unlocking the secrets of the human psyche—and the power to help others do the same.

As the stars emerged overhead, the soft glow of peace settled over Elizabeth's heart, illuminating the path to a brighter future.

The moonlight filtering through the trees cast an ethereal glow on the path ahead, as if guiding Elizabeth and Susan toward a new chapter in their lives. Their footsteps crunched softly against the gravel, the only sound in the otherwise still night.

"Elizabeth," Susan began, her voice quiet but steady, "do you remember that moment in the labyrinth when we first encountered our fears? The way they manifested themselves in front of us?"

Elizabeth nodded, shivering slightly at the memory. "It's hard to forget. But it wasn't just the fear that was overwhelming; it was also the realization that we had been carrying them with us for so long."

"Exactly," Susan agreed, her eyes reflecting the determination that had brought them this far. "It was in confronting those fears head-on that we started to break free from their grasp. We learned that the monsters lurking in the shadows of our minds could be overcome."

As they walked, Elizabeth replayed fragments of their journey in her mind, marveling at the resilience she and Susan had displayed in the face of unimaginable adversity. Elizabeth thought of the intricate layers of her psyche, peeled back one by one like the petals of a flower, each revealing a deeper understanding of herself and the human condition.

"Sometimes, I can't help but wonder what would have happened if we hadn't embarked on this journey," Elizabeth mused, her words trailing off into the night air.

"Perhaps we'd still be trapped in our mental prisons," Susan replied, her gaze meeting Elizabeth's. "But instead, we chose to step out of our comfort zones, challenge ourselves, and confront our deepest fears. And now, here we are—stronger, wiser, and more capable than ever before."

"Indeed," Elizabeth whispered, her breath visible in the cool evening air. "I've come to understand that our minds are not fixed, unchanging entities. They're malleable and adaptable, as long as we're willing to confront the darkness within."

"Exactly," Susan affirmed, her eyes shining with an unwavering belief in their shared purpose. "And as psychologists, we must help others navigate that darkness—to guide them toward the light that lies beyond."

As they continued down the moonlit path, Elizabeth couldn't help but feel a profound sense of gratitude for the trials they had faced together. Each harrowing encounter, each heart-wrenching revelation, had served to strengthen their bond—a bond forged in fire, tempered by adversity, and ultimately transformed into something unbreakable.

"Thank you, Susan," she murmured, her voice thick with emotion. "For everything."

"Thank you, too, Elizabeth," Susan replied, her smile a testament to the enduring connection they shared. "We've come so far, but I know there's still much work to be done—and I can't imagine facing it without you."

In the quiet of the night, as the stars above bore witness, Elizabeth and Susan moved forward, their hearts lighter and their resolve stronger than ever before. Side by side, they walked toward a future filled with hope, healing, and the knowledge that together, they could overcome even the darkest corners of the human psyche.

Chapter 23

Elizabeth tapped her fingers on the sleek, holographic desk, her eyes flitting between the photographs of Anna and Mr. Thompson. The uneasy feeling in her chest refused to dissipate, and she realized that she needed a break from the darkness engulfing her patients' lives. She snatched her sleek, transparent phone from the meticulously organized holographic workstation. and dialed Sarah's number, an old friend who had always been a beacon of light during her darkest moments.

"Hey, Colleen, it's Elizabeth. I know it's been a while, but do you want to meet up for coffee? I could use some company."

"Of course! It's been too long, Elizabeth. Let's catch up at Café de Lune tomorrow afternoon around three?"

"Sounds perfect. See you then," Elizabeth replied, a genuine smile tugging at the corners of her lips. They exchanged a few more pleasantries before ending the call.

The following day, Elizabeth stepped into the warm embrace of Café de Lune afuturistic haven where holographic displays shimmered with interactive menus, and sleek, levitating drones served steaming cups of synthetically brewed coffee. The air was filled with a gentle hum of technology, and the soft glow of augmented reality projections adorned the space. . Its inviting atmosphere was a welcome respite from the cold winter's day. The café sparkled with sleek, minimalist furniture and holographic displays, creating an ambiance that seamlessly blended comfort with cutting-edge design. Virtual reality books floated in mid-air on levitating shelves, their covers changing with a touch to suit the reader's preferences. An ethereal, synthesized melody accompanied the soft hum of advanced coffee machines producing steaming cups of specialty brews. Aromas of molecular gastronomy-inspired treats, synthesized to perfection, filled the air, enhancing the sensory experience in this haven.

"Elizabeth!" Colleen exclaimed from a corner table, waving her over. Her golden hair framed her face like a halo, casting a soft glow against her pale skin. Elizabeth couldn't help but notice how little Sarah had changed since their college days—still the bright, warm presence she had always been.

"Colleen, it's so good to see you," Elizabeth said, embracing her friend. As they settled into their chairs, a hovering service drone, equipped with holographic menus, gracefully approached to take their orders: : a cappuccino for Elizabeth and a chai latte for Colleen.

"Tell me everything," Colleen urged, her eyes shining with curiosity. "How's life treating you?"

"Where do I even begin?" Elizabeth sighed, rubbing her temple. She launched into an account of her professional accomplishments and the challenges she faced in her work as a psychologist. However, she carefully avoided mentioning the shared nightmares haunting her patients, unwilling to burden Sarah with her growing obsession.

As they sipped their drinks, the conversation shifted to their shared past. They laughed about their youthful escapades, reminiscing on late-night study sessions that turned into impromptu dance parties, fueled by equal parts caffeine and adrenaline. They exchanged tales of heartbreak and triumphs, weaving a tapestry of memories that bound them together.

"Remember when we snuck into the observatory freshman year?" Colleen asked, her eyes twinkling with mischief. "We spent all night stargazing and talking about our dreams for the future."

"Of course," Elizabeth replied, a nostalgic smile playing on her lips. "I think that night was when I first realized how much I wanted to help people and understand the complexities of the human mind."

"Speaking of which," Colleen said, leaning in conspiratorially, "how are your endeavors coming along? Have you made any progress in finding answers about your sister's death?"

Elizabeth hesitated, her grip tightening around her cup. While she longed to confide in her friend, she knew it wasn't the right time or place. Instead, she forced a smile and shook her head. "Not yet, but I won't give up. I can't."

"Knowing you, I'd expect nothing less," Colleen replied, giving Elizabeth's hand a reassuring squeeze. "You've always been the most determined person I know."

As they continued to reminisce and exchange stories about their current lives, Elizabeth felt some of the weight from her shoulders lifting. For a few hours, she could forget the labyrinthine nightmares and focus on the warm familiarity of her friendship with Colleen. And for the first time in months, she felt a glimmer of hope that perhaps there was still light to be found even amidst the darkest shadows.

A gust of wind blew through the open door of the cozy café, scattering dried leaves across the floor in a whirlwind dance. Elizabeth shivered and watched as the barista hurried to close the door, trapping the warmth inside. She glanced at Colleen, who was engrossed in her steaming cup of tea, and decided it was time to delve into deeper waters.

"Colleen," she began hesitantly, "I've been going through some difficult times lately." Her words tumbled like an avalanche, each one pushing the next forward with increasing momentum. "My sister's death has left me feeling... lost."

Colleen's eyes softened with understanding as she reached across the table and placed a comforting hand on Elizabeth's arm. "I can't imagine how hard that must be for you," she said gently. "But I know you, Liz - you're strong. You'll get through this."

Elizabeth sighed, staring down at her coffee, the steamy tendrils curling up like ghostly fingers. "It's not just her death," she admitted, her voice barely above a whisper. "It's everything that's come after. The nightmares, the uncertainty... the fear that I'm losing touch with reality."

"Is that why you've been isolating yourself?" Colleen asked, her brow furrowing with concern.

"Partly," Elizabeth confessed, her fingers tracing patterns in the condensation on her cup. "But also, I've been trying to grow, to heal. I've started attending therapy sessions with Dr. Susan Park, and I've even joined a support group for people who've experienced trauma."

"Really?" Colleen exclaimed, genuine surprise coloring her tone. "That's amazing, Liz! You've always been so private about your emotions. This is such a big step for you."

Elizabeth smiled faintly, acknowledging the truth in her friend's words. "I suppose it is. And honestly, it's been helping. Slowly, but surely, I'm starting to feel more... grounded."

"See?" Colleen said a triumphant note in her voice. "I always knew you could do it. You just needed to permit yourself to lean on others for support."

"Which brings me to you," Elizabeth continued, her gaze meeting Colleen's. "Throughout all of this, you've been such an incredible friend. You're always there when I need you, and you never judge me or try to fix my problems. You simply listen, and sometimes that's all I need."

"Of course, Liz," Colleen replied, her eyes glistening with unshed tears. "That's what friends are for. We're here to hold each other up when life tries to knock us down."

"Thank you," Elizabeth whispered, feeling the knot in her chest begins to unravel. "For everything."

As they sat in companionable silence, sipping their drinks and watching the rain patter against the windows, Elizabeth felt a sense of peace wash over her. At that moment, she knew that no matter how dark her world became, she would never be alone.

"Speaking of support," Colleen said, breaking the silence between them. "There's a group of people I think you should meet. They've helped me through some rough times, and I believe they could do the same for you."

"Really?" Elizabeth asked hesitantly, suddenly apprehensive about the prospect of meeting new people.

"Trust me," Colleen encouraged, her eyes filled with warmth and sincerity. "They're a diverse bunch, but what they all have in common is their dedication to personal growth and helping others. I think you'll fit right in."

A week later, Elizabeth found herself standing outside the door of a quaint brick house, clutching a bottle of wine as a gift for the host. She took a deep breath, trying to calm her racing heart, and knocked on the door. As it swung open, she was greeted by the sight of Colleen, beaming brightly.

"Come on in, Liz!" Colleen exclaimed, pulling her friend into the warm embrace of the room. The air buzzed with laughter and conversation, the walls adorned with eclectic artwork that seemed to tell a hundred stories.

"Let me introduce you to everyone," Colleen said, guiding Elizabeth through the crowd. They stopped first at a tall man with salt-and-pepper hair who exuded an air of quiet confidence. "Liz, this is Michael. He's a writer and has some incredible insights on the human psyche."

"Nice to meet you, Elizabeth," Michael said, extending his hand. "I've heard a lot about your work from Colleen."

"Thank you," Elizabeth replied, feeling the first flicker of curiosity ignited within her. "I'd love to hear more about your writing sometime."

As the evening progressed, Elizabeth found herself drawn into spirited debates on topics ranging from the nature of consciousness to the impact of early trauma on adult relationships. She felt both challenged and invigorated, her mind whirring with new ideas and perspectives.

"Elizabeth, come join us!" called out a woman with an infectious laugh. She introduced herself as Maya, an artist who used her work to explore the complexities of emotion. "We're discussing the power of vulnerability in creating authentic connections."

"Vulnerability," Elizabeth mused, considering the word that had once terrified her. But as she looked around the room, at the faces of these strangers-turned-friends, she felt emboldened. They were all here, sharing their stories and insights, bound together by a desire for understanding and growth.

"Alright," she said, taking a seat beside Maya. And as she opened up about her struggles and the journey that had brought her to this point, Elizabeth felt a sense of connection, unlike anything she'd experienced before. These people, with their open hearts and minds, offered her a glimpse into a world where vulnerability was not a weakness, but a strength.

As the night wore on, the conversations shifted and deepened, interspersed with moments of laughter and shared joy. For the first time in what felt like forever, Elizabeth allowed herself to be truly seen, to let down the walls she'd so carefully constructed around her heart.

"Thank you," she whispered to Colleen as they stood on the doorstep, saying their goodbyes. "For bringing me here, and for believing in me."

"Always," Colleen replied, her eyes shining with pride. "This is just the beginning, Liz. There's so much more waiting for you. All you have to do is reach out and embrace it."

And as Elizabeth walked away from the house, she knew that the darkness which had once consumed her was now held at bay by the light of new friendships, understanding, and hope.

The door to the dimly lit room creaked open, revealing a circle of chairs occupied by people who wore their pain like invisible armor. Elizabeth hesitated at the threshold, the air thick with a mixture of vulnerability and empathy. The support group leader, a kind-eyed woman named Alice, beckoned her inside with an encouraging nod.

"Welcome, Elizabeth," Alice said softly, gesturing for her to take a seat in the circle. "We're glad you could join us."

"Thank you," Elizabeth murmured, lowering herself into a vacant chair. She glanced around at the faces of the others, searching for a connection in their eyes as she fought back the rising tide of emotion within her.

"Would you like to begin by sharing your story?" Alice asked, her voice gentle but unwavering. "Remember, this is a safe space. We're all here to listen and support one another."

Elizabeth took a deep breath, feeling the weight of her sister's unexplained death heavy on her chest. She began to speak, her voice trembling at first, but gradually finding strength as she recounted the harrowing events that had shaped her life. As she spoke, she watched the expressions of understanding and compassion on the faces of those around her and felt a warmth spread through her, a solace born from shared suffering.

"Thank you for sharing, Elizabeth," Alice said when she was finished. "I know it's not easy, but we've all found healing in giving voice to our pain."

"Dr. Park suggested I come here," Elizabeth admitted, casting her eyes downward. "She thought it would help me process everything I've been through."

"Speaking of Dr. Park," Alice smiled warmly, "I believe you have an appointment with her later today, don't you?"

Elizabeth nodded, a flicker of gratitude crossing her face. "Yes, she's been an incredible support for me. I don't know where I'd be without her guidance."

"Let's all take a moment to reflect on the stories we've heard today," Alice suggested, "and then we'll move on to our next activity."

As the room fell silent, Elizabeth found herself lost in thoughts of the therapy session with Dr. Susan Park that awaited her later that day. She imagined the familiar comfort of her therapist's office, the smell of lavender oil that always lingered in the air.

"Elizabeth," Dr. Park said, her voice soothing as she gestured toward her plush armchair, "please, sit down."

"Thank you, Susan," Elizabeth replied, sinking into the soft cushions and allowing herself to relax.

"Let's talk about your progress," Dr. Park began, leaning forward with an air of genuine interest. "How has attending the support group been for you?"

"Surprisingly, it's been... healing," Elizabeth admitted, a slight smile playing at the corners of her lips. "Being able to share my story with others who understand, who have gone through their traumas, it's... freeing."

"Your willingness to open up is a testament to your strength, Elizabeth," Dr. Park praised, her eyes warm with pride. "I'm so glad you've found solace in the group."

"Thanks to you, Susan," Elizabeth said, her gratitude shining through. "You've guided me toward accepting my past, embracing my present, and moving forward with hope."

"Remember," Dr. Park added gently, "healing isn't linear, and neither is life. You're making incredible progress, but there will still be challenges ahead. Just know that I'm here for you, every step of the way."

"Thank you," Elizabeth whispered, her heart swelling with appreciation. As she sat in that nurturing space, surrounded by the quiet strength of her fellow survivors and the unwavering support of her therapist, she knew that the road to healing was one she no longer had to walk alone.

"Every brushstroke is a step toward self-discovery," Elizabeth murmured, her voice barely audible above the soft rustling of the canvas beneath her paintbrush. She had long admired the works of others - the layers of color and emotion that seemed to leap from the canvas, demanding to be seen. Now, she found herself completely absorbed in her exploration of the art form, crafting landscapes and abstracts that bore the weight of her unspoken thoughts.

As she swirled cerulean blue into the tumultuous ocean scene before her, Elizabeth marveled at the transformative power of her newfound hobby. Each stroke of the brush seemed to coax forth a piece of herself that had been locked away for so long, buried beneath the weight of her past. Painting provided an outlet for expression, unlike anything she had ever experienced, leaving her feeling lighter and more at peace with each completed work.

"Your progress has been remarkable, Dr. Harmon," said her art instructor, Ms. Monroe, as she examined Elizabeth's latest piece. "The depth and intensity in your work speak volumes."

"Thank you, Ms. Monroe," Elizabeth replied, a sense of pride swelling within her chest. "It's been a journey I never knew I needed, but I'm grateful for it."

Ms. Monroe nodded knowingly, her eyes lingering on the powerful waves crashing against the rocky shore. "Art has a way of revealing truths we never knew existed within us. Keep exploring, Elizabeth. You have a gift."

With each day spent in the tranquil embrace of her studio, Elizabeth felt the frayed edges of her soul begin to mend as if the colors and textures of her creations were weaving together the fragmented pieces of her identity. It was an unexpected gift, one that she cherished with every fiber of her being.

"Remember to breathe, Elizabeth," the soothing voice of the mindfulness retreat leader instructed, guiding her through meditation exercises designed to anchor her in the present moment. Inhaling deeply, she allowed herself to be enveloped by the scent of pine needles and damp earth as she sat on a cushion beneath the towering trees.

"Notice the sensation of your breath as it enters your body," the leader continued, "and allow it to carry away any tension or stress within you."

As Elizabeth focused on her breath, an image of her sister's face emerged in her mind, no longer shrouded in darkness but bathed in a warm, golden light. The pain of losing her felt more distant now, softened by the passage of time and the healing embrace of self-discovery. She knew that her journey was far from over - there would still be days when sorrow threatened to consume her - but at this moment, amidst the dappled sunlight and the gentle whisper of leaves, she felt the stirrings of inner peace.

"By cultivating mindfulness," the retreat leader intoned, "we can learn to accept our past, acknowledge our emotions, and discover the strength to move forward with grace."

"Thank you," Elizabeth whispered, her heart echoing with gratitude, for the healing power of art, for the wisdom of mindfulness, and the promise of a future filled with hope.

A cacophony of voices filled the air, mingling with the aroma of freshly brewed coffee and homemade pastries. Elizabeth stood at the entrance of the bustling charity bake sale, her hands filled with trays of her gingerbread cookies, the delicate swirls of icing a testament to her newfound creative passion. She hesitated for a moment, her heart racing with anticipation as she prepared to immerse herself in the warmth of human connection.

"Dr. Harmon!" A cheerful voice called out, and Elizabeth turned to see Sarah weaving through the crowd, her eyes sparkling with enthusiasm. "I'm so glad you could make it! Your cookies look amazing."

"Thank you," Elizabeth replied, feeling a surge of pride at her friend's genuine admiration. "I've enjoyed exploring my artistic side. It's been quite therapeutic."

"Isn't it wonderful how helping others can also help us heal?" Sarah mused, guiding Elizabeth toward their designated table. "There's something truly special about coming together as a community for a good cause."

As they arranged the cookies alongside an array of other delectable treats, Elizabeth couldn't help but agree. The energy in the room was electric, an infectious blend of generosity and camaraderie that seemed to lift her spirits higher with each passing minute. As she exchanged pleasantries with fellow volunteers and customers, she felt a sense of belonging that had eluded her for much of her adult life.

"Remember to breathe," Elizabeth reminded herself, drawing on the mindfulness techniques she'd learned during her recent retreat. While the bustling atmosphere was exhilarating, it was also overwhelming at times, threatening to send her anxiety spiraling out of control. But each measured inhalation brought clarity and calm, allowing her to remain grounded amidst the chaos.

"Your cookies are selling like hotcakes!" Sarah exclaimed, grinning from ear to ear as she handed another satisfied customer their change. "You've made a difference today, Elizabeth."

"Thank you," she replied once more, her heart swelling with gratitude. "I couldn't have done it without your support and encouragement."

"Of course," Sarah said warmly, giving her friend's hand a reassuring squeeze. "That's what friends are for."

As the sun dipped below the horizon, painting the sky with hues of violet and indigo, Elizabeth found herself standing on the edge of a windswept cliff, the salty breeze tousling her hair as she gazed out at the vast expanse of ocean before her. The solo trip had been a spontaneous decision, fueled by a desire to test the limits of her newfound independence and self-awareness.

"Where will this journey take me?" She pondered, the question echoing in her mind like a riddle waiting to be solved. And though the answer remained elusive, the very act of asking felt like a victory, a testament to the resilience and courage that had blossomed within her during these past few weeks.

A sudden gust of wind tugged at her scarf, sending it fluttering like a wayward kite toward the waves below. Instinctively, Elizabeth reached out to catch it, her fingertips grazing the silken fabric just as it slipped from her grasp.

"Let it go," she whispered to herself, watching as the scarf vanished into the twilight, carried away by the whims of fate. "Sometimes, we must embrace the unknown to truly find ourselves."

With a deep, steadying breath, Elizabeth stepped forward into the darkness, her heart a beacon of hope amidst the shadows, guiding her toward the promise of self-discovery and the infinite possibilities that lay ahead.

The silhouette of her childhood home loomed before Elizabeth like a specter from the past, its weathered walls and ivy-clad facades whispering secrets she had long sought to suppress. She hesitated at the gate, her fingers tightening around the cold iron bars as if seeking assurance that this was reality and not some twisted figment of her imagination.

"Forgive me," she murmured, the words a fervent prayer that floated on the breeze, mingling with the distant rustle of leaves and the haunting cries of birds overhead.

"Elizabeth?" Her father voice emerged from the shadows, tentative yet unmistakable. Their eyes met, and Elizabeth was struck by the raw vulnerability etched on her father face, a mirror image of her inner turmoil.

"Dad, I—I've come back to make amends." Elizabeth took a deep breath, feeling the weight of a thousand unspoken apologies pressing down upon her shoulders. " I'd like to try and heal our relationship."

Her father's gaze softened, tears glistening in the corners of his eyes. "I've been waiting for this moment, Elizabeth. We have a lot to talk about."

As they stepped inside the house, memories swirled around Elizabeth like phantom echoes, each room a testament to the love and pain that had once filled these walls. The dining table, where laughter and arguments had intermingled in an intricate dance; the living room, where she had shared countless hours of whispered confessions with her sister; the study, where the seeds of her obsession had first taken root.

"Can you ever forgive me for the distance I put between us?" Elizabeth asked, her voice barely above the creaking floorboards beneath her feet.

"Elizabeth, we all carry our burdens and make mistakes," her father replied, his hand reaching out to rest gently on Elizabeth's shoulder. "What matters now is that we move forward, together."

As they sat in the old armchairs, sharing stories and tears, Elizabeth felt a sense of catharsis taking hold, the walls she had built around her heart beginning to crumble. She reflected on the journey that had brought her to this moment, acknowledging the challenges she had faced and the strength she had gained in overcoming them.

"Facing my past has been like navigating a labyrinth," she mused, her thoughts drifting like shadows across the room. "Each twist and turn revealed a new facet of myself, and it has taken all the courage I could muster to confront my fears and seek the truth."

"Your sister would be proud," her father whispered, his eyes glistening with unshed tears. "She always believed in your ability to heal and grow, even when you couldn't see it yourself."

"Thank you, Dad." Elizabeth reached for her father's hand, their fingers intertwining like roots seeking sustenance in the fertile soil. "I couldn't have made it this far without your unconditional love and support."

In the dimly lit room, surrounded by echoes of the past and the promise of a brighter future, Elizabeth embraced the transformative power of forgiveness and reconciliation. And as the shadows began to recede, she knew that she was finally ready to face whatever lay ahead, her heart a beacon of hope amidst the darkness, guiding her toward the infinite possibilities that awaited.

The sun hung low on the horizon, its warm golden rays casting a halo around the world outside Elizabeth's window. She stood there, taking in the serenity of the small suburban street, the quiet hum of life unfolding beyond the glass pane. The scent of freshly brewed coffee and the faint sound of her father humming a familiar tune wafted through the air, grounding her in the present moment.

"Sometimes, I find it hard to believe how much my life has changed," she said softly, speaking to herself as well as to the universe that shimmered like a mirage before her eyes.

"Change can be a powerful thing, Lizzy," her father replied, entering the room with a steaming cup of coffee in each hand. He handed one to her, its warmth seeping into her chilled fingers, anchoring her further into the now.

"Thank you, Dad," she murmured, her gaze still fixed on the tranquil scene outside. "It's just...I never thought I could find such peace and happiness after everything."

Her father wrapped an arm around her shoulders, drawing her close. "You've earned it," he whispered, his breath stirring the tendrils of her dark hair. "You fought through the darkness to reach this place of light."

Elizabeth took a slow, deep breath, allowing the realization to settle within her: she had indeed fought, and she had won. It was a victory she would savor, carried on the wings of gratitude for the support and love that had buoyed her throughout her journey.

"Hey, look who I found!" Sarah called from the doorway, a bright smile gracing her features as she entered the room, followed by Dr. Susan Park.

"Surprise!" Susan exclaimed, her eyes sparkling with genuine warmth. "I heard you were in town and couldn't resist stopping by to see how you're doing."

"Susan," Elizabeth breathed, her heart swelling with affection for the woman who had helped her navigate the treacherous waters of self-discovery and healing. "I can't thank you enough for everything."

"Think nothing of it, dear," Susan replied, giving her a gentle squeeze on the shoulder. "It's been an honor to witness your journey."

As they settled into the comfortable living room, laughter and conversation bubbling around her, Elizabeth marveled at the tapestry of connection and love that had been woven around her. Each person present had played a role in her growth—Sarah and her new friends, who had expanded her horizons; the support group members, who had shared their stories and offered solace; and her family, who had stood by her..

At this moment, she felt the full weight of her rebuilt personal life, the foundation of peace and happiness upon which she now stood. And as she let herself sink into the embrace of these relationships, the warmth of the setting sunbathing her face, Elizabeth knew that she had found something precious: a sanctuary, a haven, a place where she could finally be free.

Chapter 24

Dr. Elizabeth Harmon glanced at her watch, the ticking second hand amplifying the urgency she felt. Her newest patient was scheduled to arrive any moment now. She took a deep breath and steadied herself for the meeting. As she pressed her hands against her cold desk, the door to her office opened with a soft creak.

"Hello," the man said, his voice trembling slightly as he reached to shake her hand. He appeared to be in his early 30s, with short, messy hair and a gaunt look about him. His eyes darted around the room, never settling on one place for long—a sure sign of anxiety. Dr. Harmon noticed that his shirt was damp with sweat, despite the chill in the air.

"Please, have a seat," Elizabeth gestured toward the chair opposite her. The man hesitated before slowly lowering himself into it, perching on the edge as if ready to bolt at any moment.

"Thank you for coming in today," she began, her tone gentle and reassuring. "I understand that you've been experiencing some distressing nightmares."

The man swallowed hard, his Adam's apple bobbing visibly. "Yes," he whispered, staring down at his clenched fists. "It's always the same dream. It starts normal enough, but then... everything changes."

"Can you describe the dream for me?" Elizabeth asked, her pen poised above her notepad.

He took a shuddering breath. "I find myself in a labyrinth—an endless maze of twisting, turning corridors. The walls are made of stone, slick with moisture, like something ancient and primal. It's so dark I can barely see, but I can feel... something watching me, stalking me through the shadows." The man's voice grew more strained as he spoke, his body tensing as though bracing for an unseen threat.

"Go on," Elizabeth prompted gently, her eyes never leaving his face.

"Every time I turn a corner or enter a new passage, I hear whispers—voices that seem to be coming from the very walls themselves. They tell me that I'll never escape, that I'm trapped forever in this nightmare. And then... then the ground starts to shift beneath my feet, like it's alive and trying to swallow me whole." He paused, his breaths coming in short gasps now. "I don't know what's worse—the feeling of being hunted, or the knowledge that even if I somehow manage to evade whatever's after me, I'll still be lost in that maze for all eternity."

Elizabeth nodded slowly, her heart aching for the man before her. She recognized the fear that clung to him like a shroud, the terror that seeped into every fiber of his being. This was no ordinary nightmare—it was something far more insidious and malevolent. And she would do everything in her power to help him find a way out.

Elizabeth closed her eyes for a moment, allowing herself to fully absorb the patient's story. It was as if she could feel the cold, unyielding stones of the labyrinth pressing against her skin and hear the whispers echoing in her head. With each breath, she delved deeper into the collective unconscious, searching for connections that might reveal the nature of this haunting nightmare.

"Your dream, it speaks to something primal within us all," Elizabeth began, her voice steady and confident. "The labyrinth is an ancient symbol representing both our internal and external worlds. The winding paths and dead ends reflect the complexities of the human mind and the challenges we face navigating through life."

She opened her eyes to meet her patient, seeing the flicker of recognition there. "This maze you find yourself trapped in—it's a manifestation of your deepest fears and anxieties. The walls, impossibly high and suffocating, represent the obstacles you perceive to be insurmountable. They close in around you, making it nearly impossible to breathe. And yet, you continue to search for a way out, driven by some unseen force."

"Every step you take, every corner you turn, brings you closer to confronting the darkness that stalks you from the shadows. This entity embodies your darkest thoughts and self-doubt, feeding off your fear. But remember, it exists only because you give it power. To confront it is to face your demons."

The patient's eyes widened with a sense of revelation, but also a hint of trepidation. "But how do I escape the maze, Doctor Harmon? How do I free myself from this nightmare?"

Elizabeth leaned forward, offering a comforting hand on his shoulder. "That is a journey only you can take, but I will be here to guide you every step of the way. We will explore the depths of your mind and confront the fears that bind you to this labyrinth. Together, I will help you find the strength to tear down the walls and face the darkness that haunts you."

"Remember," she continued, her voice resolute, "the maze is a reflection of your inner self. It may twist and turn in unexpected ways, but with each step forward, you claim control over its power. By understanding the metaphorical nature of your nightmare, you can begin to unravel its mysteries and ultimately discover the key to your liberation."

As they spoke, a sense of determination began to radiate from Elizabeth's patient. Though his journey was far from over, he now had a glimmer of hope—a guiding light to illuminate the shadows of his subconscious and lead him toward freedom. And with Elizabeth by his side, he would never have to face the darkness alone.

The air grew thick and suffocating as Elizabeth guided her patient through the twisted labyrinth of his nightmare. She could feel the weight of his fear, a tangible shroud that clung to every surface like a damp fog. Faint echoes of forgotten screams hung in the air, each one a testament to the countless souls who had been lost within these walls.

"Remember to breathe," Elizabeth gently reminded him, her voice a beacon of warmth amidst the darkness. "Focus on the present moment. Each step we take together is a step towards reclaiming your power over this place."

Her patient hesitated, his breaths shallow and unsteady. "I-I can't go any further, Dr. Harmon. The shadows ... they're alive. They're waiting for me."

"Those shadows are nothing more than manifestations of your fears," she assured him, her eyes never leaving his. "To conquer them, you must confront the truth that lies within your heart. The labyrinth may be treacherous, but it is nothing compared to the strength you possess."

He swallowed hard, nodding his head with a newfound determination. "Alright, let's do this."

As they ventured deeper into the maze, the once-distant whispers grew louder and more insistent, clawing at the edges of their minds. Elizabeth could see the terror flickering behind her patient's eyes, threatening to consume him if he wavered.

"Stay close to me," she urged, her hand gripping his with reassuring strength. "We will face these challenges together. You are not alone."

"Thank you, Dr. Harmon," he whispered, his voice raw with emotion. "I don't know what I'd do without you."

Together, they navigated the labyrinth's winding corridors, flanked by towering walls that seemed to close in around them. With each turn, they were met with new obstacles—rickety bridges suspended over abyssal chasms, labyrinthine hallways that stretched on for eternity, and monstrous shadows that lurked just beyond the reach of their vision.

"Focus on your inner strength," Elizabeth encouraged him as they faced each challenge. "Remember, the nightmare is a reflection of your mind, and you have the power to reshape it."

"Dr. Harmon, I-I think there's something up ahead," her patient stammered, his eyes wide with terror. "It's... it's coming for me."

"Face it head-on," she commanded, her voice unwavering. "You are stronger than anything this maze can throw at you."

As the looming threat drew closer, its monstrous form shrouded in darkness, Elizabeth could sense her patient's resolve faltering. But she refused to let him succumb to his fears. Elizabeth stood tall beside him, her presence a fierce reminder that he was not alone in this battle.

"Together," she whispered, steeling herself against the encroaching darkness. "We will conquer this nightmare and emerge victorious."

The labyrinth stretched before them, an intricate dance of shadows and despair. It breathed life into the very walls that sought to entrap them, their cold stone surfaces pulsating with a sinister energy. Elizabeth's patient, his face pale, clung to her side as they ventured deeper into this dreamscape realm.

"Listen," she whispered, her voice barely audible in the stillness that suffocated the air. "Every step we take together is a testament to your strength."

He nodded solemnly, the weight of his fear etched across his features. As they continued on their precarious journey, the very fabric of reality seemed to warp around them. Time melted away like wax, leaving only the labyrinth's twisted embrace.

"Voices, Dr. Harmon... I hear them," he murmured, his eyes darting frantically through the darkness. The whispers clawed at the edges of his sanity, threatening to tear him apart from within.

"Focus on my voice," Elizabeth urged, guiding him through the dissonant chorus. "You control this narrative, not the nightmare."

With newfound determination, he pushed forward, his grip on Elizabeth's hand tightening as though it were a lifeline. They crossed a bridge of fragmented memories, each footfall echoing through the void. Specters of his past materialized before them, phantoms of regret and sorrow, but he refused to yield to their siren call.

"Dr. Harmon, they're showing me things... Things I wish to forget," he choked out, his breath coming in ragged gasps.

"Confront them," she replied, her tone resolute. "Acknowledge their existence, but do not let them define you."

Each specter he faced seemed to imbue him with a newfound strength, his eyes shining with a fierce defiance. They traversed an ocean of shifting sands, where the winds threatened to tear them apart, yet he held fast, his determination unwavering.

"Almost there," Elizabeth murmured, her voice tinged with awe at the resilience he displayed. "Just a little farther."

Finally, they stood before an imposing door, its surface etched with intricate symbols that seemed to writhe and squirm beneath their gaze. The patient hesitated, his courage faltering in the face of this final obstacle.

"Dr. Harmon, what if I can't do it? What if it's too much?"

"Trust yourself," she replied, her voice gentle but firm. "Remember everything we've overcome together. You are not alone in this fight."

With a deep breath, he steeled himself for what lay beyond, his resolve burning brighter than ever before. As the door swung open, revealing the darkness within, he stepped forward, emboldened by the newfound strength he had discovered within himself.

The darkness enveloped them, an inky void that seemed to pulse with malevolent intent. His breathing quickened, his heart thundering in his chest as he fought to keep his composure.

"Dr. Harmon," he whispered, his voice trembling, "I can't see a thing. What if I lose myself in this black abyss?"

"Focus on my voice," Elizabeth replied, her tone steady and calm. "Let me be your anchor. The darkness may surround us, but it cannot consume us."

Elizabeth guidance felt like a lifeline, a beacon of light amidst the suffocating shadows. As they navigated the treacherous terrain, she offered insights into the symbolism of each challenge they faced, helping him peel back the layers of his fears.

"Each step we take," she explained, "brings you closer to understanding the nature of these nightmares and what they reveal about your subconscious mind."

He paused, his brow furrowing in thought. "These dreams... they're not just random manifestations, are they? They're reflections of my innermost fears and insecurities."

"Exactly," Elizabeth confirmed gently. "And by confronting them head-on, you're taking control of your narrative. You're reclaiming your power."

As they delved deeper into the dream world, he found himself grappling with ever more complex obstacles—riddles etched in stone, impossible labyrinths that shifted with each passing moment. Yet through it all, Elizabeth remained his constant, her unwavering support bolstering his courage.

"Remember," she reminded him, "you possess the strength to overcome anything this nightmare throws at you. You've already proven that time and time again."

With every challenge he faced, he felt a growing sense of self-awareness, as though he were peering into a mirror that reflected not only his physical form but also the intricate tapestry of his soul. The fears that once held him captive now seemed smaller somehow, less potent in the face of his newfound understanding.

"Dr. Harmon," he murmured, gratitude lacing his voice, "I can't thank you enough for guiding me through this. I feel... lighter. Unburdened."

"Your progress is your accomplishment," she replied, her words tinged with pride. "I merely provided the tools and support you needed to unlock your potential."

Their journey continued, each step revealing new facets of his psyche, unearthing long-buried memories and emotions. And though the path ahead remained shrouded in uncertainty, one thing was clear: together, they were forging a new way forward, one defined not by fear, but by resilience and resolve.

The air in the nightmare grew colder, the oppressive fog thickening as the patient and Elizabeth ventured deeper into the labyrinth. The walls seemed to close in around them, pulsing with malevolent energy that sent shivers down his spine. Their path twisted and turned, revealing a landscape of decaying buildings and desolate streets, each corner echoing with the whispers of forgotten memories.

"Stay close," Elizabeth warned, her voice low and steady. "We're approaching the heart of your fears."

"Is... is this where it all comes together?" he asked, feeling both anticipation and dread coursing through him.

"Yes," she confirmed, her eyes fixed on the horizon. "But remember, you've come this far. You have the strength to confront whatever awaits us."

As they rounded a final bend, the pair emerged into a vast, open plaza, at the center of which stood a towering monolith. Engraved upon its surface were countless faces; their anguished expressions etched in stone. A cold realization gripped his heart, as he recognized each face as a manifestation of his own deepest fears.

"Dr. Harmon ... what do I do now?" His voice trembled, betraying his nerves.

"Confront them," she said softly, placing a reassuring hand on his shoulder. "Acknowledge your fears and let them go."

Taking a deep breath, he stepped forward and faced the monolith. With every ounce of courage, he could muster, he began to speak aloud the names of his fears, voicing the anxieties that had plagued him for so long. As he did so, the faces began to crumble, dissolving into dust before his very eyes.

"Loss," he whispered, the weight of his grief bearing down on him. "Abandonment," he added, his voice growing stronger. "Failure," he declared, the echoes of his past mistakes fading away.

"Keep going," Elizabeth urged, her presence a beacon of support amidst the darkness.

"Loneliness," he continued, his resolve unwavering. "Insignificance," he said, feeling the burden of his fears begin to lift. "Fear itself."

With every word spoken, the monolith cracked and shattered, its once imposing structure now reduced to rubble at his feet. As the dust settled, he stood before the wreckage, his heart pounding in his chest, a newfound sense of liberation coursing through him.

"Dr. Harmon," he breathed, turning to face her with tears in his eyes, "I did it..."

"Indeed, you did," she replied, smiling warmly. "You've faced your deepest fears, and in doing so, you've found the strength within yourself to overcome them."

As they stood amidst the shattered remnants of his nightmares, he couldn't help but feel a profound sense of gratitude for the woman who had guided him through the darkest corners of his mind. With her unwavering support, he had confronted his fears, and in the process, discovered the resilience that lay dormant within him all along.

The Patient stood firm, the remnants of his fears scattered around him like broken glass. Elizabeth's eyes shone with pride as she observed the transformation that had taken place within him.

"Your journey isn't over yet," she cautioned, her voice both gentle and resolute. "But you've made incredible progress."

"Thank you, Dr. Harmon," he said, his gratitude palpable. "I couldn't have done it without you."

"Remember," she urged, placing a hand on his shoulder, "the strength was always within you. I simply helped you find it."

As they spoke, the shattered landscape began to shift and reassemble itself, the fractured pieces coalescing into something new and unfamiliar. The air hummed with potential energy, the dream world preparing for the challenges that lay ahead.

"Dr. Harmon?" The patient asked hesitantly, his gaze locked on the ever-changing scenery. "What happens now?"

"Your mind is a labyrinth, constantly evolving and adapting," she explained, her eyes reflecting the shifting landscape before them. "There will be more obstacles to face, more fears to conquer. But know that each victory brings you closer to understanding yourself and finding peace."

"Will you be there to guide me?" he asked, the vulnerability in his voice unmistakable.

"Whenever you need me," she promised, her determination unwavering. "We're in this together."

As they watched the dreamscape transform around them, Elizabeth couldn't help but feel a sense of accomplishment. She had been able to reach the patient, guiding him through the treacherous terrain of his psyche. It was a testament to her growing understanding of the collective unconscious, and her ability to apply that knowledge to help others.

Yet, she knew that the path ahead would not be an easy one. If they were to continue unraveling the mysteries of the shared nightmare, they would need to delve even deeper into the labyrinth of the human mind. The dangers that lurked within were as immense as they were unknown.

"Let's keep going," she said, her voice steady and resolute. "Together, we'll face whatever comes our way."

"Thank you, Dr. Harmon," the patient replied, his newfound courage evident in his posture and demeanor. "I'm ready."

Chapter 25

Rain pattered against the window, the droplets leaving ephemeral trails as it slid down the surface. The room was bathed in a soft, ambient glow emanating from holographic panels embedded in the walls. A holographic time display hovered in mid-air, its digits changing with a subtle humas Elizabeth sat in her office, her gaze fixed on the two patients before her. Their hands wrung together with unease; faces etched with the same torment that haunted their dreams. It was a shared nightmare, a labyrinth they had each stumbled upon independently, and it had become the epicenter of Elizabeth's obsession.

"Doctor Harmon," came a voice from the door, jolting her back into the present. The receptionist stood hesitantly at the threshold, clutching a small package. "This just arrived for you."

"Thank you, Lucy," Elizabeth replied, taking the parcel and dismissing her patients. She couldn't shake the feeling that this delivery held some significance, some weight that could tip the scales in their favor. The box felt heavy in her hands, a sensation that seemed to defy its size.

Once alone, she carefully opened the package to reveal a letter and a file, both marked "Confidential" and addressed to her. Her heart raced, her fingers trembling slightly as she unfolded the letter. The words on the page were imbued with raw emotion, cutting through the clinical sterility of her office.

"Dr. Elizabeth Harmon," the letter began, "I cannot begin to express my gratitude for your bravery and determination in exposing the government experiment. Your tireless pursuit of the truth has given hope to those of us who have been affected by the nightmares, by the labyrinth that haunts our dreams."

A shiver ran down her spine as she read the message, confirming what she had come to suspect: these nightmares weren't merely figments of disturbed minds, but the result of something far more sinister. The stranger's words resonated deeply within her, filling her with a renewed sense of purpose. In their desperation, they had reached out to her—a stranger—connecting them through the shared pain that had brought her patients to their knees.

"Your work has not gone unnoticed," the letter continued, "and I hope you understand the tremendous impact your actions have had on our lives. You have given us a reason to keep fighting, to believe that one day we might find the truth and perhaps even justice for those who have suffered."

The words blurred as tears welled in Elizabeth's eyes, her sister's memory resurfacing like an old wound. It was a loss that had left her with a heart full of guilt and an insatiable curiosity about the unexplained—and it had led her here, to this moment. This connection was forged through whispers in the dark, through the labyrinth that seemed to grow more twisted and treacherous with each passing day.

"Thank you, Dr. Harmon," the letter concluded, "for shining a light in the darkness."

As Elizabeth sat there, clutching the heartfelt message from a stranger, she knew she had to see this through to the end. For her sister, for her patients, and for the countless others whose lives had been ensnared by the government's failed experiment.

"Darkness cannot drive out darkness; only light can do that." The quote danced in Elizabeth's mind as she reached for the file accompanying the letter, her fingertips tracing the word "Confidential" embossed on the cover. A quiet sigh escaped her lips, and she prepared herself for the revelations that lay within.

As she opened it, a cacophony of newspaper clippings, research papers, and photographs fluttered onto her desk like fallen leaves on an autumn day. Her eyes darted from one piece to another, each serving as a fragment of a puzzle she had dedicated herself to solving. The weight of the truth pressed against her chest, a silent plea to be heard and understood.

"Look at what you've started," whispered a voice in her mind—a mix of admiration and accusation—as she flipped through the documents. It was true; her actions had set off a chain reaction, pulling others into the orbit of her relentless pursuit. Elizabeth felt both humbled and terrified by the tide of human spirit that surged behind her, seeking solace in the truth she'd worked so tirelessly to uncover.

"Subject 14: Unidentified Trauma"—the headline on a research paper caught her eye. The words seemed to leap off the page, ensnaring her thoughts. As Elizabeth read on, she realized that the writer had dug deeper into the project than even she had dared to venture. It was as if they had crawled inside her mind, picking apart the threads that held her together, searching for the elusive answers that haunted her every waking moment.

"Is this what I wanted?" she asked herself, struggling to reconcile the feelings of pride and fear that welled up inside her. The answer came in the form of a photograph, tucked between the pages of a scientific journal. It depicted a group of people huddled together, their faces etched with determination and hope. They were the ones she had inspired, the ones who dared to join her in this treacherous quest for truth.

"Faith is taking the first step even when you don't see the whole staircase," the quote whispered once more in her mind. And in that moment, Elizabeth understood the power of her actions, the ripple effect that had begun with a single drop of courage. She was not alone in this fight; others were there, ready and willing to stand by her side.

"Your bravery has given us hope," the stranger's words echoed through her thoughts as she studied the documents before her. And with each new revelation, Elizabeth felt an unbreakable bond forming—a connection forged in the fires of adversity, tempered by the shared determination to expose the twisted secrets of the experiment.

"Let there be light," she whispered, her voice barely audible yet filled with purpose. For the first time in her life, Elizabeth knew that she was part of something greater than herself, a force that would not be silenced or defeated. Together, they would shine their light into the darkness, illuminating the path that led to truth and justice.

"Remarkable," Elizabeth murmured, her fingers trembling as they traced the edges of a newspaper clipping. The headline screamed in bold letters: "Whistleblower Exposes Government Experiment."

The words felt like a lifeline thrown to her heart, pulling her out of the dark abyss she had been drowning in for so long. Her chest swelled with a mix of emotions—pride, relief, and a renewed sense of purpose—as she realized that her efforts were not in vain. She had made a difference and had touched the lives of countless people who had suffered in silence.

"Dr. Harmon?" a voice called out from behind her, snapping her back to the present. She turned to see a young woman with wide, curious eyes and a notepad clutched in her hands. "I'm sorry to disturb you, but I couldn't help overhearing. Are you the one who exposed the experiment?"

Elizabeth hesitated for a moment, considering the weight of her decision. Yet, there was something in the woman's expression that told her it was safe to trust this stranger. "Yes," she replied, her voice steady and resolute. "I am."

"Thank you," the woman whispered, tears welling up in her eyes. "My brother ... he was one of them. You saved his life."

As Elizabeth looked into the woman's eyes, she saw reflected there the impact she had had on the lives of those affected by the experiment. The importance of uncovering its secrets became crystal clear at that moment, and she knew she could not turn away from the path she had set foot upon.

"Dr. Harmon, we have been desperately seeking answers for so long," the woman continued, her voice cracking with emotion. "Please, tell me how you found the courage to stand against the darkness. How did you know where to look?"

"Sometimes," Elizabeth said softly, her gaze distant as she recalled the long nights spent poring over documents, the whispers of her sister's unexplained death echoing in her mind, "you have to step into the darkness to find the light. The truth is often hidden beneath layers of deception, waiting for someone brave enough to unveil it."

"Your bravery has inspired us all," the woman replied, her eyes shining with a newfound sense of purpose.

"Remember," Elizabeth said, her voice firm and unwavering, "we are stronger together. We must continue to seek the truth, to expose the lies, and to stand up for those who cannot fight for themselves."

And with that, she knew that she had become more than just a psychologist searching for answers. She had become a beacon of hope and determination, guiding others toward the light even as the shadows threatened to swallow them whole. And in this pursuit, she would never be alone again.

The room seemed to sigh around Elizabeth, the silence bearing down like a weight upon her shoulders. The package lay before her on the table, its contents now splayed out like an intricate puzzle waiting to be solved. She traced her fingers over one of the newspaper clippings, feeling the rough texture of the aged paper beneath her fingertips.

"Thank you," she whispered to the empty room, her voice barely audible. It was time to reach out to the person who had sent her this trove of information. They deserved her gratitude and, perhaps, they could use her help in return.

Her fingers danced across her keyboard as she began to draft her response, the words spilling forth from her soul like water cascading down a mountainside.

Her thoughts were a swirling maelstrom, yet somehow, she managed to convey them with clarity and emotion.

Dear Friend,

I cannot express how grateful I am for the package you sent me. Your support means more to me than you can imagine. In my pursuit of truth and justice, I have often felt isolated, facing insurmountable odds. But now, knowing that others stand with me, I feel a renewed sense of purpose.

Your efforts to uncover the secrets behind the government experiment are both admirable and inspiring. My journey toward understanding has been fraught with challenges and heartache, but with each step, I grow closer to the truth that we all seek.

I want you to know that I am here to help in any way possible. If there is anything I can do to assist you in your search, please do not hesitate to reach out. Together, our combined knowledge and determination can make a difference.

With deepest gratitude and solidarity,

Dr. Elizabeth Harmon

As she finished typing, Elizabeth paused to read her message once more. Although she knew it would never fully capture the depth of her emotions, she hoped it would convey her sincerity and her willingness to help.

"Send," she muttered, her finger hovering over the button. She hesitated for a heartbeat before pressing it with a sense of finality.

As she sat back in her chair, Elizabeth's thoughts turned to the lives that had been affected by the experiment, their stories now etched into her very being. She could feel their pain and their longing for answers, and she knew that she could not turn away from this path.

"Stand up for those who cannot fight for themselves," she whispered, an unbreakable resolve taking root within her heart. And as the shadows of doubt and fear began to recede, Elizabeth knew that she was not alone on this journey toward truth and justice.

The faint hum of the computer's fan accompanied Elizabeth as she stared at the screen, her finger hovering above the send button. The weight of her decision pressed down on her like a vice, but at that moment, she found the strength to push through.

"Thank you," she murmured, her voice barely audible even to herself. She felt a sense of camaraderie flicker to life within her—for the first time in years, she was not alone in her quest for truth and justice.

Over the next few days, Elizabeth immersed herself in the stories of the individuals mentioned in the documents. Her office, now transformed into a haven, featured holographic displays projecting images, floating digital newspaper clippings, and virtual notes suspended in the air—an organized chaos that echoed the turmoil within her enhanced cognitive interface. The room was bathed in a soft glow emanating from sleek, luminescent panels embedded seamlessly into the walls.

As Elizabeth delved deeper into the narratives of the past, her fingers danced across holographic interfaces, manipulating data with swift gestures. Three-dimensional visualizations of historical events materialized before her, creating an immersive experience that blurred the lines between the tangible and the virtual.

"Dr. West..." she muttered, Her fingers glided over the holographic display, tracing the name that shimmered in luminescent letters on a sleek, transparent research interface. . "What did you uncover?"

Each person she researched brought forth a kaleidoscope of emotions: admiration for their unwavering determination, empathy for the burden they carried, and a renewed sense of purpose to help them in any way she could. Elizabeth's mind danced between the past and present, weaving together threads of seemingly unrelated information to create a tapestry of understanding.

"Moments of serendipity," she mused, recalling the phrase from a psychology lecture long ago. It described the phenomenon where seemingly unrelated events and discoveries converged, leading to new insights. This was what she needed to uncover the truth behind the experiment.

"Dr. Harmon?" a voice called from behind her office door.

"Come in," she replied, her dark eyes never leaving the screen.

"Your appointment is here," the receptionist informed her, peeking in hesitantly.

"Thank you, I'll be right out," Elizabeth replied, closing the file on her computer. As she rose from her chair, she glanced around her office one last time, taking in the labyrinth of information that now surrounded her.

"Keep searching," she whispered to herself as she closed the door behind her, leaving the chaos of her research behind for a moment. The familiarity of her practice, and the comforting rhythm of helping others through their struggles, provided a brief respite from the shadows of the past creeping into her present.

But even as she listened to her patient's words, her mind continued to race, seeking connections and patterns hidden within the documents and memories of those affected by the experiment. It was only a matter of time before the pieces fell into place, revealing the truth that had been shrouded in darkness for far too long.

"Thank you for sharing that with me," Elizabeth said softly to her patient, offering a reassuring smile. "Together, we can work through this."

As she spoke those words, Elizabeth knew that they held not just for the person sitting across from her but also for the strangers who had become her allies in the fight for justice.

Elizabeth's eyes traced the lines of text on her holographic computer screen, her mind racing as she pieced together the intricate web connecting these individuals. A small group, bound by a shared determination to expose the truth and seek justice for the victims of the experiment. It was almost as if fate had drawn them together, their paths converging at this critical juncture.

"Strangers in the shadows," she murmured, her fingers hovering over the keyboard. "Driven by an unrelenting quest for truth."

The room seemed to hum with energy, the air crackling with anticipation as Elizabeth composed a message to the group. She hesitated for a moment, her heart pounding in her chest, before pressing send. The die was cast, and her intentions laid bare and vulnerable before these unknown allies.

"Elizabeth?" The voice of one of her patients echoed through the walls of her office, pulling her back from the precipice of her thoughts.

"Sorry, I'll be right there," Elizabeth called out, her voice steady even as her hands trembled. Her gaze lingered on the screen for a moment longer, the words of her message burning into her memory like the embers of a dying flame.

"Forgive me, sister," she whispered, her breath catching in her throat. "But I will not rest until your death is avenged."

The hours that followed were a blur of faces and emotions, the familiar rhythm of her practice providing a reprieve from the storm brewing within her. But as the sun dipped below the horizon, a response flickered to life on her holographic screen. A simple affirmation, a welcoming embrace from the shadows: "We've been waiting for you."

"Finally," Elizabeth breathed, her heart soaring with equal parts relief and trepidation. This was the beginning, the first step toward unraveling the twisted threads of the experiment that had haunted her for so long.

"Let's meet," she typed, her fingers flying across the keys with a newfound sense of urgency. "I have much to share and we have work to do."

Within moments, an address materialized on her screen, accompanied by a date and time. The meeting was set, the stage primed for a reckoning long overdue.

"Thank you," Elizabeth whispered to the strangers who had now become her comrades in arms. As she prepared to leave her office, She glanced at the holographic display of her sister, , her eyes glistening with unshed tears.

"Rest easy, dear sister," she murmured, her voice thick with emotion. "For together, we shall uncover the truth and bring justice to those who have been wronged."

The dimly lit room pulsed with an undercurrent of anticipation, the shadows themselves seeming to breathe in sync with the hushed whispers that filled the air. Elizabeth stepped through the door, her heart pounding a staccato rhythm against her ribs. A dozen pairs of eyes turned to her, their gazes warm and welcoming, yet tinged with a steely resolve that mirrored her own.

"Dr. Harmon," a woman said, extending her hand. "I'm Sandra. We've been expecting you."

"Thank you," Elizabeth replied, her voice quivering slightly as she clasped the proffered hand. She glanced around at the assembled group, taking note of the varied faces—some young and eager, others lined with years of hard-fought battles against injustice. These were her allies, her fellow truth-seekers, bound together by a shared purpose.

"Please, have a seat," Sandra urged, gesturing toward an empty chair. Elizabeth obeyed, her fingers twisting nervously in her lap. She took a deep breath, steeling herself for what was to come.

"Allow me to begin," she said, her voice steady now, imbued with the strength of her convictions. "I've spent the past year researching the government's failed experiment, delving into the darkest corners of their clandestine operations. And I've discovered something ... something we can use to expose them."

As she spoke, Elizabeth unveiled her findings, laying out a veritable treasure trove of evidence before her rapt audience. The room crackled with energy as she detailed her insights, each revelation bringing a collective gasp or murmur of outrage from the group.

"Your work is incredible, Dr. Harmon," one man remarked, his eyes wide with admiration. "We're grateful to have you on our side."

"Thank you," Elizabeth responded, a faint blush coloring her cheeks. "But I couldn't have done it alone. It was the courage and conviction of people like you that gave me the strength to keep going."

"Then let's not waste any more time," Sandra declared, her voice resolute. "Together, we can devise a plan to bring their crimes to light."

The room hummed with activity as they pooled their collective knowledge, each member contributing their unique skills and resources to the cause. Ideas were exchanged, strategies refined, and a unified vision took shape from the chaos of individual thought.

"Remember," Elizabeth urged them, her eyes blazing with determination, "we're not just fighting for ourselves. We're fighting for the victims, for the countless lives destroyed by this experiment. And we will not rest until justice has been served."

A chorus of agreement rippled through the group, their faces etched with fierce resolve. At that moment, Elizabeth knew that she had found her purpose, her place among these dedicated individuals who would stop at nothing to expose the truth. No longer was she alone in her quest; together, they were unstoppable.

Darkness shrouded the small room, pierced only by the thin slivers of moonlight that filtered through the blinds. Elizabeth leaned against the wall, her fingers gripping a cold cup of coffee, bitter and forgotten. The others had gone home for the night, but she remained, unable to shake the urgency that coursed through her veins like an electrical current.

"Dr. Harmon," she whispered to herself, testing the weight of the name. For the past year, it had been her shield, her fortress of solitude. But now, standing among these brave souls who dared to challenge the very foundations of power, she realized that it was more than just a title. It was a symbol of hope, a beacon in the darkness that led others to seek the truth.

Her heart swelled with pride as she thought of the group—each individual with their own story, their battle scars. They were a motley crew of misfits and renegades, bound together by a shared mission and an unbreakable determination. And she was one of them.

"Elizabeth?" The voice startled her, pulling her from her reverie. She turned to see Sandra, her eyes shadowed with fatigue but still burning with resolve. "I thought I'd find you here."

"Can't sleep," Elizabeth admitted, a rueful smile playing on her lips. "Too much to do, too much at stake."

"Tell me about it." Sandra sighed, sinking into a nearby chair. "But we can't burn ourselves out before the real fight begins."

"True," Elizabeth conceded, her gaze drifted over the holographic display, projecting intricate data patterns that hovered above. The virtual documents, illuminated by soft beams of light, formed a dynamic and ever-changing collage of information in the surroundings. , each one a piece in the complex puzzle they were trying to solve. She knew that every scrap of information was crucial, every lead worth investigating. But there was something else, something deeper that fueled her relentless pursuit—a need to make amends, to right the wrongs that haunted her every waking moment. And now, for the first time, she saw a glimmer of hope, a chance to leave a lasting legacy.

"Elizabeth," Sandra said softly, her voice pulling her back from the precipice of her thoughts. "I just wanted to say... thank you. For everything you've done, and everything we're about to do. I know it hasn't been easy, but you've given us all something to believe in."

"Thank you, Sandra," Elizabeth replied, her eyes glistening with unshed tears. "But this isn't just about me. It's about all of us, fighting together for what's right. We will expose the experiment's secrets, and we will ensure that justice is served."

"Here's to that," Sandra agreed, raising an imaginary toast. "And to a better future."

As they shared a moment of quiet camaraderie, Elizabeth felt the weight of her past begin to lift, replaced by a renewed sense of purpose and determination. No longer would she be shackled by guilt and regret; she would forge a new path, one built on truth and redemption. As the night gave way to dawn, she knew in her heart that the legacy of her actions would live on, ensuring that the secrets of the experiment would not remain hidden forever.

Chapter 26

The morning sun cast long shadows across the cemetery, bathing the tombstones in an eerie amber glow. Elizabeth stood at the entrance, clutching a bouquet of white lilies—Claire's favorite flowers. She took a deep breath and walked along the gravel path, feeling the weight of her sister's absence with every step.

"Hello, Claire," she whispered, kneeling before the grave in a serene futuristic cemetery. The stone marker emitted a soft holographic glow, displaying Claire's name and dates in a sleek, digitized font..A small bird stood on the ground as if waiting to deliver a message from beyond.

Elizabeth set the bouquet carefully on the grave, As she did so, memories of Claire flooded her mind—the sound of her laughter, the way her eyes sparkled when she smiled.

"Your laughter is something I'll never forget," Elizabeth said softly. "You made me feel alive... When you left, a part of me went with you. I don't know if I'll ever be whole again."

She brushed away a tear, remembering how they had been inseparable as children. They would spend hours exploring the woods behind their house, pretending to be adventurers seeking hidden treasure. In those moments, it seemed as though there was no darkness in the world that could touch them.

"Every day, I try to be strong for my patients," she continued. "But sometimes, I can't help but think that maybe... Maybe if I had been stronger for you, things would have turned out differently."

Elizabeth shook her head, banishing the thought. She knew it led only to a cycle of guilt and self-blame, one she'd been caught in countless times before. Instead, she focused on the positive impact Claire had had on her life. Her kindness and empathy inspired Elizabeth to become a psychologist, driven by the desire to help others find healing and understanding.

"Thank you, Claire," she murmured. "I have to remind myself every day that your death wasn't my fault, and that you had a positive influence on me, shaping who I am today."

"Sometimes, I think about what our lives would have been like if you were still here," Elizabeth said softly, her voice barely audible above the rustle of leaves overhead. The autumn breeze sent a shiver down her spine. "I wonder if we could have helped each other through the darkness. You always knew how to make me laugh, even in my darkest moments."

Her eyes filled with tears, and she took a deep breath before continuing. "Claire, I regret not being able to save you. But I am grateful for the time we had together. Your memory has guided me, given me strength when I needed it most." A tear trickled down her cheek, but she didn't bother to wipe it away.

"Your death taught me that life is fragile, and I've tried to honor your memory by helping others. I've become a better psychologist because of you, Claire, and I want you to know that." Elizabeth's hands trembled slightly as she reached into her purse, extracting a holographic notepad. She gazed at the holographic interface projected above the notepad, blank page displaying a three-dimensional grid, as she gathering her thoughts.

"Dear Claire," she began writing, her words seamlessly appearing on the holographic display before her. The digital interface projected a virtual keyboard, allowing her to effortlessly compose her thoughts as if conjuring them from the ether. "Since you left, I have grown in ways I never thought possible. I have learned to listen, truly listen, to the suffering of others. And in doing so, I have found my purpose."

"Your absence taught me the importance of empathy and understanding, both for myself and for those around me. In the depths of my grief, I discovered resilience and the power of human connection. Through the pain, I forged a new path—one dedicated to healing and hope."

"Every day, I carry your memory with me, and it reminds me of who I was, who I am, and who I can become. I promise to never stop learning, to never stop growing, and to honor your name through the work I do and the lives I touch."

"Thank you for being my sister, my confidant, and my guiding star. You may be gone, but you will never be forgotten."

As Elizabeth finished the letter, she felt a strange sensation wash over her, like tendrils of mist wrapping around her heart and lifting it from the depths of despair. Her hand trembled as she folded the holographic display carefully.

"Goodbye, Claire," she whispered, her voice catching in her throat. "I will carry your light within me, always."

As Elizabeth's fingers hovered above the holographic notepad, she felt the memories of their childhood together come flooding back to her. She could almost hear Claire's laughter, rich and warm like sunlight on a cool autumn day, as they played in the park, their feet sinking into piles of auburn leaves that rustled beneath their every step.

"Remember when we used to dream about our futures?" Elizabeth whispered, her voice barely audible, as if speaking louder would shatter the delicate web of memories woven around her. "We'd lie in the grass, staring at the clouds above, each one a different shape, a different possibility. You wanted to be an astronaut, exploring the farthest reaches of the universe, while I longed to be a writer, creating worlds with the stroke of my pen."

A wistful smile crossed her face as she continued, "And then there was that time we tried to make our perfume using rose petals from Mom's garden. We crushed them up, mixed them with water, and left the concoction sitting in the sun for weeks. It smelled... awful," she chuckled, shaking her head. "But we were so proud of it. We thought we had discovered some secret recipe, the key to wealth and success."

"Life had other plans for us, didn't it?" Elizabeth sighed. "But those days, those dreams, they shaped us, Claire. They made us who we are today."

With a heavy heart, Elizabeth stood up and walked among the graves, their sleek, luminescent panels standing like holographic sentinels amidst the verdant grass. Each marker bore a name, a date, a testament to the fleetingness of existence. Some had virtual overlays flickering with memories, nearly obscured by the passage of data, while others were still stark and new, fresh wounds carved into the earth.

"Look at all these lives," Elizabeth murmured, her eyes scanning the rows upon rows of tombstones. "Each one unique, each one a tapestry of love and pain, triumphs and failures. But in the end, all that remains is this: a name etched in the holographic display, a whisper of what once was."

"Is this all we are, Claire?" she asked, her voice wavering. "Are we just fleeting moments, soon to be forgotten by the relentless march of time?"

As the wind picked up, rustling through the trees and sending leaves dancing around her feet, Elizabeth felt an unexpected sense of clarity settle within her. She knew that while life was fragile, it was also precious. It was something to be cherished, celebrated, and remembered—no matter how brief or seemingly insignificant.

"Perhaps," she thought, "it isn't the length of our lives that matters most, but the depth of our connections, the impact we have on those around us, and the memories we leave behind."

With renewed determination, Elizabeth walked back to Claire's grave, ready to face the next chapter of her life with hope and resilience. For she now understood that though her sister was gone, the lessons and love they had shared would forever remain, woven into the very fabric of her being.

The cemetery seemed to stretch out endlessly before her, a somber ocean of grief and remembrance. Elizabeth's gaze fell upon a tall figure standing a few rows away from Claire's grave, their back turned to her. She recognized the posture, the way the shoulders hunched ever so slightly as if bearing an invisible weight.

"Thomas?" she called out hesitantly, feeling a mixture of surprise and curiosity.

The man turned around, his face lighting up with recognition. "Elizabeth! It's been years," he said, his voice tinged with a bittersweet warmth.

"Indeed, it has," she replied, her mind racing back to the countless memories they all shared during their youth—Claire, Thomas, and herself—a trio inseparable by time and circumstance. But now, one of them was gone, leaving behind an emptiness that gnawed at her very core.

"Are you here for Claire as well?" Thomas asked after a moment of silence, his eyes glistening with unshed tears.

"Of course," Elizabeth replied, her heart aching with longing and loss. "I came to pay my respects and to try to find some closure."

Thomas nodded solemnly, understanding her sentiments all too well. "You know, I've never told you this, but Claire ... she saved my life once." His voice trembled with emotion as he recounted a memory long buried. "We were just kids, no more than twelve or thirteen. I remember feeling lost like I didn't belong anywhere. One day, I decided I couldn't take it anymore. I went to the old bridge, ready to end it all."

Elizabeth felt a cold shiver run down her spine, her breath catching in her throat. She had never known about this dark chapter in Thomas's life, nor about the role Claire had played in it.

"Before I could take that final step, I felt a hand on my shoulder. It was Claire," he continued, his voice barely above a whisper. "She somehow knew what I was going through, and she refused to let me go. She talked to me for hours that night, telling me how much she cared and how important I was to her. She made me promise to keep living, no matter how hard it got."

Tears streamed down Thomas's face as he looked up at the sky as if searching for some trace of Claire among the clouds. "I kept that promise, Elizabeth. I'm still here because of her. She had this... this incredible ability to see the good in people, even when they couldn't see it themselves."

"Thank you for sharing that with me, Thomas," Elizabeth choked out, her own eyes welling up with tears. She felt a sense of gratitude and profound sadness, marvelling at how Claire's impact transcended the boundaries of life itself.

"Take care, Elizabeth," Thomas whispered before walking away, leaving her standing alone amidst the sea of tombstones.

As she returned to Claire's grave, Elizabeth felt a renewed understanding of her sister's legacy. Claire had not just been a loving sister, but a beacon of hope for those who needed it most.

The scent of damp earth mingled with the fragrance of fresh flowers, as a gentle breeze whispered through the cemetery. Elizabeth took a deep breath, allowing the air to fill her lungs and permeate her very being. She could feel it, that elusive sense of peace she had been searching for, washing over her like a warm embrace. It was as if a weight, long carried on her shoulders, had finally been lifted.

"Thank you," she murmured, unable to contain the gratitude swelling within her chest. The words felt inadequate, but they were all she had to offer.

As Elizabeth stood there, she contemplated the lives that had touched her own, intertwining like the roots of the ancient oak tree that loomed nearby. Her connection with Claire had been strong, forged by blood and love, but now she realized the tendrils of her sister's reach extended far beyond their shared bond. Claire's life had mattered; her influence continued to shape the world, even in her absence.

With a renewed sense of purpose, determination burned within Elizabeth's heart. She would live her life to the fullest, not just for herself, but in honor of Claire's memory. The thought brought a smile to her face, a genuine warmth that spread from the corners of her mouth to the depths of her soul.

"Promise me, Claire," she whispered as if the wind could carry her words to whatever realm her sister now inhabited. "Promise me that you'll be with me every step of the way."

There was no answer, of course, only the soft rustling of leaves overhead. But Elizabeth knew, deep down, that Claire would always be with her—a guiding light in the darkness, a source of strength when she needed it most.

She turned away from the grave, her heels sinking into the soft grass as she walked. The sun peeked out from behind a cloud, casting a golden glow over the cemetery. It felt like a sign, a confirmation from the universe that she was on the right path.

"Goodbye, Claire," she whispered once more, her voice barely audible even to herself. "I love you."

With each step Elizabeth took, she felt lighter, as if she were leaving behind the shadows of grief and guilt that had plagued her for so long. She knew there would still be moments when those emotions threatened to overwhelm her, but they no longer held the same power. She was stronger now, changed by the journey she had undertaken—a journey that had led her not just to find closure, but to rediscover herself.

As she walked away, the wind seemed to carry with it a faint echo of laughter, a sound that lingered in the air long after Elizabeth had disappeared.

In the cool, quiet solitude of her home, Elizabeth stood before a cardboard box filled with fragments of her sister's life. Flashes of memory overtook her as she sifted through the photographs and mementos, each piece a frozen moment in time, a testament to Claire's vibrant spirit.

"Ah, this one," she murmured, holding up a photograph of the two of them as children, their faces smeared with cake frosting while they grinned ear to ear.

The picture seemed to radiate warmth as if the sun had kissed it at that exact moment, infusing it with an ethereal glow. Elizabeth traced the contours of Claire's face with her fingertips, feeling a pang of nostalgia deep within her chest.

Piece by piece, she began to arrange the remnants of Claire's life on the empty wall in her study, creating a tapestry that told the story of a soul both lost and found. It was a cathartic process, allowing her to confront the regrets and unspoken words that had weighed so heavily upon her heart.

"Here's to you, Claire," Elizabeth whispered, stepping back to admire the memorial. With a solemn nod, she picked up her phone and began dialing the numbers of her closest friends and colleagues. "It's time."

* * *

A hushed anticipation filled Elizabeth's living room as her guests arrived, each bearing their offering of memories and stories to share. The air seemed charged with a strange mixture of sadness and celebration as if the ghost of Claire hovered just beyond their reach.

"Thank you all for coming," Elizabeth said, her voice trembling slightly with emotion. "As you know, my sister Claire meant the world to me, and I wanted to gather you here today to celebrate her life."

"Of course, Elizabeth," replied a colleague, placing a reassuring hand on her shoulder. "We're here for you."

As they settled into comfortable chairs, the room was filled with a chorus of voices recounting tales of Claire's laughter, her kindness, and her unwavering spirit. Elizabeth listened intently, her heart swelling with each anecdote that revealed a new facet of her sister's character.

"Remember that time she convinced us all to stay up and watch the sunrise?" one friend reminisced, chuckling softly at the memory. "I've never seen so many people willingly wake up at 4 a.m."

"Or when she helped me through my breakup," another added, tears shimmering in her eyes. "She held me while I cried and told me it would get better—and it did, thanks to her."

As the stories continued, Elizabeth felt a sense of connection with everyone in the room, as if they were all bound together by the love and light that Claire had brought into their lives. It was a living testament to her sister's impact on those who knew her, a legacy that would continue to resonate long after her passing.

"Thank you," Elizabeth whispered, wiping away a stray tear. "Thank you all for sharing these memories of Claire with me."

As the gathering drew to a close, the friends and colleagues embraced and murmured words of comfort and support. The air seemed lighter now, filled with the echoes of laughter and conversation as if the act of remembering had breathed life back into Claire's memory.

And as Elizabeth stood alone in the quiet aftermath, surrounded by the fragments of her sister's life, she felt a sense of peace settle over her heart. She had found solace in the knowledge that Claire's spirit lived on, not just within her, but in the hearts and minds of those who had loved her.

"Goodnight, Claire," she whispered, gazing at the memorial wall that now held the essence of her sister's life. And in the silence that followed, Elizabeth could almost hear the faint echo of a voice, whispering back: "Goodnight, Elizabeth. I love you too."

The room was filled with a soft, golden light as the sun dipped below the horizon, casting long shadows across the faces of Claire's friends and colleagues. Elizabeth sat in her favorite armchair, cradling a cup of tea as she listened intently to their stories, eyes shining with unshed tears. The air was thick with emotion, charged with the energy of shared memories.

"Remember that time," began one of Elizabeth's colleagues, "when we were working on that particularly challenging case? You stepped in to help me, even though you didn't have to, and managed to get through to the patient when no one else could."

Elizabeth smiled at the recollection, touched by the genuine affection in her colleague's voice. It seemed that Claire wasn't the only one who had made an impact on those around her; she too had left her mark, helping others overcome the darkness that haunted them. As more testimonials flowed, Elizabeth felt a renewed sense of purpose swelling within her, reaffirming her commitment to her work as a psychologist.

As the conversation lulled, Elizabeth took a deep breath, feeling the weight of the moment settle upon her shoulders. She stood up, her gaze sweeping over the familiar faces gathered before her and began to speak.

"Thank you all for being here today, and for sharing your memories of Claire with me. She was such a bright, vibrant presence in our lives, and I know she would be deeply touched by the love and support you've shown me."

"Loss has a way of making us question everything," she continued, her voice shaking slightly with emotion. "But it can also bring clarity, helping us see what truly matters." She paused, taking a moment to collect herself before continuing. "After losing Claire, I realized that there is still so much left for me to do in this world, so many people who need my help. My work as a psychologist is more important to me now than ever before."

"Your stories have shown me that I too have made a difference in your lives, and for that, I am eternally grateful. I promise to continue helping others overcome their fears and nightmares, just as Claire would have wanted me to. And I hope that by honoring her memory, we can all find the strength and courage to face whatever challenges life throws our way."

As she spoke, Elizabeth felt a warmth spreading through her chest, radiating outward like ripples on a pond. It was as if Claire's spirit had somehow infused the air around her, imbuing her words with an almost tangible energy. The faces of her friends and colleagues were a testament to the power of her message, their eyes glistening with unshed tears and fierce determination.

"Thank you," she whispered, the words barely audible but resonating deeply within the hearts of those who heard them. "Together, we will continue to make a difference in this world, fueled by the love we had for Claire and the lessons she taught us all."

Elizabeth moved across the room, her footsteps muffled by the plush carpet beneath her feet. She hesitated at the entrance to her newly created sanctuary, taking a deep breath before stepping inside.

Surrounded by photographs and mementos of Claire, Elizabeth sank into the cushioned armchair that had once belonged to her sister. The fabric still held the faintest hint of Claire's perfume, a delicate scent that seemed to wrap around Elizabeth like a comforting embrace.

"Thank you," she murmured, her voice barely audible even to herself. "For everything."

She traced her fingers along the edge of a photograph, the image capturing a moment of shared laughter between the two sisters. A warm smile tugged at the corners of her mouth, even as tears threatened to blur her vision. The juxtaposition of joy and sorrow resonated within her as if each emotion was a note in a symphony that only she could hear.

"Look at us," Elizabeth whispered, her eyes moving from one picture to another, each snapshot a window into a memory long past. "We were so young, so full of dreams..."

Claire's presence seemed to hover at the edges of her consciousness, a soft whispering reminder of the love they had shared. As each cherished memory played out in her mind, Elizabeth felt the shards of her fractured heart knitting themselves back together, transforming her pain into something new, something stronger.

"Your death won't be in vain, I promise," she vowed, her voice low but resolute. "I'll continue to help others, to make a difference in their lives. Just like you made such a difference in mine."

The weight of her unspoken regrets and the guilt that had once consumed her began to dissipate, replaced by a newfound sense of purpose and determination. Elizabeth knew that she could never undo the past, but she could honor Claire's memory by embracing her personal growth and using it as fuel for her journey forward.

As the minutes ticked by, the room seemed to grow warmer, infused with the soft golden glow of the candles that flickered on the nearby table. The quiet solitude enveloped Elizabeth like a blanket, wrapping her up in its comforting embrace as she allowed herself to truly feel the peace and fulfillment that had eluded her for so long.

"Goodbye, Claire," she whispered, her voice steady and strong. "You'll always be with me, in my heart."

With those final words, Elizabeth rose from the armchair, her gaze sweeping over the memorial space one last time. She felt lighter somehow as if the shadows that had clung to her soul had been banished by the light of her sister's love. As she stepped out of the room, a renewed sense of purpose coursed through her veins, propelling her into the next chapter of her life.

About the Author

Stephanie Tyo, a rising voice in the literary world, currently resides in the quaint city of Cornwall, Ontario. With a professional background in medical assistance and personal support work, she's always had a keen interest in the intricate complexities of the human mind and societal dynamics. Currently, she is broadening her horizons further by pursuing a double major Bachelor of Arts degree in Psychology and Women and Gender Studies. Her ultimate aspiration is to become a therapist and eventually a psychologist, using her growing expertise in understanding human behavior to help others navigate their lives more effectively.

Stephanie is enthusiastically exploring various genres, driven by a voracious curiosity and love for storytelling. She is passionate about learning and self-improvement, qualities she also encourages in her readers. Her journey into writing is an extension of her commitment to continuous education—a value she holds dear.

At the core of Stephanie's world are her two teenage daughters. They provide her not just with abundant joy but also a rich source of inspiration for her narratives. Being a mother has deepened her understanding of the human experience, an understanding she seamlessly weaves into her writing.

Apart from her academic and writing pursuits, Stephanie harbors a deep-seated love for creating stories. Each plot, character, and sentence she crafts are reflections of her fascination with the diverse spectrum of human emotions and experiences.

Stephanie's unique blend of empathy, intellect, and imagination shapes her promising writing journey. Her work resonates with her life philosophy—an unending quest for knowledge and a deep commitment to service. Stephanie looks forward to connecting with readers who share her thirst for well-crafted stories and lifelong learning.

Facebook: https://www.facebook.com/StephanieTyoAuthor

Website: https://www.stephanietyo.com

Also By

ETERNALLY YOURS

Love BEYOND *Age*

Stephanie Tyo

Bone Pickers Diary

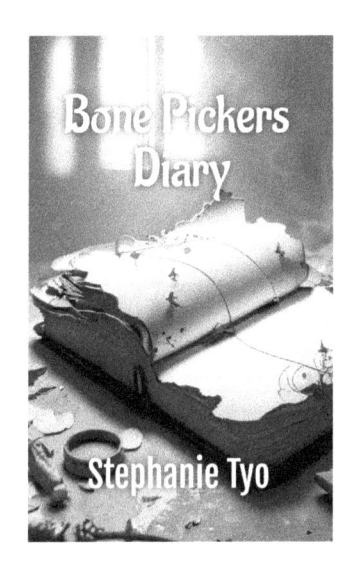

Stephanie Tyo